I0524126

SILENT SUBVERSION

Coyote Plays Rabbit

Hyrum Jones

○ ○ ◉

Silent Subversion III: Coyote Plays Rabbit

Copyright © 2025 by Hyrum Jones

This is a work of fiction. Names, characters, places, institutions, and incidents either are the product of the author's imagination or are used fictitiously. Any resemblance to actual persons, living or dead, businesses, events, or locales is entirely coincidental.

First edition: August 2021

ISBN (Print): 978-0997210750

ISBN (eBook): 978-0997210743

Interior Artwork: astrosense.net/astrology-fonts

Cover Design: nickcaldwellcreations.com

All rights reserved. No part of this text may be reproduced or distributed without the express written permission of the author or publisher, except by a reviewer, who may quote brief passages in a review.

Anxiety Publishing

Thanks again to Jim and Carlene for the tremendous amount of time they spent proofreading and providing their useful feedback. Thanks to Gregory F. Fegel for his research of ancient settlements in the Sahara. And finally, thanks to Carrie for her patience with the impact of this project on our lives.

Summary of Book 2

Here is a little recap of the story before continuing with this book.

Taylor was not too happy when Gerald told her about a high-profile businessman, Max Garner, who learned of their group from his employee, Mark Salmon, one of Gerald's old friends. Mark worked for a satellite company and Max had caught him looking at the group's website. Gerald had given Mark partial access to their website as a recruiting effort. Since Mark would not tell him anything, Max secretly hired a private investigator who traced the website to Gerald. Although Taylor had many concerns, she let Max learn a little about what they were doing in return for access to his company's resources.

After Cesar and Taylor finished converting his BMW into a high-tech escape vehicle, Max and Taylor took it for a semi-successful test flight into the vacuum of space. Afterward, Max offered to give them his old company jet to convert into a larger, more sophisticated escape vehicle. Taylor and Mark moved to Brazil and devoted all of their time to the project.

Sadi returned home with Helen and the other girl they had rescued, Daryn, and then went on a vacation. For a short while, their lives returned to semi-normal, but the authorities eventually traced the deaths to her, and she had to go on the run with the girls, staying first with Mr. Smith, then Gerald, and finally Cesar.

While Sadi was on the run, the military arrested Gerald and Max and took them to a top-secret psychiatric hospital where psychiatrists learned about the group's plans. The doctors at the hospital also learned about Taylor's new technology and Freddy's abilities and were instructed to damage Max and Gerald, psychologically, to neutralize their desire to continue fighting against the establishment.

Unknown to the authorities, Max's chief of security, Simon Thatcher, discovered the location of the psychiatric hospital and then gathered a few people for a daring rescue operation. He contacted Audrie, Max's sister, and some members of Taylor's group, including

Freddy.

After rescuing Gerald and Max, those who could, gathered in a forest in Canada where they barely escaped the CIA and then followed Freddy's instructions to travel toward Mercury in the modified jet. Sadi brought her daughter, Helen, and her semi-adopted daughter, Daryn. Dominga decided to come with Cesar, although she probably could have safely stayed on Earth. The others who escaped in the jet included Sadi and Gerald, Max and his chief of security, Simon, and Mark who also brought his wife, Susan, and their two sons.

Franklin, who built the group's website, and Gerda, the botanist, did not escape with the rest but were captured by the authorities in northwestern Washington state. Freddy and Doroteo decided to stay on Earth, hoping to help those who were left behind.

Sadi's brother, Brian, is left wondering what happened to his sister and nieces. Audrie Garner still needs to explain to the authorities how she just happened to visit her brother, Max, when his friends rescued Gerald and him from the secret hospital. The FBI agent, John Pratt, was left wondering why the hell he helped them and decided to abandon his quest for revenge on Gerald.

CONTENTS

PART I

THIRTEEN REFUGEES

While crossing the ocean

Don't look under the water

And stay in motion

ONE

Taylor

The tunnel began as tiny holes exploding in space before them, coalescing into a larger hole and quickly consuming the light from Mercury. The sharp contrast between the utter blackness of the expanding hole and its ring of plasma was mesmerizing. She felt its heat on her nose, cheeks, and forehead as though facing a new sun. Taylor knew she needed to close her eyes, but the scene grew more terrifyingly beautiful with every passing second.

Close your eyes before entering the tunnel.

The harsh voice spoke slowly and succinctly, penetrating the interior of the jet like an electrical discharge, and then the following silence felt almost like an explosion of its own. As if in a trance, Taylor's attention was fixed on the expanding blackness and the blinding ring of plasma surrounding it. When the voice crackled again, she finally closed her eyes, mostly from fright.

Now!

When the explosion of light hit them, she held her hands over her eyes for additional shielding, and then the tremendous energy required to create the black tunnel nearly knocked her unconscious. Taylor had never felt such immense energy being released. The alien machinery on Mercury was ripping apart the vacuum of space to create an even emptier void.

From her engineering experience, she knew the tunnel would have an equal amount of energy opposing it. In the following darkness, an ocean of pressure seemed to surround them, attempting to collapse the tunnel, the jet, and all of its occupants.

Once inside the tunnel, everyone slowly removed their hands from their faces and opened their eyes. During their short time there, no one spoke. Everyone was looking through the windows at the darkness, making brief eye contact with each other as if to reconfirm their own existence. Even the children were silent.

At the end of the tunnel, Taylor had to turn away from the bright lights blazing through the windows. For some mysterious reason, she noticed the time on her watch. Gerald was fascinated with that particular minute, twelve thirty-four. He had even given it a name—magic time.

—※—

When her eyes adjusted to the bright light streaming through the cockpit window, Taylor first noticed the immense horizon of a new planet. A star-filled sky stretched above the horizon, with white clouds, blue water, and dark land masses below it. For a brief moment, she almost mistook the planet for Earth. But Mark sitting silently beside her was a stark reminder of the present circumstances. Her only other view of a planet from space had been with Max in the BMW.

For nearly a minute, she and Mark just stared at the scene, their harnesses keeping them secured to their seats. When the sudden sensation of gravity pulled her forward, she jolted in surprise. Someone other than she or Mark had engaged the engines to counteract the planet's gravitational force.

Before entering the tunnel, the alien entity—or maybe just the probe—had taken control of their craft and delivered them to their current position. The sensation of gravity became an unwelcome reminder of the mysterious next phase of their journey. Taylor was still trying to make sense of their time in the tunnel, which had felt like a trip through a dimension with a different version of time.

When the warm hand touched her shoulder, Taylor inhaled in shock. She had forgotten about everyone else in the jet. Cesar's voice seemed to wake her from a trance. When she turned to face him, he was standing at an angle, holding onto the wall for balance.

"I do not suppose," Cesar began, "that either of you know where we are?"

Mark turned his head and Taylor thought he looked as confused as she felt, still disoriented from the strange experiences. He turned back to the windshield, remaining silent.

"You scared me, Cesar," Taylor said, her laugh lacking humor. She exhaled in resignation. "No, I have no idea where we are. We entered that black tunnel, then the next thing I know, we're staring at this."

Taylor waved her hand toward the cockpit's front window, at the breathtaking view of the unknown horizon. After a moment, she turned back to Cesar. While holding onto her shoulder, he also stared at the scene, his warm hand alleviating some of her stress.

Despite her excitement at reaching what she assumed was their destination, she was still experiencing considerable anxiety. She felt almost as if she lacked the ability to cope with her present circumstances. Earth, her home, almost seemed non-existent, and her fellow companions had become her only resources. She thought of Cesar as a father figure, someone who could handle the situation for her.

She noticed the awkward way he was standing, so she thought of a way to help him.

"Let me reorient this thing, so it's more comfortable for you."

While orienting the jet normal to the planet, her body fell neatly into her seat. The action helped her feel more in control of the situation.

"Much better," he said, finally standing up straight. "Thanks."

"I'm going to go check on the kids," Mark said after tearing his gaze from the view. "I'm sure you both can handle things."

Mark stood slowly from his seat, walked past them, and entered the cabin. Cesar sat in Mark's seat and spoke while looking forward. At the start of their conversation, the sound of voices from the cabin replaced the silence.

"We weren't sent back to Earth, were we?" Cesar asked. "It's kind of hard to tell."

Taylor searched for any hint of sarcasm in Cesar's voice but found none. The thought of returning them to Earth made no sense. The possibility both frightened Taylor and excited her. She looked more closely at the visible land below them and found no familiar shapes, but the heavy cloud cover obscured most of the land and water. The place did not feel like her home.

"Why would you say that?" Taylor asked and waited several seconds for him to answer.

"It just seems," he began after searching for the right words, "unlikely to find a planet so much like Earth. Doesn't it?"

"I suppose so, but Freddy said there was another planet we could escape to. It doesn't make sense to return. We barely escaped with our lives. I don't want to go back and be a refugee the rest of my life, at least not yet."

Cesar shook his head and smiled.

"This is too much for me," he confessed.

"I understand," Taylor said, her lips also stretching into a wide smile. "Try to think of this as an adventure. And when we return, you'll have quite the story to tell your daughter. My mom would freak out! I probably won't be able to tell her."

"You think we'll be able to go back?"

"If it was this easy to get here," Taylor answered, "then we'll definitely be able to return."

"It was easy for us, but we're not making the decisions, are we? I don't like this feeling of *dependence*."

The sudden tone of despair in Cesar's voice gave Taylor a new purpose, to make him feel better about their situation. She stood from her seat and stretched her legs and arms, then grabbed his shoulder.

"Because we were almost thrown into some military prison for the rest of our lives, or killed for knowing too much, I think this is a much better position. Come on, let's go see how everyone's doing. We need to decide what to do next. After two and a half days without a shower, we need to make some quick decisions."

Cesar looked up at her and his fake smile suddenly seemed slightly less fake.

"You're right," Cesar said and his tone turned from somber to sarcastic. "Let's go make our decision before we're destroyed by some orbiting rock."

Taylor led Cesar from the cockpit of the jet into the main cabin to find the remaining eleven passengers looking through the windows. Only Gerald and Max remained seated. Sadi's two little girls stood at one window and Mark's two little boys stood at the adjacent window. They were all pointing and talking excitedly. Taylor paused to enjoy their tiny voices, but not really listening to their words.

Mark and his wife, Susan, stood at the window closest to their boys. Taylor thought Mark looked excited, but his wife wore a worried scowl. Although Taylor liked Mark's wife, she suddenly felt grateful not to have a binding relationship with anyone.

Sadi was staring through one window while Gerald sat next to her, looking over her shoulder. Max sat across from him, on the other side. When Taylor looked at him, he turned to face her. He smiled awkwardly, shook his head, then looked away. During their journey, both Gerald and Max had recovered a little from when they first arrived at the campsite, their takeoff site. But neither man had returned to normal, and they spoke much less than usual. Taylor hoped their psychological recovery just needed more time.

With all of her completely new surroundings and experiences, Taylor could easily ignore some other disturbing issues, like the emotional and psychological well-being of her friends. All thirteen passengers had to wrestle with their own issues, and Taylor needed to worry less about them and try to cope with her own anxiety.

Before Taylor or Cesar took the opportunity to address the group,

Dominga turned from her window.

"Do you know where we are?" she asked, looking from Cesar to Taylor and then back to the window. She experienced difficulty finding the right words for her next question. "Any signal, from anyone?"

All of the adults turned to stare at Cesar and Taylor. Only the children continued talking. They seemed oblivious to anything but the view from the windows. Cesar waited for Taylor to speak. Maybe he thought her positive attitude would be more effective than his tension. Taylor knew him enough to read his intentions.

"We've heard no communication except for that voice before the tunnel," she said, feeling slightly uncomfortable with so many eyes focused on her. "I have a feeling though, that we need to decide our own course of action before we hear from whatever it is that brought us here."

"Too bad Freddy is not with us," Dominga said. "He would probably know what to do. That probe thing seemed to like him."

"I don't think we should expect Freddy anytime soon," Sadi interjected. "I doubt he was able to find the others so soon, and he has no way to get them all here."

At the sound of her mother's voice, Helen turned momentarily from the window and Taylor smiled at her. She returned the gesture, but only slightly, then quickly returned her attention to the window. For some reason, she could not explain at the moment, having the children with them felt comforting.

"I agree," Taylor answered after returning her focus to Sadi. "We should probably review our options first. I don't know about the rest of you, but I really need a shower, and it looks like there's water down there."

"Wait a minute," Susan said, wiping her short blond hair away from her dark eyes. "You're suggesting that we go to the surface? How do we know it's safe or that we can even breathe?"

"I don't think we have a choice," Mark answered, probably fearing that Taylor would make a sarcastic reply.

Susan looked at Mark with dangerously narrow eyes, and Taylor suppressed a smile and then looked away from her. When Susan discovered that her husband had been working very closely with Taylor, a pretty and young female, she had failed to hide her suspicion from Taylor and Mark. She liked the woman's aggressive attitude and knew they would eventually become friends.

"Well, we can go back home," Susan said, daring Mark to disagree with her.

Before Mark could reply, Dominga came to his rescue.

"I agree with you, Susan," she said, reaching her hand over the boys to grasp Susan's shoulder. When she spoke again, she addressed the whole group, giving the impression that she and Susan were on the same team. "We cannot stay here, forever. What other options do we have?"

"We are nearly out of food and water, and this craft was not designed for thirteen people." Simon spoke to no one in particular. "The bathroom situation needs to be addressed soon, too."

"What other options do we have, except to attempt a landing?" Sadi asked and directed her gaze at Taylor. "I know this craft got us here, but can we land safely? Is the gravity comparable?"

"You're feeling the gravity now," Taylor answered. "Our engines are keeping us at a constant altitude. We can measure our acceleration later to be more accurate, but to me, it feels like it could be just a little stronger than Earth."

Only the children's quiet discussion kept the silence away. Taylor understood Sadi's concern about the descent to the planet's surface. She had experienced the same worry during her test flight with Max. She remembered imagining their final descent as a ball of fire. Their current altitude and mass represented a considerable amount of dangerous potential energy.

Taylor waited for someone to answer, for anyone to offer any alternative. Other than the children, all eyes focused on her, even Susan. As she opened her mouth to speak, Cesar answered first.

"We all have the same concerns, but I doubt that we were brought to a place where we could not survive." He spoke while focusing on

Susan and Sadi. "I have full confidence that Taylor and Mark can deliver us safely to the surface. We'll look for a safe place to land and then some of us can go in search for what we need while the rest stay with the jet."

"We have instruments," Taylor began, "to help us determine what's out there. We'll probably be able..."

Taylor stopped speaking when Helen turned excitedly from the window. The little girl pulled on her mother's shirt. On the trip, Taylor had gotten a little acquainted with the kids. She loved them all like family, but she especially enjoyed interacting with Helen.

"There's something out there, Mom. It's getting darker too."

Everyone rushed to the nearest window to look. Taylor had to look through the gap between Dominga and Cesar. When she could not see clearly enough, she ran to the cockpit and leaned over the instrument panel. Her mouth hung wide open as she watched the view of the planet and stars slowly disappear.

People spoke in the background, but Taylor failed to notice anything other than the two huge panels slowly closing in front of the jet, erasing her view of the beautiful planet and sky. For the second time that day, a warm hand grasped her shoulder.

"I guess we're not going to the surface just yet."

TWO

Sadi

“What's happening, Mom?” Helen asked without turning from the window.

“Don't be afraid, honey,” Sadi said in a weak attempt at comfort, her tone in opposition to her emotions. “I really don't know what's going on, but we made it this far. This is just another part of our adventure.”

Daryn and Helen grasped each other's hands tightly. Sadi thought they looked more excited than frightened. If only she could feel the same. After leaving Earth, she constantly worried about what might happen next. A mysterious future lay before them, but she should have been more accustomed to that perspective.

“We're in some kind of hangar,” Simon said from the other side of the aisle. “A landing bay.”

Sadi watched as the two huge walls closed and then the beautiful view of the planet disappeared completely. After the giant doors closed in front of them, Sadi thought she heard a rush of wind outside the jet. She had not heard any sound outside the jet since they left Earth's atmosphere, except for the voice at the tunnel.

For the next few seconds, the walls in front of them caught Sadi's attention and she briefly forgot her feeling of dread. Their shiny surface reminded her of the probe, which had led them on the first part of their journey after leaving Earth.

The closing of the doors caused an unexpected relief to sweep through Sadi. For some reason, a descent to the planet's surface had become a palpable fear, as strong as anything from a horror movie. Was she afraid of burning up in the atmosphere, or finding something horrible on the planet's surface? Sadi was not sure. Whatever the reason, the giant doors had rescued them from an unknown fate, and she felt a strange relief.

Capture by an unknown alien seemed like less of a threat, now that a protective atmosphere had replaced the void of space. During their long journey, she had forgotten about their proximity to death, just beyond a few centimeters of the jet's protective walls.

When she sensed the gentle movement of the jet, everyone ceased discussion, even the children. On their descent to the floor, Sadi looked down and noticed the mesmerizing floor surface, composed of some swirly marble material, multicolored and surprisingly beautiful. While staring at the floor, she began to feel a little dizzy, almost as if going to sleep but with open eyes.

Another sensation of change distracted her from the beautiful floor, and she quickly recognized the feeling, a decrease in the strength of gravity. The subtle disorientation reminded her of descending in an elevator. After about twelve seconds, they came to such a smooth stop, that Sadi only realized it after the maneuver had ended. For the next few seconds, everyone in the cabin continued to stare outside of the jet, watching for someone or something to walk into view. But after failing to see any movement in the large hangar, Sadi pulled Helen and Daryn away from the window.

"You two stay close to me," she said with a forced smile. "Whatever happens, stay close and don't do anything without asking first."

"Okay," Helen said, closing her mouth and puffing out her cheeks in a mock hold-your-breath contest. "Tell us when we can breathe."

Sadi smiled involuntarily, but she quickly erased the emotion. She wanted to impress on her silly daughter the seriousness of their situation.

"Enough kidding around, Helen," Sadi scolded. "Daryn, be a good girl and help me keep an eye on your sister."

"Okay," Daryn said without any trace of joviality. She had a better grasp of their precarious situation.

"That goes for you too," Susan said from across the aisle to her two boys.

Neither of her children looked away from the window. Susan glanced at Sadi and shook her head slightly, a look of indignation. Having another mother with them helped Sadi feel much less alone. She had grown to like Mark's wife and their boys.

Almost a minute later, Taylor and Cesar emerged from the cockpit and all eyes turned towards them, even Helen and Daryn. Sadi noticed the look of concern in Cesar's eyes. When Taylor spoke, her excitement contrasted sharply with the look on Cesar's face.

"According to our sensors," she began, "the pressure outside has reached approximately one atmosphere and it seems to be composed of the right proportion of oxygen, nitrogen, and water vapor. The temperature is also a comfortable twenty-two degrees Celsius. God, I sound like a stewardess. Although we have not had any communication with whatever it is that led us here, we think it's safe to exit the jet."

Sadi felt a strange mix of emotions. Just a few minutes previous, she had looked out the window at the vacuum of space, and now they could safely go outside the jet. Despite the potential dangers of their unknown situation, Sadi experienced an incredible urge to leave what had come to feel like a prison. Alternatively, parental instincts said to keep her children in a safe environment. Brief eye contact with Susan told her the woman felt the same.

"I am going outside to make sure it is safe," Cesar said.

"Cesar and I are going," Taylor interjected.

"I think a better idea is for me to go first," Simon said.

Sadi drew a deep breath, her muscles tensing in anticipation of another confrontation. During their journey, Taylor and Simon had gotten into a few uncomfortable arguments. Their most recent argument had started when Taylor had teasingly accused Simon of cheating during a card game. The argument quickly escalated when he took her accusation seriously, claiming that sarcasm was often a subtle revelation of truth.

Sadi remembered being amused at first, but then she and the other participants in the game quickly found something else to do. Simon and Taylor only spoke again after they both took a long nap. Taylor secretly enjoyed her effect on him, Sadi suspected.

"It's not because I'm a girl, is it?" Taylor replied with exaggerated sarcasm.

"Kind of," Simon said casually. "I'm a man, and no offense, Cesar, a little younger. I'm better suited to handle any unpleasant situation."

"Ha!" Taylor laughed, eyes wide and a wicked smile. "If the alien opens those doors and throws you in a vacuum, is your manhood going to save you?"

Simon looked at Taylor without any trace of emotion in his eyes. He turned slowly to Mark.

"Come on, Mark. Help me open the door."

"I'm coming with you," Taylor said and laughed again. "You know that, right?"

"Taylor," he said, and Sadi thought she heard exasperation in his voice. "We should only open the door for as short of a time as possible. If the air outside has something in it that might affect us, I don't want it to come into the plane. *And get all of us.*"

"If that thing wanted to kill us, it could have already, Simon."

Taylor took the required steps to reach the exit door to join Simon and Mark. Sadi suppressed a smile and shook her head, but her impatience was growing. No matter who went outside to investigate the situation, she wanted the wait as short as possible. She wanted out of the jet.

"Taylor, seriously, just let me go outside and I'll give the all clear in just a few minutes. It won't be long. I promise."

"I think he's right," Mark said as he began turning the unlocking mechanism. When the seal broke, Sadi heard a quick rushing sound. "I'll hold the door long enough for you too if you really want to, but I think it should just be Simon."

Taylor turned to Mark with a renewed look of anger. For a moment, everyone waited for her to respond.

"Fine," she said in resignation and then stepped away from the door.

When Simon glanced at her again, Sadi saw no emotion there. Then he turned back to Mark who nodded and opened the door all the way. Simon quickly jumped down to the floor and Mark closed the door behind him.

Everyone stepped to the nearest window to watch as Simon took a few steps away from the jet and then looked up at the window. Sadi's heartbeat increased in excitement at the thought of joining him, to breathe different air, stand on different ground.

"He's not dead yet," Helen said to Daryn then turned to her mother in excitement.

Sadi heard quiet laughter from Dominga, Cesar, and Mark. The remaining passengers continued to watch outside in anticipation of something happening. Dominga turned to Helen and used her right hand to press the child into her hip.

"That's very good news, isn't it?" Dominga spoke while laughing, relief in her tone.

Outside the jet, Simon stood for a few minutes in the same position and looked in all different directions. When he walked out of their sight, Sadi heard movement behind her and turned to see Taylor walk to the exit hatch.

"You're right, Helen," Taylor said while stepping into the hatch. "He's not dead. It should be safe for the rest of us."

"Hold on, Taylor. Let's wait for Simon to give the all clear." Mark stepped back from the hatch and pointed through its window. "He's coming back."

Sadi looked back to the window and saw Simon come to a stop

where he first landed after jumping from the jet. He stopped and looked up at them all and gave a thumbs up. Sadi looked down from his upraised hand and noticed the multi-colored swirly floor again. With almost overwhelming anticipation, she imagined how wonderful the hard floor would feel under her feet.

When Simon helped Sadi exit the jet, she immediately noticed the familiar smell of fresh rain in the air. She breathed the cool, welcome air as deeply as she ever remembered doing on Earth.

Sadi immediately turned and helped Helen and then Daryn exit. After setting Daryn on the ground, both girls stood by her and looked around at their new surroundings. As a total surprise to Sadi and everyone else, tears immediately began to fall from her eyes.

"What's wrong, Mom?" Helen asked, hugging her mother's waist.

Sadi laughed while answering.

"I'm just so glad to be off that thing."

After Dominga joined them, she stepped to Sadi's side and hugged her.

"Oh my god! It is so nice to be out of there. I do hope this place has a decent bathroom and shower."

Susan joined them with her boys and for several seconds, they all just looked around the gigantic room. Only the jet occupied the large area, which could have held several Boeing 747 airplanes. The wall, which had opened to let them into the landing bay, had a long horizontal seam and almost looked like a giant zipper.

A long row of lights shined from high above them in a high ceiling, maybe thirty meters high, Sadi guessed. Each light resembled a large ring of plasma. Sadi could have stared at them for a long time, enjoying the different colors there. Whatever had led them through space and that frightening tunnel, at least Sadi appreciated its taste in decoration.

THREE

Josef

During a long break between speakers at the second South America-Africa summit in late September 2009, Josef Brunner, the chief of Libyan intelligence, decided to go on a walk. The sea air on Isla de Margarita in Venezuela felt cool on his skin, and especially clean in his lungs, a welcome replacement for the smell of all the humans at the summit.

As he walked away from the beach resort, on a small trail through the palm trees, the sound of the ocean and salty air partially replaced his mental exhaustion. Listening to that imbecile, Colonel Gaddafi, had really worn on his patience. At the end of the previous week, Josef had listened to him for over an hour and a half. After the short break, Josef had to endure yet another hour.

For the first three minutes on the trail, Josef fought the temptation of spending mental energy on his work, but he focused instead on the sound of crashing just beyond the trees, the crunch of the gravel under his shoes, and the rustling of the leaves in the wind. The combined sensations helped to clear his mind and prepare him for what he needed to do, digest the latest proceedings of the summit.

Colonel Gaddafi had needed more and more assistance acting as the leader of the Libyan state, and the effort was wearing on Josef's patience. While listening to his latest speech, Josef had made an unpleasant conclusion. The time had finally arrived to begin their next set of actions. Josef was partially excited to begin their plan for the region, but the thought alone nearly exhausted him.

Josef had successfully built the Colonel into a symbol of hope for an African alliance and now he would have to dash that hope to pieces and ensure that the entire region felt the message. After the summit, Josef was required to send his final decision to his superiors.

After another long and deep breath, Josef decided to suspend the enjoyment of his relaxing surroundings and return his attention to less pleasant input. He paused and turned around to wait for his silent companion, Enzo, to catch up with him. The shorter man, his chief intelligence officer, looked up from the gravel path and patiently met Josef's intense blue eyes without any intimidation.

"Ich nehme an, das ist weit genug, Euer Gnaden," Enzo said politely after arriving within a meter of the much taller Josef. "Niemand kann uns hier hören. Ich bin sehr gespannt, was Sie über die Konferenz denken und ob Sie sich entschieden haben. Ich kann..." he paused to search for the right words, "euren besorgten Verstand sehen."

Josef laughed softly but without humor and then paused before responding. He stared into Enzo's dark brown Italian eyes and attempted to determine if the younger man was worried about being attacked by some local criminal or overheard by a member of President Chávez's security. Josef had to agree with the man's concern about being overheard. If the Venezuelan leader heard that Colonel Gaddafi's top intelligence officers were speaking in German, he would suspect their covert status.

"We should continue in English," Josef said with a hint of apology. Both men spoke English and Arabic fluently, but Josef preferred to speak in English. "I desire your advice without any misinterpretation due to language. I appreciate, however, your gracious attempt to use German. As you know, my use of Italian would have the same potential for misunderstanding."

Josef allowed a quick display of humor to appear in the corner of his mouth. He felt completely capable of conversing in Italian but wanted to be polite to his trusted officer whose use of German left a sour sound in his ears.

"Of course, Your Grace," Enzo said quietly with a hint of disappointment.

Josef ignored the small emotional discharge from his second in command, a man who just wanted to please him. In Libya, they only spoke Arabic, never their native tongue. Once they had arrived on Margarita Island and found some isolation, they had agreed to speak in any other language. They felt a mutual need to take a break from speaking in Arabic. Even English held more appeal than the dirty speech of the desert.

"Although everything is going as planned," Josef began with a tone of resignation. "I anticipate the next stage with extreme displeasure. What is your opinion? Can you think of any other option?"

"Like you say, they all look to Muammar as the man with the strength to carry the project forward. I don't see any other option. All the African heads now look to him. The most effective way to destroy the dream of a Southern Union and send an effective message is to cut off the head. Libya must fall, and at the last moment, Gaddafi will fall with it. There is no other way."

Josef sighed with disappointment. He expected Enzo to give that answer but hoped for an escape from the unpleasant task of planning the downfall and restructuring of an entire country, or the appearance of it at least. They had much to do.

"I am sorry," Enzo said with a tone of real regret. "Neither of us wants to start a civil war, even if just the appearance of one, but I'm sure you will be able to minimize the suffering."

"I appreciate your confidence in my abilities."

"At least we won't have to babysit Muammar anymore," Enzo said with a smile. "He's ready for his retirement, and won't shut up about it."

Josef opened his mouth to say more but decided instead to take another deep breath of the salty air. His paltry attempt at seeking an alternative course of action instilled a momentary feeling of failure. So far, he had perfectly executed his assignment as the head of Libyan intelligence. The administration had praised his leadership, and until that point, their appreciation of his talents had sustained his motivation. But during the summit, and especially after speaking with Enzo on the subject, Josef felt the heavy weight of responsibility resting almost entirely on his shoulders. Enzo's presence offered only a fleeting comfort.

"Your Grace?" Enzo said tentatively.

"We should start walking back," he responded, ignoring the temptation to explain his momentary loss of attention. "We wouldn't want to be late. We might miss the remainder of Colonel Gaddafi's speech."

As Josef expected, Enzo laughed at the sarcasm, since they had written all of the speeches.

Just as their walk into the security of the palm trees, Enzo walked behind Josef by several meters. When the beach returned to his view, Josef's attention was drawn to a pair of women sunbathing on the beach, about fifty meters away.

Before turning to view the rest of the beach, Josef experienced an intense desire for a sexual encounter with the woman on the left. When he regained control of his thoughts, he wondered what his wife would think of his choice. For a certainty, she would laugh at him. He suddenly missed her and then felt stupid for the distraction.

A vibration from his phone interrupted his thoughts. After retrieving it from his shirt pocket, under his grey suit coat, he stared at the phone number with momentary confusion. He had expected instructions from the Colonel to return, but instead, a message came from his direct superior, who very rarely sent texts. With his heart beating wildly, Josef prepared to see the whole message. He stopped on the trail and drew a deep breath to regain his composure.

After the summit, meet us at the Library.

Prepare Enzo as your replacement.

"Your Grace?" Enzo asked, turning.

For nearly ten seconds, Josef failed to respond and just watched the horizon beyond the waves, squinting in the sunlight. A hundred thoughts passed quickly through his mind, cars on a busy highway. Enzo waited patiently.

"They have called me to another assignment," he said without emotion. "You are my replacement."

FOUR

Sadi

"I have to go to the bathroom," Mark's oldest boy said after all thirteen refugees from Earth had exited the jet.

"Why didn't you go before now?" his mother asked in exasperation.

Sadi and Susan looked down at the small six-year-old boy. His blond hair partly covered his beautiful blue eyes.

"I didn't have to go then."

"Well, your dad will have to lift you back up," she said. "But you might have to wait."

The brief exchange between Susan and her son reminded Sadi of the utter strangeness of their situation. That exchange belonged to a long car drive, not a trillion light-year journey, or whatever ridiculous distance they had traveled. The cognitive dissonance made Sadi feel as if she was in a crazy science fiction movie.

"Mark, can you lift..."

Before Susan could finish her sentence, something began making a strange clicking noise. Susan and Sadi followed the source of the sound and noticed the three large entryways leading out of the landing bay to their left. The hallways had no doors, just an opening for each in the wall, extending to the ceiling.

Sadi watched with fascination and a trace of dread as three machines approached them. Calling them robots seemed wrong to her. The only robots Sadi had ever seen all resembled some kind of life form. These did not resemble any form of organic life. Each had two appendages extending to the ground, like legs, but not touching the floor. They floated smoothly above the floor towards the group and made a soft clicking sound with a frequency just low enough for Sadi to hear the individual clicks. Several other appendages extended from a central mass of tubes, rings, rods, and other shapes she failed to recognize. Some of the appendages resembled hands but with three robot fingers in a circle, like three thumbs.

At first, everyone stopped talking and watched as the machines approached, but when they came within about twenty meters, Simon, Mark, and Cesar stepped in front of the group, forming a human shield for the rest of them. The men's reaction made her think of a more primitive civilization from the ancient past when humans lived in small tribes and the men had to protect the group.

Although none of the three *things* approaching them looked identical, Sadi could not quite tell them apart. Each had a larger central compartment protected by six separate plates of glass—two red, two yellow, and two blue. One of the yellow plates rotated randomly. The machines' lack of symmetry made them seem more mechanical and less like living creatures, making them less intimidating. The longer Sadi inspected them, the more curious she became and the less afraid.

"What are those things, Mom?" Helen asked, trying to release herself from Sadi's grasp to get a better look.

"Stay here, Helen," Sadi said while attempting to focus on the machines' approach.

All three machines stopped about two meters from the group. The closest one stretched itself taller than the others, nearly three meters high, maybe so it could see the entire group, Sadi thought. After they stopped, Helen and Daryn stepped closer to Sadi and looked at the machines with wide eyes. Sadi squeezed the girls' hands almost too tightly, but she hardly noticed. When they heard the voice, Sadi's heart almost stopped. The sound originated from inside her head, not her ears.

Welcome!

For a moment, no one answered. Sadi noticed each of the men had become tense. Before the voice, they had only seemed curious, as Sadi felt. A moment later, the front machine shortened itself a bit.

"Gracias," Cesar said, speaking for the group. "What are you?"

"No need to be worried," it said audibly, with a slightly mechanical yet female voice and a Northwestern American accent. Sadi wondered if its initial greeting to Cesar had been in Spanish. "We are here to serve you."

The sound seemed to emanate from the main compartment, but Sadi could not determine what part had produced the sound. The machine remained perfectly still, but the round yellow plate kept rotating and drew her eyes to it. She kept a tight grip on Helen and Daryn, holding them close. Although she no longer felt any threat, a strong parental instinct urged her to hold on to them.

"We will communicate through a method more suited to your experience. Sound seems to cause less anxiety. As to our identity, you can think of us as servants. We have been programmed to meet your needs. If we are not mistaken, the young one here needs to use a toilet." One of its appendages extended forward and a mechanical finger pointed between Simon and Mark at the boy. "Please follow us to the rooms we have prepared."

"Before we go anywhere with you," Simon said, "we need to know where we are and what we're doing here."

"Of course," it answered politely. "Overall, you are safe, but to answer your question, we are occupying an observation station, orbiting a planet very similar to your Earth. It has many names, which we can go over later. We have a specific coordinate system, but I'm afraid our location would be meaningless to you."

"Well, that answers all my questions," Taylor said sarcastically to Simon then stepped between him and Mark. She turned to the machine in front of her. "Right now, I'm a little more interested in seeing what this place has for us."

"Do you have any more questions before we take you to your rooms?"

"I don't," Taylor answered for the group then turned and made brief eye contact with Sadi and Susan. "But we can talk more on our way."

"Of course, follow us then."

The machines did not turn but just started floating back toward the corridor of their origin. During their levitation, they remained exactly the same distance from the floor. Sadi found herself watching their movement with fascination.

Everyone followed the machines as a cohesive group, staying in their same relative positions. The rotating yellow glass had a black sensor of some sort in the center and Sadi stared at it, wondering what kind of signal it was designed to detect or transmit. As they walked, Sadi relaxed her grip on the girls and found that Helen stopped trying to escape. When they entered the darker corridor, Sadi concentrated on breathing the fresh air.

As they walked, the machines remained silent and only the children talked with each other. Sadi had several questions to ask, but their strange surroundings consumed all of her attention.

The group walked through the tall corridor for a few minutes, passing entrances to several other hallways. After turning into one, they walked a short distance and stopped at a strangely familiar object, a human-sized wooden door set in the tall wall. The wood looked out of place in the multi-colored marble wall, Sadi thought.

The closest machine reached out and used its three-fingered appendage to turn the knob and gently push the door open, revealing a lighter area inside.

"This is where your rooms are located," the machine said.

Sadi assumed the voice came from the same machine that had appeared to do all the talking so far, but she could not positively identify either of the machines as the speaker. The first machine floated through the doorway and the two other machines moved aside so the group could see inside the new hallway.

"We have prepared a room for each of you, for your stay with us," it said.

The sound came from inside the new doorway, so Sadi had guessed correctly about which machine was speaking to them.

"You are free of course," it continued, "to group together until you feel more comfortable and familiar."

Simon stepped into the new hallway first, followed by Cesar, Mark, Taylor, and then the rest of them. Dominga entered last, after Max and Gerald who looked around with more distrust in their eyes than everyone else. Sadi was curious to know Gerald's thoughts, but at the moment she had other interests. She first noticed the much lower ceiling with the same round plasma lights. While looking up at them, she saw all colors swirling inside the fat glass tubes. Sadi made a mental note to inspect the lights more closely later.

When she looked back at the hallway, she noticed the construction material of the walls, a polished wood resembling cedar. Her next breath confirmed the material identity. She definitely smelled the familiar scent of cedar.

The new hallway had more wooden doors on each side, spaced evenly apart by maybe four meters. Sadi quickly counted at least eight doors on one side. Before she could finish counting all the doors, Dominga's voice interrupted her.

"I think I would like to have this entrance closed," Dominga said and shut the door after the other machines had moved into the hallway.

Sadi pulled Daryn and Helen close as the machines passed. Although they were in a wide hallway and there was plenty of room for movement, the proximity of the machines to her girls caused a sudden panic, but it quickly subsided. Dominga looked at Sadi with wide eyes, then breathed deeply before speaking again.

"I feel better with the door closed. It seems to separate us a little from all this strangeness."

"Yes, it does," Sadi admitted. "Do you smell the cedar?"

Dominga breathed deeply again and smiled.

"Oh my," she said. "How did they—"

"Excuse me," said one of the machines.

Dominga stopped talking and turned to look at them. Everyone in the group also became silent. It lifted one of its appendages and then pointed a robotic finger to the nearest door.

"The doors have your names engraved on them," the voice continued. "This one is for Sadi and of course, the nearest ones are for Helen and Daryn."

A small hand began pulling on her shirt. Sadi looked down while Helen spoke with obvious excitement.

"It knows our names, Mom!"

Sadi turned and noticed Susan looking at her. A silent communication quickly passed between them, an acknowledgment of warning. Sadi felt much less excitement than her daughter. Hearing her name by the alien voice caused a chill through her system.

All thirteen refugees from Earth found their doors in the hallway and stood before them, waiting for some unknown signal to indicate their next move. Simon and Taylor entered theirs first and left their doors open. Sadi did not immediately open her door but stood before it and prevented Helen and Daryn from going to theirs. She stared at her first and last name, beautifully carved in the wood. Only a machine could have carved her name with such perfection. She put her hand on the beautiful door knob, a polished silvery metal.

"Let's check out my room first," Sadi said to the girls then turned to look at the nearest machine. It stood there silently, perfectly motionless except for the rotating yellow glass with the dark sensor in the middle. She tried ignoring the sensation of being watched. "We'll go see yours if everything looks okay in mine."

"Yes, Sadi," Daryn said.

Immediately after Sadi opened the door, her eyes opened wide and she stopped breathing. A sudden dizziness caused her to hold onto the wall with her left hand for balance. Sadi found herself staring at a copy of her room from the house she'd left on Earth. She slowly stepped inside. In her state of shock, she watched as Helen and Daryn ran into the room before her. Sadi reached out in a vain attempt to stop Helen's entrance.

"It's exactly like your room back home, Mom."

Helen spoke with pure excitement and ran to the bed, jumping onto it as she would have done at their home. Daryn followed her with less enthusiasm. The neatly made bed had the pillows stacked as Sadi would have stacked them. She required several seconds for her disorientation to pass, the dichotomy of finding her room on an alien orbiting observation station. The girls seemed unaffected.

When Sadi noticed the bathroom door, the absurdity of her situation vanished. Access to a normal bathroom became her greatest desire. After opening the door, she walked tentatively to the toilet, opened the lid, and flushed. While watching the clear, swirling water, Sadi tried to recall a more beautiful sight.

FIVE

Josef

Josef watched through the window as his driver waited for the gate to open. The sight of his home estate released a tsunami of emotions and his eyes suddenly became moist. Three white spires from the main house pointed to the sky, the tallest in the center, evoking the image of stalagmites in a cave. He'd never thought of them like that before and wondered, momentarily, if the connection meant any kind of foreboding. When the gate opened, and they started traveling down the cobblestone drive, Josef's blood pressure started to rise in anxious anticipation. He fought back the tears as his emotions almost overpowered him.

A large garden with a fountain and statue of his great-great-grandfather separated him from the house. As they approached in silence, he turned his gaze from the house to watch the water trickle down the statue and into the rippling surface of the pond. If the sun were visible, he would have seen a warped reflection of the spires, but the overcast sky denied him the pleasure. For a brief moment, the statue blocked the view of the staircase, twenty-three steps to the main entrance of the three-hundred-year-old structure.

When the stairs returned to his view, his eyes ascended them one by one almost as slowly as if by foot, to see the most beautiful sight his mind could have created. His wife stood at the top of the steps, wearing a beautiful silver-blue dress with hand-woven white lace, most likely a new piece she had purchased just for his return. The bottom of the dress and her long blond hair flowed slightly with the breeze in almost perfect synchronization.

As the car rolled to a stop in front of the stairs, Josef's eyes remained fixed on the scene at the top. He waited patiently for the driver to open the door for him, almost wishing for the moment to never end. The desire to hold his wife and see his children gave his muscles the strength they needed to start moving. As he ascended the steps, he counted each one but kept his gaze upward, maintaining eye contact with his wife.

"Hello, Lise," Josef said in English before she could speak in German.

"Hello, Your Grace," she said in a respectful tone, but Josef could hear the slight inflection of sarcasm.

She spoke English with her natural Norwegian accent, but if she had desired, her acting ability would have kept any accent completely hidden. While addressing him, she bowed her head slightly and part of her blond hair fell over her right ear. Josef ignored his instinct to return those beautiful blond strands of hair to their original position.

He loved to hear her speak in her native Norwegian and regretted that he still had not found the time to gain fluency in that language. If he had allowed her to speak first, she would have chosen German for him, out of respect, but she had the same difficulty speaking his native language. Nevertheless, she spoke German much better than he spoke Norwegian.

Arabic had taken too much of his time to learn. That little contribution to his life, from his previous assignment, deepened his dislike of what he liked to call the dirty desert speech.

"You cannot imagine my relief at seeing you, and hearing you!"

She laughed, throwing her arms around his neck. The pressure of her breasts on his ribs inspired him to hug her even tighter. He released her after hearing the breath escape her lungs.

"Don't you want to see the children?" she said, her lungs refilling with air. She stepped to the side so he could see his two young daughters and seven-year-old son. As Lise smiled widely, he noticed the contrast of her white teeth with her blond hair.

"Hello, Father," his second daughter said with a heavy German accent, then she and her sister curtsied. His son remained motionless. Both girls resembled their mother, with blond hair, light-blue eyes, and sharp features. His son had the same facial features but with the piercing, dark-blue eyes of his father.

While each child came forward to hug him, Josef felt slightly awkward. He hardly knew them, regretfully, and the action felt more like a formality than a genuine sign of affection. He began speaking with them in German, asking simple questions about their lives, to which the girls returned short answers.

His son spoke with excitement and immediately began asking Josef how he liked living in the desert with the Arabs. His mother had told him exciting stories about his father as a major figure in the Middle East. In contrast, his daughters had shown much less interest in him.

After the formalities of the reunion had ended, Lise and the children followed Josef to the main entrance. An older male servant with grey hair stood on the left of the large door, and a younger woman stood on the right, her black hair wrapped in a bun. Both servants smiled politely. Josef recognized the older man. After making brief eye contact, the man bowed his head.

Once they entered the estate, the female servant took Josef's son and said he would rejoin them during lunch. The daughters curtsied and walked down a hallway, leaving Josef, Lise, and the older servant alone. The man stood out of their way, eyes averted and awaiting instructions.

"So you only have two days with us?" Lise asked while watching her daughters walk away. "What do you want to do first?"

Without saying a word, Josef looked hungrily into his wife's eyes, then his gaze traveled downward to enjoy the view of her attire and form. She smiled and turned to the servant.

"Wir werden für Sie anrufen, wenn wir etwas brauchen," Lise said but faced her husband with a smile.

"Ja, natürlich," the man said, then walked away.

—✳—

Later, when Josef and Lise rejoined their children for lunch, Josef experienced a small amount of anxiety about reconnecting with them. For years, he had only interacted with adults—often hostile ones—and only rarely dealt with young children. In some ways, he would have felt more comfortable giving directions to a group of dangerous mercenaries hired by US Central Intelligence.

But to his great relief, Josef thoroughly enjoyed lunch with his wife and three children. His daughters spoke for over thirty minutes about the summer they spent with their great aunt, the queen of Norway. Josef felt a small twinge of regret at having missed the event. He would have enjoyed seeing his Norwegian in-laws with his children and wife. He also would have had more practice speaking his wife's native language.

At the end of the meal, he was more familiar with their lives. He especially enjoyed having a conversation in German. At the pinnacle of the event, his young son asked, with some trepidation, to sit on his father's lap.

Later that night after the servants took the children to bed, Josef and Lise found some time alone. After all the discussion with the children, Josef had anxiously awaited more adult conversation.

"I saw the review of your latest film, *Intergalactic*, I think it was called," Josef said, "on that Rotten Potato website."

"Rotten Tomatoes," she chided with a slight smile, but he continued unperturbed.

"A couple of the reviewers hinted that the acting performances were the only saving grace of the film. As the lead role, I assumed they meant your performance."

Lise blushed dramatically then brushed his comment away with a graceful wave of her hand. Although he knew she acted unaffected, Josef recognized her sincere delight at his praise. The action reminded him of a former life when he lived with her and his two young girls. She had always tightly controlled her actions, and he wondered if she ever acted according to her true emotions, and not how she wanted people to think she felt. The life of an actor, he thought and smiled.

"Unfortunately," she began after taking a drink of the red wine in her crystal glass. "The script was shit. I hate to say that, but it was. I worked with some amazing professionals on that film. John was a pure delight to work with. I was very fortunate."

"I haven't watched it yet, I'm afraid, but I want to. I've been too busy, as you know."

"You're always too busy. As soon as I heard of your reassignment, I told the studio that I had to take a few days off." Lise frowned, sighing dramatically. "Oh, I wish you could have attended the premiere with me. Stewart, of course, was an acceptable replacement for you, but as a necessity only. When you return, will you watch it with me?"

"Yes, of course. I don't know when that will be. Maybe you can meet me somewhere?"

"That might be possible," she said, nodding. "Now that we'll be in the same hemisphere more often. That's what you said, isn't it?"

"I really do not know," Josef confessed. "For the first few weeks, I think."

A momentary lull in the conversation became a warning to Josef. He almost sensed Lise's next question, one he did not yet want to answer. For the present, he preferred talking about her work. He loved to see the life in her eyes while she discussed her acting hobby.

"I hope you break up with John soon."

"Not jealous, are you?" she asked with all seriousness.

"Not unless you were jealous of my desert beauty," he answered with sarcasm and then smiled. "She was a good woman. All things must come to an end."

"Of course not. If you chose her, she must have been great. It was unfortunate that I did not get to meet her."

As she prepared to answer his original question, her eyes opened wide in anticipation. For a moment, he wondered if she would inquire further about the covert Libyan wife he left behind, but he knew she would be unable to resist talking about the drama with her Hollywood husband. She loved that public acting role almost as much as her movie roles.

"We've planned a horribly tragic breakup," Lise began, pleasure almost shining from her expression. "He's going to catch me with my lesbian lover, and then he'll check into a drug rehabilitation center after getting arrested at a Hollywood party, naked and high as a kite. It's going to be in all the papers. Oh, and we'll be fighting over our poor children. It's supposed to kick-start Frankie's acting career. The papers will rave about how well he handled the stress and how hard he tried to stay out of the spotlight. In the end, they'll say he was forced to accept at least one of the subsequent acting offers."

"Sounds a little overly dramatic to me, but who am I to judge?"

"You should have heard the original plan from Alex, my agent," she said and laughed. "You're hearing the attenuated version. Who knows how the final version will be. I think it's hilarious how the public believes whatever the papers print."

"You know how it goes," Josef laughed without humor. "Anything you do outside of the movies must be real."

"So true," she said and laughed.

"I read a recent interview online," he said playfully. "I don't like to highlight this sort of thing, but you made a mistake."

"Whatever," she said, laughing even harder. "You love telling me about my mistakes. What did I do wrong?"

"You mentioned your sister."

"I did not!" she said, brows furrowed. After a moment, she sighed. "Okay, I can tell you're not lying. When and how? You're not worried, are you?"

"Of course not," he said. "It can always be called a misquote. Don't feel bad. I've read and watched all of your interviews and that was the only time you referred to your real life."

They talked about her Hollywood life for another hour. Although Josef felt less interest than he was showing, he loved watching her excitement. To keep her going, he simply needed to add the occasional comment and question or show some surprise. She didn't seem to notice how preoccupied he was with his next assignment.

During her story, his mind drifted into thoughts from his former life in Libya. Even in that remote area of the world, he had seen the occasional image of his wife in movie advertisements or on the cover of some magazine. Nowhere on the planet did Hollywood's influence fail to reach. Her image was always a stinging reminder of the physical distance between them. When he saw her with other men, he never felt any jealousy. They were just more testaments to her acting skills.

Near the end of the conversation, Lise noticed when Josef's innocent glance lingered a little too long on her exposed cleavage. When he noticed that she noticed, she stopped speaking, her mouth tightening into a frown.

"Excuse me," she said, acting like a teacher scolding a student, "but my eyes are up here."

"I'm sorry," he said with some embarrassment, a shy smile stretching across his lips. Only Lise had the power to cause that emotion in him. On some deep level, he enjoyed the sensation. "Apparently, I get distracted easily."

"You already took advantage of me this morning," she reminded him. "Was that not enough for you?"

He paused, trying to think of what to say, but a moment later, she smiled and relieved him of the necessity.

"I suppose we'll have to make a second round of things, but first," she paused again and let a moment of silence pass between them.

In those few seconds, he tried guessing what she would ask. Most likely, she saw the opportunity to inquire into his new assignment and wanted the sexual tension to build, and become the driving force to pry information from him. Josef suddenly became jealous. If only he had that power over other men. Her tactic would become stronger than any drug he could have used on an interrogation suspect.

"I want to hear about your new assignment."

In resignation, Josef knew his wife would only be satisfied after she extracted all of the information he possessed.

"I will tell you what I know," he said, focusing on her eyes.

"That's a good boy," she began and smiled deviously. "But first, tell me about your visit to the Library!"

SIX

Sadi

"We will leave you for a while so you can eat and recover from your stressful journey," the machine voice said pleasantly after it led them to the entrance of their dining hall. "We grew the food in several greenhouses on the station that you can visit at a later time. The station will enter shadow soon. We have positioned it to correspond with your circadian rhythm. We will return in the morning, but if there is anything you need, we will come. Just knock four times on any wall."

The machines floated out of the large room and disappeared into the hallway where the bedrooms were located. The group sat at a long dining table full of different foods. Two large white porcelain refrigerators sat against one of the walls next to two large ovens, a huge counter, and a long shiny metal sink. Sadi thought they all looked like normal appliances, just no manufacturer's identification. Cupboards lined the other walls. If not for the food on the table and her hunger, Sadi would have explored the contents of the cupboards.

After the machines left, Sadi returned her attention to the group at the long dining table. At first, no one spoke, not even the children. Everyone just stared at each other. The large spread on the table looked too perfect, almost unreal, but the smell of the food was difficult to deny.

"Can someone convince me that this is not a dream?" Mark asked and laughed.

"I don't care if it's a dream," Taylor replied from the other end of the table, smiling widely and staring at the salad in front of her. "I'm starving, but I have an idea. Simon should try the food first and if he doesn't die, we'll know it's safe. So go ahead, Simon. Here, have a tomato slice. That's what I want the most."

Simon leaned forward to see Taylor more clearly. She sat three seats away, out of his reach.

"An excellent idea, Taylor. I'm going to eat it slowly, just so you have to wait longer." He stabbed a red tomato slice from the salad in front of him, juice dripping as he bit it in half.

Everyone watched as he slowly chewed the tomato. Sadi had to swallow the saliva suddenly pooling around her tongue.

"Be nice," Dominga said, laughing but curiously watching him. "They're not going to kill us with food. I don't need to wait."

Dominga grabbed a slice of bread from a basket in front of her but deliberately delayed taking a bite. Sadi guessed that she preferred to wait for Simon's approval before eating any of the food herself.

"My God," Simon said after swallowing, a sincere look of pleasure in his eyes. "That's the worst tomato I've ever had. I wouldn't have one if I were you, Taylor."

Simon turned to Taylor and slowly placed the other half of the tomato into his mouth. Taylor smiled widely and started shoveling salad onto her plate, all familiar foods: lettuce, cucumber, chickpeas, red onions, several different dressings, and even cheeses.

At that signal, everyone started filling their plates with food. While they ate, the pleasant sound of conversation filled the dining room, mostly speculation about the origin of the food. For the next ninety minutes, everyone enjoyed the feast the machines had prepared for them.

Before the machines had led them to the dining room, all thirteen refugees had spent a couple of hours getting accustomed to their rooms and sharing their amazement. Sadi had taken a shower and then made the girls take one too. She had found a clean set of new clothes in her drawers for each of them. Their rooms contained all the same clothes she had left in her house on Earth. After all of her impossible experiences since ascending from her home planet, she found herself just accepting what came next. In the back of her mind, she felt that perhaps if she questioned her fortunate circumstances too much, their good fortune would stop.

Although Sadi had loved the food and relaxation during their first meal together in the orbiting observation station, she wanted the evening to end. She kept imagining the bed in her room and lying under the covers, and then losing consciousness. What would she find when they awoke?

She tried ignoring that question and focused on having a better night of sleep than the restlessness of their journey. Those two and a half days in the void had passed very slowly, and Sadi remembered feeling dread during the entire trip, a creeping fear that the craft would be hit by some floating piece of rock in space, or they would run out of oxygen, or some other life-threatening situation.

When Cesar stood from his chair, Sadi was the first to look up from the table. The others did not notice until he tapped his glass with a fork. He cleared his throat before speaking.

"If you all don't mind," he began, "I would like to say a few words before we finish our meal and go back to our rooms."

"That is a very good idea, Cesar," Dominga answered. "I have no idea what to think about any of this, and would love to hear what you and others have to say."

Sadi noticed Cesar's quick nod towards the older woman and wondered about the status of their relationship. During her time with them, they had refrained from showing signs of physical affection for each other, but Sadi thought they acted as a married couple.

"I know you all must have hundreds of questions about our situation. I do too." He paused before continuing and returned his glass to the table. "But if you all feel like I do, you're in need of rest before we try to figure things out. Our hosts, whoever they are, have been very good to us, so I would suggest that we assume the best, that they don't intend to harm us. However, they have been in control, not us, so tonight we all should think about what we want out of this situation. Hopefully tomorrow, we can come to some sort of general agreement before anything else happens. I'm not sure that I can take anything else tonight. If you'll excuse me, I'm going to my room. Good night and I'll see you all in the morning."

Cesar pushed his chair away from the table, took a deep breath, and without making eye contact with anyone, walked out of the room. He left the door open to the hallway leading to their rooms. Dominga looked a little shocked. After a moment, she stood from the table, said good night to everyone, and then disappeared through the door. In the next few minutes, everyone else left the room.

After Sadi and the girls returned to her room, she instructed them to get the pajamas from the drawers in their own room and then return. Although Sadi could see the longing in their eyes to sleep in their own beds, especially Helen, they did not complain. She did not feel comfortable with them away from her. The experience reminded her of the time after Helen's abduction.

"Mom?" Helen asked after pulling her nightgown over her head.

"What is it, Helen?"

"Can we look out the window?"

Sadi turned to the wall with the large window on the opposite side of the room and wondered why she hadn't previously considered the option. She was now very curious about what hid behind the curtains. Soft plasma light illuminated the room, enhancing the absence of light on the other side.

When Helen began walking toward the window, Sadi felt an urge to stop her, but curiosity overpowered the instinct. Helen slowly lifted her hand to part the curtains, opening it just enough for her to see.

"Wow," she said and then opened it wide enough for Sadi and

Daryn to see just a small glimpse. "You guys need to see this. It's the planet way, way, way down there."

After hesitating for just a couple of seconds, Sadi found the courage to open the curtains all the way. For the next few minutes, they just looked through the window. Curiosity and amazement immediately replaced her anxiety. The star-filled sky cast just enough light to illuminate the clouds far below them.

"I think this is a computer screen," Daryn said.

"Hmm," Sadi said with a smile, surprised at the girl's perception. The view looked like a normal window, but somehow, the emptiness of space did not seem to be right in front of them. "I think you're right."

"Look at that," Helen said, pointing to the upper right of the window. "That looks like a tiny moon."

"Sure looks like it," Sadi said after finding the small but bright light against other fainter stars.

She required a moment to notice another strange aspect of the window. When she bent down to see the satellite more clearly, the view changed, making it appear as if the image was three-dimensional. While enjoying the amazing view, Sadi made a mental note to ask the machines about it.

They looked through the window for the next several minutes, but before getting into bed, Sadi closed the curtains. She did not like the idea of someone or something looking through the window at them while they slept.

Both girls slept with her that night. Whenever either girl moved, Sadi was too exhausted to care or even notice. If she had any dreams, she failed to remember them.

Seven days later, Sadi heard a knock on the door to her room. Before responding, she quickly finished the last two sentences in the paragraph of her book. "Come in," she said, sitting up and swinging her legs over the edge of her bed. As the door opened, she laid the book face down beside her.

"Hi, Sadi," Susan said while closing the door.

"Are the kids still playing in the observation room?"

"Well," Susan began and smiled. "They're not with me are they?"

Sadi laughed. "I guess that answers my question, but they could be in the greenhouse. That's where Dominga spends all of her free time."

"Old-One-Eye is showing the kids some of the wildlife down on the planet. I don't even think that George noticed I left. They'd sleep in there if I let them."

"Old-One-Eye," Sadi said, shaking her head and still laughing. "I can't tell the machines apart, but Helen tells me that all the kids can."

Before Susan sat on the couch under the window, she took a glance at the clouds far below. She shook her head in silent amazement, and Sadi understood the gesture. No members of the group had grown accustomed yet to their position high above the planet. Sadi appreciated the fake starlight streaming into the room from the screen. She appreciated the illusion.

"I think Helen had more to do with choosing their names than she admits to," Susan said. "All the kids say that they agreed to the names together, but Helen has become their leader and I think she thought of the names all by herself. She is so funny."

"Want to switch ownership for a while?" Sadi asked, changing to a serious tone.

"I'll take your girls any day. I always wanted a girl."

"Are you going to have any more?"

"Mark and I have talked about it," Susan replied sadly. "Back on Earth, we talked about it. Now I don't know. I want to go back home."

Sadi looked at Susan and saw through the forced smile. Everyone knew of her desire to return to Earth. On the second night, Sadi had walked past Mark and Susan's room and heard them arguing. Sadi remembered feeling sorry for Mark who had almost zero control over their situation. Sadi had only heard one sentence, Susan telling Mark she thought he did not care enough to get them home.

"I'm sure you'll be able to go back," Sadi answered, then wondered if her words would entice the woman into another argument with her husband. Sadi did not want to cause more irritation. "I know this sounds weird, but I'm just trying to enjoy our time here. No one from the government is after us, or the deep state for that matter. We have everything we need and want here."

"Don't you want to go back?" Susan asked incredulously.

"I miss my brother and some of my friends." Sadi thought of Zoya, the only friend she really missed, and then she thought of Jen. "But I don't really want to go back. Ever since the start of this whole mess, my life's been a living hell. This feels like a fresh start. How many times do we get that?"

Susan turned from Sadi to stare at the floor. Both women sat in silence for several seconds.

"You're right," Susan said finally. "For now, life is good. I shouldn't complain. It's probably not safe to return right now anyway." Susan exhaled and looked back into Sadi's eyes.

"So, does Mark still feel the same about our situation?" Sadi asked. "Remember in our group discussion a week ago, when we all agreed with Cesar to wait for news from Freddy?"

"Of course, Mark likes the idea," Susan answered quickly. "I think *waiting* is the same as no plan, but I can understand how he feels. He and the rest of you have been on the run and under a lot of pressure for a long time. It must be nice to relax. Mark didn't give me much time to think when he called and said we had to leave. You can imagine my additional surprise that we had to leave Earth."

"That must have been quite the shock," Sadi laughed and then decided to persuade her to forgive Mark. He probably needed some assistance dealing with an angry wife. "I think Mark was just trying to shield you and the boys. I'm sure if he knew how much trouble we were going to be in, he would have told you sooner."

"I guess you're right," Susan said.

Hoping to change the subject, Sadi continued before her friend could.

"I've been meaning to ask you. Do you still distrust those machines?"

"We don't have any choice," Susan answered, shaking her head. "When they said to enjoy the time while waiting for Freddy to return, I thought they were just stalling before telling us something we didn't want to hear."

"Like what?"

"Well," she said, exhaling slowly. "Like I don't think our host or hosts would just bring us here and say, oh, here's a planet for you, and not want something in return. I can guess a million things they might want, but I don't think it's a good idea to let my mind wander. If I let them, my thoughts can get really dark."

"Good point," Sadi answered, making a note to remember that advice next time her mind began wandering. "You don't seem to mind the kids hanging out with them. I probably shouldn't be comfortable with it. It's funny though. After all I've been through, maybe I've learned to be more trusting of machines than humans."

When Sadi heard herself say the word *humans,* she wondered again what kind of creatures had built their machine servants, the ones watching over her children. She felt a sudden chill, an odd sensation in their perfectly comfortable environment.

"Are you okay?" Susan asked.

Sadi turned from the window and noticed Susan looking at her through narrow eyes.

"Sorry," Sadi said, forcing a smile. "I'm fine. Just blanked out for a second. I do that sometimes."

"Speaking of *blanking out,*" she said, her eyes opening wider. "So how are things between you and Gerald?"

Sadi was relieved for the change of subject but wondered if Susan still planned to throw more of her frustration and anger at her husband. Sadi did not envy Mark's position. Before responding, she took a deep breath for additional time to consider her response.

"I really don't know," Sadi began, "Things were starting to go really well, before his abduction. He hasn't been the same since."

"Do you think he's lost interest in you? Judging from the way he looks at you, I'd say not."

"No, but..." Sadi stopped, suddenly unsure how to answer. "It's like they broke his spirit. He won't talk about what happened to him at that damned hospital. I don't know how to help him if he won't talk to me. Maybe he just needs time to heal."

"That's what Mark thinks about Max," Susan said, an attempt at reassurance. "I'm sure you're right. They just need time."

SEVEN

Gerald

Gerald jumped at the sound of knocking on his door and turned from his window. For several hours, he had been staring in silence at the planet below, and the space surrounding it. Watching the planet had become the only activity taking place in the world outside of his head. Watching the alien sky reminded him of his childhood on Earth. Looking down at the sky from his current position almost had the same effect as staring up at the sky from solid ground.

"Gerald," the familiar voice said on the other side of the door. "It's Sadi. Can I come in?"

The door opened slowly and Sadi's head appeared. While trying to focus on her face, the whole scene of the door and her face shifted several centimeters to the right, then shifted quickly back to its original position. After waiting a moment to see if her image would shift again, he noticed that Sadi had already stepped completely into the room and had closed the door behind her. Although she had a beautiful smile on her face, she stopped and just stared at him, her dark blue eyes almost frozen in time.

"Gerald?"

"Yes," he answered.

Sadi was now sitting on the bed beside him. The warmth of her hand on his felt like a hot electric current and shoved the disturbing thoughts from his mind, some event happening in his imagination. The memory of their conversation suddenly returned to his awareness.

"You were doing it again," Sadi continued, squeezing his hand even tighter. "What happens when you zone out like that?"

"I don't remember," he answered, looking away from her blue eyes and pretending to focus on her neck. "It was just thinking about something."

Although he needed to focus on the conversation with Sadi, he desperately wanted to remember his waking dreams, another world existing simultaneously with the one in the orbiting space station. As usual, the memory of the waking dream was like a slippery fish, falling back into the water and completely disappearing from his memory. He often felt grateful for their escape, because they always left him with some residual emotion, usually fear or confusion. At that moment, he felt only unsatisfied curiosity.

While he and Sadi talked, his other reality kept distracting him. At some points in the conversation, he found himself looking at Sadi, and at other times, he looked elsewhere.

Gerald stood with the crowd in a large stadium, an arena for some barbaric sporting event. A pulsating amber triangle hovered in the dark sky above the stadium, each side several meters long and casting a bright glow over the entire arena. The energy of the crowd and the light matched the frequency of his heartbeat.

The rows of people in the stadium ascended high into the sky, and Gerald could not see the end of them. He stood at the very edge of the flat field, holding the wooden fence with both hands. While waiting for the games to begin, he strained to remember a pleasant daydream—a beautiful woman whose face he desperately wanted to see again.

The sudden roar of cheering from the crowd restored Gerald's attention to the present. On one side of the arena, a giant gate opened and a knight appeared from the shadow, the polished metal of its armor reflecting the amber light from the giant triangle. The large knight took several steps, his black cape flowing behind him as though caught by a strong wind. Yet the air in the stands remained still—hot and muggy—prompting Gerald to wipe the sweat from his forehead.

The knight's helmet fully enclosed his head, hiding his face from view. A long slit allowed him to see, revealing nothing but darkness inside as if the light was too weak to penetrate there. In his right hand, he held a massive sword, raised high above his head and pointing at the glowing triangle in the sky.

While holding the sword aloft, the crowd on the opposite side of the stadium cheered even louder than when the knight first appeared, and Gerald's eardrums felt ready to burst from the noise. In response, the crowd around him began booing and Gerald joined in their intense hatred for the knight of the black cape. For several minutes, the crowd fought for dominance of sound, half for the knight and half against him.

The knight held his sword pointed to the sky, standing as a statue until the deafening roar of the crowd had subsided. He slowly lowered the shining tip to point at the gate on the other side of the field. When the gate opened, he let the sword fall to his side.

On the other side, a new knight wearing armor and a cape stepped into the bright amber light, his shadow stretching on the ground behind him. He was as large as the first, but he wore a cape of pure crimson as if soaked in wet blood, the reflected light shining from its liquid surface. Gerald also could not see this knight's eyes, but instead of darkness, a bright white light shined through the slit in his helmet.

Gerald felt a wave of love for this new knight and a desperate desire for him to vanquish the knight of the black cape. The crowd continued cheering and booing, but the noise had an even stronger intensity. Gerald cheered with twice the energy as he had booed. He shook his fists at the other side of the stadium, feeling a sudden anger toward those who booed his champion, the knight of the red cape.

—※—

"Everyone daydreams," Sadi said, "but this is different. You're barely able to hold a conversation. Maybe if you talked about what happened to you at the hospital, you can heal. I only want to help."

Gerald focused his attention on her eyes, and for several seconds, he saw only the blackness of her dilated pupils. As he stared at the darkness there, he remembered children with fangs drowning in boiling water. He opened his mouth to speak, but his mind required a moment to recall Sadi's words.

"I don't remember much," he said, forcing a smile. Although he was lying to her, Gerald knew he would be unable to explain what he did remember. "They kept me drugged most of the time."

"Okay, let me ask something specific," Sadi said, speaking slowly. "Do you know what you told them? I don't care if you told them everything. I wouldn't blame you."

Gerald forced a chuckle and the sensation brought some relief. His mind was too full of horrible memories. The physical action of laughter helped to replace some of them, like pouring clear water into a glass of mud. He was suddenly grateful for his limited mental capacity.

"I think I spilled my guts on the very first day." Gerald tore his eyes away from her and turned to the window. Before continuing, he took a deep breath and stared at the view of the stars. "I actually don't remember doing it, but during some later interview, the doctor asked me some follow-up questions, which only made sense if I had already given them the information. They were tricky bastards, I'll give them that."

"Tricky bastards." Sadi laughed with him. "That's putting it nicely."

Without turning from the window, he suddenly remembered lying on a cold metal table in a bright room, feeling utterly alone and frightened of what they were going to do to him. The memory destroyed the enjoyable moment, and he had to force his smile to remain.

—※—

On the other side of the arena, Gerald noticed a specific individual standing and booing the knight of the red cape, Gerald's knight. Although he recognized the man as his fellow prisoner, Simon, he failed to remember ever liking him. When Gerald made eye contact with his new enemy, hatred swelled inside his breast. Gerald and Simon turned away from their champions and for several seconds, shook their fists in the air at each other.

Gerald suddenly wanted to inflict vengeance upon all who dared to wish harm on his champion in the red cape, especially Simon, the man across the stadium from him. With indignation flooding his emotions, Gerald felt alive, finally having an enemy to hate.

The knight of the red cape turned from the crowd and pointed his giant sword toward the other knight across the field from him. In response, the knight of the black cape did the same. For several moments, the tips of their swords reflected the amber light from the giant triangle in the sky. While remaining perfectly still, the knights waited until the noise from the crowd slowly died to silence.

"Let it begin," the first knight said, the one with the black cape, the one with darkness shining through the slit in his helmet.

At his words, the crowd began cheering again with a deafening roar, everyone in the stadium excited for the great celebration of conflict to begin. Gerald looked up at his champion, the knight of the red cape, and felt such a large amount of pride for his hero that his heart was ready to explode in his chest.

As a symbol of silent acceptance, the knight of the red cape and shining eyes took a single step toward his opponent, and the noise from the crowd grew even larger, the whole stadium shaking with the energy. Gerald turned to the crowd around him, but movement in his peripheral vision drew Gerald's attention back to the field.

The knight of the black cape was running toward his opponent. Even above the great noise of the crowd, Gerald could distinctly hear each crash of the knight's footsteps, the sound of metal crushing rock and dirt.

When the knight of the black cape came within ten meters of his opponent, he propelled himself into the air with the sword high above his head. With surprising serenity, the knight of the red cape put one knee on the ground and held his sword to the ground, bracing himself for the impact. As the black knight's sword crashed against the up-raised sword of the red knight, sparks exploded in all directions and Gerald had to shield his eyes from the incredible burst of burning metal.

Before Gerald could see again, he heard the clash of metal against metal, sword hitting sword. When he first saw the battle in progress, hot tears began falling down his cheeks. To prevent himself from exploding with the joy of watching the combat, he raised both fists into the air and screamed, joining the entire crowd in their chant.

"Take his last breath. Conflict ends in death!"

As the great swords clashed together, each impact resounded across the stadium, nearly replacing the noise of the crowd. Although the knight of the black cape initiated the battle with his great leap into the air, the knight of the red cape took his turn at offense. Whenever the knight of the black cape charged at his opponent, Gerald felt a great rush of anticipation. More than anything else in the battle, he loved to see his champion successfully deflect the enemy strikes.

After several hours of watching the battle, Gerald heard a collective intake of breath from the entire crowd. He had been looking across the field at Simon and noticed his lips suddenly pressed together in anger. When Gerald looked back to the combatants, the knights stood together, left hands on the right shoulder of the other, struggling for dominance. Gerald held his breath. After a long moment, they stopped struggling and stood motionless, the white light of his champion's eyes shining into the dark slit of the other's helmet.

When the sword of the red knight fell to the ground, Gerald inhaled in horrible anticipation of defeat. His lungs filled beyond maximum capacity, the pain of expansion eliminating all other sensations.

But the knight of the red cape had dropped his sword intentionally and then used his free hand to push away from the black knight's grasp. In a swift movement, the red knight took hold of his opponent's neck, lifted him above the dirt and rocks, and then slammed him to the ground. In another flash of movement, he retrieved his fallen sword and swiftly removed the head of the black knight.

In an act of primal instinct, Gerald raised his fists in the air and screamed in triumph until his lungs felt ready to burst again, but he could not distinguish the pain from the noise. His joy had joined the millions of other spectators. The indignation and anger from the other side of the stadium increased Gerald's joy.

EIGHT

General Franks

General Henry Franks of the United States Air Force sat at his desk in the main office building of the Air Force Space Command, headquartered at Peterson Air Force Base in Colorado. He had arrived at his office later than usual that beautiful morning. His corner office on the third floor overlooked the largest of the yards surrounding the complex. Sunlight from about thirty degrees above the horizon filled his office. Before starting his day, he liked to spend several minutes enjoying the blue sky above the green lawn.

While spreading out a group of high-altitude photographs on his oak desk, he prepared to study a report from one of his engineering managers, which required dozens of images to explain the complex conclusions of their analysis. To prevent himself from getting lost in the details, he placed the report's introduction prominently above all the pictures as a reminder. He enjoyed reading reports from that particular officer and wished every engineer at the base had the same clarity of presentation.

The phone rang during his second review of the photos, destroying the concentration and serenity he had gathered. After recognizing the caller, General Franks let it ring three more times before answering. He liked making that pain-in-the-ass twenty-four-year-old assistant

Alois wait. After slowly picking up the phone and pressing it to his ear, he silently waited for the man to speak.

"General," the young voice said confidently and then waited.

"Yes."

"We're having a special visit tomorrow morning. I'm canceling your morning appointment with Colonel Gerard and his staff."

"What do you mean, you're canceling the appointment?" The general's heartbeat increased in frequency, and his ears began getting warm, a sign of frustration. "This is a very important appointment. Tomorrow morning between ten and noon is the only time that all of our schedules coincide. We aren't canceling. You reschedule."

Before he could slam the phone down, Alois's voice rose in intensity, causing General Henry Franks to pause.

"General, this is not my decision," he said. "My new director is making a special visit, and he said it is important."

The general gulped before responding. The young man's words hung in the air between his lips and the phone, momentarily preventing his reply.

Your new director!

"You are here," the general began after gathering the strength to inflict a counter-strike, "so that your directors don't have to. You must be mistaken."

"I am not mistaken, sir," the voice said. "I will notify the colonel and make the appropriate preparations."

Click

—※—

The next morning, General Franks opened his office door before sunrise. Although he disliked getting out of bed earlier than usual, he loved the privacy of his office, in the dark and alone. He sat in his office chair, sipping coffee for about thirty minutes before turning on the light. He liked to watch the dark sky turn from black to dawn. He had a bad feeling about the day and the visit from their new director.

He needed time to prepare mentally for the meeting.

During his career, General Franks had only a few personal meetings with his intermediary's directors. He never counted the exact number of times, but it was definitely only a single digit. Those meetings always meant more work for him and his entire staff, and usually a major course correction for a large set of activities.

He suspected the reason for the visit was related somehow to the break-in of the psychiatric facility. Although the event had taken Franks by surprise and provided no small amount of wonder, he never expected the occurrence to spark the interest of Alois's superiors. He had worried more about the response from Central Intelligence. While preparing for the worst, he hoped there was a more mundane reason for the visit.

The general preferred to know the identity of his visitor before the meeting, but he would discover it soon enough and learn what kind of special accommodations he would need to make. Without even knowing the man, his status as director indicated almost everything the general needed to know, most importantly, his family's membership in the top bloodlines. The general's lineage might not have been the purest, but he took pride in how high he'd climbed up the ranks with the ancestry he was given.

Soon after sunlight had flooded his office, he heard a knock on the door. He stood from his desk, reminded himself to remain calm, and then answered loudly for his arriving audience to enter.

"Don't speak unless spoken to," he whispered with a twinge of sarcasm.

After the door opened, General Henry Franks smiled as three men entered his office. Alois walked in first, a young man in his early twenties with dark brown hair and even darker brown eyes. A much taller man followed, who Franks had never seen but immediately recognized as the new director. The man wore his height well, being slightly thinner, proportionately, but with a tight and trimmed muscular physique. He had intense blue eyes and blond hair, cut short on the sides like a military officer, but longer and ruffled on the top. The man's hair looked as though each strand had been intentionally and precisely placed.

General Franks immediately recognized the CIA officer walking behind the new director, Gordon Booth, the general's second cousin on his mother's side. The officer from Central Intelligence had command of the staff at the facility that was recently breached, the facility that General Franks had the unfortunate responsibility of guarding. Gordon Booth's presence immediately confirmed the purpose of the visit, what Franks feared.

"Good morning, General," Alois said before the third man had completely entered the room. As the CIA officer closed the door, Alois finished. "This is Josef Brunner, and of course, you know Officer Booth."

"A pleasure to meet you, sir," General Franks said without making any attempt to step around the desk and shake the man's hand.

"Likewise," Josef said pleasantly with a slight German accent. He spoke the word *likewise* as a barely discernible *likevise* and the general wondered if the man could have completely hidden his accent if he'd wanted.

After making the necessary eye contact with Josef, General Franks turned to the CIA officer, whose thick grey hair sat like a rug on his head. Although the shortest man in the room, Gordon Booth had the most muscular physique, with green eyes that seemed unusually bright.

"Good to see you, Booth."

The familiar man nodded silently in acknowledgment, then turned to see what Alois and Josef would do first.

"Please have a seat," General Franks said, extending his hand to indicate the several chairs in front of his desk.

"Yes, let's sit," Josef said and Franks heard the command in his voice, as if he had already commandeered the conversation. "But first, I would like to see the view for a moment, if you don't mind."

Josef Brunner walked behind the desk to the window overlooking the large yard. As he passed, General Franks smelled a faint but distinct scent, a mix of spices most likely including cloves. It was definitely not any kind of antiperspirant he'd ever encountered. The scent quickly dissipated when the taller man reached the window behind Franks. For a moment, the general wondered if he should join the director at the window or just sit and wait as the two men in front of his desk had chosen to do. Although he sensed the director wanted to enjoy the view alone, the general turned and joined him.

After a few seconds of uncomfortable silence, General Franks wished he had chosen to sit. He probably shouldn't have come so close to the man. Due to his age and position as a general, Franks usually cared less about social propriety than when he was younger. His last remaining aspiration was a comfortable retirement, so he did not worry as much about impressing people. But the silence was definitely amplifying the tension.

"Can I get you anything?" the general asked, keeping his gaze outside.

Eventually, Josef looked down at the general.

"I am perfectly comfortable," he said and smiled pleasantly. "Please sit. We have much to discuss."

NINE

Gerald

The knight of the red cape stepped away from his fallen opponent and raised his sword, pointing it to the sky. The amber light from the triangle reflected off the tip as though shining on its own. As the cheering and booing continued, the knight slowly turned to face the entire crowd.

"I have vanquished my foe," he said, the deep voice resonating through the entire stadium and causing the railing in Gerald's grasp to vibrate.

After hearing the voice of his champion, Gerald noticed movement on the ground. With extreme difficulty, he tore his gaze from the red knight and his sword and watched in horror as the body of the black knight began to move. The headless body rolled over slowly to lie on his stomach. Then with both hands, he pushed himself up into a kneeling position and reached out in every direction in search of his head. When Gerald saw the helmet containing the severed head, he noticed the blackness of the eye slit grow even darker.

The knight of the red cape let his sword fall to his side while looking down at his fallen companion. For several seconds, the red knight watched as his opponent searched for his head. He gave a great laugh, which shook the entire stadium again.

"Behold," he said, still laughing. "The fallen wishes to regain his head. What do you say? Shall I let him?"

Gerald and all of his neighbors joined in a single answer.

"Give him back his head. Raise him from the dead!"

The red knight laughed as the fallen knight searched for his head. When his gloved fingers finally touched his helmet, he grasped the tassel extending from the top and then raised the helmet, enclosing his head, from the ground. With his head in one hand, the decapitated knight used his other hand to push himself to his feet. The red knight stepped away from his foe, slowly and showing no fear. While the red knight watched, the black knight held his head high above his shoulders. His voice could be heard across the stadium.

"Who dishonors my memory?" The voice came from inside the helmet. He held his head out toward the red knight. "Did I not battle with honor?"

"Not I," answered the red knight. "You fought valiantly."

After the knight's answer, the entire crowd became silent. Gerald noticed millions of heads turning from left to right in search of the guilty one. When Gerald looked across the field, he found Max staring at him.

"Which one of you dishonors me?" the black knight asked again. "Instead of joy in the victory or anger at my defeat, one of you finds pleasure in my death."

Across the field, Max lifted his right hand, his index finger pointed at Gerald, and the entire crowd soon followed his motion. Millions of eyes suddenly focused on him, each eye becoming a searing pain on his cheeks and forehead. The black knight swung his face toward Gerald and held his head perfectly still for several seconds. Gerald stared into the dark slit.

When the head of the knight began shooting toward him, Gerald's eyes widened in fear and he stopped breathing. The black knight's arm stretched and stretched until his head was within a centimeter of Gerald's face. When the giant knight spoke, his hot breath flowed through the dark slit in the helmet, burning Gerald's cheeks and eyes.

"You should have stayed home, Jerry," the voice whispered.

—※—

Gerald paused to let his mind process the last words Sadi said to him. During a single blink, an entire eternity of time had passed. As she finished her current sentence, a disturbing image evaporated from his memory—a metallic face with a long black slit where its eyes should have been. He tried to devise an appropriate response before she finished.

"Old-One-Eye showed them the poles this morning," Sadi said, shaking her head, "and now she's been begging me to go there once we go to the surface. I'm cold just thinking about it."

"I'm glad they're having fun," Gerald said almost as soon as she had stopped talking.

Later that evening, when Sadi had closed the door behind her, Gerald sat on his bed and stared at where she'd stood. Although he was grateful for the solitude, he wished she had stayed. Yes, human company exhausted him, but it also helped to alleviate his emotional instability. Without someone in front of him, he had difficulty keeping focus and all attempts exhausted him.

He understood and appreciated her tactic, talking to him of pleasant subjects, hoping they would replace the memory of darker experiences from his recent incarceration. She did not directly explain this tactic, but he understood and would have done the same had she suffered the CIA psychiatrists' treatment. Perhaps with enough time, new experiences would bury his disturbing memories. Traveling to a new planet should definitely help.

He stood and walked to the window to get a closer look at the darkening sky. For a long while, he just stared at the stars, clouds, and the diminishing light on the horizon. As the room became darker, he began to feel as if some creature watched him from behind. The feeling did not really instill fear, so he turned and expected to see an empty room, which would destroy the annoying sensation.

In the part of his mind that recognized the physical world, Gerald saw only his room, the bed, the door, the small table with the closed book on top, an old copy of *Moby Dick*. Superimposed over the physical world, Sadi stood at the door, facing him. Instead of blue eyes, she stared at him with yellow eyes, each iris shaped as a triangle. He felt no fear, knowing she only existed in his imagination. Usually, he imagined worse things. He stared at her for several seconds until she dissipated into nothing again.

"Okay, Gerald," he said quietly to himself. "Get a hold of yourself. No one was there. No one was in the room with you. Take a shower and then get some sleep."

The physical action of speech helped connect him to reality and escape his mind. When he flipped the switch in his bathroom for the light, it momentarily blinded him. As he stared at the familiar surroundings, he wondered again how the alien could have made the room such an exact replica of his bathroom at home. Even after living on the platform for several days, Gerald was still dumbfounded by their seemingly impossible situation.

After undressing and stepping into the shower, he let the hot water flow over his chest, then his back, neck, and shoulders. As usual, he delayed putting his head under the water. Once the water hit his face, it would force him to close his eyes, thrusting him into a disturbing alternate reality where his imagination became very erratic. He used to enjoy showering, but after his time at the psychiatric facility, the activity always caused anxiety.

When he finally closed his eyes and let the hot water flow over his face, he focused on the sensation of his feet on the shower floor, the warm water on his skin, or any other physical sensation. His effort to remain in the physical world only lasted for a few seconds. The water on his skin and the steam in his lungs were suffocating, reminding Gerald of being a small child. Instead of remembering the pleasant memories of youth, he re-experienced the negative emotions he had learned to overcome: fear of the future, incompetence, insecurity, and an overwhelming feeling that the world was incomprehensible and dangerous.

With his eyes closed, the hot and humid atmosphere became his entire world, and Gerald was going to live in that state of suffocation for the rest of eternity. In his mind, a hand emerged from the drain, and its hot fingers wrapped around his ankles. He remembered sitting in a circle with strange children, surrounded by cement walls and hot water rising from the floor.

—※—

"Stay with us, Jerry," the smallest child said.

"Yes, Jerry, don't go up to the surface." An older girl sat on the other side of him, with long dark brown hair and striking black eyes. Gerald noticed her soaked hair, the oily strands reminding him of an otter sunbathing on its back. "They'll find you. Stay down here with us, where it's safe."

"We'll keep you safe," said another child sitting across from him.

The hot water slowly filled the space between his toes and then climbed up his ankles. All the children looked at him with a strange eagerness. When the water reached his waist, he noticed many of the children licking their lips.

The steamy atmosphere began to choke him.

The candlelight disappeared and Gerald heard the sound of splashing as the children dove under the water. He felt small hands and mouths on his ankles, legs, and when the water touched his chin, mouths began sucking his neck. When Gerald opened his eyes, he was standing in the shower, alone.

TEN

General Franks

The general detected no accent in the man's speech, suggesting his native language was American English. When he finally sat in his chair, he expected the new director to join the others in front of him on the other side of the desk. But Josef Brunner remained at the window, while all three men sat looking at each other. General Franks smiled politely, only glancing at each of them. He did not enjoy their presence in his office.

"Let me try to explain the purpose of my visit, and our current situation," Josef said casually while still looking out the window as if attempting to determine how to begin the conversation. His next sentence sounded like a reprimand, but his tone indicated a mere statement of fact. "A handful of civilians infiltrated your facility and extracted patients with very sensitive information."

Gordon Booth looked relieved, for the moment, as though the statement was not directed at him. Alois looked smug with an *I-told-you-so* kind of look. The general's anxiety about Josef Brunner's visit transformed into a welcomed anger, and he almost thanked them for it. He imagined himself as an old decaying forest at the end of a hot drought, just waiting for the inevitable cleansing fire to burn him to the ground.

In the following silence, the general directed some resentment at Josef Brunner, a man nearly half his age who had come to reprimand him for a completely unprecedented situation. After letting his initial reaction pass, General Franks decided to speak before Josef or either of the two idiots in front of him did.

"Yes," the general began. "That's what happened, but I don't understand why you are here. Why not just give Alois instructions? That's standard operating procedure."

"That's true," Josef said quickly, without turning from the window. For the remainder of his answer, he spoke more slowly. "There are two reasons for my visit. Since I have just recently been reassigned to direct this situation, I wanted to meet you all in person. The other reason is more interesting. As you can guess, this is a very unique situation that has caught the administrators' attention."

Josef paused again and General Franks could hear the rustle of his clothes as he turned from the window. He walked to the other side of the desk to stand behind the two sitting men, then glanced down at the general with narrowed eyes, as if only General Franks mattered to him. From his seated position, the director seemed even taller than he had before they were standing together at the window.

Franks had wanted to retire gracefully and quietly in a couple of years, but he feared suddenly that the man standing before him would announce an abrupt and disgraceful ending of his career.

"Before we go into all the details," Josef began.

He walked to the right side of the desk so all three of his audience could see him. He glanced at Alois and then finished his remarks while looking at Gordon Booth. The general felt relieved, temporarily free from the spotlight.

"I want to impress on your minds the importance of this situation. As far as I understand, a new technology has been developed by a group of civilians, and they have caught the attention of some alien influence. Have I accurately described the situation?"

"That was the summary of our latest report," Gordon Booth said while maintaining eye contact with Josef. As usual, the man's bright green eyes failed to blink or reveal any emotion.

"Good," Josef said with a quick hint of satisfaction. "Officer Booth, we'll discuss the security of the intelligence later, but first I want to review how we lost, not only the suspects but also the Central Intelligence psychiatrists' files on the case."

"I believe," Gordon began, "that we have already provided this information in our report. Do you want me to go into the details again?"

"Yes, if you don't mind," Josef answered with polite impatience.

"A man named Simon Thatcher," Booth began after blinking once, "an employee of one of the patients, Max Garner, entered the facility with an obscure civilian named Freddy Carlson. From security camera video, we know these two individuals overpowered the guards and doctors and retrieved the patients. Although we don't have video evidence, we believe they entered the facility in the vehicle that other members of their organization built. Other evidence suggests that this Freddy Carlson has some kind of special psychic abilities, which may have assisted them in the break-in."

General Franks looked at Gordon Booth, attempting to hide his frustration. He fought the tension by tightly pressing his lips together.

"That facility is minimum security," Franks said calmly, hoping to convey his confidence in the situation. "If you were concerned about security, you should have told us about their friends, and especially of Mr. Carlson's ability. What do we have to do? Ask specifically for this kind of information? We have different levels of alert status for this situation."

Gordon met the older man's gaze without any hint of intimidation. He answered just as calmly. "We tell you what we feel is important for you to know, nothing more."

"In all my years," General Franks said after taking a short breath. "No one has ever attempted a break-in of a facility such as this one, on American soil no less. Let me reiterate, we depend on intel to determine the necessary level of security, otherwise, it will remain the same as what has been shown to be sufficient in the past."

General Franks turned to Josef, hoping his initial investigation was correct and the CIA had not provided such information. His level of awareness did not include that specific facility. Lower-level officers took care of its maintenance and defense.

"With respect, sir," he said to Josef, "you must understand my position. Officer Booth left out an important detail. We believe that other CIA assets, Miss Garner and her friend Ms. Zhang, led the offensive. They were also present on the night of the incident."

"Yes," Booth answered with some irritation, and a hint of vindication. "One of our assets and Max Garner's sister, Audrie, used false authority to visit her brother on the same night of the incident. Although we do not believe this to be a coincidence, we do believe that Simon and Freddy followed them, using her visit to coincide with their plans. I know Ms. Garner personally and do not believe she had anything to do with it."

Due to his lack of information, the general was a little uncertain about how to proceed. He had intended to catch Officer Booth off guard with his counter-accusation of the CIA having a conspirator to the event. He should have suspected the man was prepared for the attack, but since the general honestly felt vindicated from any blame, he decided to take that route.

"Doesn't seem very plausible," General Franks said without any hint of irritation, or fear of being wrong, "for intelligence agents to be followed by a couple of civilians. They would not have been able to locate the facility without her help."

Gordon Booth failed to show any negative reaction to this accusation as Franks had hoped. He answered quickly and spoke with an angry pleasure in his unblinking wide eyes.

"That is possible, and we have not entirely excluded that possibility, but did you know that Simon Thatcher discovered the location of your facility by accessing one of your own satellites when we apprehended his boss, Mr. Garner? While going through his company records, we discovered the log of his access."

Before answering, Franks took a short breath to steady his emotions. He would not acknowledge how the Central Intelligence Officer had successfully backed him into a corner. He only needed a few moments to process the damning information and devise a defensive answer.

"TerraWatch has several contracts with us for communication systems development. As such, they have clearance to access some of our devices, for diagnostic purposes." Before finishing, he took a deep breath, as if he had grown tired of explaining something obvious. "As I said before, this information would have been useful before you had apprehended him, then we could have restricted their access until you concluded your business with them."

"Hindsight is twenty-twenty, gentlemen," Josef said as if breaking up a childhood squabble. He walked slowly around Alois and Gordon to stand on the other side of the desk. "Like you already said, this has never happened before. For a group of civilians to make such a bold attempt is yet another indication of this situation's importance."

General Franks breathed in relief. He really disliked arguing with Booth. Maybe he was getting old. As a younger man, his blood would have been boiling with anger, invigorated instead of drained. Josef's next words caught him off guard.

"What this does indicate, General, is the state of affairs under your command. Your staff lacked discipline, you must admit. You have a valid point, however, that more appropriate intel should have been provided."

Josef glanced at Gordon Booth, whose eyes widened in anticipation of another reprimand. When Josef returned his attention to General Franks, Booth exhaled in relief, almost imperceptibly. Before the onslaught continued, the general experienced a moment of satisfaction at the other man's discomfort. When Josef did continue, he spoke politely, but the general could sense the feeling of disappointment.

"I don't want you to think of my presence as a negative event, gentlemen. Think of this as a positive opportunity for all of us. Although the situation shows your attention to be lacking in effectiveness in this particular situation, it has proved to be extremely interesting. The administration has entrusted the ownership of this issue to me, and I am here to assure that it is given the proper care and attention."

"Of course," General Franks said.

"So," Josef continued as though there had been no interruption. "What I'm hearing is that we don't know for certain how they found the facility, but they most likely used the satellite links. Please make sure that TerraWatch's access is monitored very closely. Cutting them off completely would cause too many ripples in the pond. We want as little attention as possible."

"We will provide a weekly report of their activities to Booth," General Franks said with a glance at the Central Intelligence officer, "and an immediate notification if any abnormal connections take place."

Alois sat forward and placed a notebook on the desk in front of him. He retrieved a mechanical pencil from his pocket and used it to write a reminder on the notepad. General Franks glanced briefly at the younger man then looked back to Josef.

"Good," Josef said approvingly. "We'll talk about what to do with Ms. Garner and Ms. Zhang later, but what do we know happened to Mr. Carlson, Simon Thatcher, and the two patients after they left the facility?"

While waiting for Booth to respond, General Franks felt impressed by Josef's memory of all the relevant participants' names. Even the Central Intelligence officer who had prepared the reports seemed to require more time to recall their names.

"Like I already mentioned," Gordon said, "we don't have any video from after they left the facility, but we were able to locate their rendezvous site in Canada just as they departed. The satellite images show the scene just before the craft began its ascent."

Gordon Booth opened his eyes wider, then nodded to the desk, suggesting that they look at some of his images. Earlier that morning, General Franks had separated all of the pictures into different groups. A small paper clip kept each group of photos from mingling with the others. He took the top group, unclipped it, and spread the photos across the desk. Each image showed the craft at a different altitude.

Josef leaned over the desk from his position and the other two men leaned forward to get a better look.

"One of our platform stations, EZRA, was within range to capture images of their craft." General Franks emphasized the term, *Platform Stations,* contrasting it with Gordon and Josef's use of *Satellite.* "As you can see, we had a twenty-eight-degree view at ground level and captured images until they passed EZRA's viewing altitude of forty-three kilometers. We, unfortunately, did not have any other platforms with skyward sensors within range to see higher resolution shots than our ground telescopes had acquired."

While waiting for the men at the desk to assess the information, General Franks wondered how well they knew the actual assets at his disposal. Their use of the word *satellite* indicated that he might need to educate them. The men under his command knew better than to use the term in his presence unless they were actually referring to one. He preferred the use of more correct terms for the particular instrument of discussion, but he understood the convenience of using the generic reference.

"It's the Hawker 400 they converted in Brazil," Gordon said in explanation to Josef. He retrieved a photo from the desk and held it up to the light. General Franks thought he saw admiration in the man's eyes. "The windows are too dark to see inside."

General Franks gathered the remaining pictures on his desk, except for the one in Gordon Booth's hands, and set them aside in a neat stack. He then took the next group of photos and spread them out like the first.

These are the close-ups of the plane on the ground. Due to the low light conditions and light cloud cover, they were not that clear. These ones in IR show the last scene in the best detail. Their craft had just begun its ascension."

For some reason, General Franks was excited to describe the remainder of the scene. He reminded himself not to display excitement about the human casualties, but knowing their effect on Booth seemed to boost his emotions a bit. The general filtered through the photos and found one with a wider view of the scene, including the dead Central Intelligence agents.

Here are the bodies of the two agents," he said, pointing at the two spots on the ground." Even though the image was taken in infrared, he could see blotches of dark blood all over the bodies and ground around them. "And here's the unknown character from the report. We still have not identified him. All we know is that it appears to be a man and he had dark hair, but the exact color is unclear."

Josef leaned down to retrieve the photo from the desk. He held the piece of photo paper closer to his eyes so that General Franks could no longer see his face.

"Could this be Mr. Ortiz?" Josef asked.

"We don't know," Gordon Booth said, sitting back in his seat. "From the hair color, we can eliminate Mr. Thatcher, Mr. Carlson, and Taylor Evans. Since they were able to escape the scene, we doubt they would have left behind Mr. Foster or Mr. Garner."

Gordon Booth paused to take a short breath, and Josef spoke before he could continue.

"From your report, I did not understand the basis for your conclusion that Freddy Carlson, Simon Thatcher, and the two escaped patients were at the scene. How did you come to that conclusion?"

"Our certainty is not one hundred percent," Booth began slowly, "but before they were killed, the two agents did make a specific communication that they had subdued Mr. Carlson, so we know he was there. Sorry, I must have forgotten to include that detail in my report. And due to the speed of their arrival after leaving the psychiatric facility, we do not believe they made a stop to deposit any other passengers."

"Of course, you are basing all of this on the assumption that the two patients and Mr. Thatcher all left the facility together."

"Yes," Gordon said confidently. "We believe that is a safe assumption. We know they were at the facility from our video footage. Their craft is the only way they could have escaped."

"And yet, you have no photographic evidence that this craft was at the scene in Canada?"

Josef asked his question while looking at the photo again. General Franks wondered if the director was making an accusation. In the uncomfortable silence, he decided to come to Gordon's rescue. He pulled the next group of photos and unclipped them. Each picture showed an aerial view of clouds at night with a dark spot growing in size with each one. In total, he spread out ten pictures.

"After we delivered our summary to Central Intelligence," the general said, spreading several photos of a dark object, "we found these images, which contain what we believe to be their first craft. As you can see, the images are not clear enough to be one hundred percent certain, but it is in the shape of an automobile and it was in the sky just a few miles from their location. These were taken before their jet began its ascent."

"We found these images just yesterday afternoon," General Franks said, turning to meet Gordon's eyes. "I decided to inform you at our meeting this morning."

"Okay," Josef said and dropped the other photo he was holding back on the desk. "Then it's confirmed. Both of their craft escaped the scene together. I need you to continue working on the identity of the occupants, but we should focus more on where the craft went, since you only have very flimsy evidence that only their converted automobile returned to the surface."

"We lost them both after they ascended above EZRA's view angle," General Franks said in disappointment.

"We are fairly certain," Booth said in a defensive tone, "of a positive ID on the craft at Cesar Sanchez's estate in Seattle before the break-in."

"But your agents watching the home reported no such evidence."

Josef's tone was one of curiosity rather than accusation. General Franks thought it sounded like an unspoken apology.

"We evaluated those agents," Gordon said with confidence, "and we believe their memories were altered. I suspect Mr. Carlson's influence."

Josef retrieved the aerial photo with the automobile at its highest elevation, a picture with the most clarity. He looked at the picture for a few seconds before speaking. General Franks thought he noticed excitement in his voice.

"The administration is most interested in capturing the new propulsion technology and energy source, and containing the information of course," he said, still looking at the photo. He walked towards the window and paused a moment. "But I'm coming to suspect this Freddy Carlson to be of equal importance. We must find him."

ELEVEN

Gerald

For several seconds after hearing the knock on his door, Gerald continued to stare at his window screen, trying to determine the wisdom of turning around to verify if anyone was at his door or if he was just imagining things again. Although their new planet's star Dzalm had risen already, Gerald switched the view to show the stars instead of the bright view of the surface. The starry sky kept his room in darkness. He felt comfort inside his room. It separated him from the strangeness of the alien corridors, but even in his room, he still felt as though he'd never escaped the psychiatric institution. His grasp of reality seemed forever broken.

Previously, in the middle of the night, a similar, quieter knocking had woken him from a fitful sleep. Although he was grateful for the end of his nightmare, he simultaneously hoped for a visit from Sadi but also dreaded such an encounter. In his damaged mental state, he would invariably continue to disappoint the woman he desperately wanted to see and touch. For several minutes, Gerald had lain in bed and waited for Sadi to enter his room, but no one had, and he'd fallen back into his strangely disturbing dream of living in a universe devoid of other creatures, a universe composed merely of geometric shapes.

"Good Morning, Gerald," Sadi said pleasantly through a partially opened door. Then Gerald heard soft footsteps. "Looking at the window again, huh? It's such an amazing sight. Isn't it."

He took a breath before turning. When he saw Sadi closing the door behind her, his lips stretched into an automatic natural smile, sparing him the necessity of making an effort.

"Good morning," he answered, mimicking her pleasant tone.

"Did you sleep any better?"

Gerald paused before answering and required less than a second to decide on a lie. He turned back to the window.

"A little better than normal."

"That's good."

"I took a shower after you left last night," he began and opened his mouth to continue. He prepared to lie again and say how the shower had helped him sleep, but the faces of children in a sewer suddenly appeared in his mind, causing him to pause. "I, I, it felt good. I think it helped."

"Showers always make me feel better."

Sadi turned from the window and smiled. He could feel her watching him.

"I often forget that I'm not looking through normal glass."

"I know," she said and turned back to the window. They stared in silence for several seconds. When Sadi spoke again, Gerald noticed a deep intake of breath, as if she had prepared a speech. "Gerald, I wanted to ask you something."

"Okay, what is it?"

"I was talking to Old-One-Eye," she began.

"The machine?" he asked, somewhat shocked.

"Yes," she answered bluntly, "the machine."

"Did you initiate the conversation?"

"Helen did," she said, smiling. "The kids love talking to them. In fact, it's giving the kids some lessons about the planet right now. It's pretty interesting. You should hear about it, but I wanted to ask if you would consent to talk to it. I think it might be able to help you."

"Help me with what?"

"I was talking about what happened to you," she cleared her throat. "About what happened at the psychiatric hospital. I know you don't like talking about it with me, but if I can't help, they might. You haven't been the same since. I'm sorry, but you need help."

Before he could stop himself, Gerald revealed his true thoughts on the subject.

"We don't even know what they really want with us," he said in frustration and a bit of anger. He made brief eye contact with Sadi before continuing. "I just need time. Talking is only a band-aid."

"Is that how you feel about me?" Sadi asked. For the first time since he had known her, Gerald thought he heard her anger directed at him. "Is my *talking to you* just a band-aid? I'm trying to help you."

"That's not what I meant," he said, attempting to sound apologetic. "I'm sorry. Okay, I'll talk to it, but will you be there too? I don't trust it."

"Of course, I'll be there if you want."

Her tone indicated acquittal, giving Gerald some relief, and he realized at that moment how much Sadi's opinion meant to him. In the back of his mind, he wondered if she had used an angry outburst as a tool for manipulation, but he immediately abandoned the suspicion. Sadi would not have planned an angry outburst. That came naturally. He really did not want to talk to the machine, especially about what had happened to him, but he would feel foolish to withdraw from the commitment now.

"What did it, I mean, Old-One-Eye say?"

"Well," she began, smiling as though about to laugh, "Helen was asking if it could make people happy or sad, since it can talk directly to our minds, and it claimed to have the ability to influence our emotional state. That's when I got the idea to ask about you."

Gerald gulped. Old-One-Eye suddenly seemed even more dangerous than before he knew it could influence his emotional state. Although in a way, Gerald thought, any sentient creature could influence another sentient creature's emotions just by talking or revealing information in other ways.

"What did it say about me?"

"All it said was," she paused briefly to recall the exact words, "to call them if Gerald agrees."

Gerald was tempted to postpone the meeting indefinitely and say he would tell her when he felt ready, but he knew she would not let him do that for long. He also did not want to disappoint her. Before he could respond, Sadi broke the silence.

"Do you want to have breakfast first?"

"I," Gerald said, about to answer in the affirmative but then changed his mind. He disliked postponing the inevitable. "Let's do it now."

"Okay," Sadi said slowly.

Gerald thought he understood the reason for her hesitation. She had probably expected him to have breakfast first. She turned to the right of the window, stepped closer to the wall, and knocked four times. After fifteen seconds of silently waiting, Gerald jolted when he heard the response in his mind.

I am at the door.

TWELVE

Gerald

When Gerald heard the voice in his mind, he and Sadi turned to face each other. He did not have to ask if she had heard the same words in her mind. Although Gerald knew he should be the one to open the door, he felt paralyzed. Sadi smiled weakly.

"I'll get it," she said while taking the first step. Before grasping the door handle, she looked over her shoulder at him. "There's no need to worry."

Sadi stood to the side and waited for the machine to hover into the room, but it just continued to levitate a few centimeters above the floor, remaining perfectly still. Not even the yellow glass was rotating. For several long seconds, Sadi and Gerald just stared at the machine. Gerald's gaze was drawn to the dark area in the middle of the yellow glass. The dark reflections on the surface reminded him of the crystal spider with the multi-colored rocks for eyes.

"I have come at your request." The machine spoke, using sound waves now, and then its yellow glass with the dark area in the center began to rotate.

"Thank you," Sadi said. "Please come in."

The machine glided into the room and Sadi closed the door, then walked to stand beside Gerald. As the machine moved toward him, Gerald tensed. The machine stopped at the bedside about two meters from his location by the window. Sadi slid her hand into his, giving him the strength to start breathing again.

"Which one are you?" Sadi asked. "Old-One-Eye?"

"We are all the same," it replied in the same female voice Gerald remembered from the first day they arrived. "But the children call this machine Miss Poofie. The name probably influences your opinion just a bit on the negative side, or as you might say, you wouldn't take someone named Miss Poofie seriously. Am I right?"

"Yes, definitely," Sadi said with a little chuckle. "Miss Poofie is not a very dignified name."

For the eight days of their stay, Gerald had only seen the machines talking to other members of the group, mostly the children. He had never stood this close to one or conversed with one directly. The jovial way Sadi spoke with Miss Poofie helped Gerald feel a little less anxiety, but he still held onto Sadi's hand, although a little too tightly probably.

"As long as the adults approve, I am happy to be called whatever will please the children."

"You have been very good to them," Sadi said with genuine gratitude in her voice, then she cleared her throat before continuing. "Thanks for coming. Can you help Gerald and Max? They were incarcerated before we got here and were hurt in some way."

"Gerald," the machine said, perfectly imitating a female's voice and matching his accent. "I cannot fix what they did to you, but I can offer an improvement to your condition."

"What is my condition?"

"The military psychiatrists damaged your barrier to the background, causing your difficulty focusing. You are not configured to process the background simultaneously with information from the corporeal."

"What is the background?" Gerald asked, curiosity replacing some of his anxiety.

"The background is another part of reality, the part you cannot see with your eyes, what you cannot touch or taste. Your interpretation of background information is often called a dream."

The machine's answers failed to satisfy all of Gerald's curiosity. The answers caused even more confusion. While he attempted to formulate the next question, Sadi spoke.

"So chemicals can interfere with this barrier?"

"Your bodies are chemical," Miss Poofie said as if explaining to a child. "Creatures, such as yourselves, already exist in the background and use the corporeal chemical body, specifically the neural network to interpret the physical universe. Due to the complexity of the situation, I cannot adequately describe it to your satisfaction with the limited time we have. Suffice it to say, Gerald and Max have been damaged and we can only offer temporary relief. We have been instructed to let Freddy explain the situation to you."

"So, why did they do this to Gerald?" she asked. "To learn what he knows?"

"They had two purposes," the female voice said calmly. "Like you say, they wanted to acquire information, but they also wanted to neutralize Gerald and Max." The machine spoke without turning or making any other movement except for the rotation of the yellow glass. "The intelligence network considered them a security risk and decided to impair Gerald and Max so they could not cause any more trouble. They didn't exactly know what they were doing, only the effect of their actions."

"Okay," Sadi began, pausing to decide on her follow-up question. "So how can you help him?"

Gerald appreciated Sadi's help and wondered about the direction of the conversation without her participation. He wanted to learn more about what had happened to him, but Sadi was focusing on his recovery.

"Only your host can cure them," Miss Poofie continued. "I can provide a method to relieve some of their symptoms."

"And when will we meet this host?" Gerald interjected.

"Sometime after Freddy arrives."

The conversation with the machine felt so strange to Gerald and was causing yet another distraction. In a usual three-way discussion among humans, the speaker would turn to look at the target conversation partner, but in this conversation, Gerald kept wondering if the machine spoke to him or Sadi. Probably both, he assumed.

"What is this method?" Sadi asked.

"A mixture of chemicals during a special sequence of music will help them focus on the physical universe," it said.

Gerald was disappointed. He had expected the machine to offer some kind of device. Since the doctors at the psychiatric hospital had used mind-altering drugs on him, the use of chemicals frightened him. But after further consideration, he felt more curious than afraid.

"Can we do this treatment together?" Sadi asked, turning to Gerald. "I want to make sure it's okay."

"Of course," the machine responded.

"How will it affect me?"

"The music will be designed for Gerald's configuration. You will only feel an emotional response, but nothing more. I suspect you will not like it."

"And what about Gerald?" she asked quickly. "How will it affect him?"

"I'm sorry to say," Miss Poofie said apologetically. "Gerald will experience some anxiety with the first treatment, but subsequent treatments will be less unpleasant."

"Will it cause physical pain?"

"No."

Despite Gerald's instinct to reject the offer of help, he preferred to experience the first treatment immediately. He wanted to feel normal again, no matter the cost. Since the procedure involved no physical pain, just mental, he felt less afraid than he would have otherwise. Although he found humor in the irony, he lacked the strength to smile.

"What do you think?"

"Let's get it over with," he said, looking into her blue eyes, but a sudden movement from Miss Poofie caused them both to turn.

With its mechanical hand, the machine reached inside itself to open a box-like compartment. Both Sadi and Gerald stared as Miss Poofie retrieved a small round pot, maybe fifteen centimeters in diameter, filled with a grey-packed powder.

"Get a cup of warm water from the bathroom," Miss Poofie said.

Before Gerald could move, Sadi turned and walked into the bathroom, emerging only twenty seconds later. She carried a dark glass cup, steam rising from it.

"Pour water into the pot until the material becomes saturated," it said.

Before obeying the instructions, Sadi turned to look at Gerald, and he needed a moment to understand her expectations. She was waiting for his approval to proceed. He nodded silently, his eyes fixed on the pot. Sadi poured the water slowly and the grey powder absorbed it almost instantly.

"That's good," Miss Poofie said.

"Now what?" Sadi asked.

"Keep watching."

Miss Poofie remained motionless while Sadi and Gerald watched. After nearly a minute of silence, Gerald noticed movement in the center of the pot. The grey mud slowly parted to reveal the top of two tiny green leaves pointing away from each other. The growth process reminded him of clouds drifting in the sky, an almost imperceptible movement. As the green leaves slowly emerged from the mud, Gerald grew more curious about the plant's final appearance.

"It needs more light to complete the process," Miss Poofie said while gliding closer to Gerald's bed and placing the pot on the small table there. The lamp on the table had a long flexible neck for variable positioning. The machine carefully adjusted the light to shine straight down on the plant. Without any further movement or audible command, the lamp began to shine, dowsing the pot with an intense white light, stronger than Gerald thought the lamp could produce.

"While the plant grows to maturity, I will explain the procedure,"

Miss Poofie said after turning towards Gerald and Sadi again, the yellow glass facing them and spinning back and forth. "The plant will produce a flower with a strong scent. You should place the flower directly in front of you and then close your eyes. Then the music will begin."

"Specific instructions will interrupt the music at certain points, which will direct you when to inhale the fragrance of the flower. You can open your eyes at any time and stop the music, but you should inhale the flower scent at least three times. For optimal effectiveness, keep your eyes closed and listen to the music for as long as you can endure."

"What do you mean, for as long as he can endure?"

"There is no need to worry," it said almost apologetically. "When the procedure is complete, Gerald can try to describe it, if he wants."

While listening to the conversation, Gerald kept glancing at the pot. The two first leaves of the plant had grown to the size of his thumb, and two more began growing in a perpendicular orientation from the dark green petiole below them. The leaves looked like little green arrows with bright yellow veins.

"Why won't you tell us?" Sadi asked.

"Anxious anticipation will enhance the effectiveness," it said. "I can explain if you really want me to."

"No need to explain then," Sadi said reluctantly with a glance at Gerald. She waited in vain for him to comment. "How will we listen to the music? Do you have a music device of some sort?"

Gerald turned from the plant to look at the yellow glass on the machine. He wanted to give Sadi the appearance of paying attention, but he just wanted to watch the plant grow.

"The windows in each of hyour rooms can respond to voice commands. All you need to do is look directly at the window and command it to play Therapy-One. That's what I have named this piece, Therapy-One." Miss Poofie turned from them and started moving to the door. "I will leave you now. The flower will be ready when you can smell the fragrance."

Its mechanical hand silently opened the door to Gerald's room. While exiting, the yellow glass stopped rotating.

"Remember to inhale the scent at least three times."

—※—

After the door closed, Gerald looked into Sadi's eyes, then they returned their attention to the flower. A third level of leaves had started growing above the first two levels. The dark green leaves reflected the strong light of the lamp, glistening as though coated with a thin oil, and the yellow veins seemed to pulsate with life. When Sadi spoke, the sound of her voice brought Gerald back to reality, breaking the spell of watching the accelerated plant growth.

"I was not expecting this," she said while sitting on the bed next to the table with the flower. "I don't know what I was expecting."

Gerald took a step closer. Instead of sitting with Sadi, he crouched on the floor to watch the plant continue to grow. Although he felt the need to respond, to give Sadi the illusion of his attention, he really just wanted to watch the plant. Speaking words might somehow break the spell.

They watched in silence for a couple more minutes. Maybe Sadi felt the same as him and just wanted to watch the growth of new life, or maybe she did not want to make another attempt at conversation. While staring at the pot, he imagined the flower growing in the middle of a large barren field, completely devoid of life except for the plant. After two knights in metallic armor walked onto the field from different directions, Gerald jolted.

Sadi was holding onto his arm.

"Everything okay?"

"Oh," he said, flustered. "I'm fine."

"That's probably the flower bud," Sadi said, pointing to the small growth at the top of the plant, shaped like a green, slightly opaque water drop. "I want to touch it, but don't know if the oils on my skin will damage it."

To lessen the temptation, she pulled her hand away. During the next minute of silence, the flower bud grew about one centimeter in diameter. When the flower began to open, Gerald's eyes grew wide in anticipation. He had been enjoying the experience but knew the end would soon come, and he would have to begin the therapy procedure. The experience reminded him of waiting at the doctor's office for the nurse to come and call his name. He would soon have to put the magazine down and face reality.

The flower opened much more quickly than any other stage of the plant's growth. The beautiful flower rested at the top of the plant, about fifteen centimeters above the pot. Four levels of leaf pairs extended from the single dark green petiole, their yellow veins carrying light energy to the flower at the top.

Gerald found himself holding his breath while watching all the layers of petals unfold. Each layer of long oval petals sat atop the lower layer, forming a circle. The first layer of large black petals rested on the two leaves at the top of the plant and seemed to suck the light from the room. The next layer consisted of bright orange petals in a slightly smaller circle. The layers alternated between black and orange. At least a dozen long white stamens extended from the center of the flower in different directions. Light blue spheres covered in pollen rested atop the delicate filaments.

When the growth stopped, Sadi leaned forward and inhaled the scent. The light blue spheres covered in pollen seemed to balance on top of the tiny black filaments as small, separate balls.

"Smells like some kind of spicy candy, a mixture of blueberry and cloves," Sadi said and then leaned back to make room for him. "Really sweet."

Gerald leaned forward with some trepidation. He did not expect to experience anything other than a scent, but in the back of his mind, he feared the alien flower would cause some horrible vision.

"Hmm, very strong," he said in surprise, "almost too sweet."

"Are you ready to try it?"

Gerald took a deep breath before answering.

"Let's get this over with."

Sadi stood from the bed and grabbed a small chair from the corner of the room for Gerald. While he sat down and got comfortable, Sadi returned to her original position on the bed. As a final preparation for the procedure, Gerald leaned forward to make sure he was positioned to smell the flower when the time arrived in the music.

"I'll be right here," she said, placing her warm hand on his knee.

Gerald held eye contact with Sadi for just a moment and tried to smile. He turned to the window, took another breath, and then closed his eyes. After the music began playing in his head, he remembered only one thought—the name of the treatment lacked creativity.

"Play, therapy-one."

THIRTEEN

General Franks

“What have your doctors learned of Freddy Carlson’s abilities?” Josef asked.

General Franks turned slightly so he could see Josef at the window. The man’s constant movement irritated the general who had to switch positions just to keep him in view. He wondered if the man intentionally kept moving for just that effect. Josef returned to his position standing at the left side of General Franks’ desk.

Gordon Booth breathed deeply before responding. When he finally answered, his anger seemed to shine as bright as the sunlight spilling through the windows.

“We lost the doctor’s files with information regarding Freddy Carlson. What I do know, however, is that my two agents who met him at the takeoff site are dead, and the last message they sent was that they had apprehended him. Due to Mr. Carlson’s earlier incident with the FBI, my agents were informed to take extra precautions when dealing with Mr. Carlson, but apparently that was not enough.”

“Well,” Josef said and paused, probably hoping to give him time to regain his emotions. “In your report, you only mention a few things about his history. He grew up in foster care and has little contact with his family, a mother and sister. You also assert that he was involved with some incident in a hotel in which he single-handedly overpowered several armed guards, and killed several other people. What is your evidence?"

"We have positive confirmation of his presence at the time and location of the incident." Booth's emotions suddenly transformed from anger to curiosity about his two dead agents. "The two homeland security agents who were following the case are missing, and we believe they were last known to be with Mr. Carlson at his employer's home in Portland, Oregon."

"Does he have any combat training? Is there any way to account for his abilities?"

"His official history does not indicate any," Booth answered definitively. "From the few files we do have from my doctors working with Gerald Foster, we know they are getting help from an outside influence. Although Taylor Evans is exceptionally talented and intelligent, we find it unlikely that she was able to single-handedly develop this new science. I suspect that Mr. Carlson is the link between them."

"The link?" Josef said, but more to himself.

During the following few seconds, Gordon and General Franks exchanged eye contact. The general looked for signs of deception in the man's unblinking eyes. He would never completely trust the information from an intelligence agent, even when that information was being transferred to a commanding officer. Perhaps his second cousin kept something from them, something he would reveal later.

Josef's next question brought their eyes back to him.

"Is Freddy Carlson a human?"

Gordon Booth faced the much taller man standing over them, his eyes wider than normal. While waiting for the Central Intelligence officer to answer, General Franks wondered if their new director had been fooled by their own psyop programs. The general directed a whole department, whose only job was to spread disinformation to the public, including fake leaked documents about alien contact and other secret programs, to keep a certain demographic in a constant state of confusion about the real activities of the military.

"What do you mean, not human? Some sort of alien?" Gordon said with a respectful tone of incredulity. "He has the physical attributes of a human."

"If he was an insect, we could waste our time arguing about the species," Josef returned with some impatience. "He does not exhibit natural human abilities, and since your report on his history does not include any mention of these special talents, that indicates he had none before, and he has them now. This person you call Freddy Carlson is not consistent with the same character as the historical one you have identified. Do you agree with this assessment?"

"Yes, that seems fair," Gordon said.

"I don't think we should make any conclusions yet about Mr. Carlson, but let's keep this as a possibility, that the Freddy Carlson in the group is not the same as the United States citizen that the state records describe."

Josef paused to take a deep breath and look out the window. In the short moment, General Franks suppressed a smile. His curiosity about where the conversation was leading matched his enjoyment of Gordon Booth's discomfort. He imagined the Central Intelligence officer felt as he looked, embarrassed to be following the lead of their new director instead of leading the conversation about his own intel.

"Before we discuss how to proceed, I just want confirmation about the success of your doctor's work at the facility. From your report, the escape happened after a successful deconstruction."

"The lead doctor has confirmed it," Booth said as if he had lost all hope of leading the conversation. "He believes the deconstruction was successful, but they did not have the proper ramp-down for the patients' emotional recovery. If they survived their journey beyond our influence and were not destroyed by an orbital, Gerald Foster and Max Garner would appear obviously damaged. Their companions might not trust them anymore."

—※—

The conversation continued for twenty more minutes. General Franks mostly listened as Booth and Josef discussed how to proceed with the investigation. Josef wanted them to focus on finding Freddy Carlson. He believed that Freddy would then lead them to the remainder of the group. Gordon mentioned a report he had received about Mr. Ortiz and Freddy possibly going to Mexico. His agents were currently working with the Mexican authorities to find them. Josef suggested that if they found Mr. Ortiz, of course they had to interrogate him, but that he might be a valuable asset if he could be persuaded to join their ranks.

From the way he talked, the general could feel their new director's excitement about the situation. General Franks also began to feel the same. Although he had little interest in promotion, he could see the potential uses for the new propulsion, which would revolutionize the world and make further exploration possible, something he never thought would have happened in his lifetime. Of course, it also meant another layer of activities to conceal.

As expected, Josef gave the general the responsibility to use his resources to find the specialized jet and BMW. This was to be his top priority. He also needed to invent a convincing cover story for his staff who would be helping with the project. Josef suggested a possible story about tracking one of the low-orbiting asteroids but deferred to General Franks to make the final decision.

After the discussion about General Franks' responsibility, Alois made an unexpected interruption in the conversation. During the entire morning, he had remained mostly silent.

"Does the American administration know of this situation?" asked Alois.

General Franks, Gordon Booth, and Josef Brunner all looked at Alois with curiosity, as if none of them understood the question. Although General Franks knew the answer to the younger man's literal question, he waited for Josef to answer, since Alois was his direct subordinate. While waiting, General Franks remembered his indignation at being overseen by the much younger and less experienced man, despite his higher bloodline.

"I doubt the general or Officer Booth would have notified them without your awareness," Josef said with a hint of admonishment. "Why would they need to be involved? This is a case for the administration, not any nation-state bureaucrats."

"Yes, of course," Alois said, somewhat apologetically but without any hint of embarrassment. "I just wanted to make sure."

Josef paused for a few seconds, and the other men in the room waited for him to respond. He lightly stroked his chin with his index finger and thumb.

"Perhaps this is a good place for us to stop," he said while taking a few steps away from the table to stand closer to the window again. He looked through the window, squinting slightly from the bright sunshine. "We all have a good deal of work to do if we're going to get control of this situation. We all need to prove to the administration that we are worthy of our positions. Come Alois, we have more to discuss."

Josef looked down at Alois who stood silently, as an obedient pet.

"Of course," he said, standing and then walking to the door. He put his hand on the door handle and waited for Josef to move.

Josef maintained eye contact with Alois for a moment then returned his attention to the men sitting at the desk. General Franks and Booth stood, but only the general smiled. Booth remained expressionless with unblinking eyes.

"Gentlemen," Josef said, nodding, then joining Alois at the door. Josef exited first without looking back, and Alois closed the door behind them, leaving General Franks and Gordon Booth alone in the office.

The sudden calm in the room, due to the absence of his new director and intermediary, reminded the general of being able to hear the breeze again after witnessing the recent launch of an F-16 Fighting Falcon. The greater the disturbance, the greater the following calm.

"Well," General Franks said after the silence began to feel a little awkward. "That went better than I had anticipated. I did not fully understand the importance of it all. To be honest, I was more worried about the negative aspect of our fuck-up, not the positive aspect of what can be learned from it. I like this new director."

The look in the Central Intelligence officer's green eyes reminded Franks of when he had first met his young cousin. Gordon's mother had introduced him to the general, then a colonel, at a dinner party for one of his nieces in Bari. The party had taken place in a beautiful manor overlooking the Italian coast. The pleasant memory seemed to lessen his general dislike for the man, if only for a moment.

"You don't know who that man is, do you?" Gordon asked in an irritated tone, instantly destroying the positive memory of their introduction.

"No," General Franks grunted. "Should I?"

"I suppose you wouldn't necessarily know him, but his grandfather was also known as Adolph Hitler, for a while at least."

Gordon paused, probably intending to engrave the information in General Franks' memory. "Hmm," General Franks said, trying to act less impressed than he felt. "Is that so?"

"Josef Brunner is also the brother of some duke, but I can't remember the name of the Austrian province."

"So Adolph Hitler was really a Brunner?" General Franks asked but more to himself. He doubted the officer from the Central Intelligence Agency would feel inclined to answer, honestly at least. He had always wondered about the true identity of the most hated man in history.

"That information is classified," Gordon responded in a bloated tone of self-importance.

The general often heard that tone from men privy to secret information, but he experienced no insult since he often used the same tone. As the gatekeeper of all aerospace knowledge, General Franks probably possessed even more classified information than anyone from Central Intelligence. He would allow his second cousin to momentarily feel his own importance.

"Just for your information," Gordon continued, "he was not a Brunner, but was from Josef's mother's side."

"Well, I won't be giving Josef any undue consideration just because of his bloodline. My first impression of him, I must admit, is a positive."

"We can't make any mistakes," Gordon said seriously. "This is a very important case. We need to act with more—"

"You think I am unaware of the importance?"

"You seemed to be more interested in impressing him."

Gordon looked up at the general, blinking once before turning and walking to the window. While looking down at the green lawn, he waited for the general to reply. He was probably looking for Josef and Alois walking away, but General Franks knew he would fail to locate them. The parking lot was located on the other side of the building. A driver would then take Josef to the airfield. Very few would witness his departure.

"I'll be seventy years old this year, *cousin*," General Franks said as he returned to his seat. Although the younger man's welcome had already expired, the general chose to reply calmly. His lack of emotional injury might even cause annoyance. "I don't need to impress anyone, and I really don't care who Josef's ancestors are. Wouldn't a man in your position and age have more to gain by impressing a man like Josef Brunner?"

In the following silence, General Franks began gathering the pictures on his desk. After clipping the first group of photos back together, the general gathered the second group and waited for a counter-accusation, but he received only silence. Perhaps his last remark had hit home.

FOURTEEN

Gerald

Gerald recognized the instrument, a piano. Although no images had appeared in his mind, he imagined a pianist playing on stage in a dark lounge. Tables surrounded the piano and its player, with a man and woman sitting at each table. The pianist began by gently pressing one of the keys and holding it down.

While the volume held steady, the tone ascended slowly in pitch and then gradually descended again. The smooth cycle continued at a constant frequency until he started breathing in sync with its rhythm. He inhaled at the start of each cycle, when the pitch was at its lowest, and then exhaled at its peak. After several cycles, the simple act of breathing became his entire existence, replacing thoughts of the flower, Sadi, and the hovering machines.

While the original note continued its peaceful cycle, the pianist hit the next keys harshly, almost completely drowning the rhythm of his wave. The new melody fought for his attention, but with some focus, the gentle first note continued to control the steady rise and fall of each breath.

After several breathing cycles, Gerald recognized the structure of the harsh melody. It was a repeating pattern of scales, falling in sync with the original wave, which matched his breathing pattern. At first, Gerald missed the simplicity of the original wave, but as the cycles repeated, he began to appreciate the skill of the pianist and a world of more complexity.

Without his notice, the frequency of the wave crests began to decrease, the cycles stretching longer until his breaths became longer. When Gerald recognized the change, he felt a momentary panic. If the cycles continued to lengthen, his lungs would burst from inhaling so much air. To calm himself, he focused on enjoying the beauty of the complimentary waves.

The wave cycles stretched until Gerald felt a little lightheaded from the long inhalations and the surge of oxygen entering his blood. He wanted to breathe at his own pace but his body insisted on matching the wave's rhythm, unconcerned about making him dizzy.

At the end of a particularly long exhale, the flower's small stamens touched his nose, startling him. At first, the sweet scent was pleasant, but as he continued to breathe it in, its sickly sweetness quickly disgusted him, and he wanted to stop breathing altogether. The horrible smell nearly made him lose consciousness.

When Gerald began exhaling again, he felt instant relief, but he felt as though he'd entered a different dimension. Although he had no sense of sight, he felt the presence of other beings, creatures like himself. They were aware of his existence just like he knew of theirs, but they did not know how to communicate or interact with each other.

After a long time in his new world, Gerald felt the emotions of the other beings, especially their excitement. He soon discovered the cause of their great anticipation—the creation of a single point—a portal to another reality. None of the creatures knew how to access this point. They just felt its existence. At some future instance, the portal would become strong enough for one of them to enter, but only one.

Near the end of his long exhale, Gerald's awareness of the other beings disappeared, replaced by the pain of expelling the last remaining air from his lungs. And soon, he would inhale the horrible fragrance again. He wanted to open his eyes before bringing the disgusting smell inside of him but remembered the instruction to inhale the scent at least three times.

After the wave descended to its lowest point, where Gerald had to inhale, the horribly sweet smell began again to overpower all of his senses. But during the second half of the cycle, when the scent was no longer present, Gerald entered the other world again where he felt the presence of other creatures and the portal, which had grown in strength, bringing their excitement into a frenzy of anticipation. Gerald felt as if he were swimming with a group of sharks that smelled the blood of a wounded fish, hidden somewhere in the murky water.

When the intensity grew strong enough, Gerald got sucked into the portal, into another world where he was warm, protected, and alone. He enjoyed the new sensation until his awareness faded again, and then Gerald smelled the dreaded flower.

"Just one more time," he told himself. "Just one more time and I can open my eyes."

During this cycle, the scent of the flower failed to bother him as much. After the sweet scent dissipated and he began exhaling, Gerald was delivered for a third time into another realm. Although the presence of the sharks had vanished, he did not feel alone anymore. He felt the presence of a new creature, stronger and more intense than all of the others combined. It was the only other creature in that universe other than Gerald. At first, the new creature seemed far away, too far to cause harm. Then the face of the creature emerged from the darkness.

—❈—

Gerald opened his eyes before the face could fully materialize, bringing the beautiful music to an end. He found himself bent over the flower with his nose touching it. Before he started to breathe again, he moved away from the flower and faced the other direction. As fresh air filled his lungs, his memory of the face disappeared, replaced by a more pleasant sight, Sadi.

"Are you okay?" she asked, still sitting on the bed next to him.

"Yes," he said and stood from the chair to get further away from the flower. He took a couple of steps backward. "That was crazy."

"How do you feel?"

"I feel," he began, then paused to decide. "I feel a little more like myself, actually."

Sadi stood from the bed and stepped next to him. He turned to meet her gaze while she inspected him. He understood the look. She was looking for signs of sincerity. He took her hand in his and squeezed reassuringly.

"I really do feel a little better."

"What happened? What was it like?"

"It was like an intense meditation," he said while still holding her hand. "With a horrible smell."

His own words made him laugh genuinely for the first time since escaping the psychiatric hospital. He prepared to tell her about the impression of the other world, but his memory of the experience had mostly vanished, leaving him only with impressions. But surprisingly, his memory loss was a relief.

"It doesn't smell that bad," she said, smiling.

"It did up close."

"Should I try it now?"

"Actually," he said before she could continue. He did not want her to have the same experience. Instead of trying to explain his reasoning, he would use a diversion. "I'm starving. Let's go have some breakfast. We can tell Simon and Taylor about it. Maybe it will help Max too."

Gerald left the room holding Sadi's hand firmly in his own. While closing the door, he glanced briefly at the beautiful flower sitting by his bed. Although the plant filled his room with life, the flower reminded him of two eyes emerging from the darkness. The memory brought a sudden chill, so he focused on the warmth of Sadi's hand.

PART II

VIKINGS

Don't dive too deep

Into a dream

You might wake from sleep

FIFTEEN

Freddy

Freddy spent several minutes searching through the immense room, finally stopping in front of the crystal container of the creature he'd chosen. Like all the others, the creature was suspended inside the silvery liquid, motionless. It was covered in short white fur, speckled with small patches of grey and green.

He peered through the crystal at the lifeless face, partially visible through the translucent liquid. Long white lashes extended from its closed eyelids. Freddy thought they looked like the wings of some exotic butterfly or moth. When the white eyes flapped open, Freddy jumped in shock. The creature had only appeared to be alive, and then it suddenly was.

Freddy and the furry creature on the other side of the glass stared at each other. He felt afraid at first, but the barrier seemed like sufficient protection should the creature decide to attack. While suspended in the dark liquid, it looked at him with wide eyes, tiny black pupils in the middle of snow-white discs. It seemed to be studying him, patiently, unbothered by its liquid prison. Freddy was looking at more than just an animal in a cage.

The level of the silvery fluid began to recede, and the spotted fur shifted with the downward flow, clinging more tightly to the creature's body. Within a minute, no more liquid remained, and the container transformed into a wind tunnel, the air flowing swiftly from bottom to top. The creature's fur was completely dry in just a few seconds.

Freddy held his breath as the container walls were raised. Soon, only the air separated them.

The creature bent over and spent several seconds expelling the silvery liquid from its lungs, which drained through small holes in the pedestal. The sound of its first deep breaths reminded Freddy of a panting dog.

"Hello, Freddy Carlson," the alien creature said in perfect English but with a slurred accent, as though speaking with a mouth half-full of food. While waiting for his response, the creature stood fully erect and raised both hands in the air, stretching.

"Hello," Freddy answered, confused. He was unable to read the creature's emotions.

Unlike his dealings with other humans on Earth, Freddy felt nothing from the creature, no emotions or instincts. Ever since his first contact with the woman from his vision, Freddy had grown accustomed to perceiving emotional states. He required some time to remember the skill of reading a partner's body language and predicting their likely reactions.

When the furry little creature deftly hopped from the pedestal, landing softly on the hard surface, Freddy instinctively took a few steps backward. Its small mouth curved into an extremely severe smile, the ends of the lips almost vertical. The open mouth revealed rows of tiny but sharp teeth. If not for the friendly hello, Freddy would have thought it looked angry. For several seconds, Freddy looked down and the smaller creature looked up.

"Did you choose me because of my benign appearance?" it asked curiously. "I probably look like a cute little walking weasel."

Freddy suddenly recognized its resemblance to a weasel and then wondered about the extent of its knowledge of Earth. What else did it know? Did this creature originate from the planet below them? Freddy was even more curious to learn about it.

"I," Freddy began, attempting to think of a way to respond without causing offense. "Maybe I thought you looked the least intimidating. What do I call you?"

"Hmm," it said, stroking its furry chin. "What to call me, what to call me? Do you have any preferences?"

Freddy paused in confusion. At that moment, he did not feel particularly creative, not enough to invent a name to call a member of an unknown species.

"Don't you have a name?"

"Well, it's been such a long time," it said and smiled again. "How about Dod? Yes, Dod. That's very easy to say. You can call me Dod. I'll show you my signature when you're ready."

"Okay, Dod," Freddy began, suddenly wondering what a *signature* meant. Somehow, he knew the creature did not intend to show him writing. He felt uncomfortable calling it an arbitrary name.

So many questions were flooding his mind, Freddy did not know where to start. Did it not have a name? The furry creature just stood there, waiting patiently.

"Can I ask you questions?" Freddy asked. "I have a lot of them."

"Sure, let's get this out of the way. I don't promise to answer them all, but let's see what you've got. Throw 'em at me."

While waiting for Freddy to respond, Dod stretched again. It extended both hands high above its head, reaching almost to the level of Freddy's chin. After a few seconds of stretching, Dod yawned, revealing the sharp white teeth again, then rubbed its eyes. Freddy watched Dod's movements with fascination, momentarily forgetting his first question.

"Are you male or female?"

"There, I feel better now," Dod said after opening its white eyes again. "This, I mean, is a female."

She looked up at Freddy and blinked, her mouth remaining flat and expressionless. Freddy waited for her to say something else. When she blinked again, he somehow knew the action meant she expected him to continue his interrogation.

"Okay," he said after rubbing his eyes. "Let me start with why you brought me here?"

Dod blinked again, and Freddy found himself focusing on the tiny black pupils, which seemed to float in the middle of a white sea.

"Oh, Freddy," she said and laughed, sounding like a high-pitched cackle. "I'm not the one who brought you here."

Freddy began to feel frustrated with how his questions always seemed to get thwarted. Every response urged him to ask a completely different question, getting further away from what he really wanted to learn.

"Then who brought me here?"

"Hmm," Dod said, stroking the fur on her chin.

She paused and focused her white eyes on the space just above Freddy's right shoulder. He waited for several seconds, fighting the urge to turn and see if she saw something behind him. After returning her attention to Freddy, Dod continued speaking, slowly as if attempting to remember her lines.

"Now that is a very good question, Freddy," she began. "The one who brought you here, the woman from the plane, invited me to this corporeal world to explain some things to you. Come, let's go to the viewing room. We can continue this fascinating discussion there."

Dod smiled quickly, showing her sharp teeth again, then turned and started walking away. While following her, Freddy appreciated her form, slender and graceful. He wanted to reach out and touch her back. The green and grey spotted fur looked extremely soft, reminding him of a cat.

As Freddy followed Dod past all of the strange creatures in the crystal cases and then through the dark corridors, he tried to organize his thoughts and determine what else he wanted to learn from her. What was the woman from his vision? Or who was she? Where was he? What did they want from him? He soon quit making the list and realized that Dod would probably control the conversation.

—※—

They arrived back in the dark observation room with the viewing glass in the floor, which showed the planet below the orbiting station. Dod stopped at the edge of the glass, and they gazed in silence at the view. Puffy white clouds drifted across the surface. Freddy focused on breathing, waiting patiently for the creature to speak.

"Okay, this is a very simple situation." Dod was speaking without looking at Freddy, her eyes remaining fixed on the beautiful view below them. "*She* wants you to join her and in return, she'll help you rescue Sadi from her unfortunate predicament."

The unfortunate predicament she created for Sadi, he thought.

Freddy felt as if frozen fingers had closed around his heart. Now, his focus shifted to Sadi.

"How will she rescue Sadi?"

"Well," Dod began and Freddy wondered if he should already know the answer, "she gave you a gift, and you can use that gift to help Sadi, and whatever else you want. You can help her up to a certain point at least."

Dod extended her right arm, pointing her index finger at the planet's surface. Freddy noticed the short claws at the end of her furry fingers. Very sharp claws! He imagined shaking her hand and accidentally getting sliced.

The view suddenly changed and zoomed closer to the planet's surface, sending a wave of vertigo through him. After only a few seconds, the view had focused on a large mountain, causing Freddy to feel as if they had moved that much closer but without the physical sensation.

"If they want to come, she can bring your friends here," Dod said, then moved her hand slowly to the right and the snow-covered mountain flew away to reveal more mountains and then a green valley. Again, Freddy felt as though they had moved. "It's safe here. If they want, they can live here permanently or just stay for a while."

Sounds like a trap, he thought, but the planet's surface distracted him. He required several seconds to regain his sense of balance. Beyond the valley, he saw an ocean, then the scene changed and he saw only clouds.

"Actually," she said, turning to face him again. "If you're successful, she will give this place to you. Then you can decide who comes."

"Give this place to me?" he asked but did not wait for the answer. He pointed at the giant lens. "This planet?"

"Yes," Dod said and smiled.

He did not want to accuse Dod of lying, but owning a planet seemed too unreal. Did the woman from the plane just want to lure him and his friends to the planet? If she had been lying to him, maybe she was manipulating Dod too. He liked her.

"Why does she want me? How will I join her?"

Dod looked again to the air just above his left shoulder, pausing for about three seconds.

"I can't answer that, exactly."

"You are not allowed to answer, or you do not know how to answer?" Freddy asked, frustration beginning to taint his tone. She seemed to lack a complete answer to every single question. He suddenly wondered how she knew the English language.

"Freddy Carlson," Dod said, his last name sounding like the hiss of a cat. "Before you completely lose your cool, I'd just like to say what an honor it is to speak with you."

She paused and smiled. Freddy glanced at her sharp teeth again and then at her claws. Before he could consider the significance of her words, Dod continued.

"*She* is running the show here and has given me the honor of acting on *her* behalf, for now at least. Like I said already, she will help you help your friends, but only if you *decide* to join her. You don't know what that means now, but you will later."

"What do I need to do?"

Dod's eyes widened, and she clapped her hands. After looking away from the glass in the floor, her pupils also grew larger. The only light in the room came from the glass, the bright sunlight reflecting off the clouds.

"Now that's a question I can answer." Dod looked back to the glass, her hands still clasped together. She rubbed them excitedly. "Before I get to that, can I ask something?"

"Okay," Freddy answered, disappointed by another delay but curious too.

"Can I hold your hands?"

Freddy hesitated for a moment before extending both hands toward her, palms down. With a wide grin, she grasped his hands, her claws resting gently against the back of them. In contrast to the softness of her fur and the warmth of her touch, the claws felt like cold, sharp metal. If she had wanted, she could have torn his hands to shreds.

After spending a few seconds acquiring a comfortably tight grip, she squeezed but kept her claws from piercing his skin. A spectrum of emotions accompanied the sudden pressure, almost overpowering his consciousness, ranging from anger, to hate, to confusion, to awe, to love. Freddy understood the hate and anger. Alternatively, Freddy had felt love for Mr. Smith, for Sadi and her girls, but he never had experienced such intense love, the kind he imagined a child felt toward its parents, a strange kind of love for a father or mother figure he never knew.

The emotions began swirling together like colorful dyes in a glass of water, not mixing just circling each other. While the emotions swirled, a memory appeared in his mind, a memory he did not seem to own. He remembered standing in an arid desert, staring at a hole in the ground, an entrance to the earth.

When Dod squeezed tighter, his gaze shifted from his hands to her eyes. Her tiny black pupils in the sea of white reminded him of the hole in the ground from his new memory.

"Close your eyes," Dod commanded, closing her own but keeping her tight grip on his hands. She breathed deeply as though enjoying the experience. "Tell me what you see."

Before Freddy could obey, her claws dug into his flesh. Small streams of blood ran down his hands, but he lacked the strength to look away from her closed eyes and the white fur of her face.

"I see a hole at the bottom of a dark pit," he said after closing his eyes. Attempting to ignore the pain, he inhaled deeply and the scene from his memory came into sharp focus. "It is the entrance to a cave. I want to go away from here."

Dod's voice answered from the pit.

"If you want to save Sadi and her family, you must descend here into the earth." The voice from the real world united with the imaginary. "You will meet us there. The decision has already been made."

Despite his fear and the physical pain in his hands, Freddy knew how he would respond. He would do whatever the woman from the plane demanded. She alone had the power to help Sadi. Even his new abilities originated from her. His choice felt like accepting a pre-existing decision rather than making a new one.

Before opening his eyes, Freddy somehow understood their connection. He and Dod were experiencing all of the same sensations, including the pain from her claws digging into his skin. The pain in his hands brought a strange kind of euphoria, causing her to squeeze even tighter.

"Return to Earth," she said, and Freddy heard drops of blood splattering on the floor. "We will guide you to the cave. After your journey through the earth, you can help Sadi and the rest of your friends."

SIXTEEN

Doroteo

After leaving their friends in the upper atmosphere, Freddy and Doroteo traveled in the BMW to Juarez, Chihuahua, flying into Mexico beyond the detection capabilities of the military, according to Freddy. The thrill of being so high and traveling so fast provided a pleasant escape from the traumatic events of the evening. The vehicle felt like an extension of Freddy's body, and he controlled it effortlessly.

They landed in a remote part of the desert before driving the rest of the way to his friend's house in Juarez. To Doroteo's relief, they had traveled mostly in silence both in the air and on land. On their journey together, he had quickly come to understand the redundancy of speech, the need to tell or ask Freddy anything. He had known where Doroteo wanted to travel without even asking a single question or even a questioning glance.

Doroteo admired Freddy and was never jealous of his abilities. Freddy could not physically compete with him, but he could not compete with Freddy in other ways. In his life, he'd come to appreciate the skills of other people and always looked for ways of taking advantage of them or ways they could complement his own.

Several times during their flight, the events of the evening had replayed in his mind especially his conversation with Freddy in the Canadian woods.

"John Pratt, the FBI agent, is coming from that direction," Freddy had said, pointing to the shore, west of the lake. "If you can get him to feel like he is in control of the situation, he will facilitate our escape. I will make sure of it. The other intelligence agents are already there and one of them just grabbed Taylor."

Doroteo remembered feeling overwhelmed by all of the enemies who had stood against them. He'd wanted to run off by himself to see what he could do, but a great calm had settled over him, producing trust in the boy.

"Okay, what do I do?"

—※—

"Let me get us something to eat," Doroteo said. "My friend will give us anything we want."

"Sure," Freddy answered, remaining seated on the sofa.

Before Doroteo closed the door to the basement of his friend's home, he nodded at Freddy, his equivalent expression of a smile. Freddy met his gaze without emotion. The boy looked even more exhausted than Doroteo felt.

As Doroteo rummaged through the refrigerator for something to eat, he talked with his friend who owned the house. Besides Freddy, only they remained awake. The man's wife and two grandkids had gone to bed. If they had arrived earlier than midnight, his friend's wife would have made them a meal and they would have eaten together. Doroteo looked forward to interacting with them again. He had become friends with the man and his wife when they worked together in the police department before he worked for Cesar. Only Doroteo and this man had remained friends from that time. The drug cartels had murdered the rest of those friends.

Despite the late hour and his physical and mental exhaustion, Doroteo preferred to remain awake and talk with his friend. Spending time with Freddy had failed to decrease his tension from the horrific events of the night. Speaking in Spanish with his old friend helped him to feel more at ease, helped him focus on the future, and put his mind to work replacing the pain of losing his best friend, Cesar.

For the immediate future, Doroteo would stay with his friend. The basement would be his new home for as long as he wanted, forever even, or until Doroteo decided to help Freddy and the group again, or just disappear to some other place for a while.

After looking through the refrigerator for a while, he decided to take the leftovers from that evening, half a pan of enchiladas, still lukewarm when he touched the glass. Instead of using the microwave, he put the pan in the oven. He hated microwaved food and preferred to use a more conventional heat source. While they waited, he focused the discussion on mundane matters and said they could talk later about what caused him to seek refuge.

"I hope you like enchiladas," Doroteo said when he saw Freddy in the basement again. He placed the plate and cup on the coffee table.

"Yes," Freddy replied, his look of exhaustion easily recognizable. "Thank your friend for me."

"I will. If you don't mind, I'm going to eat upstairs and might not be down for a while. Take either bedroom and I'll take the other one. It doesn't matter to me."

"Sure."

Freddy smiled weakly and then turned to his food. Doroteo stayed long enough to see the boy retrieve the fork from the plate.

When Doroteo returned to the basement two hours later, he found Freddy asleep in one bedroom, so he took the other one and lay in the bed. As he fell asleep, the faces of his friends helped expel consciousness. His dreams that night did not help him feel rested. In the morning, he woke with the vague memory of disturbing nightmares. Instead of escaping with Freddy, he had gone with the group and watched Cesar depart with Freddy. He remembered sorrow for never seeing Mexico again.

Doroteo did not find Freddy in his room, only a note on the bed. While reading it, the memory of his dreams vanished.

Thank you for the meal and place to sleep. If I need any help or have news for you, I will come back to this place. If you are not here, I will let your friend know and perhaps he can deliver the message.

Good luck, Doroteo! It has been a pleasure knowing you. You will see your friends again. Please take a break and try not to worry about anything. The situation is out of your hands for now.

~Freddy

Doroteo read the note a couple of times, then stared at it for a few seconds. After neatly folding the paper, he placed it in his wallet. The lines of ink were the only physical connection to what had happened for the past year. Everything else existed only inside his head.

The next few days, Doroteo read Freddy's note at least a dozen times, each reading renewing his respect and trust in the boy. As the days passed, he tried focusing on building a new life in the home of his friend and thought often of his time in Cesar's home with Dominga and Taylor.

After a few weeks in his new life, another hope began to form. Although he loved his homeland and the peace of his situation, he wanted to join his friends again. Thoughts of seeing them helped the future seem just a little brighter. Of course, he wanted to see Cesar again, but he had an almost equal desire to renew the battle with Taylor.

SEVENTEEN

Brian

Brian Jacobsen rolled over in his bed and wiped perspiration from his forehead. He had another dream of his sister, Sadi, and his two nieces, Helen and Daryn. In this dream, they were running from a pack of monsters with sharp teeth and glowing eyes. As usual, Brian hovered over the scene, silently watching and unable to help them. For the following hour, Brian lay in bed, trying to return to sleep but unable to rid his memory of the dream. Whenever he closed his eyes, several pairs of glowing eyes stared back at him.

After trying in vain to sleep, he finally decided to regain control of his imagination. He grabbed the cell phone from the top of the covers and then shielded his eyes when the light illuminated the bed around him. He opened the photo application and swiped through several photos until he found the last picture he had of his sister. She had one girl on each side, her arms pulling them close. Both Sadi and Daryn were smiling, but Helen was making a funny face.

"Blahhhhh," he remembered her saying loudly as he took the picture, her mouth remaining open.

Brian stared at the picture for almost a minute, his lips spreading wide. If he stared long enough, the image might replace the memory of his nightmare. He focused on the memory of when he had taken the picture, the last time they had all been together. He wished she would have let him help her.

He planned to turn off the phone and go back to sleep, but he heard a knock on his door.

"What the hell?" he whispered.

At first, he was afraid that a policeman was standing outside his apartment door, then he decided against that possibility. The police would have announced their identity. He knew that all too well, having experienced it a few times in the past. Then an exciting thought came to him. Maybe Sadi stood at the door.

He jumped out of bed and ran to the door, not bothering to slip a t-shirt over his bare chest. After looking through the peephole, he felt a little disappointed, but he opened the door without hesitation.

"Freddy?" he asked in confusion. "Oh my god!"

"Hi, Brian," Freddy said. "Can I come in?"

"Of course," Brian said, pushing the door open wide.

After Freddy walked past him, Brian looked outside in the hopes of seeing his sister, but he saw only an empty second-story stairwell. When he shut the door, he found Freddy sitting on the chair by the couch. Brian was embarrassed at seeing his blue t-shirt draped over the back of it, just behind Freddy's shoulder.

"Sorry about the mess," Brian said while taking the shirt from the chair and slipping it over his head. "I wasn't expecting company, especially at almost two in the morning. What's been happening? Where is Sadi?"

"I'm not sure exactly," Freddy answered vaguely, "but she and the girls are safe."

Brian walked to a table by the wall and flipped the switch to the lamp sitting there. He turned to Freddy and saw him shielding his eyes from the light. He was silent and seemed distracted.

"How are you so sure they're safe?" Brian asked. Before sitting by him on the couch, Brian had to remove the acoustic guitar. "You have to tell me what is happening. When I went back to your employer's home a few weeks ago, no one answered."

"Mr. Smith's in the hospital, and I've been gone."

"Okay, so what happened to Sadi?"

"She's out of their reach," Freddy said, looking directly into Brian's eyes.

For the next few seconds, Brian stared back at his childhood friend as if seeing him for the first time. Brian had planned to keep asking about his sister, but the look in Freddy's eyes changed his course of questioning.

"What happened to you, Freddy?"

"Too much to explain now," he answered, breaking eye contact and looking toward the door. "I should not have come here. They were hiding from me, watching."

Brian felt a chill pulsate through his core, a warning of danger.

"Who's hiding from you?"

Instead of answering, Freddy jumped from his seat, ran to the door, and looked through the peephole. After opening the door and stepping outside, Brian quickly joined him, the cool night air enhancing his sense of foreboding and making him shiver. He was glad for the shirt.

"There is no time to explain," Freddy said, then spoke more quietly to himself. "Did they find a way to hide from me?"

Freddy shut the door and turned to Brian. Instead of speaking, he stared as if unable to decide on the course of action.

"What's wrong?"

"You need to come with me," Freddy answered finally. "Hurry and get dressed. People are coming to take us, not just me but both of us. We might have enough time to escape. Meet me in the parking lot."

Freddy exited the apartment before Brian could turn around and head to his room. In less than a minute, Brian had gotten dressed in shorts and shoes. He paused at the door and looked back at his apartment with a disturbing thought. He might not return.

He ran back to his room and grabbed his favorite hat from its place on the bedpost, the plain tan hat that Helen had decided to mark with a smiley face. Then he grabbed his guitar and left the apartment without a backward glance.

When Brian reached the bottom of the stairs, he started walking down the path to his covered parking space, about ten meters away and past some small trees. When Brian reached the trees, he stopped. Freddy stood in the middle of the street by the BMW, the engine humming. Two men stood between Brian and the street, two large brutes, each with a gun in his right hand, aimed at the ground and looking at Freddy. Brian looked at them briefly, then at the path he would have to take to join Freddy, past the two men.

"Come on," Freddy said, waving for Brian to continue walking. "They won't hurt you."

"What the fuck!" Brian said, not moving.

"Hurry," Freddy said. He closed his eyes, and then the two men stepped away from each other, making enough room for Brian to easily pass between them. "More of them are on their way."

As Brian walked between the men, he could almost hear his heartbeat, and his instinct demanded that he run the other way. He imagined walking between hungry lions. Both men looked at him curiously as he passed, as though he did not interest them, only Freddy. When Brian reached the other side of the BMW, he grasped the door handle. Then he heard footsteps behind him.

"Put your hands in the air," said an angry male voice.

Instead of obeying the command, Brian obeyed his instinct to turn and see what confronted him. He found two more men standing on the other side of the street, just two meters away. They looked almost identical to the first men. He looked into the closest man's eyes, the white parts reflecting the streetlights. For a moment, he felt as though his heart had stopped.

"Get into the car, Brian," Freddy said from behind him. "They won't hurt you either."

"Show us your hands," the man said, angrier now. "I said put your goddamn hands in the air. Now!"

When the man lifted the gun and pointed it directly into Brian's face, Brian almost dropped his guitar in panic. For several seconds, no one moved or said anything else. Then Brian felt a mysterious rush of courage. He turned to face Freddy and noticed the sweat glistening on his face and his closed eyes. Brian suddenly had the courage to open the car door and sit slowly in the seat. He carefully placed his guitar in the back seat, afraid of making sudden movements or sounds.

After shutting the door, Brian expected Freddy to get inside too, but he just stood in the same spot. He turned to face the men who had pointed their guns at Brian and they slowly lowered their guns, pointing them at the ground as the first men had done. While trying to understand what was happening, Brian had only one thought. Freddy needed to get inside the BMW so they could drive away.

A sudden noise from the front of the car dashed this hope to pieces. Two large black Hummers pulled into the parking lot. One of them stopped at the entrance, blocking any hope of escape. The other Hummer stopped about fifteen feet away from the BMW. In horror, Brian watched as nine more men exited the vehicles, each one holding a gun.

As the men formed two lines, Brian guessed their identity, soldiers dressed in civilian clothes. All of them had short military haircuts. One of the men even wore a military hat. He stepped in between the two rows, his gun pointed to the ground. The other men had their guns aimed at Freddy.

"Put your hands in the air, please," the man with the hat said calmly as if he spoke to his mother or father, and not an enemy.

When Freddy failed to comply, the man spoke again, louder but just as calmly.

"If you don't put your hands up, we will shoot your friend. The glass will not stop the bullet."

Brian gulped but did not move. From his vantage point in the passenger seat, he could see only Freddy's lower half, hands held tensely at his side.

Freddy remained silent, and then Brian noticed his hands clenching into fists as if in anger. After another few seconds, Brian saw movement in his peripheral vision. The first four soldiers to confront them started moving. They slowly stepped between Freddy and the soldiers from the Hummers.

"Get out of the way," the man with the hat yelled, his voice filling with anger, but the men just stood between him and the BMW.

"Fasten your seatbelts," Freddy said and then slowly descended into the vehicle, the car door remaining open.

Outside of the car, all of the soldiers stood in the same positions. Only the man with the hat began moving. He lifted his gun and aimed at the closest man between him and Freddy. The man took slow steps forward.

"Get the fuck out of the way," he yelled, but the men just stood silently.

"What is happening, Freddy?" Brian asked in panic as Freddy closed the door. Brian heard a quiet rush of air as the door sealed itself. "There's no way out of here. They have the exit blocked."

Without answering or looking away from the scene in front of the BMW, Freddy put his hand on what resembled a modified stick shift. His hands were shaking.

"Hold on," Freddy said, almost hyperventilating, as if he'd just run a long race. "This might hurt so hold your head tight against the back of the seat."

Brian obeyed Freddy's command and held his head tightly against the seat, preventing a dangerous whiplash as they suddenly shot away from the earth. Brian remembered seeing the four men in front of them begin turning towards the BMW and then he heard gunshots. Without realizing it, Brian held his breath and the grips on the side of the seat.

After about four seconds of ascension, Freddy slowed the vehicle a bit and Brian began breathing again. He turned from facing the windshield and attempted to see through the passenger window, but the dark tint prevented him from clearly discerning anything. He had to press his face to the glass to see the outline of the clouds as they entered the fluffy whiteness.

"That was too close," Freddy said to himself, taking quick gulps of air. "We can stop for a while and I can try to explain things. Are you okay?"

Brian turned from his window and stared at Freddy. Before responding, he watched as Freddy wiped the sweat from his forehead and brushed his wet blond hair to the side. Light from the control panels and the computer screen illuminated his sweaty face. Brian thought his hair looked whiter and messier than normal.

"Holy shit, Freddy!" Brian said as the blood returned to his brain. He took two deep breaths before finishing. "Holy shit. I'm not dreaming, am I?"

"No, this is real."

"So we're actually in the sky?" Brian said to himself, turning from Freddy's intense brown eyes to look through the window again. He could only see darkness. "In a car that can fly?"

"Yes."

"Did you make this thing?"

"No, a couple friends made it," Freddy answered. "This is what got us all in this whole mess."

"What the hell happened down there?"

Brian shuffled in his seat to get more comfortable. He began to feel better about the situation, even though he still had no idea how he should feel.

"I am sorry about that," Freddy said, exhaling in frustration. "I should have known they would be watching you. I just assumed that I would be able to detect them."

"Okay, but what happened? I mean, those were soldiers, right?"

As Brian spoke, his excitement began to rise. While waiting for the response, he attempted to make a mental recording of the experience and produce some possible lyrics for his band's next song. He sang the lyrics in his mind.

Shooting into the sky,
a funny way to die?
As the bullets fly?

No. 'Sky and fly' is too cliché.

"Damn it," he said to himself, just as Freddy began to speak. "I forgot my notebook."

"What about *sky* and *lie*?" Freddy asked seriously.

Brian stared at Freddy, squinting with sudden suspicion.

"How did you know I was thinking of a song?"

When Freddy failed to respond, a realization materialized in Brian's mind, and his eyes widened in shock. Had Freddy entered the minds of the soldiers and scrambled their thoughts? Brian suddenly felt as though he sat with a stranger.

"I am your friend, Brian," Freddy said in answer to his thoughts. "I am the same Freddy you have always known. And yes, I can influence people's perceptions. I wanted to help relieve your mind about your sister. That is why I came to you. I am sorry you had to leave with me. They probably would have left you alone if I had not come."

"You said you didn't know where Sadi is," Brian began, trying to remember their conversation in his apartment. "But she's safe, right? Can we find her?"

"I do not know exactly where she is," Freddy began.

Brian wondered if Freddy really did know and just did not want to say. Maybe the information would upset him.

"Just tell me where she is," Brian said, pleading in his voice. "I just want to see her."

Freddy took a deep breath before answering.

"I really do not know where Sadi is, but I do know how to find her. We cannot go to her just yet though. She is no longer on Earth."

"Not on Earth?" Brian asked in frustration. He felt unable to handle any more confusion. "Then where the hell is she? Are you trying to tell me she's dead?"

"No," he answered quietly and calmly. "Your sister is alive and well, and so are your nieces." Freddy opened his mouth to say more but turned quickly to the computer screen in front of him. His eyes narrowed so tightly, Brian could see only darkness between his eyelids.

"What is it?" Brian asked with a sudden sense of panic, a new anxiety replacing his other questions.

"They," Freddy began, but he let several seconds pass in silence. "They are watching us. We cannot stay here."

Freddy typed on the keyboard near the dashboard then grasped one of the control sticks with his right hand, his knuckles turning white. He closed his eyes and took two slow breaths.

"Where are we going?" Brian asked, not sure he wanted to know the answer.

"Up," Freddy said, then opened his eyes and smiled. "I'm going to reorient the car. Try to relax."

Freddy tapped a key on the keyboard and the car began to rotate. The pressure from gravity on his butt and thighs slowly transferred to his back. He stopped breathing until the motion stopped. He still could not see outside the vehicle, but he knew they were facing the sky above them. The experience reminded Brian of going up the steep tracks of a roller coaster.

When they began ascending, they accelerated at a more comfortable rate than when they had first left the ground. Brian did not have to press his head against the seat to keep his neck from snapping. Gravity did the work for him.

As the pressure increased, the pull of Earth became more real and stronger than ever before in his life. Their connection to the ground reminded him of a stretched rubber band. At some point, they would no longer have the energy to fight against the force and would fly back to reunite with Earth.

"I can imagine worse ways of dying," Brian said, laughing to himself in an attempt to fight the panic.

After only a few seconds, they left the safety of the clouds and Brian saw light in his peripheral vision. With some effort, he turned his head toward the window to see a thin glow on the horizon, and another light moving just below his view. He had to lift his head to see the blinking light more clearly.

"That is a military helicopter," Freddy said, almost like a tour guide explaining some historic site. "We can ignore that, but we do need to worry about the surveillance planes above us."

Brian let his head rest against the back of the seat again, switching his view to the front window above him, which showed only darkness. Despite the dangers above them, Brian had complete trust in Freddy, the guide on his crazy tour. *Good thing I have no problems with vertigo,* Brian thought, smiling. He preferred to have the contents of his stomach on the inside.

"So we're going above them?" Brian asked. "How high can this thing go?"

"We can go higher than they can," Freddy said without taking his eyes from the control panel. "They are going to try to capture us, but they do not want us dead, not yet at least. They want this vehicle, and me."

Brian gulped.

"How in the hell are they going to capture us?"

Instead of answering, the BMW moved to the right, hard enough to jerk Brian's head to the left. He had to hold his head against the back of the seat until Freddy reoriented the car to face their direction of travel.

"What's going on?" Brian asked.

"They sent something after us," Freddy said in panic. "It is fast."

For the next several seconds, they accelerated upward in silence. The force against his back and head began to make Brian feel light-headed. He just wanted to close his eyes, but curiosity and fear kept them open. When he noticed the stars through the window, his fear momentarily disappeared. He stared at their bright brilliance against the black until the following explosion of light and sound destroyed his awareness.

EIGHTEEN

General Franks

At a few minutes past midnight, General Franks was following a soldier through the bright lower-level hallways of building seven. The soldier stopped at the door marked B11, placing his hand on the scanner. After a quiet click, he opened the door and stepped aside to let General Franks enter.

"You're dismissed," General Franks said after he noticed the soldier standing with his back against the door, facing forward vacantly.

"Yes, sir," he said.

For the next few seconds, General Franks assessed the condition of the room, looking for evidence of organization and discipline. Two men sat with their backs to him at the large oval table in the center of the room while another man stood behind them. One of the seated men typed on a keyboard built into the table while he faced the illuminated monitor next to it. The other man had his left hand on a complex control board while holding onto a control stick with his right hand. He kept his eyes fixed on the central flat screen on the wall in front of the table.

General Franks approved of the general condition of the room, taking special notice of the empty office chairs arranged neatly under the desk, and the documents on the table also organized to his satisfaction. The appearance of orderliness gave General Franks confidence in his staff. He glanced at the screens in front of the room, which showed a live view of some clouds.

The man standing behind the desk stood with his hands behind his back, staring at the illuminated screens in the front of the room. Before turning to address the general, he finished some instructions to the man who had his hand on the control stick.

"Keep going, just a few more percent. Okay, hold it there," he said, then glanced back at the general. "Good evening, General Franks. Sorry to wake you."

"Good evening, gentlemen," General Franks replied casually to the men at the desk. "Remain at your posts."

The man on the left turned first, nodding before his companion did the same. General Franks thought only the second man seemed surprised to see him.

"At ease," the general said, turning to the man he had placed in charge of the Freddy Carlson case. "Thanks for notifying me, Lieutenant Hinckley. What's the status?"

"You're welcome, sir," he answered, smiling and turning back to the illuminated screen. "Like I said on the phone, we're tracking the BMW. I suspect he's on his way to Portland, Oregon. That's him there."

Before returning his attention to the screen, General Franks glanced at the back of Lieutenant Hinckley's head, which was covered by his hat. The video, shot in IR, showed a clear image of a BMW flying through the clouds. Seeing the ridiculous flying car made General Franks shake his head in amazement. In his lifetime, he never expected to see such a thing.

"Do you have a positive ID on the driver?" he asked. "Is it Mr. Carlson?"

"That's just an assumption, sir," Lieutenant Hinckley answered with a hint of disappointment. "We haven't had a good enough angle to make a positive identification. And in the clouds, it's also difficult to determine."

"So he thinks he can hide in the clouds, does he?" General Franks smirked.

"Perhaps."

"Where did he go after you lost him in Mexico?"

General Franks used the word *you* instead of *we*, not to blame the officer of failure but to balance his motivation. He had to give Lieutenant Hinckley special treatment. For proper motivation, humans needed both positive and negative feedback, and the general felt as though he had given Hinckley too much motivation lately on the positive end of the spectrum.

"I lost him," he answered, "after he entered the ionosphere. He likes to go all the way above the atmosphere before traveling to a new location. I failed to find the correct sensors in time. It won't happen again. We will be able to successfully resolve his signature in the future."

"Good," the general said, trying to hide his satisfaction. "Are the special forces ready in Portland?"

"Officer Booth has notified them and says they will be ready as soon as we provide the exact location." Hinckley turned to the men at the table. "Any change to the ETA of the target?"

The man on the left tapped on the keyboard.

"He should arrive in about twenty-one minutes."

"Okay, be prepared to zoom in so we don't lose him. Thank you."

For the next minute, the general and lieutenant watched the screen. The camera had locked on the vehicle so that only the land and clouds moved. Although General Franks liked watching the clouds passing between the camera and BMW, he wished they'd had a clear sky.

The view through the IR camera showed the heat trail following the vehicle. General Franks had expected a much larger thermal output. He hoped that when they captured the BMW, he could personally investigate the machine before Central Intelligence confiscated it. He desperately wanted to know how it worked. Gordon Booth, his cousin, probably had more interest in the driver.

"Any word from Alois?" the general asked while keeping his eyes on the screen. "Will Mr. Brunner be joining us, or is he with Booth?"

"I have no definite information about that." Lieutenant Hinckley turned to look at the general, but Franks kept his eyes on the screen, hoping to appear unconcerned. "All I know is that per your instructions, I notified Alois *after* notifying you."

"Good."

Two minutes later, the camera controller zoomed in on the BMW, and they watched as Freddy descended closer to the ground. The image became more blurry the lower his elevation.

"What drone is closest?" Lieutenant Hinckley asked. "Let's activate those cameras."

"Both drones are within range, sir," said the man holding the control stick. "I'll show both."

The man punched some keys on the control board and then put his hand on another control stick. When the two other screens on the wall showed new images, the room suddenly became much brighter. While the IR camera tracked the BMW from higher above, the drone operator zoomed in from two new angles, one clearer than the other, but both with more detail than the IR camera showed.

"The windows are too dark to make out the driver," Lieutenant Hinckley said with disappointment. Then he spoke to the controller. "Do we have a filter to show the driver?"

"I can try, sir," the man answered, then quickly clicked some keys. The view of the BMW switched through several filters, but none showed much improvement. "Sorry, sir. Looks like it's got some complex tinting."

"Damn," the general whispered to himself.

The sudden click of the door behind him brought a rush of blood and instant anxiety. The general knew who had arrived even before he recognized the voice. Before turning, General Franks waited impatiently for the sound of the door closing.

"Good evening, General Franks," Josef Brunner said with his slight German accent.

Josef joined the general's side and scanned the three screens in front of him. After making quick eye contact with the man, he returned his view forward. Although the general had expected to see the man, seeing non-military personnel in the operations room displeased him.

"Good evening, Herr Brunner," Franks said, remembering at the last moment to follow Alois's recommendation to address their director as *Herr Brunner*. "He's just dropped out of the clouds and will be arriving shortly, we suspect, in Portland, Oregon."

"Excellent," Josef said with his hands clasped together, fingers tightly interlocking. "I want to talk to Officer Booth. Have you connected with him yet?"

"Lieutenant Hinckley," General Franks said with a nod to indicate Josef. "This is Herr Brunner. Please do whatever he says."

"Yes, sir," Lieutenant Hinckley said and nodded, his hat briefly hiding the view of his eyes. He turned to the man at the computer. "Initiate a connection with Officer Booth."

Before the man answered, he looked up at the Lieutenant.

"Do you want him on the speakers, or a personal line, for privacy?"

"Put him on the speakers," Josef Brunner answered, keeping his eyes on the screen.

A few seconds later, the general heard a click after the soldier established a connection. Gordon Booth's voice filled the room, adding to General Franks' irritation at his lack of complete command.

"This is Officer Booth," answered the man on the other line, and General Franks thought he heard excitement in his cousin's voice.

"Good evening, Officer," Josef said with unusual cheerfulness as if he had just woken from a refreshing mid-day nap. "We're following our target and he is almost at Portland. Are your men ready?"

"The men are ready, and waiting for the location, Herr Brunner," Booth said

General Franks could almost hear the man's attempt to impress Josef.

"We will keep you informed," Josef said. "Keep this line open."

For the next few minutes, they continued watching the BMW while the soldier at the computer provided updates to Officer Booth.

When the vehicle finally landed safely on a side road just south of Portland, it then traveled to Interstate 5 and turned northward.

General Franks watched with some admiration as the driver, presumably Freddy Carlson, wove expertly through the late-hour traffic. When the soldier at the controls calculated his speed at over a hundred miles per hour, the general felt as though they were watching a high-speed car chase without the pursuing law enforcement officer. At one point, the general saw a highway patrol vehicle a mile ahead of the BMW and waited for the inevitable pursuit, but when Freddy passed the patrol car, it remained parked on the side of the road.

"Interesting," Josef said, rubbing his chin.

"Do you think the policeman didn't see him?" Lieutenant Hinckley asked, addressing his question to General Franks.

"Or they saw him," Josef said without turning from the screen, "and didn't notice him."

Lieutenant Hinckley turned to look at his commanding officer, the tense corners of his eyes transforming into a silent question mark. The general just nodded, almost imperceptibly. He had neglected to tell Lieutenant Hinckley about Freddy's abilities. He made a mental note to explain at a later time.

They watched him drive for another five minutes.

"He's taking exit 34 to Rosa Parks," the soldier said after the BMW left the highway. Before continuing, he waited until the BMW came to a stop. "He's heading eastward on Rosa Parks."

While waiting for Gordon Booth to respond, they watched the BMW accelerate. During the silence, General Franks felt his pulse quicken.

"The unit will start heading in that direction," Officer Booth answered finally. "The closest assets can be in that area in fifteen minutes."

"We'll give you more details," Lieutenant Hinckley said after waiting for Josef to answer. "Just as soon as we know his final destination."

Ten minutes later, the BMW pulled into the parking lot of an apartment building. Before it came to a stop, the soldier told Officer Booth the address. Streetlights illuminated the parking area, revealing a human wearing a hat. Their target walked at a steady pace toward the building.

"Open an additional IR view and start recording that profile," Lieutenant Hinckley said to the soldier who obeyed silently by clicking on the keyboard. "We need to record the target's heat signature when he comes back out."

When the red infrared trace of their target disappeared inside the building stairwell, Josef turned to General Franks. Despite his attempts to appear stoic, Josef wore an animated smile.

"It's out of our hands now," Josef said, grabbing the general's shoulder and squeezing quickly before releasing. He turned back to the screen. "Officer Booth."

"Yes," Booth answered.

"Are scanners in place for when the target returns outside? Remember, we want a recording of his physical state during the confrontation."

"Scanners are ready."

"Good," Josef said. "Also, give us access to the conversation between you and the unit. We want to hear everything."

"Yes, sir," Officer Booth said with surprising confidence and an excitement of his own.

The occupants of the control room at Peterson Air Force Base in Colorado listened in shocked silence as the soldiers in Portland, Oregon, confronted Freddy Carlson and his companion, a man yet to be identified. To the general's surprise, Josef Brunner listened patiently as Officer Booth communicated with the soldiers who had surrounded Freddy and the BMW.

In the excitement of the situation, the general almost expected his new superior to intervene with instructions, especially when they failed to apprehend the targets when Freddy and his accomplice escaped in the BMW.

After General Franks listened to the soldiers give their final report to Booth, the general glanced briefly at Josef Brunner, afraid of what he would find. His new superior just watched as the BMW ascended from the scene, a haunting look of satisfaction in his eyes.

"Your orders?" Gordon Booth asked with a voice of stone, totally devoid of life. "Herr Brunner?"

"Good work, gentlemen," Josef said with a slight nod and a glance at the men around him. "We now have a better assessment of Mr. Carlson's abilities and limits."

General Franks felt a slight satisfaction at guessing his cousin's disappointment. From his point of view, the mission had probably been a total failure. The general had a better view of the situation. The ball had landed in his hands now.

"Don't let him out of your view," General Franks said to the men, then turned to Lieutenant Hinckley. "Are we still ready for retrieval?"

"Retrieval is standing by."

"Good, send the missile."

"Yes, General."

NINETEEN

Brian

Brian floated on an ocean of cold water, his body rising and falling with the waves. While relaxing on the surface, he enjoyed just staring at the sky and the faint outline of the sun behind the clouds. As the sky traveled slowly over him, he felt like the one moving, traveling on a peaceful journey to an unknown destination.

Autopilot enabled

After a long time of riding the gentle waves, he quietly and peacefully slipped under the surface and began sinking, unaware of the need for breath, and uncaring. As the light faded, he enjoyed the distinct sensation of falling, slowly and steadily. Then Brian began to feel alone as more and more water separated him from the air and light. When the darkness became complete, all hope seemed to vanish and he resigned himself to an eternity of darkness, under an infinite weight of water. After a while, the pressure did not seem to matter anymore and Brian felt safe again. There was nothing under the water that could hurt him and nothing from the surface could reach him.

Autopilot enabled

The sensation of falling eventually ended and Brian just floated peacefully in the darkness. At first, he felt completely alone and isolated from all other life, but after a long time of stillness, he felt the presence of another prisoner in the dark depths, his dead nephew, Jacob. Sadi's son, who had died as a young child, was there with him. After realizing the identity of his companion, he was afraid at first, but when that passed, he felt a great urge to extend his hand and make physical contact. When the small hand clasped around his own, Brian's eyes burst wide open.

—※—

"Autopilot enabled," said the friendly female voice, originating from the dashboard.

While rubbing his eyes, Brian inspected the dark interior of the BMW. He was sitting in the passenger seat with Freddy next to him in the driver's seat, his head hanging forward and eyes closed. At first, Brian thought Freddy had died, but then he noticed the gentle breathing. And then he felt the weight of his own body. For some reason, the familiar sensation of gravity seemed significant.

Through the windows, he saw a star-filled sky. As the memory of the dream faded, Brian gazed at the stars and thought they looked much brighter than he had ever seen. He leaned closer to the window and felt a sudden panic. The breathtaking view of Earth revealed his location, farther away from the ground than he had ever been.

Although Brian failed to recognize any land mass, mostly clouds and blue ocean, he could see the Earth clearly even in the darkness of night. The sun had not yet risen, but Brian could see the bright horizon. While watching the peaceful scene, Brian remembered the last moments before losing consciousness, a loud explosion followed by some kind of shock wave.

"Autopilot enabled," repeated the voice, causing Brian to turn from the window. He noticed a blinking icon on the computer screen in front of them, a picture of small robot hands holding a steering wheel.

"Freddy," he said, turning to his companion.

When Freddy failed to respond, Brian touched his shoulder and squeezed. While gently shaking him, Brian noticed his messy blond hair, frozen in place with dried sweat. "Freddy," he repeated, afraid for his friend's health. With Freddy incapacitated, Brian might have difficulty surviving the situation. "Are you okay?"

When his head jerked up, the quick motion startled Brian and he released Freddy's shoulder.

"How long have I been unconscious?" Freddy asked, turning toward Brian. He extended both arms forward, stretching then wrapping his fingers around the steering wheel. While staring out the window, he took a deep breath.

Before responding, Brian looked out the window again.

"Long enough for us to get up here. I woke up just a few minutes ago." He glanced at Freddy then whistled. "Tell me I'm dreaming. Please tell me I'm dreaming."

"Autopilot enabled," the female voice said again.

Freddy turned his attention to the screens on the dashboard. He clicked a button and the icon of the autopilot disappeared.

"No, you are not dreaming, Brian."

"Why do I feel gravity? I mean, shouldn't we be weightless or something?"

He leaned closer to the window, and looked outside, slowly changing his view downward. The sensation reminded him of looking over the edge of a tall building. Although he did not usually fear heights, Brian had a healthy respect for the danger of their great altitude. The thin glass separating him from the vacuum of space made him feel particularly more vulnerable.

"The engines are still moving us away from Earth," Freddy said while typing on the keyboard. "We are not in an orbit."

"Oh," Brian said, not fully comprehending the reason and too confused by the entire situation to ask any follow-up questions.

"That was a close call. I think they used an EMP on us," Freddy said after another glance at Brian. He continued as though talking to himself, more softly. "Unless those are just bloated propaganda too."

"What," Brian began, but Freddy interrupted.

"An EMP is a strong *electromagnetic pulse*," he said. "Normally, that would have disabled all our electronics, but she apparently added protection against that."

"She?" Brian asked in confusion. "Someone in the military?"

Freddy paused for a deep breath.

"Listen, Brian," he began, looking directly into Brian's eyes. "I will tell you everything, but for now, I need to determine our next course of action. I was not planning to have you with me. Let me think out loud. Maybe you can help me think straight."

"No problem," Brian said and laughed. "I'm very patient, and at your complete mercy."

"Okay," Freddy said, turning to the control panels again. "So they wanted to disable us, but that would have caused the engines to stop and we would have started falling."

"Seems reasonable," Brian said after turning to the window again. The view began to frighten him less.

"But they want me and this car, alive and functioning, so they must have been prepared to retrieve us."

"Retrieve us?" Brian asked, not intending to interrupt. "How the hell can they catch a falling car? Maybe they were hoping we'd have an emergency parachute or something?"

"The military never bases their decisions on hope," Freddy said with a sneer. "They have the capabilities to capture a falling object of our size. They have the equipment to retrieve very heavy instruments on high-altitude balloons where no plane or helicopter can go. Now they know we can withstand an EMP blast. That is not good."

Brian was tempted to ask how Freddy knew so much about the military but decided to let him reveal what he wanted on his own schedule. Then he wondered if the military had somehow recruited the strange kid from his childhood, and that had started the whole mess. Although the idea seemed too ridiculous, the incident on the ground burned in his memory, when soldiers had surrounded them and mysteriously let them escape. Brian remembered the look on the soldiers' faces and wondered if their state of mind was similar to his own.

While waiting for Freddy to continue, Brian decided to keep his focus on Earth, the stars, and whatever else he could find. With every passing moment, the situation became more real to him. As his mind tried to resolve the situation, his excitement and horror mixed, causing some adrenaline to enter his blood. The experience reminded him of the final moments before a concert when his band would make their first appearance.

"So they will be looking for us if they have not already found us," Freddy continued finally, then turned to look through the window at his left. "They were tracking me the entire way to your apartment. Sorry, Brian, I led them right to you, but I thought I was hidden."

"I have so many questions," Brian said then sighed when the first one materialized in his mind. "How the hell did we get away from them? They could have stopped us, but they didn't. What did you do to them?"

"It is difficult to explain because I do not fully understand it yet," Freddy began, avoiding eye contact. "When this all started, *she* gave me the ability to experience the emotions of others. That helped me rescue Helen and Daryn."

"Okay," Brian said, pausing to process the information. "How did that stop them?"

"I am just beginning to understand how it works," he continued, still looking forward. "I can sense people's experiences through a back door. And now I can influence people from the back door, from behind their minds. It is like making them live in a dream and the physical world simultaneously. Human brains are not programmed to function that way and it makes people confused."

"The power of confusion," Brian said, laughing.

He turned from Freddy to the beautiful view again. The explanation kind of made sense and reminded Brian of a superhero movie. He suddenly felt sorry for his friend. His new ability seemed more like a burden and had made them a target. The concept frightened Brian. He wanted to talk about something more concrete.

"Can they see us now?" Brian asked. "I mean, they have all these satellites out here, right?"

"The world is different than what you have been told," Freddy began, pausing as though deciding to continue or not. "We cannot know if they see us, but it is better to assume they do."

Brian turned back to the window at his side and looked at Earth again. A bright light had begun to shine from the horizon. Freddy silently extended a pair of sunglasses to him. After putting the dark lenses between his eyes and the rising sun, he breathed deeply, enjoying the beauty of the scene. Two breaths later, a new calm spread through him.

While Brian watched the rising sun, Freddy typed on the computer, punching buttons and flipping switches. He explained his actions, but Brian only half-listened. He heard the word *radar* a few times and Freddy mentioned giving away their position to someone. When he heard Freddy say *asteroids*, Brian turned from the window and removed his glasses.

"Asteroids?"

"Yes," Freddy said without looking away from the screen. "I am searching for any large objects within our range. Something could appear at any moment and destroy us."

Brian prepared to ask what they were going to do, but Freddy spoke first.

"Before we go back," Freddy began, then turned to face him, "I will teach you how to fly. You may need to control this thing at some point."

Brian's first instinct was to protest. Pilots required years of training. But after a second of thought, he decided to reject his instinctual reactions and trust Freddy. Thoughts of flying seemed more fun than returning to Earth where the military wanted them.

"How much time are we going to be up here," Brian asked.

"We might need only a couple hours to teach you the basics."

While considering flying lessons, Brian remembered a more important topic—his sister and nieces—which were his primary motivation. In all the excitement and anxiety, he had forgotten about them. He experienced a moment of guilt.

"Okay, you can teach me," Brian began, "but first…"

"I know, Sadi," Freddy said. "I already told you. Sadi, Helen, and Daryn are safe, but I cannot take you to their location just yet."

"I remember. You can't tell me where they are, but please tell me something. I need to know." Brian drew a deep breath. "I need my guitar."

Brian unbuckled the safety straps and reached into the back seat. His fingers closing around the neck of the guitar brought instant relief. At that moment, his guitar became the link to Earth, to his life there. Since waking from his strange dreams, his life seemed farther away than Earth appeared. Before he plucked the first few strings, he noticed the sunlight illuminating the side of Freddy's face.

"Sadi and some others escaped to an alien planet," Freddy said, pausing as if that explained everything.

The word, *alien*, reminded Brian of the movie, *Alien*, which he had watched as a kid, the source material for many vivid childhood nightmares. Before responding, Brian needed a replacement for the memories, so he began playing the melody from his favorite song from his new band's first album. He stared at the strings while playing the ballad's introduction.

"Alien planet huh," he said, attempting to conceal his concern. "I don't know much about space travel, so please tell me how they got to this *alien* planet, and what are these aliens? I thought aliens weren't real?"

Freddy turned to the dashboard as though trying to decide what to reveal. Although Brian played the notes softly, the sound filled the BMW and even started resonating with parts of its interior. He suddenly imagined the vacuum of space as a living thing, just a meter away, desperately wanting to open the car like a soda can and suck the air away to stop the music. Brian shivered.

"When I said alien, I was not talking about creatures," Freddy said as clarification. "I meant, alien, as in a place, not Earth."

"Oh, right."

"Did you write that?" Freddy asked.

"Yep," Brian said without looking away from the strings. "Our band's first hit. Playing really helps me chill."

"Funny, I do not remember you playing that before," Freddy said wistfully. "I like it."

"Dude, I mean my new band. You should come hear us."

Brian shook his head slightly and almost stopped playing. When would he see his mates again, he wondered. The current experience should inspire a kick-ass new song or two, or maybe even a whole album. Playing the guitar helped him think.

His band desperately needed some new material. Ever since his sister disappeared, apparently from the face of the earth, Brian had lost most of his motivation. Now that he knew his sister and nieces were safe, he could start thinking about new material. As he approached the end of the introduction, Brian was excited to begin singing the lyrics. A celestial audience awaited.

"I will," Freddy said and smiled. "When this is all over, I will come to hear your band."

"So, tell me what's going on."

While Freddy explained the situation, Brian switched between quiet singing and humming. In contrast to the soft and peaceful melody, he usually sang more harshly, like crashing waves, but in the cramped interior of the BMW, he sang softly. As Freddy spoke, he imagined the beat of the drum. The stronger tempo seemed fitting to his old friend's story.

"So you don't know what this alien wants?" Brian asked while continuing to play.

"This *being*," Freddy said, "is using Sadi and our other friends to motivate me to do what it wants."

"And you don't know why," Brian said, stopping finally and taking a deep breath.

Since Freddy had failed to mention anything about fangs and acid blood, Brian felt a little better about the alien creature, but with his sister and nieces so far from his reach, he could not feel at ease about them. Brian needed to see his sister, even if he had to visit this alien planet himself.

"No," Freddy said, closing his eyes, "but I have a bad feeling that I will discover the reason after I go to my next destination."

At that moment, Brian felt worse for Freddy than he did for his sister. At least she had managed to reach a safe place, thanks to Freddy and the alien creature. He thought suddenly of their own escape from the surface, all the men with guns and the military waiting for their return.

"Okay, so where is this next destination?"

"We need to visit an ancient settlement in the desert," Freddy said, shaking his head. "But first, let me teach you how to fly."

TWENTY

Freddy

Freddy had no difficulty teaching Brian how to fly the BMW. Brian had quick reflexes and learned fast. Freddy remembered when Cesar had taught him how to fly. He had required more time, but Brian had a completely different learning setting. Although they felt the pull of gravity, Brian did not have to worry as much about crashing as Freddy had. Perhaps he would have learned more quickly if he could have flown in the security of relatively infinite space.

No asteroids came within range of their radar so Freddy could relax a little bit. The machines on the alien station had enhanced the BMW with more advanced detection capabilities and even added some protection via an electric field generator, which could deflect small objects, but only within a certain speed. He remembered their advice to minimize any time near large bodies in space, such as Earth, outside the protection of an atmosphere.

Overall, Freddy needed only three hours to feel comfortable with Brian's abilities. He learned the physical action of flying to Freddy's satisfaction but would need more time than they had to learn all of the computer controls. Freddy taught him the basics of the flying maneuvers that Taylor had programmed. The autopilot features and his skill would probably suffice if Brian had to take control.

While practicing, they spoke mostly about flying the craft but a little about what had happened since Freddy had reconnected with Sadi. Freddy skipped most of the disturbing details, hoping the flight lesson would distract Brian from noticing the gaps in the story. Freddy's ability to detect and direct Brian's emotional state helped that plan succeed.

When he could, Freddy searched for signs of the probe, possibly watching them from a distance. While the sensors in the BMW detected nothing within hundreds of kilometers, he knew the probe had sensors capable of detecting them from thousands of kilometers away, probably farther. The alien machines had equipped the BMW with advanced technology but not as advanced as the probe. Freddy suspected the probe could detect dimensions other than space and see them from any distance.

After all of his experiences with the alien woman and Dod, Freddy suspected the existence of another reality, one where other creatures resided, what he would consider aliens. He had initially referred to the other reality as an alternate dimension, but that term felt inaccurate. The concept of alternate dimensions suggested other physical worlds, separate from his own. But now, the physical world seemed as if it was only one aspect of the universe.

He thought initially that the crystal spider, hidden in the compartment under the seat, gave him access to another aspect of the world. A different theory now seemed more likely. Looking into the eyes of the spider had probably placed him in a different state, one susceptible to an alien hijack. Although he always kept the crystal spider close, Freddy decided against using it to confront the alien. He disliked the idea of having experiences he might forget.

After his struggle to understand the alien woman's purpose, Freddy came to a few other conclusions. He would probably die in the end. He accepted that. If his death benefited his friends, at least his life would have had meaning and they would appreciate his memory. His dealings with the alien woman had also given him a very unique life, a different set of experiences than most humans would ever receive. He preferred to remain alive, of course, but at least he could die overflowing with interesting memories.

His next conclusion concerned the alien woman's purpose. He would be used as a pawn in some high-level struggle with other creatures. Every creature Freddy had ever encountered, ultimately cared most about its own desires and needs. Freddy suspected the alien dream woman wanted him to do what she could not, or what she preferred not to do. After the horrors he had experienced, Freddy could handle one final horror in a dark cave.

"This is fun," Brian said while making the BMW spin, first a side rotation and then front to back.

Freddy was glad he had an empty stomach. During the spins, Brian kept the vehicle free from the sensation of gravity and the changing orientation of the sunlight streaming through the windows became the only indication of their rotation. The sunlight seemed to originate from a giant flashlight moving outside the car rather than from their movement.

"Yes," Freddy said, looking away when the sun hit his eyes. "This is probably the most fun I have ever had."

"Almost competes with sex," Brian said, laughing.

"Brian," Freddy cleared his throat, attempting to eliminate the sudden mental image of Audrie Garner removing her clothes. "We need to figure out where to take you."

"You're going to take me to see Sadi," he said, the smile disappearing. "You said I could go see her."

Brian's resemblance to his sister suddenly caught Freddy's attention. He had the same dark blue eyes and thick dark hair. He looked like a male version of Sadi. Freddy could see why the girls always surrounded him.

"Yes," Freddy said after the brief pause, "but first I need to do something alone, and I really need to use a restroom."

"The bathroom's a good idea," Brian said, looking into Freddy's eyes suspiciously. "What do you have to do alone?"

Freddy felt a sudden distrust from Brian, and he understood the reason. Freddy would have felt the same.

"I have to visit someplace in the desert first," Freddy said while clicking the map program icon. A moment later, the screen filled with a map of Earth's surface.

"Is that the Pacific Ocean?" Brian asked, pointing with his index finger at the blue on the screen.

"And this is our position over it," Freddy said, pointing to a small red dot, two hundred miles from the Oregon shore.

"How does the program know where we are?" Brian asked, his eyes squinting slightly.

"The computer tracks our speed and direction from multiple sensors, and can calculate our position from the data." Freddy experienced a new appreciation for Taylor and Cesar's programming skills. "It should be accurate to within a few meters."

While Brian's mind digested the answer, questions replaced his suspicion, questions about their next destination and what Freddy had to do. Instead of answering the questions before Brian asked them, Freddy waited patiently.

"So you need to drop me off," Brian began, leaning closer to the window so he could see Earth below. "And you'll come back to get me when you're done? What do you have to do?"

"Yes, and I only know where to go, not what I have to do. We should probably take you far away from your home, far from the US military. I have more than enough money to pay for your stay anywhere. Do you have a preference?"

"My grandparents were from Norway," Brian said after a short pause. He squeezed the control in his left hand and the muscles in his forearm tightened. "I've always wanted to go there."

"Okay, Norway. Take us there," Freddy said, noticing the tattoo of a woodpecker on the inside of his wrist. He liked acting as a flight coach. "Do you speak Norwegian?"

"Nope, and I don't have a passport either."

"Hmm," Freddy began, "you should only need to show a passport while traveling through security checkpoints. Everyone will assume you have one. I should only be gone for a few days."

They spent the next thirty minutes flying to the upper atmosphere of Norway. On the video footage, their dot stopped halfway up the coast with the nation's border showing as superimposed lines on the video. They hovered there for a few minutes while Brian prepared for the descent. Freddy quickly showed him how to use the computer to program the appropriate descent pathway, a journey without vaporization.

"Where should we go?" Freddy asked himself, then clicked on the closest city. "The map program says the nearest city is called Bergen, the second largest city in the country. Do you know where any of your relatives live?"

"I can't remember," Brian said as he held tightly to the controls. "I know we have a couple aunts here, but I haven't seen them since I was a little kid. The city name doesn't sound familiar though, but I wouldn't know."

"Okay good," Freddy said with some relief. "We probably would not want to lead anyone to your family here, to implicate them too."

"Wouldn't a large city have more military and police?" Brian asked. "Maybe we should find a small village or something?"

"I think it will be easier to hide in a bigger city," Freddy said without taking his eyes from the dashboard.

"Makes sense."

When they felt the heavy force of deceleration, Brian almost began to panic and Freddy remembered feeling the same with Cesar. While Brian controlled the vehicle, Freddy monitored the skies, both with their sensors and with his extra-sensory abilities. Neither set of sensors detected any military presence, but Freddy felt the all-too-familiar paranoia of being watched. Despite his feelings, he could only trust the data and concluded that no one from Earth was watching them.

Freddy enjoyed feeling Brian's excitement when he first noticed the sound of the wind outside the car. Freddy loved that part of the journey when his ears could detect the presence of their mother Earth, and not just his eyes. Only when they heard that first sound, could they fully appreciate the complete silence of space, the absence of airflow. When they finally entered the clouds and their bright view through the windows turned to a white haze, Brian's anxious anticipation climaxed, an intense desire to see the land with his own eyes again.

"Nice and steady," Freddy said as they exited the clouds and Brian tilted the car so they could see the land through the front window. The transition of pressure moving from the seat to the straps on his chest brought a wave of dizziness.

"Now that's a beautiful sight," Brian said, his lips stretching into a wide smile. "I never thought I'd be so happy to see the ground again."

A few minutes later, snow began sticking to the windows, quickly melting and then turning to rain as they descended lower. While they watched the land become more distinct, they greatly anticipated the sensation of standing on the ground again.

"Look, there's the city center." Freddy pointed to the bridge crossing a wide channel of water. He had never seen so much water before, not even in Seattle, and he imagined the ancient Vikings, living in a small settlement on the shores. "Head towards the northeast, over there. I see a forested area with some smaller roads."

"Okay," Brian said.

He tilted the car to align horizontally with Earth, so they could prepare to land on all four tires. Freddy felt better with the pressure of his body resting on his butt again. After they aligned horizontally with the land, Freddy began looking for signs of his fellow humans. He sensed a limited human presence near a small lake with a road on its northeastern edge. After looking for an isolated spot to land, they found a connecting road with pine trees on either side, effectively hiding the car from aerial view.

Once securely on the road, Freddy took control of the vehicle since Brian had not yet learned how to transition to road driving in a two-dimensional environment. He parked on the side of the road and kept the engine running just in case they had to quickly fly away again.

"Okay, we can get out but stay close to the car," Freddy said, pushing the button to equilibrate the interior air pressure with the outside atmosphere. He opened his door first, the rushing air sounding loud and harsh in his ears.

"I really need to take a piss," Brian said, quickly exiting the car.

"Me too."

Before stepping away, they looked at each other over the BMW. A light rain landed softly on Freddy's face and arms. The sensation felt amazing. Brian looked up to the sky and raised his hands, stretching.

"Back on solid ground! I don't even mind the rain."

After relieving themselves a short distance away at their own private trees, they returned and discussed the plan. Neither of them wanted to get back into the vehicle just yet, so they talked outside. The cold rain quickly sucked the warmth from their bodies, so both men hugged their arms against their stomachs for warmth. They would drive into the city and find a place for Brian to stay. Freddy would provide him with enough money for several days.

"We should find a bank quickly," Freddy said, glancing at his wrist. He spoke while adjusting his watch to the local time. "It is almost four p.m. here and the banks should be closing soon. We need to find a bank to convert Dollars to Kroner."

"How are we going to find a bank?"

"Fortunately, the map program in the car is up-to-date as of a year ago," Freddy said. "One of our friends provided the program from his company."

The computer would save them from the need to ask for directions. Even with his enhanced senses, Freddy would still need to converse in English to communicate without causing suspicion. He could easily alleviate any suspicion, but thinking about the required effort mentally drained him. Freddy still felt exhausted from his experience manipulating the minds of several determined men with guns.

At his request, Freddy let Brian drive. It took only a few minutes before he felt comfortable driving the spacecraft on the road, though the BMW initially jerked forward and stopped too quickly. When they passed the first car, Freddy felt relieved for their subconscious decision to drive on the right side of the road, apparently the correct side of the road. For all Freddy knew, people in Norway could have driven on the left side. He hoped they would not make an incorrect assumption on another important decision, one which might draw unwanted attention.

They drove through the forest, following directions from the map program until they reached the city. Freddy enjoyed watching the homes and businesses as they passed. In addition to the goodwill he felt from the people, he loved the sanitary condition of the city and the solid architecture. No structures looked derelict and every surface seemed to have a fresh coat of paint, clean at least. Maybe the weather helped keep everything clean.

If Freddy managed to return safely to get Brian, he hoped to stay for a few days. If he could not return, Brian would have to get help from his relatives.

They found the bank easily and Freddy felt surprisingly relieved to be in the presence of other humans. All the negative emotions of the soldiers at Brian's apartment left him with a tainted memory of other people. Despite the gloomy and dark skies, the people felt happy to be alive. He began to feel a little better, more at ease. Maybe they had successfully landed without the notice of those intent on capturing him.

The currency exchange at the bank proceeded smoothly and without drawing any special attention. The only interruption was when the teller had to get another bank employee to handle the exchange, a man who spoke English. Freddy was a little surprised when the man did not notice anything special about the four thousand dollar exchange or ask for identification.

They quickly chose one of the more expensive hotels in the city, a five-story grey building overlooking the bay. Freddy liked the idea of having water on one side, just in case a hostile ambush prevented an air escape and they had to escape laterally.

"The hotel looks nice," Freddy said, glancing up at the grey brick walls.

After parking, Brian prepared to exit the car, but Freddy stopped him.

"I will stay out here," he said while looking out the window at a young couple walking past them. A light-haired man glanced at the BMW, trying to see through the tinted glass. "I think we are safe, but I would rather stay with the BMW, just in case anyone comes."

"You went into the bank," Brian said, suddenly feeling worried about going alone.

"That was just for a couple of minutes. This will take longer." Freddy drew a deep breath for some extra thinking time. "Get a nice room facing the bay, or fjord, or whatever it is called. After what I put you through, you deserve a nice place to stay. Besides, they treat rich guests the best and will probably overlook any irregularities."

"I hope someone speaks English," Brian said just before he opened the door. He paused briefly, considering the option of taking his guitar as if the object might offer comfort. "Money speaks every language, right?"

Freddy waited in the BMW while Brian went into the hotel and checked into a room. With his extra sense, Freddy monitored Brian's interaction with the hotel staff, which proceeded as expected. After paying cash for the room, Brian's anxiety decreased significantly. When he entered the fourth floor room, Freddy felt Brian's new emotion, excitement to stay in such a nice room. Before returning to the BMW, Brian spent a minute enjoying the view from the window. The large body of water offered a feeling of general peace.

"This is definitely the nicest place I've ever been in," Brian said after rejoining Freddy. "You should see some of the shit holes my band and I stayed in. Come on."

"Okay," Freddy said, the thought of leaving the car filling him with a sudden anxiety. During the wait, he had scanned all of the humans within the vicinity and discovered nothing out of the ordinary, no suspicious intentions. But even when he entered the room, the anxiety remained with him.

Brian took a long shower and emerged wearing the same clothes. During the wait, Freddy began to feel a little better. He still felt no signs of warning from the people near the vicinity of the hotel so he decided to take a shower as well. Before entering the steamy bathroom, he felt like an animal in the wild getting a drink of water with the probability of an alligator waiting under the surface.

Although he had grown accustomed to living in luxury with Mr. Smith, he quite enjoyed taking a shower in the large Norwegian bathroom. He loved being surrounded by the stained-wood walls, the ceramic-tiled floor, and all of the exposed chrome piping. At the end of the shower, he was more relaxed than before, but he would still feel safer in space.

He returned to the room while running his fingers through his wet hair and found Brian sitting on the bed, playing the guitar. After the hot and steamy environment of the bathroom, the colder air in the room was rejuvenating. Through the opened window he could see the sailboats in the bay. He stood at the window and drew a long, deep breath of the cold air.

"What if the police would have pulled us over," Brian asked while playing the guitar. "I know you have the strange ability to read minds and that's how you helped rescue Helen."

Before answering, Freddy felt a rush of painful memories almost overwhelm Brian. The subject of Helen's kidnapping had frightened him, and the act of plucking the guitar strings helped calm his nerves. Brian pretended to act only mildly interested.

"At first I could only sense the emotional state of those around me." Freddy remained standing by the open window. "Now I can influence their emotional state. I am much better at it now, but you saw me reach my limits back at your apartment."

"Can you show me?"

"You mean do something to *you*?"

"Sure," Brian said with a wide smile. His curious excitement replaced his anxiety a bit, surprising Freddy. The possibility of a new experience replaced the disturbing thoughts of Helen's kidnapping. "I mean, don't hurt me or anything."

"Okay," Freddy said, shaking his head slightly and taking a deep breath. He immediately thought of an action. "This will not hurt, but you will not like it."

Brian's smile suddenly disappeared and so did the pleasant music. Instead of playing a melody, Brian's fingers struck random strings, filling the room with a very unpleasant noise. He attempted to play for a few more seconds but then pulled his hand away as if afraid to touch the instrument.

"What the fuck?" Brian said in frustration, staring at the guitar in his lap, then turning to Freddy. "You can stop whatever you're doing now."

"Sorry," Freddy said, resisting the sudden urge to laugh. "Go ahead. You can play again."

Brian looked back at the guitar and began playing again, hesitantly. After the first few notes, Freddy felt Brian's rush of relief and then his laughter.

"Oh my, you beautiful creature," Brian said to the guitar, continuing with the same melody. "Don't ever do that to me again. Sorry for getting mad, Freddy. It was my instinct talking. I won't ever doubt you again."

"I should probably go now," Freddy said. The thought of leaving suddenly made him depressed.

"What are you talking about?" Brian asked. "You should at least stay the night. We need to eat breakfast too, or I mean, dinner. This place has a restaurant and it looks nice. I know I need to eat."

Brian looked out the window, at the darkening sky.

"It is probably not safe for me to stay here, for you at least."

"You haven't felt anything strange have you?"

"No," Freddy answered, tempted by the thought of a good meal and a soft bed. "I do need to eat though."

"You can't rescue my sister on an empty stomach."

While riding the elevator down to the restaurant on the ground level, Freddy concentrated on the thought of an uneventful meal with his friend. The waitress, a beautiful girl in her early twenties, spoke perfect English with only a slight accent, which Freddy thought was charming. Although she showed obvious infatuation with Brian, she was excited to speak with both of them in English.

They had a pleasant dinner together. Freddy loved the food and ate duck for the first time in his life. Brian had steak. While Freddy inhaled the steam rising from the roasted vegetables, he wondered what foods Sadi and the others were having on the orbiting platform. At the end of the meal, Brian had convinced Freddy to stay for one night.

TWENTY-ONE

Brian

"Wake up," a soft voice said from the darkness, rescuing Brian from a bitter dream.

Brian opened his eyes to a dark room and a warm hand on his shoulder. On the table by his head, he noticed the digital readout of the time, thirteen minutes after one in the morning.

"What's wrong?" he asked, pushing himself up in the bed. Images from a disturbing dream quickly evaporated from his memory.

"I should have left earlier," Freddy said and stepped closer to the edge of the window. He pulled the curtains apart a few centimeters to look outside. Light from the full moon illuminated the cream curtains, filling the room with a soft glow. Brian's eyes required only a moment to distinguish Freddy's features.

"Someone's here?" Brian asked, swinging his legs over the edge of the bed.

"The hotel is surrounded by soldiers," Freddy said bluntly, sounding as emotionally detached as an anchorman reporting the news. "They are discussing the situation with the hotel management. They are calling us terrorists."

Brian could hear the confidence in his friend's voice as if he knew exactly how to handle the situation.

"What are we going to do?"

"I am trying to determine that," Freddy answered.

When Brian knew there was no plan yet, he felt the beginnings of panic, not for himself but for Freddy. He doubted the military had any interest in him at all. Freddy suddenly turned to Brian, and he experienced an immediate rush of tranquility, reminding Brian of the guitar when Freddy had ruined his ability to play, and he realized the source of his new emotions, Freddy.

"Just tell me what you want me to do," Brian said. He stood and quickly dressed himself then paused to stare at Helen's drawing on his hat. In the darkness, the markings were just an indistinct shadow.

"Okay, I know something we can try," Freddy said after going back to the window. "But we need to do it quickly. They know I can trick people, so they are waiting until reinforcements arrive. I will not be able to handle too many of them."

"How many are out there?" Brian asked. He joined Freddy at the other side of the window and peered through the crack between the curtains.

"At least twenty men."

Bright moonlight reflected off the water in the fjord. Brian leaned as close as he dared and noticed at least four men walking in random directions in an empty car lane between the hotel and the water. From his view, he saw only the tops of their heads, their military hats. When one of the men turned to look up at their floor, Brian looked away from the window, his heart rate accelerating.

"Oh my god," Brian said to himself. "What's this plan of yours?"

"We are going to trick them," Freddy said. "Give me a minute though. I need to make sure to account for all of them."

While Freddy stared through the parted curtains, Brian left the window and walked quietly to the door at the front of their suite. He put his left eye on the peephole and saw the bright hallway illuminated as if it was daytime. As his eyes adjusted to the light, sleep completely fled.

"No one in the hallway," Brian said, hoping to be helpful.

He turned and found Freddy sitting on the nice loveseat, eyes closed. In the low light, he looked like a statue, motionless. Brian watched him for a few seconds then suddenly wished he could play his guitar to break the disturbing silence.

While waiting, Brian had an unexpected regret. The world did not have to be so complicated, so full of contention. If he could play a song for the soldiers, they would realize the stupidity of the situation. Everyone would enjoy listening to good music much more than fighting with each other. People rarely got hurt at a concert. That was a true win-win situation.

The next two minutes of silence seemed like an hour. Brian listened to Freddy's quiet breathing and watched his chest expand and contract with each breath. In the end, Brian began to feel a little more calm, until he heard someone knocking on the door.

"Open the door, Brian," Freddy said calmly, his eyes still closed. "Do not be afraid."

Brian hesitated only a moment before complying. The door seemed like the only barrier to the evil outside. The unlocking mechanism made a soft click before the door swung open. When Brian saw the two soldiers, his eyes opened wide. For an awkward moment, the three men just stood motionless, staring at each other.

The two soldiers wore camouflage army attire with a matching hat and looked almost identical. Brian stood several centimeters taller than one of the men and only slightly taller than the other, but his larger physical frame failed to make him feel any better about the situation. His gaze shifted immediately to the pistols resting in the holsters at their hips.

"Please move aside for them," Freddy said, "and close the door after they enter."

Brian moved to his right, keeping his hand on the door handle and making room for the soldiers to enter. As they walked past him, he turned to see light from the bright hallway illuminating Freddy's face. Brian was surprised to see his eyes still closed. He shut the door, immersing the room in darkness again. He felt more at ease in the dark, more safe.

Both soldiers walked silently toward Freddy and stopped in front of him. For several seconds, the scene reminded Brian of a secret meeting between two vicious henchmen getting instructions from their evil leader.

When the men suddenly dropped to their knees, Brian jolted in surprise. The three individuals had seemed frozen in place, and the sudden motion was like a splash of cold water in the face. After falling to their knees, the taller man put his hands on his head as though he had a migraine. The other man simply fell backward, crashing on the soft carpet with a heavy thud. The taller man swayed with his hands on his head for a few seconds and eventually fell to his side, making a quieter thud than the shorter man. The men looked conscious, squirming as though they suffered from insomnia and were trying to find a comfortable sleeping position.

After the men fell to the floor, Brian took a few steps toward Freddy. For some mysterious reason, the scene became distressingly surreal. As he stood there watching, he imagined waves of light distortion surrounding his childhood friend. But with his physical eyes, he saw no such disturbance. *Strange*, he thought and shook his head.

"Freddy," Brian whispered without taking his eyes from the soldiers on the floor. "What the hell is happening?"

"We are getting out of here," Freddy answered, opening his eyes finally and making eye contact with Brian. "We must hurry before more people come."

"So you somehow made them come up here," Brian began, trying to explain the situation to himself, "I don't need to know how you did that, but what are we going to do with them? Hold them hostages?"

"Take their clothes off," Freddy answered.

Brian's instincts told him to refuse, but the look in Freddy's eyes warned of a danger greater than possibly fighting with another man for his clothes. After inspecting the men for a moment, he slowly bent down and began undressing the taller one. To his surprise, neither man struggled as he removed their camouflage army fatigues. After taking their jackets, he felt even more uncomfortable when he had to remove their green undershirts and pants. He hated touching their skin.

Brian saw sweat on Freddy's face, reminding him of their narrow escape from Portland. While he removed their clothes, Freddy watched and tried to explain the plan. They would switch clothes and everyone would think they had been captured. Brian refrained from asking questions about how they could fool the other soldiers. He preferred to remain in ignorance. Surprisingly, the game began to sound fun.

Five minutes later, Freddy and Brian had exchanged clothing with the soldiers. Neither man had made any attempt to protest or struggle. Brian felt strange wearing army clothing and not just due to their crazy situation. The army fatigues were too restricting and formal. He preferred casual clothing at all times. To look the part of a soldier, Brian had to stuff his longer hair under the hat. Freddy had an easier time hiding his short blond hair.

"If I met you on the street, I wouldn't recognize you," Brian said while tucking the last bit of his hair under his hat.

"Good," Freddy answered, then turned to the men on the floor, the taller one wearing shorts and a t-shirt while the shorter one wore Freddy's jeans and his plain blue buttoned shirt.

Brian dreaded the next set of events. Somehow, Freddy would get the soldiers to stand and then they would all leave the apartment together. While staring at the men, he had a disturbing thought.

"They both have dark hair," he said.

"Hmm," Freddy said, taking a deep breath and answering after exhaling. "We can do what they did to me at the takeoff site, where Sadi and the others escaped. They were afraid of what I could do and thought that a bag over my head would cause me to feel disoriented."

At the mention of his sister, Brian felt a renewed source of courage and energy. He took a deep breath while looking around the apartment for something to use.

"I can use one of the pillowcases."

After placing a white pillowcase over the head of the shorter soldier, Brian stood on his feet and stepped back, giving Freddy some room. Somehow, he thought Freddy would need extra space to wake the soldiers from their semi-conscious stupor, and he did not want to get in the way. While waiting, Brian slipped his fingers around the pistol in the holster at his hip. He squeezed the grip for a moment before removing the weapon and keeping it pointed at the ground.

The gun was like a living creature in his hands, a creature wanting to kill. In the dark silence, Brian imagined a disturbing situation where he was the gun and could see from its perspective. He could feel its desire to shoot someone, to shoot anything. The gun begged for someone to squeeze the trigger. Brian suddenly remembered a quote from one of his favorite movies, *Happy Gilmore*, the words on the popular t-shirt.

Guns don't kill people.

I kill people.

The memory caused a smile, but the quote's meaning made Brian decide to keep his finger off the trigger unless absolutely necessary.

"Let's get started," Freddy said, looking down at the soldiers on the ground. They began moving suddenly. The soldier with the bag over his head began speaking first, his words muffled by the pillowcase. Although Brian failed to understand the meaning, the words sounded like a question. He suddenly felt sorry for the frightened soldier and hoped no one had to get hurt.

The taller soldier spoke next, his words clearer than his companion's. With wide eyes, he stared at the gun in Brian's hand, pointed to the floor in front of him. From their tone, Brian could almost feel their fear and confusion. He imagined they were asking for mercy, for Brian and Freddy not to hurt them.

"Get up," Freddy said in a stern tone, "both of you."

After only a brief hesitation, the tall soldier stood first and then helped his companion stand. They held their hands in the air, the shorter one facing Freddy and the taller one facing Brian. With his left hand, Freddy grabbed the shoulder of the soldier with the bag over his head and pushed him towards the door.

"Now move," Freddy said and nudged the man forward with his gun.

Wordlessly, both men began moving, taking slow steps toward the door. Brian turned from the men and looked into Freddy's eyes. In the low light, his eyes appeared cold, without emotion and the confidence in his voice filled Brian with confusion. What had happened to his friend, the kid afraid to make eye contact with people? Freddy now seemed totally in control of the situation, afraid of no one, not even a whole army unit intent on capturing him.

When Brian opened the door and the bright light from the hallway illuminated the room, he stood aside for the men to exit, the taller one leaving first. Freddy kept his gun pressed against the back of the shorter soldier. He waited in the hallway for Brian to close the door.

"Do we need the room card key?"

"Go get it," Freddy answered without looking at him, "but I do not think we will need it."

He ran back to the bed and grabbed the card key from the night stand then returned before the door had swung all of the way closed. As the door clicked shut, Brian felt as if their only escape had just disappeared. They had only one way to go now, forward.

"Are we taking the elevator?" Brian asked. He imagined one of the hotel guests exiting their room and seeing him. He felt an urge to scurry from sight, like a cockroach seeking shelter from the light.

"We will take the stairs that way," Freddy answered, pointing. "Soldiers are guarding the exit at the bottom, but I can handle them."

They walked through the hallway, their hostages moving silently in front. Before arriving at the door to the stairwell, Brian kept worrying about someone seeing them, but when he imagined the scene from the perspective of a hotel guest, he felt a small relief. A hotel guest would only see army personnel guarding prisoners down the hallway. He was confident in Freddy's ability to keep their prisoners from attempting to expose the truth of the situation.

On their way down the stairwell, Freddy took the front position and Brian took the back with the soldiers in between. The taller one helped the shorter one navigate the steps since he could not see. At the bottom, Freddy stepped to the door and turned to Brian. The back of a soldier appeared through the door's small window.

"Brian, come here," Freddy demanded. "Knock on the door and wait for them to open it. Let me do the talking."

"All right," Brian said and stepped to the door.

He took a deep breath, then quickly tapped the glass three times with his knuckles. Before the door opened, a soldier's face appeared in the glass, looking into the stairwell. He made eye contact and Brian attempted to present a serious smile, but he felt foolish. The door slowly opened and the man said something in Norwegian. With his eyes on the ground, Brian stepped through the door and walked past the two soldiers there. He waited while Freddy pushed their two captives into the first-floor hallway.

"We got them," Freddy said, looking at one of the soldiers and pointing his gun down the hallway. "Go tell the captain."

Brian could see only one of the soldiers' faces, eyes squinting and staring at Freddy in confusion. He turned to his companion, shook his head as if clearing his mind of a disturbing thought, and then smiled strangely. A moment later, he turned and walked briskly down the empty hallway.

"Move," Freddy said to the three men in front of him. The remaining soldier, the one who still looked like a soldier, grabbed the taller captive by the shoulder, and after pulling him forward a bit, the man began walking on his own.

Brian turned and made brief eye contact with Freddy, wondering how he kept the soldiers from recognizing each other. He saw no sign of emotion or recognition in Freddy's eyes. He seemed too preoccupied mentally to notice the attempt at communication.

Brian walked silently alongside Freddy, his gun pointed at the captive in front of him and his index finger held away from the trigger. As they walked down the hallway toward the hotel lobby, Brian dreaded the thought of coming within view of more soldiers.

To Brian's surprise, Freddy did not hesitate or even show any trepidation before turning the corner and entering the lobby. After entering, they stopped walking and Brian immediately noticed four groups of soldiers in the large open area, three or four men to a group. One of the groups stood by the front desk with a civilian standing behind the counter while the other groups stood in other random locations. Brian could not imagine exiting the hotel successfully.

Immediately after entering, everyone in the lobby turned to stare at the new arrivals. Nearly all eyes were fixed on the captives, but Brian noticed one man look at him, squinting as if attempting to determine his identity. He looked like the man in charge. He wore a different hat, but Brian looked away before he recognized any other differences in attire.

"Vi fikk dem," said the soldier who was leading them.

The ensuing silence almost made Brian's heart stop, and he nearly stopped breathing too. He had no idea what the soldier said, so his imagination interpreted instead.

Shoot them, the soldier said in Brian's imagination. *They switched clothes. These are the men you want!*

TWENTY-TWO

Brian

The silence was replaced by an unexpected sound. Most of the soldiers began cheering as if they had just seen their favorite sports team score a goal. Some of them turned to their companions and clapped while others raised a fist into the air. One man ran to the main entrance and disappeared into the night. Their looks of joy caused Brian to feel as if he had just entered an alternate dimension.

The soldier at the front desk, likely the commanding officer, approached the captives, his gun pointed to the ground. He stood almost as tall as Brian and had light blue eyes, the only person in the whole room who was not smiling. After stopping in front of Brian and Freddy, he looked at the two prisoners and raised his left hand to the pillow covering the shorter soldier's head, about to lift the cloth, but suddenly changed his mind.

When he turned to Brian, his eyes narrowed to small slits, squinting in concentration as if trying to see a distant object. After an uncomfortable silence, he extended his left hand and grabbed Brian's shoulder, smiling finally. "Utmerket arbeid, soldat," he said.

When Brian failed to respond, Freddy replied in English.

"We need the prisoner to open his vehicle."

The man removed his hand from Brian's shoulder and turned to Freddy, his smile disappearing, replaced by a look of confusion. Brian feared someone would notice his sudden transformation or the English words, but the man quickly nodded and moved aside for their group to move past him.

The commander barked something to the men in the lobby, too quickly for Brian to differentiate any distinct words, and all the men became silent. The cheering had stopped already, but everyone Brian could see kept smiling, showing obvious pride in their fellow soldiers. Many of them nodded to Brian and Freddy as they walked toward the main entrance, congratulating them for a successful capture. In acceptance of their praise, Brian made a weak attempt at smiling and felt as though someone would notice his obvious tension.

When they reached the main entrance to the hotel, Freddy stopped with his hand on the glass door and turned to Brian. Sweat glistened on his forehead, but he still looked confident. The commanding officer held his gun pressed into the back of the hooded captive, patiently waiting behind them.

"We need to move quickly," Freddy whispered, leaning closer so only Brian could hear. "I cannot keep this up for much longer. There are more people outside and more people coming. It is difficult to keep track of them all."

Freddy held the door while the group exited the building, and the crisp air outside helped Brian feel a little better, but he still felt exposed and vulnerable. For the first time since waking, incarceration or even death seemed likely. Brian glanced at the captain who stood with his gun pressed into the back of the Freddy impostor. He turned away before the man could make eye contact, fearing to make any sort of personal connection, which might somehow break the spell.

When the door closed completely, Brian felt as though that retreat had disappeared forever, leaving them with one less option. Freddy paused to assess the scene. They stood at the main entrance, under an enclosure supported by cement columns and facing the open space, which separated them from the parking garage. A nice open area with benches, tables, and chairs occupied half of the space with a short lane on the other side for cars to enter the parking garage. On their left was a railing overlooking the water with the main road on their right.

Brian could feel the cobblestones under his feet. The electric lights on tall poles kept the area illuminated, casting distinct shadows from the chairs and tables in front of them. Brian experienced a brief disappointment. He had looked forward to sitting out there and playing his guitar.

"Shit," he whispered, knowing he could not run back to the room and grab his guitar.

Brian suddenly was afraid to leave the safety of the partial shelter. He turned to Freddy and found him scanning the area in front of them as though unable to determine the best way forward. Then Brian looked at the main street to their right and noticed flashing lights from police cars parked in the road, blocking both directions of traffic. To his surprise, he failed to see any police officers, only their vehicles.

As Freddy wiped the sweat from his forehead, the commanding officer snapped Brian's attention back to his immediate vicinity.

"Hvorfor venter vi?" he asked, turning to Freddy with suspicion.

"Come on," Freddy answered without looking at the man, and Brian noticed the soldier's sudden relaxation. He reverted to the role of taking orders rather than issuing them.

Freddy and Brian carefully led the group into the open area. As they passed the cement columns, a wave of fear hit Brian, but he did not understand the specific reason. He remembered the same emotion as a young child when his mother would release his hand and leave him feeling exposed and vulnerable.

A couple of seconds later, Brian noticed that the soldier wearing the pillowcase was acting strangely. He was stumbling and then the soldiers around him had to help him stay on his feet. After a few more seconds, the group stopped and laid the man on the ground. Then Brian noticed the small dart in the side of the man's neck.

The commanding officer immediately stood to his feet and grasped his gun with both hands then aimed the weapon at the building across the street to their right, some clothing shop Brian thought. When the captain fired the weapon, Brian cupped his ears with his hands, including his right hand with the gun. The metal was cold on the side of his head. Even with the ringing in his ears, he heard the shattered glass.

After the deafening noise of the gunshot, the soldiers from the hotel flooded the area, surrounding Brian and the group around him. Some men joined their captain by aiming at the building across the street while others pointed their weapons in different directions. They stood as a cohesive unit and formed a protective barrier for Freddy and Brian. As Brian looked at the men around him, he noticed their attention was focused entirely on the buildings in the near vicinity.

"Their snipers shot him with a tranquilizer," Freddy whispered.

"What are we going to do?" Brian asked, not afraid of anyone overhearing him. Many of the men were yelling at each other and had their attention elsewhere.

"We need to get to the BMW," Freddy said over the noise of the soldiers. "We should move as fast as we can!"

Freddy took a few steps toward the building where they had parked the BMW, ready to push through the soldiers blocking their way. But he stopped after a pair of soldiers emerged from the inside of the parking area, effectively blocking the entrance. These new soldiers looked different to Brian and held machine guns, pointed at the ground.

The situation suddenly seemed completely different. Freddy now stood motionless and just stared at the new soldiers blocking the entrance to the parking garage. They looked at Freddy and Brian, also motionless. The group of soldiers surrounding them suddenly stopped talking and tightened the circle, each man keeping his gun aimed in an outward direction.

When Brian heard the police sirens in the distance and the distinct sound of a helicopter coming from the direction of the bay, he turned to face the water and waited for what felt like the longest thirty seconds of his life. He expected to see the helicopter flying over the water toward them, but it appeared suddenly above the hotel and then another helicopter was right behind it.

A spotlight from the first helicopter shined on them and Brian had to shield his eyes from the intense light. While the helicopter hovered thirty meters above them, the other helicopter landed in the street next to the police cars. The incredible wind threatened to remove their hats, but Brian and Freddy managed to keep theirs intact. His fear and amazement helped him ignore the frigid wind.

The street lights illuminated the helicopter on the street, allowing Brian to see the dark grey metal. He was instantly amazed at the strength of the engines to lift such an immense weight into the air. As the metal doors slid open, he and Freddy could only watch.

Ten new soldiers jumped out of the helicopter onto the street and formed a line, each soldier with a machine gun aimed at the soldiers surrounding Freddy and Brian. These new soldiers wore lighter camouflage with heavier military gear and their heads exposed. Brian noticed how each new soldier stood several centimeters taller than him with a lot more muscle bulk. He thought they looked like soldiers from some special forces group.

The final man who emerged from the helicopter looked like their commander, the only one wearing a camouflage hat. Although not the tallest or the most physically intimidating, he looked at least ten or more years older than all of the others, maybe in his mid-forties. He walked confidently behind the row of soldiers and stopped on their left.

Brian was unable to take his eyes off the man. He stood without a gun and his gaze swept across the entire scene, stopping on the group of Norwegian soldiers in front of the hotel. The helicopter rotors above him began to decelerate.

"We know you're in there somewhere, Freddy Carlson," he yelled in English over the intense noise of both helicopters.

No one made any indication of understanding him and Brian waited with dread for the commander to make eye contact with him. But he seemed to stare at the entire group, not focusing on any individual. Behind the row of soldiers standing next to him, Brian noticed a shorter man sitting in the helicopter, watching the scene.

Brian leaned closer and spoke to Freddy without turning away from the line of soldiers.

"He doesn't know which ones we are?"

"I am sorry. There are too many of them," Freddy answered then placed his hand on Brian's shoulder to steady himself.

Brian tore his eyes away from the men before them and noticed Freddy's knees beginning to shake. He suddenly realized how fast the scene could change. Only one shot from any of the soldiers could start a shower of bullets from both directions. In just a few seconds, Brian and all the men around him could be dead.

Freddy suddenly fell to his knees, putting his head down close to the ground and holding his hands on the cobblestone. After Freddy fell to the ground, Brian began to feel different. The sound of the helicopters became much more distinct and some of the soldiers in his view began to look around them in confusion. The commander in front of the helicopter kept staring at the Norwegian soldiers as though looking through them, not at them.

"There is no more light," Freddy said just loud enough for Brian to hear. Then all the light vanished and Brian saw only darkness. He could still feel the cold wind on his exposed eyes, but they no longer detected any light. The experience reminded him of grade school when they were taken on a field trip to the Ape Caves near Mount St. Helens. His teachers had instructed everyone to turn off their flashlights, leaving him and his friends in complete darkness.

Brian wanted to ask what had happened, but the intensity of the darkness left him speechless and disoriented. The soldiers around him had also stopped talking to each other, but Brian still felt their presence. He heard only the whirling helicopter rotors and the intense wind. Without the input from his eyes, he could even hear the waves hitting the shore. In one instant, a world full of light had transformed into a world of only sound and the cold wind.

A strange new possibility added to his disorientation, stretching the next few seconds into what seemed like many minutes. For the first time in his life, Brian imagined a world where light did not exist and had never existed. His eyes were just part of a grand illusion. In reality, he had existed in an ocean of blackness and had only imagined the light. The objects and people near him suddenly seemed more real and their images were mere illusions. He desperately wanted to touch something to confirm its existence, but he stood frozen in place.

Without his sight, Brian depended on his remaining senses. The intense noise above him meant that the helicopter still hovered there, inundating him with sound and cold, a mass that could crush them all if the engine suddenly stopped. He imagined the men inside, machine guns aimed at him.

"Stand steady," the commander yelled, focusing Brian's attention on the sound of his voice. "Branson, what do you see?"

"I see nothing, sir," someone yelled in English, a man with a deep voice. Brian fought the temptation to move away, thinking no one would notice but also afraid someone might rush him.

"What about you, Jones?" the voice of the commander asked, his voice pushing through the intense wind.

"I cannot see anything, sir."

Freddy's next words exploded in Brian's mind, bypassing his ears. He spoke as though the effort had required his last breath.

"All the air is gone!"

TWENTY-THREE

Taylor

October 1, Earth time, passed as all the others since they arrived on September 20. Taylor awoke just before daylight, remembering finally to refer to the rising of their new star correctly. Instead of calling the event sunrise, she had used the proper name for the star, Dzalm.

Before noon, Taylor spent some time with the children, taking lessons from one of the machines, Miss Poofie. Taylor always enjoyed the geography lessons. They spent at least an hour in the observatory studying the surface of the planet. As usual, she kept her questions to a minimum, preferring to let the children's curiosity direct the flow of information. Taylor enjoyed the experience, both learning and spending time with the kids. Even though she had little direct experience with children, they reminded her of life, home, and her mother. On that day, no other adult participated in the lesson. Other adults often participated, but Taylor never missed at least part of the day with the children.

Taylor spent the remainder of the day visiting with others, reading, and making little improvements on the jet. She and Simon visited Max during one of his treatments with the flower and music. After the experience, he acted more normal. She hoped the effect of the treatment would last until the next morning, but during dinner, he began to zone out again. He excused himself and returned to his room to do whatever he did when he was alone.

Probably just stare out the damn window, she thought.

Taylor showed more indifference to his condition than she felt. She did not like showing too much concern for Max, ascribing her feelings to pity, not hope for a romantic relationship. She even felt a little guilty. If not for her invention, nothing would have happened to him, or any of them. When he left the room, she forced herself to keep looking at her plate, pretending not to notice. Simon watched him leave, and then Taylor felt his eyes on her before he returned to their conversation.

While the group continued to speculate about Freddy's return, Taylor attempted to make sense of what the machines had told Sadi of Max and Gerald's condition involving their connection to the background. When Taylor had asked the machines to give more details about the background concept, they had said Freddy might explain more if he desired.

Sadi thought the background was just another way to explain an inability to focus on the present, the result of damaged minds. But Taylor suspected that the machines had spoken literally and the background referred to an actual place or separate reality. Their present situation had shattered her potentially naive assumptions about the universe. Anything seemed possible now.

The machine's explanation about Max and Gerald's condition made sense to her. Existing simultaneously in two different places could account for their behavior. Perhaps the implication was correct and consciousness existed apart from the human body. On some level, she wanted to trade places with them, to gain some empathy and maybe just to have the experience. The thought also scared her.

After their group dinner, Sadi and Susan left the dining hall to put the kids to bed, leaving Simon, Mark, Cesar, and Dominga with Taylor. Even though the machines would have cleaned the dishes and utensils for the next meal, the adults usually took turns cleaning them. One or two days per week, Sadi and Susan made the children do the dishes, probably to keep them from thinking of the place as a vacation, Taylor suspected.

"We have a visitor," Simon said, looking across the table, between Taylor and Dominga.

While turning, Taylor expected to hear a request for her to visit the children. They had grown to think of Taylor as an older sister and often wanted her to read them a story before bed. In disappointment, she found one of the machines about four meters away, hovering motionlessly above the floor. Everyone stopped talking and waited for the machine to announce its intentions. If the children were present, they would have greeted the machine by name. None of the adults could tell them apart.

"We have an announcement," it said with the familiar female voice, waiting only a moment before continuing. "The time has come to visit Bodn. Tomorrow morning, we will begin enhancing your spacecraft. We expect you will want to participate."

"Is Freddy back?" asked Cesar, excitement in his voice.

"No, but your host will arrive in a few days to accompany you to the surface."

While Taylor waited for Cesar to speak, she wished again that the machine would resemble another human instead of just sounding like one. Its complete stillness while communicating, other than the rotating glass plate, made her uncomfortable. She always wondered why Sadi and Susan trusted their children with them.

"Can you tell us anything about Freddy and the others?" Dominga asked.

"We do not have that information."

"So you want to make improvements on our vessel?" Taylor asked, knowing they would fail to acquire any more information about their friends.

"Yes, improvements," it said. "We have been instructed to show you how to give it more efficiency and endurance."

Taylor turned from the machine, looking at Mark. She had noticed his attention on her and then saw him smiling. A rush of adrenaline accompanied her faster heartbeat. Excitement to learn something new quickly replaced her initial annoyance at the machine.

"Why are we going to visit the surface?" Simon asked. "I mean Bodn?"

"Those of you who are considering living there," it began, "are almost ready to experience the environment personally, more than just an inspection from the observatory. After a visit, the rest of you may reconsider your position."

Taylor had already decided to move there indefinitely so the reminder failed to disturb her. A visit to the planet brought as much excitement as the enhancement to her jet. After she and Simon had argued about staying, Taylor decided not to speak about the topic with him again. Despite the danger, Simon had expressed a strong desire to return home.

"When do you want to start with the jet enhancement?" Taylor asked before Simon or anyone else could ask another question about visiting Bodn.

"We will begin whenever you arrive in the landing bay."

"Thank you," she said with a tone of finality and a glance at Simon. "We'll see you tomorrow morning. Good night."

"Good night," it repeated and Taylor winced in anticipation of its usual wish for their comfort. Their artificial consideration always annoyed her. It seemed convincingly sincere.

"Sleep well," it said.

Without turning or any other warning, the machine began floating towards the exit. Everyone at the table silently watched as it moved smoothly across the floor. Before it exited the room, Taylor turned back to Simon.

"I'm sure they can hear everything we say," Taylor began. "So there's no need to wait before we can have a discussion."

Despite her words, no one responded until the machine had disappeared. Cesar made brief eye contact with Sadi and smiled almost imperceptibly. He spoke first.

"Things are beginning," he said. "I'm excited to see what they do to the ship, but I'm not sure how I feel about meeting our host."

"What did it mean by *almost ready?*" Dominga asked. "Is there anything else we need to do before visiting Bodn?"

TWENTY-FOUR

Brian

After Freddy's last words, all the sounds and the cold wind vanished. Their disappearance seemed as though the world had just exploded, causing an expansion of empty space. Nothing existed apart from his consciousness.

After the sensation of expansion, Brian tried to sense something. He tried blinking but failed to feel his eyelids move. He tried reaching up to touch his face, but his arms did not respond. He attempted to squeeze the pistol, but he felt nothing in either hand. He felt no hands. He could not even feel gravity pressing his feet onto the cobblestones. Somehow, Freddy had disconnected all physical sensations.

Brian responded in several different ways, one after another. At first, he experienced even more disorientation mixed with a small amount of panic. Then he wanted to complain about the situation while also questioning Freddy's tactic, wondering how he accomplished the disturbing feat. But Brian soon realized the futility of complaining. He had no control over anything, so that seemed like a stupid thing to do. In the end, he decided to accept the situation and wait for something to happen.

While waiting in the silence and the darkness, Brian had difficulty trying to remember his most recent experiences in the physical world. Without any input from his senses, the memory of the scene began to fade. The cold wind and his fear of the soldiers were being erased, like a strong breeze eroding a sandcastle.

"Stay calm, dude," he imagined saying. "You're not dead. You're standing outside in the cold. Freddy's on the ground right next to you, and another group of soldiers with machine guns are in front of you. Freddy is taking care of the situation. Freddy will get us out of this."

Another memory soon began to materialize, redirecting his attention away from the present. Without questioning the reason, he welcomed the memory of Sadi and him sitting together in their parents' home in Portland. Freddy had visited that day, a warm and pleasant afternoon in late spring. Without the distraction of any physical senses, the memory of their conversation remained fresh in his mind.

—※—

That afternoon, he and Sadi were sitting in their living room and had the house to themselves. He had excitedly said goodbye to his parents as they left on their trip, so he and Sadi could smoke the marijuana he had recently acquired from one of his bandmates.

Although he had not planned to include Freddy, when he arrived unexpectedly on their doorstep, Brian followed his impulse to invite him. He wanted to see if Freddy would smoke a joint for the first time and hoped for the experience to help him relax, and maybe help him cope with his shitty life.

"Hi, Brian," Freddy said when the door opened. After Freddy's glance at Brian, his eyes darted toward Sadi who sat on the loveseat in the front room. She wore shorts and sat with one leg over the other. Brian noticed Freddy's eyes focus on Sadi's bare legs, then he quickly turned away to stare at some picture on the wall.

"Hi, Sadi," Freddy said in the same flat and emotionless tone he always used.

Sadi was holding a joint between her index finger and thumb. Before responding, she took a drag and blew smoke into the room.

"Come in, Freddy," she said pleasantly. "Have a seat and relax with us."

"Is that marijuana?" Freddy asked, turning to Brian with wide eyes, and looking like he wanted to run away.

"Dude," Brian said with a big smile and closed the door. "Some friends hooked me up! You should try it."

"Okay," Freddy said and his demeanor changed suddenly. The shy kid they knew transformed into someone older who had no emotional reservations. "If you do me a favor."

How strange for Freddy to take advantage of a favor, Brian thought, but at the same time, he was excited for his acceptance.

"We need to get Sadi to my car," Freddy said and pointed toward her, his finger held motionless. "She might be in need of medical care."

When Brian turned back to his sister, he was shocked to see her sprawled in the chair, eyes closed, head back, and arms lying lifeless on the armrests, palms up. The joint had fallen on the loveseat by her leg, smoke rising from the end. Brian even noticed the small pile of ashes there, as if his sister had dropped the joint several minutes earlier.

Instead of running to the couch to help his sister or prevent the smoking joint from causing a fire, he put the joint to his lips and inhaled deeply. As the smoke filled his lungs and the calming effect of the THC washed through him, he just stared at her as if she was sleeping.

"What's wrong with her?" Brian asked casually. "I mean, she was fine just a second ago."

Before answering, Freddy took the joint from Brian and put the smoking stick to his lips. He inhaled and held the smoke in his lungs for several seconds. He looked like a man trying to think of the solution to a complicated situation, and using the marijuana to help him relax.

"That is nice," Freddy, smiling widely and blowing the smoke into the air. "I guess you can just carry her to my car."

Brian took a deep breath before stepping to the loveseat. After bending down, he looked back and saw that Freddy was watching while taking another drag. Brain gently pulled his sister from the loveseat and put her over his shoulder in a fireman's carry, surprised at how little she weighed. He felt as though he had picked up a kitten instead of a twenty-year-old woman.

"She's so light," Brian said.

Brian took Sadi outside and began walking with her to the curb. He stopped after noticing their neighbor across the street in her front yard, an ancient woman who was looking at him suspiciously. At first, Brian was embarrassed to be seen carrying his sister and did not want the woman to see Freddy standing behind him with a joint in his hand. To prepare for the confrontation, Brian smiled wide.

"Hello, Freddy Carlson," she said loudly while stepping into the street and then walking slowly toward them. As the old woman passed Brian, she did not even glance at him or his sister slung over his shoulder. Brian could smell her perfume, a disgustingly strong scent of artificially sweet roses.

The old woman stopped within arm's reach of Freddy who was suddenly motionless and silent. The woman was balancing herself with a cane, pressed against the cement at her left, and extending her right hand into the air. She held her open palm a centimeter away from Freddy's forehead.

"It's very nice to meet you. Let's get more acquainted."

When the old woman placed her fingers on Freddy's forehead, an explosion filled the world with blue light and cold. Brian shivered and almost dropped Sadi. When he looked into the woman's eyes, their brilliant blue light blinded him.

—※—

When his eyes readjusted to the light from the world again, Brian found himself holding Freddy over his left shoulder and the special forces commander standing between him and the parking garage. The horrible sound of the helicopter above them hurt Brian's ears, and the cold wind was making him shiver. He required several seconds to readjust to the world of physical sensation with the added burden of bearing Freddy's weight.

Although he feared to look away from the soldier who blocked his path, he saw in his periphery all of the other soldiers standing motionless in the last place he remembered them. Before he had lost all of his senses, the sound of the soldiers yelling at each other made the scene too chaotic. Now the scene seemed eerily absent of intelligent life.

The special forces commander standing in front of him spoke suddenly, breaking the silence. Brian felt a strange relief to hear another human voice. But when Brian failed to respond, the commander raised his pistol to Brian's eye level, just a meter away. Brian gulped.

"Drop the gun, Mr. Jacobsen," the commander said.

"What happened?" Brian asked.

"I don't know," the commander answered with irritation. "But you need to place Mr. Carlson on the ground. If you cooperate, no one's going to get hurt."

Brian stood motionless, not knowing what to do. Until that point, Freddy had told him what to do. He was tempted just to start walking and ignore the man. But as he stared at the weapon in the man's hand, someone grabbed him from behind, holding him tight.

Another soldier appeared and removed Freddy from his shoulder. Then they forced Brian to the ground with his hands behind his back. With his cheek pressed to the cold pavement, Brian could see only their boots.

TWENTY-FIVE

Brian

"It looks like Freddy to me," the commander said, the only voice Brian recognized. After tackling Brian to the ground, they seemed to ignore him. "Jones, can you confirm?"

"Yes, that's him," said a deeper voice.

"Get the tranquilizer. We need to inject him."

"I have it right here," said another voice.

Tranquilizing Freddy meant the end for them, Brian thought, then a sudden panic gave him a burst of adrenaline, so he tried pushing against the soldier on top of him. Despite his extra strength, he failed to move more than a centimeter off the ground.

He stopped struggling a moment later when a bright light began illuminating the ground all around him. As the light intensified, the shadows from the soldiers standing above him became even darker, looking like black paint on the ground. Brian wondered initially if the helicopter had shined a spotlight on them to help the soldiers see better, but he was wrong.

"What the fuck is that?" someone asked.

No one answered, then after an audible click, the commander spoke.

"Monson, fall back to point B. Monson, fall back."

Then he heard only radio static.

Brian watched the shadow of the soldier standing closest to him. His hands moved upward and merged with the shadow of his head, an attempt to shield his eyes from the intense light. Although Brian could not see the light directly, he eventually had to close his eyes due to the brightness of the ground and soldiers' boots.

The cold wind suddenly disappeared and the sound of the helicopter faded as though a final gust had blown it away. Then Brian heard only radio static, and the soldier stopped pushing him to the ground. He began pushing himself up, but an explosion destroyed his hearing and shoved him firmly to the ground again. The soldier who had been holding him down suddenly collapsed on top of Brian and expelled all of the air from his lungs.

Brian barely held onto consciousness. The following silence lasted for several seconds, and then the light penetrating through his eyelids suddenly disappeared, and the body on top of him became limp. After waiting in vain for some kind of signal, he opened his eyes, lifted his head, and scanned the vicinity.

Brian slid the unconscious soldier off his back and then stood painfully on his feet. Although the intensely bright light had disappeared, a fainter light still shined from the sky, illuminating everything in a soft glow. Before looking upward, he visually scanned all of the soldiers lying on the ground around him. None of them looked conscious or made any movement, and Brian felt as though he was the only living creature in the area. The cars and even the police sirens had all become silent. In the distance, he could hear the lapping of the waves against the rocks.

Freddy lay on the ground in front of him with the commander's arm lying on top of his chest, as though he had made a final effort to restrain Freddy. Before crouching down to inspect his friend, Brian looked up at the sky at the source of the light, the only other thing that seemed alive, other than himself.

Squinting, he attempted to discern the shape of the light source. It seemed to originate from a single point as if it were a star, and bright enough to make the sky appear as a black abyss with an infinitesimal flicker of light in the center.

For the next several seconds, he just stared until a noise diverted his attention to the parking garage five meters in front of him. Someone was walking in his direction. Except for his breathing and the waves, the footsteps were the only other noise.

While staring into the dark garage, Brian wondered if he should feel frightened or just curious. Had the old woman from his memory materialized in the real world? Strangely, he preferred for the special forces commander to wake. But when the small figure materialized in the light, Brian stopped breathing and his heart began racing. His niece, Helen, stopped at the entrance and looked at him with her lips spread in a wide smile.

"Hi, Uncle," the little girl said, smiling sweetly.

In a more normal situation, Brian would have opened his arms to prepare for an impact. His niece would also have called him "Uncle Brian", not just "Uncle". She failed to make any further movement toward him and just stood motionlessly with the smile of a much older girl.

He saw a higher intelligence in her eyes. This little girl wore her hair in a tight ponytail, not how Sadi usually did her hair, looser and messier. Although the young girl resembled Helen in almost every other conceivable way, Brian did not know the identity of the creature before him.

"Are you Helen?" Brian asked tentatively.

The little girl laughed, throwing her head back slightly as though she could barely restrain herself.

"Don't be silly," she said, then looked at the ground in front of Brian. "You know I'm not your niece."

Brian followed her glance at the ground before him, at Freddy's unconscious body. Not only did Freddy appear unconscious, he appeared frozen, as though not even breathing. The body of the commander lying next to him appeared the same.

"Is this a dream?"

"Not a dream," the little girl said, beginning to walk toward him.

Her movement contrasted sharply with the stillness of everyone else in the vicinity, as though the whole scene had been transformed into a memorial of a famous battle. The girl stopped within a meter of Freddy's body. For the next several seconds, they just stared silently at him. The little girl's presence somehow helped dissipate Brian's sense of urgency.

He took a deep breath, and his body relaxed.

"Is he gonna be okay?" Brian asked.

"He'll be fine," she said but shook her head as if indicating the opposite condition. "He is a little preoccupied at the moment, so you need to help him."

"We need to get out of here, right?"

"No, just Freddy. You need to stay here."

Brian looked up from the ground and made eye contact with her. Seeing the replica of his niece made him want to see his real nieces and Sadi. He wanted to ask about them, but the present situation seemed more important.

"I can't stay here," Brian said defensively. "They know where I am."

"Well, you can't go with Freddy." The little girl laughed as if he had said something ridiculous. "Don't worry, Brian. You'll be fine. You can visit your aunt and uncle. You know, connect with your roots. I'll clean up this mess."

"You're the one who gave Freddy his abilities aren't you?" Curiosity helped him forget about the present situation. "Who are you?"

"I'll tell you what you want to know," she said then nodded to the ground at Freddy's body, "but pick him up first and take him to the car."

"Okay," Brian said and took a deep breath before bending down.

He lifted Freddy from the ground and began carrying him toward the garage. The stretching of his muscles caused a rush of endorphins to enter his bloodstream. While listening to the girl, he felt almost euphoric.

"I've been helping Freddy," she began, but Brian interrupted her.

"You call this helping?"

"You were never in any danger."

Brian ignored the temptation to let anger taint his words. He could not show anger to such a beautiful creature, especially a replica of his niece. Besides, anger frustrated him. He preferred to chill.

"If you can save us from them so easily, then why did you let all of this happen? And why bring him here, if you wanted him to go somewhere else?"

"Freddy needs more stretching." The little girl shrugged before continuing. "You shouldn't complain. Focus on the positive. You had a relaxing evening before all of this, and now you get to vacation for a few days in the land of your ancestors."

"What's going to happen to Freddy?" Brian asked. "Where are you taking him?"

"Believe me. You really don't want to know," she said, turning away from him and walking into the garage. "What's the fun of that?"

"What's the fun of that?" Brian repeated, squinting in confusion. He finally noticed the BMW, right where he had parked it. That time seemed like a different life. "I'm trying not to get angry, but this doesn't feel like a fun game you're making us play."

"If you can't have fun in life, what's the point?"

"I guess so," Brian said, suddenly feeling the heavy weight in his arms. He focused on breathing and took two more steps in silence.

"Freddy has finally caught their attention," she said sweetly, reminding him of his niece even more. "It's kind of funny actually. They're trying to determine what's going on and Freddy's learning what he's up against."

The little girl led the rest of the way to the BMW, letting Brian consider her answer. He knew their conversation would soon come to an end, and he was probably not going to fully understand what she had told him. Freddy's fate seemed out of his hands anyway, so he decided to ask about what really mattered to him.

"Will I be able to visit Sadi?" he asked as they arrived at the car.

The girl placed her little hand on the handle and the door opened. Brian thought the action looked fake, almost as if her hand had not made contact with the handle. He suddenly wondered if the girl was just a hallucination or a ghost.

"Possibly, Brian," she answered while holding the front door open for him, "but that'll be up to Freddy. Set him in the seat, please."

"At least tell me they're okay," he pleaded and felt as though he was asking his parents for permission to play with his friends. After setting Freddy in the seat, he sighed with relief from losing the extra weight. Brian adjusted his legs and locked the seatbelts.

"Your sister and Helen and Daryn are fine," the girl said and shut the door, the tinted windows shielding his view of Freddy. The vehicle rose into the air and began floating away from them. While watching the BMW float toward the parking garage entrance, Brian wondered when he would see Freddy again.

—❋—

The next morning, Brian woke up in the suite they had rented. His whole body felt sore, especially his shoulders. After rising from the bed, he stretched with his hands above his head, high enough to touch the ceiling. Stretching released an exhilarating deluge of potent chemicals into his bloodstream.

He got dressed, wearing the same clothes from the previous day. His memory of recent events seemed like a mixture of reality and dream. Brian spent a few minutes walking through the apartment, then he went to the window and looked at the bay. Several sailboats sat on the water in the early morning light. People on the sidewalk were acting as though nothing out of the ordinary was happening. The peaceful and pleasant environment conflicted with his memory of their dangerous interaction with the soldiers.

Then he remembered standing in his front yard, Sadi slung over one shoulder and Freddy talking to his neighbor, the crazy old woman who had always scared him as a child.

"That's not right," he said after shaking his head and re-examining his memory. He and Sadi had liked the old woman. She had never frightened them and had often invited them into her house for cookies.

"Oh man," he said, running his fingers through his hair. Then he noticed a little piece of paper on the table next to his bed. The name and address of his aunt and uncle were written on it. At the bottom of the paper, someone had written a note to him.

Go visit your aunt.

Try to enjoy yourself until Freddy returns.

TWENTY-SIX

Freddy

High above Earth, Freddy stared at the Orion constellation through the front window and imagined the BMW floating as a leaf on the water. Although he felt only seventy percent of normal gravity, he felt almost weightless, and his muscles relaxed.

While part of Freddy admired the beautiful view of the stars, another part of him walked in a foreign desert. Each component of Freddy was more aware of the other now. After his recent experiences with Brian in Portland and then in Bergen, Freddy could imagine different worlds while also living in the physical, corporeal one. Those traumatic experiences had enhanced his consciousness.

The static view of the stars allowed Freddy to concentrate more easily on his walk through the hot desert, where red and purple clouds floated in the dark blue sky above him. He walked alone and had only to concentrate on avoiding the cacti.

Although the sun was frying his exposed head and the lizards scurried from sight, Freddy just wanted to continue walking. The hot air flowing past him was rejuvenating. He enjoyed drawing the heat into his lungs and becoming a part of the desert, becoming another desert creature. A rainbow shadow occasionally passed over him, becoming a colorful reprieve from the intense sunlight.

Freddy could have reached his final destination sooner, but he wanted to enjoy the desert experience for as long as possible. He loved how the surroundings contrasted so sharply with the only climate he had ever experienced, the green and wet Northwestern United States. For the present, he concentrated on enjoying the walk.

He constructed the North African desert landscape from the vision Dod had given him, recreating the details as accurately as possible. He made everything around him a shade of beige with the occasional light green of a small desert tree or bush. Freddy spent so much of his concentration on the landscape, he failed to stop the clouds from becoming whatever color they wanted. The red and purple clouds looked like cotton candy in the sky and reminded Freddy that he had limited control of his own imagination.

When he walked past an ancient stone hut, he wondered if his imagination had created the object or if it actually existed and some creature had projected the details at him. He did not remember Dod's vision including the hut. Freddy stepped through a pair of bushes to inspect the structure.

The hut had retained its structural integrity, mostly. Only a few red bricks had fallen from the archway and lay in the entrance. A large, striped lizard waited on top of the hut, staring at him and appearing unconcerned.

Freddy stopped two meters from the entrance and attempted to see inside, but he saw only darkness. For the first time, he was afraid. He sensed the presence of another sentient creature, which was hiding inside the hut. Until that moment, only Freddy had existed in his desert world, and now it had an intruder.

He tried imagining a giant snake lying in the dark interior, but that seemed wrong. A more intelligent creature waited inside and Freddy felt a strong curiosity to know its identity. He took a step toward the entrance, thinking that nothing in his imagination could harm him. But he stopped after taking just one step and his curiosity submitted to fear. He did not want to see what was hidden in the dark. Freddy stepped carefully backward until his distance from the hut seemed sufficient.

When Freddy felt out of danger, he decided to stop stalling and find his destination. After losing consciousness in Norway, he awoke knowing what he needed to do and where he needed to go. He would be entering the earth in the Sahara Desert, through the pit from Dod's vision. But before he traveled there in the physical world, he would prepare himself by visiting the place in his imagination.

After beginning to walk again, the physical world tugged at his awareness. A bright object had just entered his view, replacing the light of Rigel. The probe from the barn moved directly in front of the windshield, then turned so the open end faced the BMW, the filaments of light extending toward him.

Reflected sunlight from the probe's mirrored surface hit his eyes, nearly severing his awareness of the imaginary desert. In an attempt to distance himself from the probe, Freddy pushed against the back of his seat. His heartbeat rose instantly to a painful rate and he almost began to panic.

To help counteract his reaction, Freddy drew a deep breath.

"It is just the probe," he told himself, the sound of his voice helping to restore reality. The desert experience remained in his awareness but had deteriorated into a simple daydream playing in the background. "It is just the probe."

The radiant filaments flowed gently in the void of space as though moved by an ocean current, momentarily causing Freddy to feel as if water surrounded the BMW. Freddy rubbed his eyes, drew another deep breath, and slowly exhaled. For the next few minutes, he let the beauty of the glowing filaments rebuild his state of calm. Only the memory of the hut tainted his serenity.

"What is happening to me?" he asked after a few minutes, thinking about the desert experience and the hut.

Freddy jolted when the filaments suddenly stopped flowing and the speakers burst to life.

"Your awareness is expanding, giving you more control of the background."

The female voice sounded too familiar, but he could not place the identity. Despite its animated quality, he sensed no life in it.

"What is the background?" he asked, his heart rate accelerating.

"Before I answer," the voice said. "Know that I have limited capacity to help you understand."

"Do what you can."

"Dreams are the interpretation of background information," the voice said, pausing to mimic the sound of taking a breath. "Your brain converts information from the background like a computer forms a picture from an image file."

"Is it another dimension?" he asked, not sure exactly what his question meant. When he spoke the term, *another dimension,* he wondered if he was acting as a computer and following a program.

"It has no dimension," the voice responded flatly. "The corporeal world contains the only dimensions."

"Okay," Freddy answered, pausing to think of his next question. "So how did I get control in the first place?"

"The crystal with the spider unlocked part of your mind," the voice said, "and provided a greater connection to the creatures around you."

"And that is how I can feel their emotions?"

"Yes," the voice said. "You began receiving the information their bodies were sending to the background."

"Am I just getting better at sensing others?" he asked. "Because it changed at Brian's apartment."

"It's a process," the probe said through the speakers. "Just like other abilities, growth comes through anxiety."

"I know more than just their emotions now," Freddy said, recalling his first experience outside Brian's apartment. "I can imagine what they are, and I can imagine things for them."

"All creatures reside in the background while experiencing the corporeal world through their bodies," the probe said. "Most creatures have very limited attention, and information from the corporeal world overwhelms their brains' processing capacity. You confuse them by interfering with their information flow."

"I have difficulty differentiating between the real world and my imagination."

Freddy waited in vain for the probe to say something else. After a few seconds of silence, he turned from the colorful filaments extending from the back of the probe to gaze at the stars again. The beautiful view caused Freddy to forget momentarily why he cared about anything else.

In his peripheral vision, he noticed a change on the dashboard. The screen on his navigation monitor had changed to a map of North Africa. The destination icon, a five-pointed star, appeared at 22.004 degrees North and 19.161 degrees East in southern Libya, just north of the Chad border. The map program showed no towns anywhere near it but a mountain peak to the southwest called Bikku Bitti.

"Can you tell me what happened at Bergen," he said while staring at the map. Although silent, the probe had remained in front of the BMW. "I don't remember how I got here."

"What do you remember?"

"We were surrounded by the soldiers," Freddy said and closed his eyes to help remember. "I imagined a world of darkness for them all, but there were just too many. And what I imagined for Brian turned into some sort of nightmare."

"Please explain the nightmare," the voice said.

Before answering, Freddy drew a deep breath and opened his eyes. He had difficulty finding the words to describe the experience, so he tried thinking of a comparable experience from the world he could visualize.

"There was an old woman and she made the entire universe collapse around me, or into me. I do not know how to describe it." Freddy inhaled so he could finish and grasp reality again. "I was suffocating. I wanted to open my eyes and see, but I had no eyes. I wanted to breathe but had no mouth or lungs, or anything anymore and I knew there was nothing to see or breathe. After realizing all of that, I felt as though other creatures were watching me, billions of other creatures."

"Doesn't sound too pleasant."

Freddy thought he heard amusement in the tone as if a sentient creature was mocking him. But the tone became a welcome distraction from his disturbing memory.

"When I woke up, I remember looking at the stars, and I started thinking about going to the Sahara Desert."

After taking a breath, silence filled his confined world and the universe outside the BMW threatened to collapse on him again. He gripped the armchair tightly, flexing his muscles, and the physical sensation quickly dispelled the sensation. Eliminating the silence would also help, he thought.

"You still have not explained how I got here."

"You required intervention," the voice said and the tone of amusement vanished. "Your friend placed you in the vehicle and I took you here."

"Where is Brian?" he asked. "You did not just leave him there?"

"We restored equilibrium at the hotel, and then he went to visit his relatives," the voice answered. "No need to worry about him. You should go."

The star on the map began blinking more rapidly, returning his attention to the screen in front of him. He watched the icon blink and wondered if the horrible collapsing sensation would begin again, but the universe outside the BMW seemed stable. He needed to avoid thinking about the experience.

Freddy had several more questions and considered interrogating the probe further, but he needed to stop delaying and perform the next task. But while considering his upcoming walk in the desert, Freddy thought of something he wanted to have with him. A sunburn in the physical world suddenly seemed worse than a sunburn in his imagination.

"I need a hat," he said.

He expected the probe to respond, either in affirmation of his plan or to advise him not to delay again, but the probe turned and shot out of his sight, quick enough for the filaments to move like a whip. It reminded him of a rock star with long hair, swinging his head to a heavy drum beat.

Before engaging the engines for the descent, Freddy wondered about his motives.

Am I stalling, or do I really need a hat?

PART III

END OF THE LINE

The end of a line
Or the beginning
Of a new time

TWENTY-SEVEN

Taylor

While Taylor showered the next morning, her dreams of the night began to fade. By the time she was finished dressing for the day, her memories had diminished to a blurry descent through the clouds in the intense light of Dzalm. She needed to focus on the exciting activity of the day, the enhancement of the jet, but the imminent visit to Bodn was competing for her attention.

Before leaving her room, she glanced through the virtual window at the dark planet below her. As usual, clouds covered most of the surface, showing only partial views of land and ocean. The light from one of Bodn's three natural satellites showed as a glimmering reflection from the water. She couldn't wait for the chance to see the satellites from the surface.

While Taylor walked through the silent hallway to the dining room, her mind raced through all the possible improvements to the spacecraft, and she expected the machines would surprise her with something she had not considered. When she entered the dining hall, she found Helen sitting at the large table alone, eating something from a bowl. Taylor thought she would have the room to herself for a while before anyone else. Of all the children, she liked Helen the most and smiled while approaching her.

"Good morning, Helen," she said from the entrance, not wanting to frighten the young girl. "You're up early."

"Hi, Taylor," she said, her lips stretching into a wide grin then a yawn. "I was hungry."

Taylor walked to the table and sat across from the little girl. While Helen shoveled spoonfuls of oatmeal into her mouth, Taylor quickly assessed her condition. She still wore her pajamas, shorts, and a plain white t-shirt. Short blond hair fell just below her shoulders with wisps of hair in her face. Taylor usually saw the girl with her hair bound by some sort of clip.

"Does your mom know you're here?"

"She's still asleep," the girl said while chewing. "Sometimes I like to get up early and eat by myself."

"Me too," Taylor said. "It's strange we've never run into each other before."

"Yes, a very strange scenario."

Taylor suppressed a laugh and waited a moment for Helen to say something else. When the girl put another spoonful of oatmeal in her mouth, Taylor turned to the food preparation area, focusing on the refrigerators. Oatmeal seemed like a good choice but so did the left-overs from the previous evening.

"You've got an amazing vocabulary," Taylor said, looking into the girl's eyes. "Where did you learn *scenario*?"

"Miss Poofie said it yesterday," Helen replied with eyes narrowed in confusion. "I asked her what it meant."

"Good girl for using it in a sentence," Taylor said while rising and walking to the refrigerators. "There's something exciting happening today."

"What?"

"The machines are gonna work on the jet," Taylor said while pouring an oatmeal mix into a bowl and then some water. Before leaving Earth, Doroteo had purchased a large supply of the stuff and several boxes remained. Most of the refugees refused to eat any more of them after arriving. "Last night, they said we could visit the planet after they're done making improvements."

"You mean we're going to Bodn?"

"Yes, in a few days."

"Can I come?" she asked, excitement in her voice. Helen turned so she could see Taylor more clearly. "Or is it just for the adults?"

"Hmm," Taylor said, wondering if she should have revealed the information. Maybe Sadi would not want her to attend. "Actually, I don't know about that. Maybe just some of the adults will go first, you know, to check things out. You'll have to ask your mom."

"She says we probably can't go back home," Helen said without any trace of disappointment. "So, she'll probably let me and Daryn go with her."

"How do you feel about that?" Taylor asked while waiting for her oatmeal to heat in the microwave. "I mean, about not going home."

"This is way better than going back to school," Helen said with excitement. "We're having a lot of fun. Mom says we're having too much fun."

"It is fun," Taylor said with a chuckle, then thought of her mother and returning to Earth to visit her. She often imagined attempting to explain her experiences and her journey to Bodn. In every imaginary attempt, her mother just laughed at her.

"You seem to like school here."

"School's fun here," she said while turning to the entrance.

Taylor followed her gaze and noticed Mark walking toward them. He made eye contact and smiled.

"Good morning, ladies," he said on his way to the refrigerator. He opened the closest one and removed a pan with a plastic lid. "You are both my witness. I'm eating Susan's casserole from last night. She thinks I didn't like it."

"I didn't like it," Helen said seriously.

Mark laughed.

"Thanks for not telling her that."

"How does she feel about the latest news?" Taylor asked.

"Well," he said after a moment of contemplation. "She's not excited about visiting the planet. That'll make this whole adventure even more real. But she thinks it might indicate a kind of progression, which translates into a faster journey home."

"Long story short?"

"It didn't upset her."

"Well that's good," Taylor said. She gave Helen a quick smile, then turned to Mark again. "What about you? After sleeping on it, are you still as excited as I am?"

"Definitely," he said. "But I'm more anxious now to see Freddy again. Susan expects Freddy to tell us all it's safe to return. I'm not so sure he can fix the situation back there."

"Earth's fucked up," Taylor said, covering her open mouth with her hand. "I'm losing interest. I don't think anyone can go back. Sorry for my language, Helen."

"You mean vocabulary."

"Yes, my vocabulary."

"Don't tell Susan that," Mark said seriously. "I'm dying to know what's happening. It's so weird not knowing anything."

"We're too addicted to instantaneous information, aren't we?"

"Yes, we are," he said. "I'm kind of nervous about meeting our host, and would rather see Freddy, or at least have him here."

Taylor put a heaping spoonful of oatmeal in her mouth, thinking suddenly about the internet and smartphones. She hated to admit missing Google, even though it could not help them find Freddy. In Taylor's opinion, they had already discussed all of the possible reasons for Freddy's absence, and she agreed with the general consensus. The alien would not let Freddy fail. Their escape from Earth was nothing less than miraculous and had required too much effort to let him fail. Unless Taylor had made a gross error in judgment, they were only safely orbiting Bodn because of Freddy and for Freddy. Besides, Sadi trusted him and that was sufficient for Taylor.

They waited twenty more minutes for the rest to arrive and then went to the landing bay as a group, Simon and Taylor walking behind

Cesar and Dominga. Taylor thought they looked cute together. They walked close enough to touch shoulders.

They had made Helen remain in the dining hall until her mother and the other children arrived. "If your mother comes and doesn't see you here," Dominga had said, "she'll begin to worry. She needs to know where you are."

Taylor expected to see everyone in the landing bay eventually, except maybe for Max and Gerald. Their absence would not surprise her. Everyone would want to see what the machines had planned. She even expected to see Susan. Her two boys would likely complain if Helen and Daryn were doing something without them, not wanting to miss any potential fun. Taylor remembered feeling the same about her older brother.

—※—

"Are all those present who want to watch our work?"

Taylor tried to determine which of the two machines addressed them. Both of the machines stood side by side between the refugees and the jet. Large stacks of shining metal sheets stood close to the jet, along with other items Taylor could not name. Some looked like tools and others looked like materials.

"I think so," Mark answered. "You can start."

"We could have built a new vehicle," the machine said, and Taylor thought the sound originated from the one on the right. "But we decided to modify your craft because of possible sentimental links. We also wanted your presence to allay any concerns for the craft's integrity."

"We appreciate it," Cesar said.

"This is boring," said Mark's youngest boy.

"Shh," Susan said, putting her hand over the little boy's mouth.

Taylor and a few of the others looked down at the boy and smiled. While keeping him in her peripheral vision, Taylor turned to the machine as one of its appendages rose into the air.

"You will not find this boring, George," the machine said. When an electric arc jumped between two of the fingers, Taylor and the rest of the group jumped in surprise. "We will first cover the frame with a grid of stronger alloy, which is also a more protective electromagnetic shield."

"Before you begin," Taylor said, raising her hand. Curiosity urged her to keep quiet so they could begin, but a question suddenly materialized. "Are you programmed with an artificial intelligence or did you receive instructions on what to do from somewhere? I mean, do you understand how to make these modifications or are you just receiving instructions?"

The machines were silent for several seconds, longer than Taylor had anticipated, and she wondered if they were communicating with their host. During the pause, Taylor noticed Cesar and Mark looking at her, probably wondering what she meant.

"The phrase *artificial intelligence* is a complex concept. But to answer what you likely meant, we possess several engineering data sets and mimic creature language processing. We have received instructions from your host to fortify your vehicle, not how."

"That was my question," Taylor said. At some future time, she hoped to view their programming code. "Thanks."

While dismantling her NMG engines, the machines explained their instructions to retain them instead of building more powerful engines with a different thrust mechanism. She was a little insulted at first but quickly recovered after accepting that her invention could not possibly be the most powerful or most efficient method of generating thrust. After the machines rebuilt the engines, she wondered if they sensed her damaged pride, because they complimented the design, saying it was more efficient than anything else developed on Earth.

Conversely, they removed the fusion reactors and built completely new energy generators, then explained how the fusion reactors generated an unstable energy supply and left a trail too easy to trace. Taylor wondered who would be interested in tracing their path, but a brief lesson on the operation principles temporarily derailed those concerns.

The new generators created an energetic form of matter, a new fuel, in a process too complicated to explain in sufficient detail with their limited time. The new generators extracted or created the fuel from the electromagnetic field, which permeated all space, a concept they knew as space-time or aether. The more stable power supply also generated a trail, but it was more difficult to trace and dissipated quickly.

While the machines built the new energy generators, Mark had asked his only question. He wanted to know if the mass of the spacecraft would increase due to the new matter. The machines explained that the new matter was only temporary and had no accumulation, and the generators provided a safe path for expulsion. The answer to that question reminded Taylor of a lesson she kept relearning. Questions generated endless other questions.

Taylor was surprised they didn't need to ask that many questions. As the machines worked, they explained everything with sufficient detail. Even when the noise became almost unbearable, they communicated effectively. When the machines had finished all their modifications, several hours later, only Taylor, Mark, and Cesar remained in the landing bay. Taylor felt mentally exhausted but considered the morning as the most thrilling mental experience of her life.

In the end, the shape of the spacecraft looked the same except for the new skin and several collapsible antennae extending about three meters from the surface, functioning as an electric shield. The new grid material covered the entire surface of the jet, including the windows, and had the color of polished silver with small squares carved into the surface. Taylor had the impression of looking at the scales of a reptilian robot.

"Your vehicle is ready," the machines said after closing the door and stopping three meters in front of them. "Please tell your group that your host will arrive on the morning of October 6, four days from now, and accompany you to Bodn. We suggest you take some time to test your vehicle to prepare yourselves for the visit."

"Sometime the day before, we will perform a non-invasive physical examination with a likely purification for those who want to visit Bodn. We will leave you now, so you can discuss among yourselves."

TWENTY-EIGHT

Freddy

Freddy began flying toward US airspace from his position over the Atlantic Ocean, a few hundred miles away from the coast of Mauritania where the probe had brought him. Surprisingly, Freddy realized that increasing the distance from the North African desert helped him feel more at ease. After traveling to Mercury, such a long distance over the Earth seemed insignificant.

Before re-entry, Freddy decided on the general location, New Mexico, a place in the desert away from a large population. He chose the United States because it was his home and the people spoke English. After his brief stay in Norway, he wanted the freedom to converse with people in his native language. He expected to have only a short while before the military relocated him. He would quickly purchase a hat and only worry about his enemies if necessary.

At an altitude of six hundred kilometers, Freddy could not locate his exact location over the surface of Earth without the help of the navigation program. He could not even determine when he crossed the boundary between ocean and land.

Freddy began his descent when the navigation program showed his position over Chicago, Illinois. If the military possessed the capability to track him, Freddy would delay their discovery of his final destination. Instead of traveling straight down, the navigation program set a parabolic trajectory to Albuquerque, New Mexico.

As the computers controlled the BMW and the outside air pressure increased, Freddy used his extrasensory abilities to search for sentient creatures. He sensed the first group of humans traveling in an airplane, and had a sudden realization—distance seemed like a limitation existing only in his mind.

Freddy could project his sense as far as he desired, it seemed, but that came with a price. The experience overwhelmed him. The number of humans and other creatures he encountered increased exponentially. Then he began losing his ability to distinguish each individual separately and they transformed into a single entity he could not comprehend. He decided to test his limits more later.

Near the end of the descent, he regained control from the autopilot and directed the BMW southeast of Albuquerque. He saw a few small towns where he might land and quickly decided on a town the navigation program called Mountainair. The local time in New Mexico was fourteen minutes after one in the afternoon.

He landed on a dirt road called Rocking RI. After confirming the absence of other cars, he felt satisfied that no sentient creatures had noticed a BMW descend from the sky. When the tires finally connected with the road, he breathed a sigh of relief. Reconnecting with the earth felt extremely satisfying, like walking through the front door of his home and seeing Mr. Smith.

Sagebrush and yellow grass covered the flat desert landscape, reminding Freddy of the vision Dod had shown him. Compared to the North African Sahara, New Mexico looked like a lush garden. But not compared to his home in the Pacific Northwest.

He drove half of a kilometer before stopping at Route 60 where he would turn left toward Mountainair. His navigation program indicated a distance of seven kilometers to his destination. When he stopped at the intersection, he drew a deep breath and prepared to turn left. While looking through the front window, he visited the imaginary desert again.

—✳—

Freddy stood directly before the hut. After realizing his position, he scrambled backward and tripped over a piece of brick that had fallen from the archway. After landing on his butt in the soft sand, he scooted backward until he felt safe from whatever waited in the dark interior.

While still on the ground and gasping for breath, he heard a hiss from inside the hut, followed by the harsh sound of a rattlesnake shaking its tail. Suddenly paralyzed, Freddy waited for the venomous creature to hurl itself from the hut and into the sunlight. The snake stayed in the hut, however, so he gained the courage to start scooting backward, attempting to move without sound.

—✳—

He returned his focus to the view through the BMW front window. Although he felt a great urgency to hurry, he sensed no immediate danger of discovery from any of his pursuers. He pulled onto the road and quickly accelerated to 130 km/h until he saw the first signs of civilization, and then he slowed to a more normal speed. If any policeman were out there, he felt confident in his ability to detect them before they could catch him on radar, but if he failed to do even that, he would make sure they recorded the wrong vehicle description and license number on their ticket. Or even better, he could make them only imagine giving him a ticket.

After driving to the center of the small town, he parked in front of a single-story consignment store, clothing and hats visible in the front window. He opened the door, stepped onto the street, and the bright sunlight immediately hurt his eyes. The heavily-tinted windows had shielded his eyes for so long, he needed time to re-adjust to unfiltered sunlight. While squinting, he decided to better prepare for his journey to Africa and purchase more items, including sunglasses and water. His detour to the small town no longer felt like a mistake.

He drew a deep breath of warm air, stretching his legs and arms satisfactorily for the first time since leaving Bergen. The rush of endorphins reminded him of life's physical pleasures, but then he smelled an unusual yet pleasant scent in the air, the dry smell of the desert.

Must be the sagebrush, he thought, taking another deep breath through his nose.

Before entering the store, Freddy glanced across the street at a small gas station, at the old-style gasoline pumps without credit card readers. He tried to remember the last time he had filled a vehicle with gasoline. While still squinting, Freddy stepped into the shadow of the store and then pulled the door open for a tall elderly woman who was exiting.

"Thank you," she said and smiled.

"No problem," he replied, enjoying the interaction with a normal human again. He remembered the probe and its lifeless voice.

The woman felt little curiosity about Freddy, but she did notice the BMW behind him and wondered why a man who could afford such an expensive vehicle would shop at a consignment store. The ding of the tiny bell on the door brought his focus to the store occupant, a single woman, and Freddy was relieved to deal with only one person.

A young girl about his age stood at his right, behind a worn wooden counter. After the door closed, the girl smiled and prepared to say hello if he looked at her, but Freddy kept his gaze directed at the ground to avoid making eye contact.

He quickly identified the area with the hats. Although the store had other kinds of hats, Freddy saw mostly cowboy hats. After placing one on his head, Freddy wondered if cowboy hats had another name. He would discover the proper name later, maybe even ask the girl at the counter when he chose one.

Freddy wondered briefly if he looked silly but quickly realized that he did not care. For the present, he just needed something to prevent the sun from burning his head and ears. The hat seemed good enough, and he planned to purchase it, then hurry to the gas station across the street for drinks, food, and maybe a cooler.

But before turning to the cashier, he felt her intention to approach him. She stepped away from the counter, heading in his direction and preparing to speak. Freddy reminded himself to act like a normal person and wait before responding to her comment.

"Hi, I'm Melissa," the young woman said, stopping about two meters away from him. "That's a nice hat."

He glanced at her then removed the hat and turned his gaze to it as if inspecting the quality. He forced a smile.

"Seems good," he said, noticing her blue eyes, beautiful and large in proportion to her face. "I just need something to keep from getting burned."

The girl had full cheeks and seemed healthy and strong, a farm girl, Freddy guessed. Thick blond hair fell over her shoulders, slightly curled and completely covering her neck and collarbone, reminding Freddy of his own hair, which was intractable. Her freckled face and bleach-blond hair indicated a lot of time in the sun.

Despite her attractive smile and cheerfulness, Freddy perceived her other emotion, a sincere desire to help a fashion-blind customer. She thought the brown leather hat looked ridiculous on him and was deciding how to handle the situation. Freddy would usually wait for her to speak, but he had limited time, he suddenly realized. A man was driving on the road toward the store and preparing to confront him.

"Do you think I should get something else?" he asked. "I just need something for the sun. I am not from the desert."

Before answering, she looked at him curiously. In her opinion, she complimented Freddy convincingly, successfully hiding her real opinion of the hat. When he had blown her cover, she experienced a momentary loss for words.

"Well, it doesn't really go with shorts and a t-shirt," she said, feeling a little relieved for not hurting his feelings. "That hat is kind of like for going out to dinner in, not a working hat if that's what you want."

"Yes," Freddy said. "A working hat is what I need."

"Well." She stepped past him and grabbed a different wide-brimmed hat. "This one has lots of life left in it. You don't plan on dying anytime soon, do you?"

"Not planning on it," he said and chuckled appreciatively for her sake.

—※—

While Freddy remained on the ground in front of the hut, the snake hissed again, quiet at first but growing louder. Paralyzed by fascination, Freddy watched it slowly emerge from the harsh shadow at the entrance, gracefully cutting through the sand. The head was massive, with scales like nickels reflecting the sunlight. As the head ascended into the air, its black tongue wiggled free of its mouth as though a creature trying to escape.

—※—

"Here," the girl said, holding the hat between them and shaking it slightly. "Hey, you okay?"

"Oh, sorry," Freddy said and took the hat from her extended hand. "Zoning out for a moment."

He stared at her blue eyes, and the black pupils seemed larger than normal, enhancing the surrounding color. The vibrant life he saw there helped return his attention to the physical dimension. The desert and snake transformed into a background memory.

He suddenly liked the girl and wanted to know her better, so he focused on what she was experiencing behind the curtains of her awareness.

—※—

Melissa was walking on a wide city street surrounded by high buildings and attractive people in professional attire. She walked confidently and comfortably, enjoying the human activity around her. She had no particular place to go but enjoyed just walking amidst all of the majestic architectural achievements of her fellow creatures.

Freddy inserted himself into her world, on the sidewalk next to her. They were walking side by side and continuing their casual conversation.

"The hat looks good on you," she said with a glance in his direction, then she returned her attention to one of the tall buildings.

Freddy nodded.

"Thank you."

TWENTY-NINE

Freddy

Back in the consignment store, Melissa picked a new hat for Freddy to try. After placing it on his head, heard a car door close outside the shop. Without showing any sign of noticing, he pulled the hat tighter and twisted it slightly until the fit was more comfortable.

"Now that looks much better," she said, smiling with satisfaction.

Her sincere desire to assist him became an invigorating sensation and contrasted sharply with the frustration and anxiety of the man who had just parked in front of the store, a local law enforcement officer. Freddy sighed with resignation at having to deal with another round of people attempting to stop him. He felt surprisingly rested and ready for the confrontation.

"I'll take it," Freddy said, stepping ahead of her toward the cash register near the entrance. He glanced through the window as a tall policeman put his hand on the door handle. Freddy quickly looked away and stopped at the counter, waiting patiently for the girl to walk around him and begin the financial transaction.

Melissa paused at the ding of the entrance bell then turned to the police officer. Freddy noticed his hat, something he thought a forest ranger might wear.

"Hi, Chief," she said sarcastically, then returned her attention to the cash register.

"Good afternoon, Melissa," he answered in a deep voice without any hint of cordiality.

Melissa looked up at Freddy and smiled, ignorant of the policeman's suppressed anxiety.

"That will be $31.65."

Freddy sensed the man looking at him and pretended not to notice. While Melissa tapped on the register and then opened the till, the police officer just stood at the door with his hand hovering above the holster at his hip, effectively blocking the exit.

Freddy handed her two twenties.

"Keep the change."

"No," she said and laughed. "I couldn't."

"No, really," Freddy answered with a smile of his own. "I really don't want any more cash."

"Well, okay then. Thank you!" The girl pushed some hair away from her left cheek and turned to the police officer. She spoke with some impatience. "Can I help you, Chief?"

Before turning to face the man, Freddy took a deep breath and sighed again. As expected, the police officer chose not to respond to Melissa. In the following uncomfortable silence, Freddy decided to speak.

"You won't need your gun," he said, taking a step back and distancing himself from the officer. He hoped the action would increase the man's sense of security.

—※—

In the beautiful city, Freddy and Melissa walked together on the sidewalk. When Freddy grabbed her hand and stopped, people had to walk around them, a continuous flow of people like water going around an exposed rock. She followed his gaze to a small shop where a young man was buying a hat from the store attendant.

An angry man in a police uniform stood just inside the entryway. He had removed a gun from his hip, aiming it at the ground, ready for use at any second. The young man at the counter turned to look at him.

"Please excuse me for a moment," Freddy said, then stepped to the shop front window. He knocked on the window and the policeman turned to look outside. After making eye contact with the man, Freddy extended his hands into the air. "What are you doing in there? I'm out here."

While facing the window, the policeman stood like a statue. Freddy peered into his eyes from two places, the real world and the background. Freddy was beginning to enjoy the experience of dual consciousness.

—※—

"Why would I need my gun?" the man asked, attempting to hide his sudden confusion. He did not want to look foolish in front of Melissa. She stepped back from the register.

"Because," Freddy said, extending both of his hands in the air. "Because I will stay in here like *they* want. I will also not disobey any order you give me."

"What's going on here?" Melissa asked, addressing the police chief. After Freddy had given her the extra money, she felt the need to protect him. All customers were her jurisdiction. Besides, Freddy seemed completely harmless and nice. He also seemed familiar to her in some way, as though they had spent time together in the past.

"You should leave, Melissa," the police chief said forcefully.

"Not until you tell me what's going on."

"Just go," he said, barely curbing his growing anger.

"I'm not going anywhere," she said even more resolutely. "I can't leave the store unattended."

For the first time since entering the shop, the police chief turned to make eye contact with the girl. In preparation for a much louder demand, he inhaled deeply and wrapped his fingers around the butt of his pistol.

"Officer," Freddy began, breaking the sudden tension. "Will you do me a favor before they arrive?"

"Do what?"

Melissa and the police chief looked at Freddy in surprise.

"I promise that this is all going to end peacefully and very soon," Freddy said calmly. "But I need a few things first. Would you go to the gas station across the street and buy two liters of water? They don't have to be refrigerated."

The police chief stood speechless for a few seconds.

"And you'll just stay here," he said as if trying to convince himself.

"I promise."

—※—

On the busy city street, Freddy stepped to the right of the window and opened the shop door. The police officer watched him with narrow eyes.

A pair of handcuffs appeared in Freddy's right hand. He shook them and made a loud clanking sound, which resonated with the glass around them.

"Here," he said while shaking them. "Cuff me to this bike stand."

From inside the store, the other Melissa and the other Freddy watched as the policeman walked out the front door. He grasped the handcuffs from Freddy-on-the-street and then cuffed him to an iron bike stand.

During the process, Melissa-on-the-street folded her arms in protest, her lips pressed together tightly in a scowl aimed at the police officer. Handcuffed-Freddy smiled politely and then the man stepped back, feeling extremely pleased with his work.

—※—

"I'll be back in a few minutes," the police chief said, then turned tentatively and opened the door. "But I'll be watching this place."

The bell rang as the police chief opened the door. Through the glass, Melissa and Freddy watched him walk across the street and disappear inside the gas station. Freddy waited for the girl to speak.

"I thought he was going to laugh at you," she said seriously. "I've never seen the chief take orders from anyone. Will you please tell me what's going on?"

"It is better the less you know," Freddy said, feeling guilty for not satisfying her curiosity. He also felt as if he owed her for staying with him. "There will be some soldiers coming in just a few minutes and they will probably make you tell them everything I said to you. My name is Freddy, by the way."

Melissa opened her mouth to speak but required a moment to comprehend the information. Rather than fear, she felt only curiosity and a little excitement. She had enjoyed disobeying the police chief.

"Soldiers?" she asked. "What are you talking about?"

"Okay," he began, chuckling despite the serious situation. He liked the girl. She helped him feel more at ease. "You will just think I am crazy. And they will probably convince you of it too."

"Soldiers?" she said again, one eye squinting more than the other in confusion.

"I have some technology that the military wants," Freddy said bluntly. "That is basically what is going on."

"Wow," she answered, rubbing her chin. "I'm sorry they caught you."

"They have not caught me yet," he said, still smiling.

Melissa was more curious about why the police chief left than she was about the technology Freddy possessed. As she prepared to ask for more details, he interrupted her.

"How much more money do you need before you move out of Mountainair?"

"What?" she asked, suddenly suspicious.

"You are saving money so you can move," he said quietly. "Am I right?"

"How did you know that?"

"Listen," Freddy began and glanced out the window again to see if the police chief had left the gas station yet. The man was standing in line at the register, but then he suddenly stepped back and disappeared from view again. "We do not have much time. I would like to make a donation to your plans. I have some cash that I do not need."

Freddy reached into his back pocket and Melissa's eyes followed the movement. He removed his wallet and then all the large bills he had taken from the BMW. He extended the cash to Melissa. She remained motionless, so he placed the money on the counter.

"No strings attached," he said, then looked through the glass door as an old pickup truck passed the shop. "Consider it as a thank you for helping me pick a better hat and waiting with me. You could have left."

"Am I safe?" she asked finally, worried for the first time, and looking away from the stack of hundred dollar bills. "Should I leave?"

"You have nothing to worry about," Freddy said confidently. "Tell me, what do you want to do when you get to the city?"

While answering, Melissa squinted in suspicion.

"I don't know," she said. "I just want to get away from here. It's a nice place, don't get me wrong. It's just, this is where I grew up. I want to see the world. If I stay here, I'll just end up as a farmer's wife."

"The Earth is an amazing place," he said, thinking about his recent travels. "Can I give you some advice?"

"Sure," she said tentatively.

"If you need to choose between two lines, get in the shorter one. The number of people in a line does not necessarily mean it is the best line. And I am not talking about a line in the grocery store."

"Makes sense," she said with complete insincerity.

"When the time comes," he began, "you will know what I mean."

As he finished speaking, a deafening sound shook the store, loud as thunder. It originated from outside, a jet flying over the town, low and fast.

"What was that?" Melissa asked, visibly frightened.

"They are here," Freddy said, turning to the front window. "You should put the money out of sight, in a safe place."

Melissa scooted the money off the counter and into her hand. When Freddy looked through the front window, he saw the police chief exit the gas station and then step to the end of the sidewalk. He looked up, holding his right hand over his eyes as a shadow quickly flew down the street. After the shadow passed, he ran back to the shop with a plastic bag swinging from his hand.

"Are you okay, Melissa?" the police chief asked after entering the store, his eyes on Freddy.

"I'm fine. What's going on out there?"

"A large military cargo plane just went by," the chief said and put his head close to the glass door, looking upward. "People in parachutes are coming down."

"Oh my God," Melissa said, excitement replacing fear. She reached down and Freddy heard the click of a latch as she put the money away. She wanted to leave the store and see, but she also feared for Freddy and did not want to abandon him. For a moment, she stood with indecision.

"You can go watch," Freddy said. "I will just stay here."

"I'll be back," she said as she left the cash register and walked past the police chief. The man stepped out of her way. He wanted to stop her but decided to stay with Freddy and prevent him from leaving.

"You stay here with me," the chief said, handing the plastic bag to Freddy. Although Freddy had already agreed to stay, the man wanted to retain some authority in the situation.

"Yes, sir."

Freddy glanced in the shopping bag and saw two water bottles and the other object he wanted, a flashlight. After the police chief had left him with Melissa, Freddy thought of the flashlight. The dark pit from his vision would be a little less daunting if he had one. While talking with Melissa, Freddy had added the flashlight to the shopping list.

Freddy watched the scene outside from the counter and the chief watched from the front door. At first, he saw only Melissa in the street, but three other people soon joined her from the gas station. They were all looking into the sky, their heads slowly descending in unison. The people who had joined her simply watched, but Melissa was recording the scene through her cell phone.

"What the hell do they want you for?" the chief asked, breaking the silence.

"What did they tell you?"

Without turning from the window, the chief answered.

"They didn't tell me anything, only to keep you in the store, and to handcuff you to something."

"Why did you not?"

"You didn't look like a threat," he said with a snort. "And I don't like to be told what to do. Now you tell me, what is this all about?"

"I have something they want," Freddy said. "My car."

The chief prepared to ask another question, but as he opened his mouth, the people on the street started taking steps backward. They looked frightened. Two held up their hands as if they were under arrest, but Melissa turned and ran across the street, back to the consignment shop. The police chief pulled the door open and stepped out of her way.

"There's several soldiers coming this way," she said, gasping for breath. "They have machine guns."

Melissa felt more excited than frightened, waiting impatiently for the soldiers to reach them, and also waiting for a good time to post the pictures she had taken on her Myspace account. In the back of her mind, she was only a little concerned for Freddy.

The police chief felt curious and also anxious. He disliked the military entering his town. The situation made him feel powerless, and Freddy understood his predicament. With his heart pumping adrenaline throughout his body, the chief had difficulty identifying each individual emotion.

Less than a minute later, the first soldier entered their view through the window. He was wearing light green military fatigues and walked in the middle of the street without even a glance in their direction. He wore a specialized black helmet with two small cameras attached, one facing forward and the other facing forty-five degrees to his right. An antenna extended vertically from his left ear and he had a tiny microphone in front of his mouth. He was walking and holding up his right hand as if directing traffic. After passing the shop, he yelled at the people in the street.

"Get back, this street is closed."

"The rest of them are staying over there," Melissa said, her face pressed to the glass. "No wait. There's one coming."

She watched for a few more seconds, then stepped away from the door and stopped on the right side of Freddy. After the next soldier appeared in front of the store, the police chief pushed the door open and held it.

"He's in here."

"Thanks, chief," the soldier said while looking at Freddy.

The new soldier wore the same helmet with the cameras as the first soldier, but he had no weapon visible. He stood the same height as the police chief and the same age, both much taller than Freddy. The soldier smiled confidently and politely. Even though he disliked the camera recording him, Freddy returned the smile.

"Good afternoon, I am Major Summers," he said, holding both hands in the air, just above his shoulders. He turned away from Freddy and spoke to the police chief. "I just want to talk to Mr. Carlson. May I join you?"

"Sure," Freddy said. "It is nice and cool in here."

As the soldier passed the police chief, Melissa fought the temptation to step away from the men. Despite the addition of a soldier, she still felt the need to protect her customers. Melissa preferred to stand with Freddy against the military, he realized with a smile, someone she only just met.

I like this girl, Freddy thought as the soldier stepped inside the shop.

"You are recording this encounter," Freddy said. "Correct?"

"Yes," the soldier answered after the door closed and the bell dinged.

"And you are unaware of what happened at Bergen?" Freddy asked.

Major Summers paused while voices spoke to him in his headset. Although Freddy could not hear the voices, he could sense the questions the man prepared to repeat. Freddy did not plan to let them control the conversation.

"You want to know about the car, so I will tell you," Freddy said and smiled.

"I'm not authorized to know that," the soldier interrupted, hoping to stop Freddy. "Above my security clearance."

"It can fly without the assistance of aerodynamics," Freddy continued. "And your leaders do not want the public to know about it. But for all of your sakes, I will not give any more details."

Freddy decided that he liked the man and enjoyed satisfying his sincere curiosity, while simultaneously hoping to anger his superiors. The soldier had no desire to harm Freddy or incarcerate him. But Freddy still worried about the consequences of revealing too much information to people who could get into trouble, like Melissa.

"The military took some of my friends to a secret psychiatric facility and severely damaged them." As Freddy spoke to the police Chief and Melissa, an unexpected anger urged him to turn to the soldier and speak into the camera. "I am not happy with whoever is responsible for sending them there. I got them out and can find you."

"I'm sorry about your friends," the soldier said, following directions from his headset. He was suddenly afraid.

"You have nothing to worry about," Freddy answered after looking into Major Summers' eyes, away from the camera. The man felt like a sacrificial pawn on a chess board and Freddy wanted to offer some comfort. "I do not blame you."

"I appreciate that," he said without any instructions from his leaders. "Let me just get to the point. We're here to invite you to come with us and answer some questions. I will escort you personally and assure your safety."

"You came with guns and several soldiers," Freddy said. "How am I supposed to believe you?"

Freddy suddenly realized that Major Summers sincerely believed his own statement. He knew nothing about the intentions of the soldiers who stood outside, waiting for Freddy to appear so they could incapacitate him. He briefly considered revealing the information to him but then decided against it. They were also testing the major in this situation.

Major Summers chuckled.

"If you knew more about the military, you'd know that we like to over-prepare. We didn't know what to expect." The major turned from Freddy to the front window and continued speaking. "There's a helicopter on the way with some recording equipment where we can talk privately. We just want to ask you some questions."

"I will consider it," Freddy said. He made eye contact with Melissa and opened his eyes a little wider just for her. The action reminded her of high school and getting scolded for passing notes.

"Before they get here," the major continued, "would you mind showing me your vehicle."

"Okay," Freddy said, but he did not move when the major opened the door and stepped onto the sidewalk.

Major Summers stood with his back to the open door and held his hand in the air as a signal to the soldiers standing there, out of Freddy's sight. When he spoke, he used a more commanding voice than he had used in the shop.

"We're coming out."

Freddy remained standing by Melissa as the police chief stepped out of the shop and onto the sidewalk with the major. Without looking back into the store, the police chief and Major Summers walked to Freddy's car and stood still while looking at it.

"It was nice to meet you, Chief," Freddy said with a snicker, just loud enough for Melissa to hear.

As the shop door swung closed, Melissa prepared to ask a question. Her sudden confusion mixed with his excitement.

"Just stay in here with me for a bit," Freddy said and put his hand comfortingly on her shoulder. "Things may get a little weird."

The next instant, they saw a dart suddenly appear on the police chief's neck. Melissa jumped in surprise and Freddy increased the pressure of his hand on her shoulder until her muscles relaxed. They watched the following scene as though watching a movie. The glass door muffled the soldiers' conversation, but Freddy and Melissa could clearly hear them.

"What the hell are you doing?" Major Summers yelled as two soldiers appeared and grabbed the police chief to steady him. "He was under my protection."

The police chief looked at the men in surprise, his eyes wide and silent. They began to droop, and his shoulders grew limp.

"New orders, sir," said one of the soldiers.

"Goddamn it! I gave him my word," Major Summers said in anger, completely losing the polite attitude he'd shown in the shop. The two soldiers laid the police chief on the ground and Major Summers watched him with indifference as voices spoke in his headset. After a moment, he turned to the soldier at his right. "See if you can find his car keys. Look in his pockets."

One soldier remained standing while the other bent down and put his hand in the police chief's pocket. He removed a set of keys and handed them to Major Summers who had turned his attention to the BMW. He took the keys and attempted to open the door.

"Do they think the chief is you?" Melissa asked in a whisper, squinting while Major Summers fumbled with the keys, glaring frustration in his eyes. "Or, did they really come for him? I'm confused."

"Yes, Melissa," Freddy said without taking his eyes off the scene. "They think the chief is me, and so do his superiors communicating with him."

"How is that possible?"

"Just listen," Freddy answered quietly, putting his index finger over his lips, attempting to concentrate.

"None of the keys work," Major Summers said without emotion.

He looked at the ground with a blank expression while his superiors gave him orders. After a moment, he turned to his left and yelled.

"We need to clear a landing area." Major Summers stepped away from the car and stopped in the middle of the road. He looked up at the power lines running along both sides of the street. After taking a deep breath and turning almost a complete circle to view the situation, he pointed to the other side of the gas station and then pointed at the empty parking lot across the street. "Johnson, that might work. Go and keep the civilians out of the way."

While Major Summers waited for the soldier, Melissa turned from the window to stare at her phone. Freddy turned to watch her.

"What the heck?" she said while sliding her index finger across the screen. "What happened to my pictures? I was going to upload those to Myspace. Darn it!"

"They handicapped all the smartphone cameras," Freddy said with sudden understanding. "Sorry." Her disappointment made him smile. In a potentially dangerous situation, which should have frightened her, Melissa had set aside some of her attention for social media.

Just then, an old man appeared out of nowhere and pulled the front door open, causing Freddy to turn and stare at him in shock. He stood in the partially opened door, using a black cane with a silver handle for balance. He was wearing an old baseball cap covered with fly hooks, a tattered grey button shirt, new blue jeans, and nice cowboy boots. Freddy felt no emotions from the old man. Light and sound were the only evidence of his existence.

"Hi, Mr. Cummins," Melissa said, confusion evident in her eyes. "How did you get past the soldiers?"

"This is my store," he said, laughing and leaning his cane against the counter. "That's all I had to say, and that nice soldier just let me through. But I did have to park down the street."

The old man walked past them, stepped behind the counter, and stopped with his hand resting on the till. Melissa smiled at the old man and then turned her attention to the scene outside. Major Summers had stepped next to the BMW again, attempting to see through the windshield. He aimed his head camera at different angles, and at one point, got on his hands and knees to see the underside of the vehicle.

As Melissa watched the scene outside, the old man turned to Freddy. His old eyes were moist and slightly swollen with age. He spoke with his lips stretching into a wide grin.

"Hi there, friend," he said, revealing crooked yellow teeth with a few of the back ones missing. "It looks like you're having fun." The old man glanced briefly at the place where Melissa had placed the cash and continued without looking at Freddy. "Very nice of you. A present for Little Missy. Oops! She hates when I call her that."

The man laughed loudly at his blunder, almost a cackle, and Freddy expected to feel a negative emotional reaction from Melissa at his right. But the old man's use of the despised nickname caused no reaction. She kept her gaze on the street, and Freddy realized that he no longer felt any emotions from her.

— ※ —

Freddy broke eye contact with the old man to face Melissa, hoping to reconfirm her existence. The experience became a crushing reminder of his old problem—not recognizing identity by a voice and needing visual confirmation. Without emotions, his fellow humans seemed like lifeless puppets. Although Melissa stood motionless, at least her beautiful eyes still glistened with vitality.

When Freddy turned to Major Summers, he was standing next to the BMW, motionless like Melissa with his hand on the driver's side window. While attempting to comprehend the situation, Freddy drew a deep breath but held the air in his lungs. Without warning, the old man was now standing next to Freddy and grasping his shoulder, pulling him to the ground as though he weighed a ton.

How had the old man come to stand by him so quickly? Freddy remembered him standing in a different location just a moment before. He was suddenly afraid to look into the man's eyes, so he kept his gaze on the street.

"Yer keeping Little Missy in a big city, eh," he said while they stood watching the scene outside. "What a wonderful imagination you possess."

The old man spoke sweetly, like a loving grandfather, but Freddy heard the sarcasm.

"That is where I found her," Freddy said defensively.

Before releasing his grip on Freddy's shoulder, the old man squeezed tightly, his fingernails puncturing Freddy's shirt and skin. With throbbing pain, Freddy grasped his shoulder, blood seeping through the holes in his shirt. He held his hand in front of him and watched as blood dripped from his fingers onto the floor. In confusion, Freddy looked from his bloody fingers to the old man.

"I understand," the old man replied, the sarcasm remaining. Instead of standing right next to Freddy, he was now standing a few feet away and holding a tall wooden staff. An ornately carved baby doll head sat on top of the staff, just above the man's grip. Freddy found himself staring into the empty eyes of the doll.

"Understand..." Freddy said then forgot what he wanted to say.

"Whatever works," the old man said. "At least, that's what Pop used to say. He also used to say it's rude to intrude without a proper introducing. And that's what ya ain't done yet, Freddy Carlson. Who are ya?"

While smiling politely, the old man waited for Freddy to answer. Was he talking about the town or something larger? As Freddy desperately tried to think of what to do, the world he had created for the soldiers outside began to slip from his grasp.

"I'm waiting, young man," the old man said softly then slammed his staff against the floor.

When the staff crashed into the ground, the store shook and Freddy's whole body stiffened. He turned from the baby's head on top of the staff and looked into the old man's eyes. The baby winked at him.

"You seem to know who I am already," Freddy said finally.

"Your name ain't your identity." The old man shook his head and sighed dramatically. "You ain't nobody. I'll find you."

He slammed his staff on the floor again, three quick stabs.

—※—

Freddy was standing in the street next to the BMW, his hands cuffed behind his back and two soldiers standing next to him. To prevent him from walking away, one soldier held tightly onto Freddy's shoulder. They were waiting as Major Summers searched the BMW. He sat in the front seat while looking at the back seats. When finished, he turned to face the dashboard.

The windows of the BMW looked different, and Freddy inspected them until he realized the reason for his confusion. They were not as tinted as he remembered, and he could not recall seeing through them so well. But now he could see the inside easily, the dashboard with a speedometer, a radio, a glove compartment, all the usual items in a typical automobile. Somehow, it did not make sense.

There was an explanation, he realized. Someone had removed him from the physical world and placed him in the background. But he was not sure when that had happened. Many of his recent memories did not feel like his own. After realizing that he did not know the way back to the corporeal world, he began to panic.

Perhaps if he could identify the last time he was in control of the situation, he could break free from the illusion. He closed his eyes and breathed deeply through his nostrils. The scent of sagebrush saturated the warm air and reminded him of opening the BMW doors and feeling the desert around him. That was definitely real, but he was not so sure about afterward.

This is fake, he whispered to himself. *I am imagining this.*

He still could not fully grasp the concept of a shared imaginary realm, although he was getting used to going there and bringing others with him. Previous to his current situation, he had been the one in control. He did not like having another creature do the same to him.

The woman from the plane had never explained anything about his ability, only that she had given him a gift. She had wanted him to discover the answers himself. He wished she would have explained the situation to him, but then he recalled her words.

You don't really want me to answer all your questions do you? What's the fun of that?

Freddy was not having fun. With eyes still closed, he tried again to recall his last memory of the physical world, but the experience was like trying to remember a fading dream. Until that point, Freddy had always retained a connection to his body. He needed to retrace his steps.

He remembered landing in the desert outside of town, then entering the store with Melissa and buying the hat. Then the police chief had entered the store, and then the soldiers came, and then the old man. He also remembered the police chief exiting the store with the soldier, but that contradicted his present predicament. He had stayed with Melissa and did not go outside.

Who put me here? Why can I not return?

For the first time since acquiring his new abilities, he felt like an interloper in another person's dream, an unwelcome guest. The feeling reminded him of something the old man had said, something he could not recall.

Freddy suddenly felt foolish with his eyes closed for so long, so he decided to just follow his usual routine—manipulate the world for his benefit. Then maybe he would feel his physical body again. After opening his eyes, Freddy found himself staring at the store window.

The buildings seemed closer to each other now. In his peripheral vision, everything else looked closer too, as if the world had partially collapsed around him. Even the clouds in the sky seemed to be lower in altitude. As a test, he blinked slowly and the world became even more compact. He drew a deep breath to help calm himself.

When Freddy noticed the three people staring at him through the store window, he momentarily forgot about the collapsing world. Melissa stood on the right, the muscles in her face contorted with concern. In the middle, the police chief stood with a look of intense impatience. The only thing he wanted was for Freddy and the soldiers to leave his town.

The old man on the left was looking at Freddy with chilling indifference. He reminded Freddy of a lizard preparing to eat a cricket. While holding the old man's gaze, Freddy had an idea. He imagined his handcuffs out of existence and they immediately, and unexpectedly, disappeared. In the back of his mind, he thought he would fail. He breathed a sigh of relief.

But when he attempted to pull his hands apart, an invisible bond still held them together. The more he tried to imagine his hands free, the more tightly they were pulled together.

Freddy groaned in pain and clenched his teeth. He felt wet blood flowing from his wrists to his fingers.

"Stand still," said the soldier at his side, shaking Freddy to reinforce his point. "I'll tell you when you can move."

Before Freddy could devise his next action, he noticed the world collapsing again. The pain in his wrists fled to the back of his mind as Freddy focused on the old man in the store and then his staff. They were getting closer. His heart rate accelerated and each breath became a desperate gulp for air.

The wooden baby head on the top of the staff suddenly came to life, smiling at Freddy sweetly, but its eerie effect on him lasted only a moment. As the world continued to shrink, the store and its occupants were coming closer. When Freddy attempted to back away, the soldier grabbed the back of his neck to immobilize him, oblivious to the collapsing world around them.

"I told you to stop!"

When the shop was close enough to touch, the world suddenly stopped collapsing, and Freddy saw something big and dark step from the shelves behind the old man, a giant creature covered in black hair. When Freddy recognized the species of the beast, he drew a deep breath without exhaling.

A gorilla had appeared in the store, but Freddy was not the one who imagined the creature into existence. The soldier holding Freddy turned to the shop and stared at the intimidating beast.

"Major Summers," he said pointing at the store just a meter away. He began stepping backward and pulled Freddy along with him. "Look!"

"What the fuck!" Major Summers said, quickly exiting the front seat of the BMW and retrieving his gun, then aiming the weapon at the store window. Neither of the men seemed to notice how everything was closer together.

The old man suddenly looked confused and turned around to see what had caught the attention of those outside. When Melissa and the police chief turned, she screamed in terror and was the first to run for the exit, immediately followed by the chief. They left the store and quickly joined Freddy and the soldiers.

Major Summers stepped in front of the group protectively, holding his gun with both hands and aiming the weapon steadily at the massive gorilla.

"Stay behind me," he said, then addressed the soldier standing by Freddy. "Yu-Chi, get up here with me."

"Yes, sir."

The gorilla breathed steadily, its hairy chest rising and falling with each breath, and its long arms almost touching the floor, while its head was the same height as the old man. More curious than afraid, he faced the beast. When the gorilla opened its mouth, exposing curved, white fangs, Melissa gasped.

"Oh my God!" she said.

The next few seconds passed slowly, accentuating every detail. The gorilla stood to its full height, clenching both hands into fists and then raising them high into the air, almost touching the ceiling. When its hands came crashing down on the old man's head, he collapsed out of sight, and the universe suddenly returned to its original dimensions.

When the beast roared next, the sound of its voice filled the street with rage and the windows shook. It raised both hands again and smashed them on the ground, blood splattering on the window. The gorilla picked the man up effortlessly and then violently smashed him to the floor, spraying even more blood on the glass door and preventing everyone in the street from seeing what Freddy imagined was a bloody pile of flesh and bones.

"Mr. Cummins, no!" Melissa screamed, covering her face as the tears began to flow. She reached toward the store while the chief held her in place.

The police chief began pulling Melissa away from the scene, distancing her from Freddy and the soldiers. The violence they had just witnessed put Freddy into shock, and it was compounded by the terror of those around him.

"Shoot that thing if it leaves the store," Major Summers barked. "And aim for its head."

The silverback gorilla was now a giant shadow behind the bloody windows, standing motionless in the same spot. Other than Melissa's quiet sobbing behind them, the scene became eerily silent. After several seconds, it began moving toward the store entrance. Using both of its hands, the beast hit the door, causing an explosion of glass onto the sidewalk.

Then the shooting began and the roar of gunfire hurt Freddy's hearing. He cupped both ears with his hands and closed his eyes. With his hands against his head, Freddy realized that the bonds around his wrists had vanished. When he opened his eyes again, he saw the front of the store being shredded by bullets but none were hitting the gorilla.

With his hands finally free and the store at the correct distance, Freddy decided to test his control over the environment. Before turning his attention to the soldiers, he sent Melissa and the police chief into the city where he'd found her. He needed to determine what to do with the soldiers and how to wake up.

When he turned to see if the chief and Melissa were still behind him, they had vanished. Only the soldiers and gorilla remained. Nothing else seemed to exist in the little town.

"Hold your fire," Major Summers said, keeping his gun pointed at the beast. He quickly replaced his empty clip with one from his belt. "We need to get Freddy out of here."

After the gunfire stopped, the gorilla stepped from the shredded store entryway, crunching glass under its bare feet, then it paused on the sidewalk to look at them. The soldiers stood their ground for its first few steps toward them, but they eventually abandoned their positions. Freddy pulled away from the soldier's grasp and the sound of their footsteps faded until he could no longer hear them anymore. He was alone with the creature, and then it started walking toward him.

When the gorilla stopped a meter away and rested the back of its hands on the ground, Freddy was only slightly afraid and decided to wait. Even with all four appendages touching the floor, the creature stood high enough to stare directly into Freddy's eyes.

A low growl rumbled from deep within its chest. When the gorilla did it again, Freddy's whole body vibrated with the sound. It was oddly comforting.

"Hmmmm," it growled, extending its right arm forward. Freddy expected its black fists to smash him to the ground. But the creature just pointed to the BMW and then lumbered toward it.

"Hmmmm."

After opening the driver's door, it stepped out of the way, keeping one large hand on the top.

"Hmmmm, hmmmm."

Freddy waited several seconds before remembering to breathe.

"They're putting the chief into the helicopter," Melissa said, her hand on the car door and looking down the street where all the soldiers had gone. Wind from the rotors of the helicopter blew her hair wildly around her face. She used her other hand in a futile attempt to keep hair from her eyes. "What's going to happen to him?"

"After I leave, they will discover his real identity and let him go," Freddy said, strapping himself into the seat. Sometime in the past, a gorilla had stood in Melissa's position, but the memory seemed like a lifetime away. "Thank you for your help."

"I didn't do anything," she answered.

"You stayed with me," Freddy said and waited for her to release the door. He forced himself to focus on the present and remember all the other events as dreams. He suddenly felt pity for the people he had manipulated and hoped that his interference did not cause any harm.

"Wait a minute," she said, turning and running back into the consignment shop. When she returned, she was carrying his bag of supplies and his new hat. The wind attempted to rip it from her grasp. "Here you go. It's a nice hat."

"Thank you," he said, remembering why he had visited the town in the first place. "I will need this."

"I still can't believe you're getting away," she continued, wanting to delay his departure so she could get more information. "They're going to keep chasing you, right?"

"They cannot capture me," Freddy answered, although he felt less confident now. Another creature posing as an old man had trapped Freddy in the background. "I need to go, Melissa. Remember what I said about the shorter line."

"I will," she said reluctantly then released the door. "Good luck, Freddy."

After shutting the door and backing into the street, Freddy positioned the BMW with the soldiers behind him, then paused to watch as Major Summers entered the helicopter. Melissa stood on the sidewalk and waived, and Freddy waved back.

"Good luck to you, Melissa," he said quietly.

Without the distracting helicopter noise, Freddy noticed the absence of something pleasant and then realized what it was. The vehicle scrubbers had removed all scent from the air, and Freddy wondered if he would ever smell sagebrush again. He hoped so.

When Freddy started driving away, he noticed an old man with a black cane walking toward the shop. The cane's silver handle caught Freddy's attention first, becoming a vivid reminder of the bloody gorilla attack. As the old man approached, Freddy avoided eye contact, afraid of getting trapped again. But instead of looking up, he kept walking, his gaze fixed on the ground.

Before his confrontation with the old man, Freddy had begun to feel invincible. Now he knew that other creatures could trap and manipulate him, and they were much more skilled than he was.

THIRTY

Sadi

“I’m sure he’s fine,” Sadi said. “Remember what Taylor said last night?”

“I know,” Susan said, shifting her weight on the couch, opposite Sadi. The two women sat alone together in Sadi’s apartment. “Just because their first test flight went well, doesn’t mean this one would. But I couldn’t say no. He was very disappointed about missing the first one.”

“He’ll get over it,” Sadi said.

“I just don’t want him to get comfortable with the idea that we’re going to stay here, even for a little bit.”

“I understand how you feel,” Sadi answered, trying to sound sympathetic. “I don’t expect to return to Earth unless some miracle happens.”

“How you can be comfortable with moving here is beyond me.”

Susan smiled as sincerely as she could, but Sadi knew her well enough to see the act. Every conversation with the woman included a comment or two about returning to Earth, or what she planned to do first after getting back to her home. How would Mark handle the situation, she wondered.

If Sadi returned home, the military or whoever controlled the military would deal with her as they had dealt with Max and Gerald. Sadi could not imagine Freddy successfully making her pursuers abandon the chase.

She looked at her watch and recalled when Cesar said the test flight would end. She had another thirty minutes before Mark, Simon, and Taylor would return, just in time for dinner.

She expected another lively discussion that night and hoped the details of their experience would decrease her anxiety about the upcoming events, which included the medical evaluation, the arrival of their host, and the visit to the surface—her potential new home. Susan liked to deal with anxiety in the comfort of her living space, but Sadi had to get up and move.

"It's almost dinner time," Sadi said, standing. "According to Cesar, they should return at five. I'm going to get the girls. Want to come with me? It should make the time go by faster."

"No thanks," Susan said as Sadi stretched. "I'm going to finish my tea. I'll meet you all at dinner."

Sadi walked through the hallways toward the observatory, meeting no one on the way. As usual, she walked quickly past a certain corridor, which ended at a closed door, the only part of the space station they could not access. The same bright lights lit the forbidden hallway as all the others, but Sadi always felt a little uncomfortable there. A couple of times, Sadi dreamed about the door opening and strange creatures emerging.

When she arrived at the observatory, she found Susan's two boys and her girls working with clay at a table while one of the machines talked to them. The machine stopped talking when Sadi appeared and then hovered silently. Daryn was the first to turn from the table and smile at Sadi.

"Your Mom's here," she said, elbowing Helen in the ribs.

The children stopped working on their clay projects and looked at Sadi. As she expected, all of them began showing her what they had made. Each child had several items sitting on the table next to them, most small figurines, but Helen and Daryn had larger ones. Sadi recognized most of their creations, wild animals from Bodn and Earth. She noticed that all of the children were currently working on the same object, the giant predator bird from Bodn.

"You all are so talented," Sadi said with exaggerated emphasis for the younger boys. "What's that called you're working on now?"

"The Solka," Harvey said, Susan's oldest boy. "It can crush a bear's skull with its claws."

"Old-One-Eye was just telling us about it," explained Daryn, pointing to the wall ahead of them to a rotating, three-dimensional image of the bird. Her eyes widened in admiration and awe at the giant white bird with spotted wings and a black beak. "She was giving us a lesson on Solkas while we try to replicate one."

"Yeah," said the younger boy, George, holding up his lump of clay for her to see. Sadi barely recognized the beak and wings, much less distinct than the other children's clay creations. "They're the top predator on land."

"Scary! I hope we don't run into one of those," Sadi said with fake alarm but then wondered if she would ever need to worry about them. "It's about dinner time. Are you almost finished?"

"Almost," said Helen while working on the body of her bird. She had created the most detailed one of them all. "We had a question first. What do you think about evolution?"

"What?" Sadi asked. "Why do you ask that?"

"Helen asked Old-One-Eye what the Solka evolved from," Daryn interjected. "She said they didn't evolve from anything. The host created them."

"Then I asked if anything here evolved like they did on Earth," Helen finished. "She said to ask you about that because of religion."

"What do you mean, Old-One-Eye?" Sadi asked, turning to the machine. She always felt silly addressing it by that name, but the children expected it.

"We only teach verifiable information, as originally requested," it said in the usual female voice. "Parents reserve the right to teach non-verifiable information, such as evolution, a subset of religion."

"A subset of religion?" Sadi asked with squinted eyes. The machine did not immediately respond, allowing Sadi more time for thought. She would have to think about that more later but admitted for the interim that religion was unverifiable, a concept similar to faith. "How can that be verifiable? Telling them that our host created those birds."

"She can create one for you," Old-One-Eye said. "Then you can see for yourself."

"Is she a god?" Sadi asked without thinking.

"According to some definitions," the machine answered without moving. "I don't know your definition, so I cannot answer that exactly."

"Can she make Jacob?" Helen asked with excitement, looking up at her mother.

Sadi's pulse accelerated and her throat suddenly constricted.

"No," she answered before the machine could respond. She did not want to hear the machine answer. "No, she can't."

"Why not?"

"Stop it, Helen," Sadi said with more anger than she had intended.

She was tempted to tell Old-One-Eye to stop teaching the children about the creation of life but then wondered what that demand would imply. She also did not want to generate any further questions for the children. For the time being, Sadi would change the subject and attempt to stop thinking about Helen's question.

"What other subjects are reserved for the parents?"

"All non-verifiable information and anything you specifically request," it answered. "For example, we have taught a lesson on how to examine historical data, as you already know, but not what conclusions to make from the data."

"How much do you know about the history of Earth?" she asked, genuinely curious. The question about Jacob began to fade.

"We have only limited information about Earth's history, as it pertains to humans, which is what you probably meant. Information about your historical records is full of inconsistencies and lacks suffi-cient supporting evidence, so we will not teach that. For some reason, the children have not asked many questions about history, so this has not been an issue."

"My history classes were so boring," Sadi began, sneering at the memory. "I don't blame them. From what the kids have told me, you don't teach a lot of what they were taught."

"Your children believe in many concepts not included in our data sets, things we suspect are human fabrications. We will only teach what is observable and verifiable. For example, in our astronomy les-son, the children became upset when we did not verify the existence of black holes, which have never been observed."

"They don't know about black holes," Helen said, laughing then turning to the machine. "Sorry, Old-One-Eye. You don't know every-thing."

"No one knows everything, Helen," Sadi said after another glance at her watch. "We should go to dinner. Dominga and Cesar are cook-ing tonight, and we shouldn't be late. Come on, boys, your father should be back very soon."

"Before you go," Old-One-Eye said to the children, "cover your birds with the wet cloth so they won't dry."

THIRTY-ONE

Freddy

Freddy aligned the BMW's trajectory with the rotation of Earth, eighty kilometers over his destination—22.0 degrees North, 19.2 degrees East—on the north side of the Libya-Chad border. The arid yet beautiful Sahara Desert stretched below him.

When the probe appeared in his view through the passenger side window, Freddy felt no surprise. He had sensed the object's presence before the reflected sunlight even caught his notice. After leaving Mountainair, New Mexico, Freddy had expected a visit. He wanted more information.

"It is safe to descend," the female voice said and Freddy suddenly recognized who the probe was mimicking—Audrie Garner.

"Am I being tracked?" he asked while Audrie's face floated in his memory.

During his last conversation with the probe, it had used the same voice. Why had he not recognized it? He suddenly wanted to see her again.

"They lost track of you in North America," it said. "They don't know where you are and will not be able to find you."

"Before I go," he began, then paused for the right words to continue, "can you tell me more about what happened back there?"

"I don't know what happened. If you tell me some details, maybe I can help."

"Okay. Everything was going as I planned, but then I could not find my way back to reality. Another person trapped me in the background, I think. Then a giant gorilla saved me, and I did not plan that either. It was all very strange."

"It looks like her friend has finally noticed you."

"Her friend?" Freddy asked, suddenly feeling a chill. "This thing was not friendly."

"I'm not allowed to explain the situation," she answered. "You would not understand anyway. If you want to save your friends, you should hurry to the surface."

Freddy almost asked about the identity of the friend or what to expect on the surface, but he knew the probe would keep the information from him. In the following silence, Freddy began to worry about remaining in one place for too long.

"Will you be accompanying me any further?" he asked.

"I will guide the vehicle to the proper location," she answered and Freddy felt the BMW reorienting vertically so he could see Earth through the windshield. "Then you are on your own."

Freddy took a deep breath and initiated the descent. The probe remained in his view for the first few seconds then disappeared. As the engines increased in power, the support of his mass slowly transferred from the straps to his seat, and he felt as though gravity had flipped and was now pulling him away from Earth. Descending vertically was not his usual orientation.

As Freddy descended, the large geological feature directly below him became more distinct, an elliptical area about 10 kilometers wide, slightly wider in the East-West direction.

"Is that a caldera?" he asked, not expecting an answer. Large rocky hills formed the most distinct border on the Southeast side and smaller hills formed the rest of the boundary. The whole area reminded him of a giant eye. To the Southwest, he noticed an isolated mountain that the map program called Bikku Bitti.

When close enough to notice the color of the river beds, he wondered if water still flowed through them. Their lack of water soon became apparent and reminded him of the location, one of the driest places on Earth. A large number of ancient river beds wound their way through the entire area and almost all of them were filled with a vibrant blue material. Freddy was excited to explore the area, momentarily forgetting about his vision of the pit.

During the final seconds of his journey, the aerial view became burned in his memory. The navigation program directed the BMW toward an area just south of the caldera center, bounded on the West by a curved portion of a river bed and on the East by massive rocks at the top of a large hill.

Before landing, he reoriented to a horizontal position relative to the earth and stopped at five meters above the ground. He quickly surveyed the area and then landed the BMW in the shade of a large rock jutting from the earth.

While Freddy unstrapped himself from the seat, he inspected the dashboard monitors to verify the normal operation of all the systems and to check the outside temperature. The 29.7C reading surprised him. Freddy had expected the desert to be hotter, especially at three pm in the afternoon. But after considering the season, the weather for October in the northern hemisphere seemed reasonable.

Taking his first step in the desert of southern Libya reminded Freddy of the moon landing videos from NASA but without thick dust covering everything. He placed the hat on his head and began viewing the entire area. The hat blocked the sun, but he still needed to squint heavily due to the brightness. He immediately noticed the absence of vegetation, seeing only rock, sand, and the blue river bed about 50 meters away.

Freddy retrieved his backpack from the passenger seat, the water bottles and flashlight making the bag slightly heavy. While swinging it over his left shoulder, Freddy heard water sloshing and wondered how quickly the water would disappear into the ground if he spilled any.

He inhaled the warm, dry air but failed to identify the distinct scent. With the absence of plants, he had expected to smell nothing, but he could only describe the smell as *dusty*.

"So this is how dirt smells," he said quietly, "after being baked by ultraviolet radiation for thousands of years."

Although the landscape looked completely barren and the sterile air was devoid of life, Freddy felt the absence of other humans the most. He had never felt more isolated, not even in the void of space. The realization left Freddy feeling invigorated. Isolation filled his mind like the warm air filled his lungs.

After quickly surveying the entire area, Freddy returned his attention to the giant cluster of rocks higher up the hill. He knew the pit lay up there somewhere. He drew a deep breath, preparing to start climbing, but then looked down to the river and decided to walk there first.

"Just one more detour," he said.

At the bottom of the hill, Freddy stood on the ancient river shore and looked across to the other side, maybe forty meters away. He closed his eyes and imagined the time when water had flowed past his location. After about thirty seconds, he opened his eyes again. When he looked back at the dirt and rocks in the riverbed, they looked less blue than he remembered from the view high above.

"Probably copper sulfate, slightly hydrated," he said.

For the next five minutes, he stood there and tried to imagine people coming to the river to fish, get a drink, or just play in the water. He was tempted to close his eyes again and create the scene in his mind, but he sighed and decided to continue with his next task. On his climb back up the hill, Freddy passed the BMW again and only a few minutes later, he found the hut from his vision.

When he first noticed the small structure, his heart rate almost doubled in frequency and he had to stop, fear suddenly immobilizing his legs. Freddy continued walking slowly until he stood three meters away from the entrance. Although it was dark inside, Freddy could clearly see the interior of the ancient habitation.

"No snake," he said, chuckling. He stepped to the door and considered entering, but the structure seemed too insecure, and he also felt like an intruder in a place potentially sacred to some people.

"Not so menacing," he said, "in the real world."

With his heart pumping faster, he continued climbing the hill until he found the pit. He stopped at the edge and looked down. The hole looked similar to what he saw in his vision, except the opening in the earth looked more like a large crack than a circular pit.

The bottom was concealed in shadow, reminding Freddy that real snakes liked to hide in the dark, but he could not imagine a snake surviving in this place. He saw no source of food, no life. He inhaled deeply and began his next descent. The jagged rocks in the walls would make the climb easy.

THIRTY-TWO

Freddy

As Freddy descended into the hole, his eyes adjusted to the lower light level and he could see the bottom, no snakes. After about a minute of climbing, he reached the bottom, stepping onto cool sand in front of a wide hole in the wall, which extended from the floor to his hips. The bottom of the pit was quieter than the top, eerily quiet. Even the sound of the breeze had vanished. He glanced up at the sky and noticed a solitary cloud against a dark blue, then he turned to the opening in the wall.

He could see for almost a meter before the tunnel became completely dark, so he retrieved the flashlight from his backpack. While taking a drink of water and then shining the light into the tunnel, his feeling of unease dissipated a little when all he saw was more rock. The eerie silence was another indication of safety.

"This is for you, Sadi," he said, kneeling in the sand and removing his hat. He would leave it at the entrance. With the flashlight beam aimed forward, he entered the tunnel. "Remember, Freddy. You are invincible."

Freddy crawled through the narrow tunnel, moving forward on his elbows against the rough rock. He soon wished he'd worn a long sleeve shirt, and pants instead of shorts. His elbows and knees were covered in scratches and some were bleeding. After several minutes of crawling, he entered a large cavern, stood on his feet, and wiped the dust from his arms and legs. His imagination filled every shadow with a monster, but he could not sense any, thankfully.

Freddy stretched, inhaling deeply, then noticed the moisture in the air and the lower temperature, a comfortable 20C according to his watch. The silence almost hurt his ears, and he could hear his heart beating. He shined his flashlight at the far wall in front of him, maybe sixty meters away, but at such a distance, his flashlight could illuminate only a portion of the wall.

The floor sloped down to his right. Just three steps away from his current position would mean a painful death falling down the jagged stone wall. With his heart racing even harder, Freddy took a couple of steps away from the ledge. The ground sloped upward to his left, leading to the ceiling of the large cavern. There were openings where the floor met the ceiling, large enough for him to enter, but he had the impression they led nowhere. Walking forward on the sloped floor seemed like the right thing to do. It generally remained level.

Before moving forward, Freddy suddenly wished he could share the experience with someone. Sadi's little girls would have loved it, Helen at least. Although Mr. Smith could not have made the journey into the hole and through the short tunnel, he would have loved it too. If possible, he would return with the girls someday, and take some pictures.

If I ever get out of here again.

When he reached the far end of the room, he was surprised to find a rectangular opening carved into the rock wall, half a meter taller than Freddy. The opening had rounded corners and smooth surfaces. A closer inspection with his flashlight and fingers revealed small grooves covering the entire surface. One possible method of creating the opening, Freddy could imagine, was scanning the surface with a laser beam, vaporizing the rock away one layer at a time.

He shined the flashlight into the opening and squinted to see better. After a few meters, the short tunnel turned to the right at what looked like a 90-degree angle. Before stepping inside, he shined the flashlight directly at the ground to double-check that there was a ground. The floor had the same grooves as the walls and ceiling.

Freddy still could not feel the presence of other creatures, so he took another deep breath and walked into the tunnel. After turning the corner, he found a jumble of shiny metal appendages connected to two rectangular metal boxes on the floor. The shiny pieces of metal scattered his flashlight beam all over the grooved rock walls.

After a few seconds, the bundle of metal appendages began moving, and Freddy remembered his visit to the facility orbiting the alien planet. He waited patiently, and unafraid, as the machine reconfigured itself and then stood erect on two metal legs, resembling a pair of crutches.

It began walking away from Freddy toward the end of the short hallway. As its metal appendages hit the stone floor, the soft and rhythmic clicking noise helped Freddy feel more at peace. Although he felt no life from the machine, the vibrations in the air made the place feel alive.

How long had the machine been waiting on the floor, Freddy wondered.

While shining the flashlight ahead of him, he quietly followed and felt better about walking on the smooth ground. In the large cavern, he had watched his steps carefully or he would have fallen.

The machine stopped at a bare stone wall and appeared frozen for a few seconds. During the pause, Freddy wondered what would happen next and then began to feel a little nervous. He felt like an actor waiting for the signal to enter the stage.

"What now?" Freddy asked.

While Freddy inspected the wall with his flashlight, the machine stepped to the side of the hall and extended a long metal arm to the stone wall in front of him. Three metal fingers at the end of the arm separated themselves at 120-degree angles and then almost touched the stone. The fingers began to vibrate, becoming a steady hum, and then the wall began to swing open.

When the hidden door opened completely, the machine backed against the wall to give Freddy room to pass. He waited only a moment before stepping past the suddenly motionless object and stopping at the top of a steep staircase, which descended into another dark tunnel. When he pointed the flashlight down, he could not see the bottom.

While staring into the darkness, the humming began again. Freddy turned around and watched as the machine slowly pulled the door shut behind them. The flashlight beam's reflection from the metal cast sharp-angled light on the tunnel walls. Freddy turned and drew a deep breath before walking carefully down the stairs with the machine following. The sound of its metal appendages on the steps quickly became hypnotic, making the experience dreamlike.

During the long descent, Freddy wondered who had constructed the stairs and how they disposed of the debris. He saw no loose rocks, not even dust. For such a long tunnel, he expected to see piles of rubble somewhere. He did encounter fissures in the walls and ceiling, some extending deeper than his flashlight could completely illuminate. After a while, his thoughts shifted from the tunnel to its destination. He also had to keep his arms folded across his chest due to the decreasing temperature.

He eventually reached the bottom to find another short tunnel ending at a bare wall again. He had descended hundreds of meters and suddenly felt even more isolated from the outside world. The Sahara Desert far above seemed a different world now, as far away as Mercury. After his momentary reverie, he stepped aside and let the machine move past him. In the same manner, as before, it opened the next hidden stone door, leading into a rectangular room twenty meters wide and already illuminated with a soft light.

When Freddy entered, he looked up at the lights in the low ceiling, several glowing white crystals embedded in the stone. Freddy immediately wondered what gave them power. They seemed electrically isolated from each other. He wanted to inspect the lights, but the machine kept moving forward. Freddy followed, feeling like an obedient puppy.

They approached two metallic boxes sitting on large blocks next to the wall. One was the shape and size of a coffin, the other only half as long but both were high enough to reach Freddy's chin. After stopping a few meters away, Freddy noticed another object between the boxes, perched on a thick stone pedestal and humming with energy. It was a black sphere, the size of a basketball, cut in half, with the flat part on top polished and reflecting the lights from the ceiling. A tiny green dot pulsated in the center.

The machine placed its three-fingered appendage over the green dot and swiped to the left. While flying to the edge of the circle, the green dot expanded to the size of a fist. Freddy stared in wonder at the beautiful object until the smaller box to his left began to open.

The stone lid swung open and rested softly against the wall. For several seconds, Freddy was paralyzed with fear. He knew the machine wanted him to approach the box and look inside. After taking a deep breath, he attempted to use his ability to sense life in the box but could not.

"You want me to look inside?" Freddy asked. He was hoping for more information, something to help prepare him for what he would see. The machine waited silently.

Freddy stepped to the box, looked inside, and was instantly confused. He never expected to see a large black bird lying motionless on a soft white bed. For the next several seconds, he stared at the creature. Upon closer inspection, he noticed the rise and fall of its breast, and the small tubes in its body. When the black eyes opened, Freddy jolted and so did the bird.

The creature stood on its feet, and Freddy stepped back. After shaking all the tubes away, the bird squawked loudly, hopping onto the edge of the box. It glanced around the room, emitted a low gurgling noise as if clearing its throat, and then slowly turned toward Freddy.

"Freddy," the bird said in a high-pitched voice, extending its beak forward. "Hello."

"Hi..." Freddy said tentatively.

"Who am I?" it said. "Who am I?"

"Do I know you?"

"Yes," it said and the feathers around its neck ruffled. "Need to find me. I fly."

Before Freddy could respond, the bird leaped off the box and began flying around the large room, rather clumsily Freddy thought. As the bird circled him, the movement of air gently brushed his face, and the harsh sound of flapping wings filled the room with life.

"Fun," it said while flying behind him, and then all around the room. "Fun, fun, fun, fun."

THIRTY-THREE

Sadi

Dominga and Cesar cooked the meal that night, cheese enchiladas, and some without tomatoes for the kids. All the children professed to hate tomatoes, even Daryn who usually ate whatever they provided. Sadi loved it when Dominga and Cesar cooked. Sadi liked cooking for herself and the girls but felt some anxiety preparing the meal for the entire group. She helped Dominga grind the corn for the tortillas and then she showed Sadi and Susan how to make them.

Except for dairy products provided by the machines, they grew all of their food in the huge greenhouse. According to the machines, the cheese, milk, and butter came from an animal similar to cows that lived on the planet. The dairy products tasted the same, and maybe even a little better. At first, Sadi was uncomfortable eating the dairy foods, due to an instinctive distrust of the alien machines. But after no one became ill or dropped dead, she felt safe to eat all of their food and allow her girls to stay in their care.

Sadi loved to visit the greenhouse. In their artificial atmosphere several hundred kilometers above the planet, seeing familiar plants helped restore a sense of normalcy. Even though the dirt in the green-house came from the alien planet, Bodn, seeing and touching it offered another comfort. During their first few days on the station, the machines answered their questions about the origin of the seeds. The probe had brought them from Earth.

For their entire stay on the station, food preparation helped to pass the time and became therapeutic to Sadi from all the trauma she had experienced on Earth. Although food preparation required a lot of their time, Sadi could not remember when food had satisfied her as much. They did not eat any meat and Sadi soon forgot about having that as an option. Only when she had overheard Simon and Cesar discussing a possible hunting trip on the planet did she think about eating meat again.

Ten minutes after the rest of the group had begun eating, Mark, Taylor, and Simon entered the dining hall. They shared their experience of flying the upgraded spacecraft and talked excitedly about flying into the atmosphere and under the clouds, farther than their first practice session the previous day. Sadi enjoyed listening to them, but she began to worry about all of the upcoming events—the visit to the planet, the medical examination the following morning, and then the arrival of their host the next day.

"Can we go back and finish our birds?" Daryn asked from Sadi's right, next to Helen. Both girls looked up at her expectedly.

"That's fine," Sadi answered. "Remember to stick together, and bedtime is nine thirty tonight. No staying up."

Without any complaint, Daryn led Helen and the boys from the room. Sadi and Susan watched them go, then returned to the conversation about the test flight and what Taylor, Simon, and Mark had seen of Bodn. While listening, their excitement began to replace her anxiety and she hoped Susan felt the same. Sadi highly anticipated feeling the solid ground under her feet again with the sky above her head.

Sadi spent that night waking from dreams and then returning to sleep. Many dreams involved their visit to Bodn, some pleasant, some disturbing. In one dream, they hiked to a lake in the mountains while giant birds flew overhead, trying to snatch the children. Only Sadi had acted concerned about the situation and fought the birds.

After the most disturbing dream, Sadi got out of bed for a drink of water and then checked on the girls in their rooms. As she fell asleep again, the dream lingered for the remainder of the night.

Sadi was a fish in a warm, dark fluid. After swimming for a long time in darkness, she saw a light in the distance and moved toward it. When close enough, she recognized the object as a giant sphere. A transparent membrane surrounded a baby, glowing and curled in the fetal position. Although the thick membrane was only semi-transparent, Sadi instantly recognized her son, Jacob. His glow provided the only light in the liquid universe.

Sadi swam all over the surface of the sphere in a futile attempt to find an opening or weak point in the surface. After a while, small bursts of light began exploding all over the membrane surface, each burst leaving a thin trail of light, which quickly dissipated and reminded Sadi of shooting stars. The lights frightened her, so she swam away from the object and watched from a distance.

As the impact frequency increased, Sadi began to worry. One of the meteors might rupture the membrane and hurt her son. But she could only watch. Over time, the meteors grew in size, and each impact sent a shock wave traveling through the liquid.

Eventually, the membrane began to tear, revealing an even more intense light within the sphere. When a large meteor ruptured it, the brilliant light blinded Sadi. When she opened her eyes, she found herself in bed and turned toward the artificial window, the light of Dzalm shining over Bodn's horizon.

All thirteen refugees ate a quick breakfast together and discussed the upcoming medical examination. Cesar wanted Sadi to take the lead due to her professional and educational background and should make the final decision if any disagreement arose between them. After everyone agreed, Sadi experienced some additional anxiety, but she felt confident since no one else had any background in biology. After the short discussion, Sadi knocked on the wall to call the machines.

One of the machines came and led the group to a room connected to the observatory, through an entrance Sadi had never noticed. Only after the door began to slide open did she notice the edges on the smooth surface of the wall. Were there any other hidden entrances, she wondered.

"Did you know that door was there?" Sadi asked Helen.

"No," she answered, watching the machine.

Helen showed no concern, just the same excitement as the other children. Sadi had expected to see signs of fear in anticipation of a medical examination.

"The kids probably wouldn't be scared even if Old-One-Eye was holding a syringe," Sadi said, turning to Susan.

"That's Miss Poofie," Helen interjected.

"They trust the machines," Susan said sarcastically, "more than they trust us."

After the door slid open, their machine guide, Miss Poofie, floated into the new room. Simon entered first with Max, followed by Cesar, Dominga, Taylor, and Gerald. Susan and Mark entered last with their two boys, after Sadi and her girls. Sadi first noticed the other machine waiting for them, hovering before a wall of open cupboards and small machines on a bench.

She recognized only one set of objects, syringes and vials, on a shiny metal counter. Several other objects she did not recognize sat next to them. Everything looked clean and orderly. On the right of the bench was a small room, enclosed by glass walls with an examination table inside and large enough for a single person. The glass walls had small metal boxes attached to them, forming a grid with about three centimeters separating each one.

"Bodn has very unique biological populations," one of the machines said after the group had formed a semi-circle around them. "As you can probably guess, any ecological system is very sensitive to foreign invaders and must be protected from such. Before you can travel to the planet, you will be cleansed."

"Cleansed from what?" asked Mark's oldest boy. "Do you mean we have to take a bath?"

The machine turned to him before answering.

"You're full of bugs."

Helen squeezed her mother's hand more tightly, but no one immediately responded. Until that point, Sadi had felt a bit excited to see how the medical examinations would proceed. The room reminded Sadi of her lab at Pantra and her friend, Zoya, which brought an unexpected nostalgia.

Although Sadi was shocked to hear about bugs, she was even more surprised that none of the children acted disturbed. Henry, Susan's oldest, just smiled and looked at his younger brother who returned the gesture. Susan turned to her, eyes narrowed suspiciously.

"Do you mean parasites?" Sadi asked the machine. "Bacteria?"

"Mostly parasites," it responded. "Once we remove them, your body can eliminate some of the foreign bacteria."

"How do you know we have parasites?" Taylor asked.

"We have detected them in your waste products," it responded, and Sadi had difficulty determining which machine answered. Both machines stood too close together.

"Gross," Helen said loud enough for everyone to hear. Many members of the group smiled, but only Dominga laughed audibly.

"And we all are infected?" Dominga asked, her smile vanishing.

"Yes," it answered. "Some of you more than others, but don't feel bad. This is a common consequence of a diet high in toxins and other factors, which we can discuss at another time. While on the station, your condition has improved, but not sufficiently."

"I want to see the data you've collected," Sadi said, attempting to mimic the tone of a polite demand. She wondered how well the machines detected tone.

"Of course," it responded. "We can share all of your data, but this morning, we need to get some additional biological samples before we determine your treatment."

"I can wait," Sadi answered. "What samples do you need?"

For the next forty minutes, Sadi followed their instructions and collected a sample of saliva and blood from each person. She first acquired a single capillary collection tube of blood and was surprised to learn that they did not need a larger quantity for analysis. Only Susan's youngest boy complained. His mother held him in her lap while Sadi pricked his finger and Daryn told him the pain would only last a moment. Sadi inserted each sample into a small instrument on the table and had to wait less than a minute for the results. She used a different instrument to analyze the saliva.

"How much time do you need to review the data?" Sadi asked.

"We have already made the necessary determinations from the data," they answered directly. "We require a sonic analysis next."

"Is that what the room is for?" Sadi asked, pointing to the examination table inside the glass enclosure.

"Yes," they answered, then continued before Sadi or anyone else could respond. "The procedure is painless and lasts about a minute. Who will go first?"

No one responded immediately and the room filled with an uncomfortable silence. Sadi did not want to go first and felt a sudden urge to get between her girls and the enclosure. During the biological sample collection procedure, she had felt confident about the examination, but the mysterious sonic analysis frightened her. Susan put a hand on each of her son's shoulders and pulled them close to her.

"I'll go first," Gerald said, taking two steps toward the enclosure and then looking at Sadi. "Sonic is just sound waves, right?"

THIRTY-FOUR

Freddy

"Where have we met?" Freddy asked, hoping for a clue. He failed to recognize its identity, but he did feel its living presence.

"Not human," it said while still in flight, each word separated as though its own sentence. "Won't find human."

Freddy focused his attention on the black half-sphere between the boxes, and the green dot in the glass surface. The small dot had returned to the center, pulsating. While staring at the tiny light, he imagined the scene from a different perspective. Freddy saw himself and the open stone door on the other side of the cavern, and then the flying black bird. After the experience in New Mexico, his imagination seemed more real, as though he existed in multiple places, simultaneously.

"Good," the bird said while making another complete revolution. "Good, good, good."

The creature returned to its box, successfully grasping the edge of the stone with its claws. But instead of landing gracefully, momentum carried it into the box again. Freddy laughed as the bird squawked inside the box, out of his view.

"Ahhh, ahhh, ahhh!"

A few seconds later, the bird hopped back onto the edge of the box, wings flapping for balance. After steadying itself, the black wings folded to its side again and Freddy suddenly recalled his visit to the station orbiting the alien planet. He had met the creature there.

"Dod," he said, smiling. "You are a bird? How did you get here?"

"Yes. I am Dod," the bird said with obvious pleasure. "Hungry."

During the following silence, the machine began to move again, walking to the open box where Dod was perched. The machine retrieved a smaller box from inside the larger one and extended the open container to Dod who dipped her head inside and grasped a large pellet with her beak. She raised her black head and the pellet disappeared down her throat.

"I am raven," she said after swallowing the pellet. "Got permission."

"Permission for what?"

"Sorry, small bird brain," she began, then quickly dipped her head. "Wanted to witness, cheer you up. Probe brought bird. Modified brain. Practiced speaking. Speech good?"

"You are very good at speaking," Freddy said, trying to sound congratulatory, then he paused to contemplate her other short phrases. "So, the probe modified the brain of the raven so you could use it?"

"Yes," she answered, then plucked another food pellet from the box still held in front of her. She continued after swallowing. "Ravens are smart. Easy to tune."

The machine stood motionless and Freddy imagined it as a post-modern piece of furniture. He smiled, remembering how much Mr. Smith hated anything resembling post-modern. Freddy prepared to ask more about the brain modification.

"Questions later," Dod said, interrupting his thoughts.

"Okay, so what next?"

"Open," Dod answered, pointing her beak at the larger box. "I fly. Nice bird, flying relieves stress."

Before leaping from her perch into the air again, Dod retrieved another food pellet. The machine kept the box of food motionless while extending another appendage to the half-sphere on the pedestal. One of its metal fingers swiped the green dot to the right and Freddy saw the larger stone box lid begin to rise, his heart rate rising along with it.

Freddy tried again to feel for any sign of life but failed. The scene reminded him of a vampire movie when some young girl in a trance had opened the coffin of Count Dracula. He half-expected to see a body rise out of it. When Freddy took his first step, he heard Dod fly from the room and the harsh sound of her flapping wings faded. In the silence, the room felt like a crypt.

The short journey to the open stone box seemed like a dream, and when he looked down at the contents, he forgot about Dod. He forgot about his location deep under the Sahara Desert. When he recognized the sleeping child, all conscious thought vanished.

At the moment of recognition, all of his unpleasant childhood memories merged with the present. Freddy had spent much of his adult life burying those unpleasant memories. Now his nine-year-old body had returned to haunt him.

"Disturbing?" the raven asked.

Freddy jumped in surprise at the sound but remained motionless, staring at the small body. Without his notice, Dod had hopped across the floor and now stood next to him. With a single flap of her wings, she hopped from the ground to the edge of the box. Dod turned toward Freddy and looked inside the box with her right eye. For several seconds, they stared silently at the body.

"Is this me?" Freddy asked finally, holding onto the edge of the box and fighting waves of nausea. "Why would you do this?"

"Can only reach destination," Dod answered, "as child."

Freddy understood what Dod and the woman from the plane expected, but his rational mind refused to accept the challenge. They wanted Freddy to control the body of the child and see through his eyes. He considered the option of running back to the BMW.

I cannot be a child again.

"Too disturbing?" Dod asked and the feathers under her neck rippled. "You are adult now. Body does not matter. This is gift!"

Freddy turned away from the sleeping child and looked at the large raven next to him. While her words replayed in his mind, he concentrated on breathing. He still wanted to run away.

"What exactly do you want me to do?" he asked.

"Take child on final descent," Dod said. "Body tuned to you."

"I have to go deeper?" Freddy asked incredulously.

"Yes, tunnel." Dod dipped her head again in one graceful swoop, reminding Freddy of a wild bird. "Almost finished, almost finished, wake first!"

"You mean, wake up as the child?"

"I will help," Dod answered. "Imagine cavern first. Close eyes if needed."

"I can do it with my eyes open," Freddy said, afraid of what he might find in the dark.

"It's different," she said, "when so far down."

Freddy was tempted to ask what she meant, especially about how their depth in the earth affected the situation, but he was sick of asking questions. They all led to more questions and he just wanted to finish whatever he had to do.

He drew another breath as if preparing for a deep dive underwater. Then he closed his eyes. For the first few seconds, Freddy heard nothing and saw nothing. He felt only the beating of his heart.

"Create the cavern," Dod said, her voice echoing all around Freddy. "Yes, good, walk to box. Look inside."

"I am looking," Freddy said, exhaling slowly. He had imagined walking to the box and looking down. The cavern seemed darker in his imagination, in the background. "I do not see the child."

"What is inside?" Dod asked.

"I see nothing."

"Not what you see," Dod scolded. "What inside box?"

"Only darkness."

"Inside is water," Dod said flatly.

"A whirlpool," Freddy said in sudden panic, seeing dark water below him as if it were a vast ocean. He wanted to move away from the box. The whirlpool frightened him. He imagined holding onto the edges and seeing the white skin of his hands.

"Just breathe," Dod said and briefly paused. "Good, now reach inside water and place hand on child's forehead."

"Not yet," Freddy said. He felt sweat forming on his own forehead.

"Do it," Dod screeched and then squawked like a wild raven again. "Ahhh, ahhh!"

Freddy reached into the water and expected the whirlpool to pull him into a suffocating darkness, but he felt a warm forehead instead. At the moment of contact, Freddy felt a large hand touch his forehead. Although he expected the hand to exist only in his imagination, he reached out of the box and grasped his adult wrist.

"Good good," Dod said. "Now open eyes."

Freddy opened his eyes and discovered two different scenes, the cavern ceiling with his adult head staring down at him, and a child lying inside the box with his adult hand on the forehead. He was paralyzed, seeing the physical world from two perspectives, two brains separately interpreting the data from two pairs of eyes. He did not know what to do first.

Dod stood on the edge of the box, balancing awkwardly and her head swiveling side to side as a normal bird. Freddy did not know how to remove his hand from the child's forehead and simultaneously release his adult arm. Adult-Freddy managed to look away from the child's face and blond hair to examine the rest of the small body. The child wore a plain sand-colored shirt and slightly darker pants woven from thick thread. The same material covered his feet.

"Just let go," Dod said while hopping on the side of the box toward the child's feet, "one at a time."

From inside the box, Freddy turned his child's head and watched the bird hop toward his feet. While holding his breath, Freddy slowly released the adult's arm and then removed his adult hand from the child's forehead.

"This is extremely disorienting," two mouths said in unison. The voices reminded Freddy of a cult ritual where everyone repeated the lead narcissist.

"Let me help," Dod said, then dipped her head into the box and gently pecked the child's right foot. "Now answer, Child-Freddy. Feel that?"

She pecked again.

"Yes, I feel it," Freddy said with the child's voice. The nine-year-old sounded like a stranger to his adult ears and failed to recall unpleasant memories of his childhood. Instead, the voice reminded Freddy of how much he missed Helen and Daryn.

"Practice time," said Dod, "just a bit, just a bit."

—※—

For the next ten minutes, Freddy alternated controlling his child and adult bodies. Initially, he could do only one at a time, but the trick took only a few minutes to master. He focused first on sensory input, then control was easy. He thought of the situation as a physical therapy session, not as an extremely disturbing transcendental experience.

"I am both now," Adult-Freddy said after Child-Freddy had climbed from the box. He no longer felt a preferential connection to either body. He felt the same connection to each, but he preferred to speak as the adult. "Will I be like this forever? Did she want this all along?"

"Exist outside the body," Dod said from her perch at the end of the box. "Easy to see. Ha! Time to go, you both."

The motionless machine suddenly became animated again. While holding Dod's food box steady, it walked between the adult and the child, arriving at a smooth part of the rock wall. It opened another hidden door and Freddy enjoyed listening to the hum of the machine's fingers. The frequency sounded more pure and beautiful through the ears of the child.

On the other side of the door, he saw only darkness, so Adult-Freddy removed the flashlight from his backpack and stepped to the entrance with Child-Freddy. With four eyes, he stared into the large open cavern, shining the flashlight on the ceiling far above and then the ground immediately before them. The eyes of the child saw much farther and with exceptionally more detail than the adult, more even than Freddy remembered as a child. He wondered if the body was more advanced.

When he saw the edge of the cliff about five meters ahead, a sudden chill sent shivers through his adult body. He focused the flashlight beam on the other side of the chasm, on another rock wall maybe forty meters away. The raven suddenly landed on his adult shoulder, her claws digging into his skin as she fought for balance. Her weight surprised him almost as much as the sudden intrusion.

"Light," she said with a turn of her head.

For a brief moment, Freddy wondered if Dod expected him to reply, but the machine extended its appendage to the ceiling and pulled one of the glowing stones from the rock. After it placed the stone in the hand of Child-Freddy, the cool surface surprised him and reminded him of an opal. He thought it would be warm.

"Where do we go?" Adult-Freddy asked while Child-Freddy rubbed the smooth stone.

"Down," she answered, flying from his shoulder and landing on the machine. "Step careful."

The child followed the adult through the door while Dod and the machine stayed behind. The ground was smooth and devoid of loose rock. When they reached the edge of the chasm, Freddy noticed stairs carved into the rock on the right.

Before his descent, the child looked back at the entrance where Dod sat perched on the machine. The raven raised her head and squawked twice, bird echoes filling the cavern. The child and adult drew deep breaths together and then turned back to the stairs.

"Hungry," Dod said from the doorway. "Ahhhh! Ahhhh!"

The adult Freddy took his first step down and the child followed.

THIRTY-FIVE

Sadi

The closest machine to Sadi floated to the enclosure and then waited for Gerald to reach the room. After a soft click, the glass door swung slowly open, but instead of entering, Gerald turned and asked if he needed to remove his shoes or wear a gown.

"Just lie on the table," they said and waited for him to obey.

After the door closed, everyone watched as Gerald reclined on the table. Helen and Daryn joined Sadi at the glass door for a closer look.

"What exactly are you doing?" Sadi asked.

Before the machine answered, she heard a high-pitched hum through the door. Gerald remained on his back, motionless and staring straight at the ceiling. The noise stopped about a minute later, and then Sadi heard a muffled voice from inside the enclosure, probably instructing Gerald to exit, she guessed. He slowly stood from the bed and opened the door.

"He's not dead," Taylor said from behind Sadi, and Mark's oldest boy laughed.

"Did you feel anything?" Sadi asked, trying not to smile at Taylor's quip.

"The table felt like it was filled with liquid, and there was a slight vibration from it," Gerald said. "I also heard high-pitched humming from the walls, but no pain."

"The wave amplitudes of the first scan were intended only for imaging and to determine organism resonance," the machine said.

"So are you saying that the parasites can be killed by finding their resonant frequency?" Sadi asked, squinting. "What if a species has the same resonance as our tissues?"

"Yes, to answer your first question," it said. "Most of the foreign organisms can be killed in this manner. And if a particular species shares the same resonance with your tissue, a different modulation program will be used. But some of you might have larger specimens in your intestines, which may require surgical removal. We will respect your privacy and not share the information with others if you so wish. If you require a surgical procedure, we will inform you later privately. But our assessment of your waste products does not indicate such an issue."

Sadi had read about a similar study sometime in the past but could not remember the specifics. She trusted the machines and felt tempted to just let them proceed, but she also felt the responsibility to acquire more information so the others could understand and make a more informed decision.

"From what I know of parasites," she began, pausing to better form the question, "they produce toxins while alive and while dead. How can you assure that by killing them, they won't overload our system with toxins from their death?"

"Yes, this is a concern," it answered. "We have prepared a simple dietary method of mitigating the side effects."

"So you haven't killed them yet?" Gerald asked, and several of the others began talking quietly.

"We will do that next," it answered. "For the next procedure, you will need to wear some ear protection. We do not want to damage your hearing."

"Very kind of you," Gerald said, sarcastically.

"Will you find any disease?" Cesar asked.

"These procedures are specifically designed to detect and destroy foreign organisms," it said. "This, combined with a nontoxic diet will vastly improve your functioning. But toxins often damage an organ or a system permanently, especially during development. We can fix those by destroying then rebuilding, but you probably don't trust us enough for that kind of repair."

The machine on the other side of the enclosure turned and extended an appendage to a small cabinet on the wall. After it opened the cabinet door, Sadi noticed a row of curved strips of material the width of her hand and covered in what looked like sandpaper.

"When you lie on the bed again," the machine said to Gerald. "Put the strip under your head so your ears are covered. We will first show you the results of the analysis and give you instructions from there."

"I'm okay if you are, Sadi," Gerald said.

"They haven't let us down yet," she said, slightly uncomfortable with his trust in her judgment.

Gerald took one of the strips from the cabinet and entered the enclosure again, the door closing behind him. After lying down with the band under his head and curved to cover his ears, Sadi watched his mouth open, and then she heard a muffled, "I'm ready."

For several seconds, Gerald stared at the ceiling, which was not visible to those outside the enclosure other than Sadi and her girls. His eyes narrowed, sweeping from side to side as he watched the ceiling. Sadi felt a sudden excitement to experience the same procedure. After a few more seconds, he turned his head slightly and made eye contact with her, his lips stretched into a tentative smile.

He exited the enclosure three minutes later and turned to Sadi.

"That was interesting."

"What do you mean?" Sadi asked, thinking he looked tired.

"They mapped out my entire body and showed me more than I wanted to see." He laughed uncomfortably and then paused for breath as if speaking required too much energy. "I prefer looking at the outside of people."

The machines gave Gerald a container of liquid, saying its contents would help him recover. They advised him to drink all of the liquid and rest for the remainder of the day, and to do a treatment later. He agreed.

Sadi focused on his post-procedure behavior, hoping to see evidence of improvement in his mental state, but she failed to notice anything different. He probably needed more time, she thought.

"I'll go next," she said.

"Don't forget the ear protection," the machine said.

After Sadi closed the door and lay on the examination table, she noticed the sensors and some kind of screen on the ceiling. The rectangular screen directly above her head looked like a thick layer of black sand—seeming to defy gravity—and the sensors covering the remainder of the ceiling resembled small oval speakers. Glowing dots of red and blue covered the sensors, briefly distracting her from the purpose of the procedure.

The initial scan required less than a minute. During the procedure, she heard the high-pitched humming Gerald had described and felt the slight vibration of the liquid-filled blanket on the examination table. Before the next procedure, the black sand on the ceiling began to hum, then vibrate and ripple, finally becoming a blur of light and displaying a three-dimensional view of her body with the results of the first scan.

The machine quietly explained the scan results and color-coded map of her body. When it said she did not require any surgical procedure, she was relieved, and excited to examine the results in more detail later.

During the final treatment, the vibration in her back was more pronounced and the humming from the walls was significantly louder. When finished, she felt slightly feverish and a little weak. After exiting the tiny room, the machine gave her the same liquid as they had given Gerald. She suddenly wanted a nap.

Helen and Daryn surprised her by begging to go next. She decided to let them but said they could not go on the first trip to Bodn. The adults would go first and see if it was safe. Surprisingly, they did not complain. After the girls had finished, she sent them back to their rooms and told them to follow the machines' instructions.

Sadi wanted to see the girls' scan results but decided to review them later with hers. She also wanted to inspect all of the instruments more closely and interrogate the machines about them. Although her body begged for sleep, she felt a responsibility to stay until the rest of the group had finished.

At first, Susan did not want her boys to do the procedure, needing more time to think about it, but after seeing everyone else do it without incident, she relented. With considerable effort, Sadi had refrained from laughing at her boys' emotional outbursts, complaining about Helen and Daryn having all the fun.

After everyone had finished with the procedure, the machines gave final instructions. Those planning to visit Bodn should have another scan the next day to confirm the results. They had nothing to worry about and should feel significantly better the next morning. Sadi would have stayed longer for her additional questions, but she just wanted to rest.

Back in their living quarters, she found the girls asleep and their containers from the machines empty and next to their beds. When she drank the liquid, it reminded her of beef broth and tasted completely natural and devoid of artificial ingredients. She had expected it to taste like medicine.

In about ten minutes, she fell asleep, but before losing consciousness completely, she felt grateful for the procedure. It had given her less time to worry about meeting their host the next day.

When Sadi awoke several hours later—just in time for dinner—she felt rested, mostly, but still weak and a little feverish. Other members of the group claimed to have the same symptoms, but at least no one would require surgery.

They briefly discussed the plan for the next day. Sadi felt the same as many of the others, excited to visit the planet but nervous to meet their host. For Sadi, at least, excitement overpowered her negative emotions.

"I'll stay with the kids," Susan said.

"I'm staying too," Mark said quickly.

"I thought you were going?" Susan asked, failing to hide her bitter tone, and Sadi wondered if they had argued about the subject before dinner.

"I can go on the next trip," he said. "It's safer if two adults stay."

Smart move, Sadi thought, smiling.

After dinner, the machines came and gave everyone more of the liquid to drink, saying it would help them sleep and recover from the parasite cleanse. Taylor, Cesar, and Simon stayed after dinner to talk while everyone else went to their rooms. Sadi and the girls played rummy until the girls became too sleepy. They played for less than an hour.

She slept well that night and without nightmares. She had vivid dreams about flying to the planet and crashing through the clouds as though diving into water. They flew over her house and she saw Zoya, her friend from work, in the front yard with Helen and her brother Brian. They were smiling and waving at her.

THIRTY-SIX

Freddy

The stairs changed direction at regular intervals, although sometimes the cliff structure necessitated shorter or longer sections. The same small grooves covered the stone steps, making his footholds more secure on the steep incline. After the first section of stairs, Dod and the machine were too far above them to hear anymore. The only available light originated from the glowing stone in Child-Freddy's clenched fingers, the flashlight in Adult-Freddy's hand, and the digital readout on his watch.

Freddy proceeded more cautiously at first, needing practice controlling two bodies, until he felt comfortable going at a normal pace. They descended in silence for about thirty minutes until the bottom became discernible. Child-Freddy saw the rocky floor first, maybe thirty meters below them. After leaving the cavern and Dod, Freddy attempted to focus on finishing his journey. If he stopped to think too deeply about the situation, he might lose his sanity.

"Almost there," Child-Freddy said, his child's voice echoing from the far wall.

After the sound disappeared, their footsteps were the only sound again. Although he had talked to himself, hearing words helped

Freddy feel more normal.

When Adult-Freddy stopped to turn directions for the final section of stairs, he paused briefly to look up the cliff wall, to see how far they had come. He aimed the flashlight above and failed to see the top. With his adult head upturned, a wave of dizziness hit him and he grasped the wall to his right for balance. But while turning, his hip hit the rock, pushing him off balance and over the edge.

Adult-Freddy attempted to turn and grasp the edge of the steps, but he missed and fell all the way to the ground, a fall of maybe seven meters. When he hit the rock floor on his back, the blunt force eliminated almost all the sensations from his adult body. For several seconds, Freddy could see only through the child's eyes. Adult-Freddy on the cavern floor blinked several times, attempting to refocus his vision. Pain from the back of the adult's head and backside threatened to throw them both into an unconscious chasm.

"Help!" he yelled while running down the stairs, two steps at a time. He could hear only the echo of his voice. "Dod, help!"

"Okay, what do we do?" Child-Freddy asked himself after reaching the adult's side. He knelt on the rocky floor.

He placed his small hand tenderly on the adult's chest to feel his heartbeat, while simultaneously feeling it inside his adult chest. Though it was difficult to differentiate from the pain. Touching the adult body while simultaneously feeling the touch nearly overwhelmed his grasp on reality. His emotions became almost too much for his small body, and tears began forming in both pairs of eyes.

He felt extreme pain from one body and complete vitality from the other. If he had not experienced the emotions of so many others, their pain and joy, both of Freddy's bodies probably would have fainted. To help calm himself, he took deep breaths.

Adult-Freddy raised his left arm, the only arm he could move, and touched the back of his head. When he felt the broken bone and wet blood, he suddenly realized the truth. The woman from the plane had planned this scenario and Dod had also known. Her final words to him rang in his memory like a crystal bell.

Step carefully.

Child-Freddy placed his small hand on the wound and attempted to lift his head away from the sharp rock that had pierced his skin and bone, and then tried in vain to stop the flow of blood by pressing his tiny hand against the wound. For the next twenty seconds, he watched the life drain from his adult body while simultaneously staring into the eyes of the child. In the end, Freddy saw through only a single pair of eyes again.

—※—

As Freddy stared at the lifeless body—the vessel he had used up until that moment—he listened to the steady and strong heartbeat inside his small chest, his only remaining physical sensation. All pain had vanished, and for the next few minutes, all thought vanished as well.

While rubbing the sticky blood between his index finger and thumb, he realized the blood would eventually dry. He illuminated the beautiful red fluid with the glowing stone and noticed that he could see the blood in extreme detail. It almost looked grainy.

The glistening red fluid, he realized, still contained live cells. But soon, all the remaining cells from his adult body would die from lack of oxygen. He felt an unexpected sense of urgency and wanted to take advantage of the situation in the only way that came to his mind. When he licked the blood from his index finger, the salty fluid tingled on his tongue. He closed his eyes for several seconds and focused on the sensation.

"Memory is not stored in the brain," he said to himself in sudden realization. If his memory was stored in the brain, the death of his adult body would have meant the death of those memories. The death of his adult body was feeling less tragic. "Interesting!"

Before continuing onward, Freddy quickly considered several implications. He would have to experience puberty again, try to find a place to live, depend on others for all of his needs. At least his genetic identity contained his educational record should he ever want to continue that path, if he reached that age again.

If he spent too much time thinking about the future, he would never accomplish much. Those thoughts probably did not matter anymore and he needed only to decide what to do next, so at that moment, he decided to continue with the task. He felt surprisingly healthy and full of energy.

Before standing, he licked the blood from his thumb and would let the rest dry on his hands. Freddy stood on his feet, took one last look at his lifeless adult body, then turned and did not look back. It was a strange feeling.

With the glowing stone held in the air to illuminate the way forward, Freddy maneuvered quickly across the boulders and sharp rocks covering the bottom of the cavern floor. He actually had fun on the way, jumping with ease from one boulder to the next. He reached the other side of the cavern in just a few minutes and stood at the entrance of another tunnel carved into the wall.

The entrance of the tunnel stood just tall enough for him to walk through without ducking. The size disturbed him, another reminder that the woman from the plane had never intended the adult body to reach this far. For some mysterious reason, another aspect of the tunnel entrance was even more disturbing. Several parallel rows of shiny metal lined the edges of the entrance. Freddy could hear them humming loudly and when he attempted to see the lines clearly, they blurred together.

When he held the glowing stone between him and the entrance, the light failed to penetrate the tunnel interior, not even a centimeter inside the boundary. Even with his improved eyesight, the darkness inside the tunnel was complete. For the first time since his fall, Freddy was suddenly afraid. Although he felt no creatures inside the tunnel, the thought of walking into the darkness terrified him.

Freddy stepped back from the entrance, human instincts urging him to turn and run. For over a minute, he stood paralyzed with indecision. More than anything, he wanted to stand on Earth's surface again and listen to the desert silence in the bright sunlight. Light was life. Darkness was death.

After taking several deep breaths, he sighed.

"Too late to go back now," he said, the unfamiliar child's voice bouncing back from the tunnel like a mirror.

Ignoring the strange effect, Freddy stepped into the tunnel.

After crossing the boundary, darkness surrounded him. In shock, he held his breath and turned around to face the entrance. Even though he knew the entrance was within reach, he could not see the cavern outside. He looked down at the stone in his open palm and did not even see his hand or the stone. For just a moment, curiosity over-powered shock. He wondered what physical law the alien was manip-ulating to block electromagnetic radiation from his eyes. After taking two steps backward, out of the tunnel, he could see the glowing stone in his hand again.

"Wow," he said, then stepped back inside the dark.

Freddy no longer felt afraid. He noticed the same humming from all of the walls as at the entrance, a single pure tone much louder than outside. The sound was comforting in a strange way. At first, he stepped carefully, afraid of falling into a hole but then reminded him-self that the woman from the plane did not bring him this far just to kill him.

At least not to kill him again.

For the first few minutes of walking, he clutched the smooth stone with both hands, his only physical reminder of light. The cool surface was comforting, but after several more minutes of walking, the stone seemed useless and burdensome, so he dropped it and paused at the sound of the stone hitting the ground.

He was sensing the humming of the walls with more than just his ears, he realized. His whole body resonated with the sound. He stepped slowly to the side and tentatively extended the palm of his hand. The grooves on the surface of the wall were like smooth metal. The temperature exactly matched his hand, so he only noticed the physical texture without any transfer of heat.

With his hand on the wall, he suddenly felt exhausted. The vibration drained his resistance to sleep, drained the energy required to keep his eyes open. The overwhelming fatigue seeped into him from the walls like heat flowing from hot to cold. The sensation felt so good, he placed his other hand on the wall and kept them there for as long as he could. Twenty seconds later, he was asleep on the ground, resting his head on his hand.

—※—

Before Freddy awoke completely, a familiar dream replayed in his mind. The same dream had haunted him in the past and contained no images, no people, no words, just the horror of standing under an incomprehensible and impossible load. Freddy could not escape its enormity, so he attempted to imagine something else in its place. But whatever he imagined, the impossible weight remained. In the past, he could escape the dream just by opening his eyes, but now he had no such luxury. The tunnel allowed no light.

The sensation was all-encompassing and produced hopelessness and isolation from all life, as though mountains kept piling on top of him and he needed to climb through all the rock to the top, but the top never stopped getting farther away. He remembered accidentally deleting a long report for his United States history class and having only thirty minutes to rewrite what had taken days.

But the effect of the dream was so much greater than a mere lost history report. He imagined a requirement to retrace every step of an entire life or to rebuild every cell of a lifeless body. If he allowed the dream to consume his entire attention, the stress would destroy him. When he felt the hard stone under his hips again, he remembered his location and surroundings and escaped back to the physical world.

After Freddy got to his feet and stretched, the rush of endorphins completely restored him to consciousness. Sensory input had mostly separated him from the nightmare, but a small portion still lingered in the background and was almost drowned in the humming of the walls.

He felt rested and his mind clean. The death of his adult body was now like a dream, but he still knew its reality. His memory was much sharper now. After his nap, the event caused less emotional distress. He still felt like the same person, just physically stronger and more alert.

A question momentarily paralyzed him. *Which direction is the entrance?* After only a brief pause, he realized the entrance was to his right. He had no doubt about the location, and that was strange. Doubt had infected his whole life. Although he waded through complete blackness, he was confident of his direction.

Had he actually awoken or was he still asleep? The question lasted only a moment, and he immediately discarded the thought. He distinctly remembered falling asleep, waking, and the lingering nightmare. He was tempted to touch the tunnel wall longer again to determine if the action would cause another wave of weariness. To distract his mind from the temptation, Freddy began walking. He did not want to dream again.

Ten minutes later, he noticed a bright blue pinpoint of light ahead and wondered why he had not already seen it. The tunnel had no turns and seemed perfectly level. And then after a few more minutes of walking, the single point separated into two lights, each one the same vibrant blue. The closer he came, the faster his heart beat in his chest. He did not understand the reason. The blue lights looked beautiful.

When Freddy arrived within ten meters of the lights, he stopped walking. He recognized the lights, two eyes at the same level as his, two black pupils surrounded by rings of blue, black, and then white. He stared at them for a long time, wondering if they belonged to some creature, a life he could not detect.

His final destination, he realized, was just ahead. All of his suffering since acquiring the crystal spider raced through his mind. The horror of Helen's abduction, Sadi's sorrow and panic. Murdering the men at the hotel. His disposal of the federal agents. The pain of leaving Mr. Smith and Audrie in the hospitals, the stress of his narrow escape from the military in Portland, Bergen, and Mountainair. Seeing his childhood body, and his death.

"Hello," Freddy said, his heart beating painfully hard and chills coursing through his spinal column. The vibration from the walls amplified his voice. "Who is there?"

The eyes did not blink, he noticed and remained motionless at the same level above the floor. Although his eyes had already adjusted to the brightness of the two lights, their intensity had exponentially increased with his every step.

Before continuing, he noticed another strange aspect of the shining eyes. The light did not illuminate any surface of the tunnel or any part of his body. He extended his hands before him and they remained invisible. When Freddy looked at the floor and behind him, he saw no light at all.

He continued walking slowly several more meters, the eyes growing more distinct and beautiful with every step, reminding him suddenly of Sadi. But they were not her eyes or even living eyes. They had no eyelids and appeared as perfect spheres, embedded in the invisible rock wall. When the light intensity became physical pain, he looked away but kept them in his peripheral vision. They were as bright as the light from an arc welder.

Although he wanted to stop walking, curiosity kept him moving forward. When he stood less than a meter away from the eyes, Freddy slowly extended both hands in front of him, keeping the glowing eyes in his peripheral vision. His hands reached the wall and he felt the grooved metal on his skin. Instead of causing sleepiness, the walls transferred their vibration to his hands, then his whole body seemed to hum.

"It is time, Freddy," a voice said from all around him, the familiar voice of Helen. "All you need to do is look into the lights."

"They are too bright," he whispered but could not hear himself over the humming. Then he yelled. "They are too bright!"

If he looked at the light, the intensity would burn his eyes away, destroying his sight forever, and he would live in a world of darkness.

"It is time," Helen said, her voice amplifying the walls' vibration.

When Freddy looked directly into the lights, each of his eyes exploded with intense pain, spreading quickly through his entire skull. Without the walls for support, he would have fallen to the ground. To quell the pain, he was about to clasp his hands over his eyes, but the pain quickly evaporated, and to his surprise, he could still see. The eyes remained in his vision.

The blue, black, and white bands of light around the pupils shined in equal intensity. Even the pupils shined. Black had become a color of its own. His physical eyes were suddenly numb, so he released the wall and turned away. But no matter where he looked, he could see the shining lights, even after closing his eyes.

Freddy had no time to mourn the loss of his sight. The two orbs suddenly merged into one and began to expand. He turned his head to escape the vision, but the great eye now surrounded him. The black hole in the center acted like gravity, pulling him inside it, under mountains of rock and oceans of water. He sank to the ground and covered his eyes with his hands.

"I cannot escape it," he cried, gulping each breath and hot tears sliding down his cheeks. "There is no way back. Please. Please take it away!"

"Yes, there is no escape," the voice said calmly. "Embrace it. This is what you wanted!"

Freddy focused on the pain in his head and chest, the heat of his face in his hands, each intake of cool air into his lungs. Only physical sensations kept the nightmare from completely consuming him.

"It's okay," the voice continued. "Let go."

"You will save Sadi and the girls?" he cried.

"No," the voice answered. "You will."

Freddy released his grasp of the physical world and let the giant sphere pull him inside it.

The sensation from his skin faded first, then the cool air in his lungs and nostrils, then his hearing. After his heart finally stopped, Freddy felt nothing.

The brilliant bands of blue, black, and white fled from his awareness as the black in the center consumed him, and then the rest of reality unraveled.

PART IV

BODN

You have a new world here
Patterned after the old one
Where we used to live

THIRTY-SEVEN

Josef

"Good morning," Josef said when Gordon Booth came within hearing range. Josef could smell the man's cologne and forced his smile to remain despite his urge to turn away from the tainted air. "Thank you for meeting me early."

"Of course," Gordon answered without emotion. He stopped after reaching the door to the control room. At thirty minutes past seven, the underground hallway was empty and dimly lit.

"I have new instructions," Josef said flatly. "I talked with the board last night about what happened in New Mexico. We need to talk before General Franks arrives, but this morning, you need to control communication. Can you do that? It did not look difficult."

Josef waited for Gordon to process the information. At that time, Josef had not yet decided how much to reveal to Gordon. To adequately perform the function of an intelligence director, he needed to control the flow of dangerous and sensitive information. But his new instructions to attenuate the search efforts would likely cause heightened suspicion and more personal interest in the case, the exact opposite of what Josef wanted for Gordon Booth.

Although Josef trusted Gordon to contain the intelligence they had acquired, all human containers eventually leaked. So Josef had prepared a cover story for the man, a task he had spent a good portion of the night contemplating. Consequently, General Franks would require a different cover story and yet another one for his staff. Each level of misdirection needed to harmonize with the others.

The situation reminded Josef of his first lesson in intelligence. No matter how insignificant the situation, prevent the public or subordinates from understanding the full situation. Controlled misconceptions of a given situation reduced potential threats. The wrong information could transform anyone into a threat to the intelligence project.

"Yes, I can control the communication," Gordon said hesitantly, "but it could interfere with my focus on the interrogations."

"Good," Josef said, then pressed his thumb against the sensor on the right of the door.

After hearing the soft click, he opened the door, stepped inside, and held the door for Gordon. As expected, Josef noticed Lieutenant Hinckley sitting at the large oval table, preparing the communication equipment for their task that morning. No one else occupied the room. The largest flat screen on the wall showed several input selections with nothing yet on the other screens. They would need at least two screens that morning, in thirty minutes.

As they entered, the man stood from the desk, nodding slightly and making fleeting eye contact. During the incident in Bergen, Josef had asked him to refrain from saluting. Josef was not a member of the Air Force. Lieutenant Hinckley looked quickly to the door and Josef noticed his eyes growing wide when the door shut without the presence of General Franks.

"At ease, Hinckley," said Gordon Booth, walking to the large oval table and stopping between Josef and the lieutenant. "I'll be taking the controls this morning. Please show me how to make the connection to Alois and the interrogation room."

"Yes, sir."

As the lieutenant showed Gordon how to make the required connections, Josef considered the situation again. After the incident at Mountainair the previous day, Josef had notified his superiors about the status of the search for Freddy Carlson. Instead of feeling ashamed to report another failed capture, Josef had excitedly reported what they had learned of Freddy's abilities and the apparent help he had received.

Josef had shown the video of Freddy to the board when he'd spoken directly into the camera attached to Major Summers. When Freddy had threatened those in the control room, Josef had experienced chills of fear, followed by an exciting adrenaline rush. Josef remembered feeling as though he faced his first real enemy.

Despite his excitement, Josef had encountered a deeply troubled response from the board, giving him a new concern. Maybe the board had not fully appreciated the situation during his initial orientation meeting at the library. In Josef's experience, his superiors always utilized all necessary resources to understand the true scope, opportunities, possible consequences, and dangers before initiating a new project. But after reassessing the situation, they had instructed him to minimize the exposure even further.

When one of the television screens burst to life, showing an empty interrogation room, Josef focused again on the present. Several seconds later, Gordon spoke into one of the microphones sitting on the table.

"Phillips, are you ready?" Gordon asked, waiting a moment before continuing. "Phillips, check your audio feed and show yourself in the interrogation room."

"I'm here, sir," answered a young male voice through the speakers of the smaller screen on the right. "I wasn't expecting you until after eight."

Before he could respond, Agent Phillips entered the frame of the interrogation room. He looked up at the ceiling behind him and nodded for the camera. In the low light, his eyes resembled black opals set in a pasty white face. The man wore a hat, hiding all of his hair, and the uniform of an Air Force officer. Josef had never seen the CIA agent before and wouldn't have suspected the disguise.

"Is the police chief ready?"

"He will be."

"Okay, good," Gordon said after a sigh. "Stand by until we notify you further."

"Yes, sir."

"So I type the phone number here?" Gordon asked, pushing the microphone away from him and turning to Lieutenant Hinckley. "Then I click here to make the connection to Alois?"

"Yes."

During the exchange, Josef glanced at his watch. They had eighteen minutes, plenty of time to talk before the general arrived. Josef did not expect him much sooner than eight.

"Thank you for your help," Josef said suddenly to Lieutenant Hinckley, surprising the officer. "We'll be taking over from here. You can go and enjoy the remainder of the morning."

Lieutenant Hinckley glanced at Gordon Booth, then turned back to Josef.

"Should I tell the general that you're ready for him?"

"No, thank you," Josef answered politely.

Before returning his attention to Gordon, Josef watched as Lieutenant Hinckley walked to the door and quietly exited the room. He did not look back. Josef took a deep breath and sighed.

"You cut the connection to Agent Phillips?"

"I did," Gordon answered flatly.

"We need to discuss the change of plan before the general arrives," Josef began, reciting what he had prepared to say. "Tell the following to General Franks. Tell him that you have discovered the true identity of the BMW driver, a man only posing as Freddy Carlson. The real Freddy went missing, probably before he killed anyone. You're not sure. You told me all this last night, and you can't reveal the identity to him. Because of other information you cannot reveal, we will continue the chase ourselves and no longer require the capabilities of the Air Force, except for today."

Gordon looked into Josef's eyes with apparent distrust. Josef could almost feel his mind grinding through all of the possible responses.

"May I inquire of the reason?"

"No."

"Okay," he said in resignation, showing more indifference than Josef had expected. "That can't be the whole story. If we discovered the identity of the pilot, Franks will assume we learned more about the vehicle. Do you want me to just say it's classified? He's not going to take that well. He's pissed off enough as it is."

Josef chuckled softly, remembering the general's reaction the previous day after the BMW had disappeared in Mountainair. Of the three men, General Franks had reacted with the most agitation. Josef had acted as if he'd expected the outcome, but he could not hide his shock at the illusion they had all experienced.

"Here's the rest of the story. This pilot works for Max Garner and it was his company that developed the vehicle, with help from Taylor Evans, but we still don't know how it works. He'll likely believe that because of what happened with the Garners. At least, that might distract him from asking too many follow-up questions."

"Hmm," Gordon said, rubbing his chin. He drew a deep breath before responding. "Franks will want to explain the situation somehow to his people. What should they think? Do you want me to think of something, or have you prepared a story?"

"I have an idea," Josef responded, "but I would like to know your initial thoughts first."

"Well, he can tell them that the BMW crashed, and another agency discovered it," Gordon said. "Or, we can use the training exercise excuse. Those are just my first thoughts."

Josef had already considered the first story and disliked the consequences. Some of Franks' people would begin an inquiry of their own and have a high probability of discovering the deceit. The training exercise option would work on the regulars though. Josef did not care that the regulars thought they had participated in a training exercise. But some of the general's staff were of his bloodline, and Josef needed to give them more respect. They deserved at least part of the truth.

"The crash idea is good but too risky," Josef said. "For the regulars, we can say it was a training exercise. For the others, I want to give them a mystery and a real enemy. The one posing as Freddy is the mystery. The enemy is the one who betrayed us all for Taylor Evans, a girl of no blood. General Franks can tell them we need to regroup and form a specialized task force to capture Freddy."

"Sounds good," Gordon said, and Josef thought his smile indicated an appreciation for the plan. "And we'll stick with the plan today. We still need to interrogate the chief and the girl from the store to help find Freddy, *the pilot*. I still think we should have used one of my agents in New Mexico, instead of Alois."

"Alois has more training than you think and this is a good opportunity for him to gain field experience," Josef answered quickly, attempting to hide his irritation at Booth's questioning of his decision. Josef wanted to see Alois' performance. "And using Alois means less exposure. We won't have to include another of your agents in this investigation."

"You can trust my people."

"The general will be here in a few minutes," Josef said, ignoring the comment and glancing at his watch. "Open communication with Alois."

"Yes, sir."

THIRTY-EIGHT

Taylor

Taylor could not remember the last time she had slept so well, even after napping almost the entire afternoon the previous day. As everyone else, she had been a little sick after the treatment. Drinking the salty liquid from the machines had caused her to urinate multiple times, and she could feel her system improving after every visit to the bathroom. She had fallen asleep thinking about their flying practice and then had extremely pleasant dreams.

When she awoke to her dark room, she felt refreshed and ready for the day. Before getting out of bed, Taylor rolled over to face the window and saw Bodn still covered in shadow, the eastern horizon slightly illuminated by Dzalm.

She quickly remembered the significance of the day, other than the trip to Bodn. They would meet one of their hosts sometime, maybe even that morning. Before the treatment, she had been anxious about meeting an alien, but she was more excited than anxious now. She imagined hundreds of possible incarnations and only a few frightening ones.

As usual, Taylor walked alone to the dining hall and expected to arrive before anyone else. But when she arrived, she found the room already illuminated and a strange man sitting at the large dining table, his back to her. When she saw his size, she stopped walking and breathing, her heart beating hard.

The man wore strange clothing, tight-fitting material composed of blue and yellow threads, thick enough for her eyes to resolve. She immediately noticed the exposed skin of his neck, black as crude oil and almost as shiny.

"Good morning, Taylor Evans," the man said after turning toward her and transferring the spoon in his hand to a bowl on the table in front of him. The spoon made a soft metallic clink sound. "I'm not surprised to see you here first."

Taylor required several seconds to process his harsh accent and extremely deep voice. He spoke the word good, like *gut*, and morning sounded like *mrning*. He seemed to make a special effort to pronounce her name with a less distinct accent. Despite the accent, the man spoke clearly and her name flowed naturally from his lips.

"Good morning," she replied hesitantly, prepared to run from the room at any sign of aggression.

The man stood and extended his hands, palms facing her, skin as black as his neck. Even while standing ten meters away, Taylor had to look upward to focus on his face. He stood maybe two and a half meters tall, had a muscular physique, and a pronounced chin. His black hair was very short with tight curls. The whites of his light grey eyes and teeth contrasted with the dark skin of his face. Taylor failed to remember the last time she had been so speechless.

"You were not expecting to see another human," he said and laughed, a deep throaty sound, which resonated like a bell. "And yes, I am a human, but let's not get into too many details now. We should probably save those for the whole group."

"I, uh," Taylor began, then cleared her throat. "No, I was not expecting to see another human. I guess you're just another race?"

"Yes," he said. "Come and have your breakfast with me. I was just eating some of your oatmeal. It's not particularly nutritious, but it tastes interesting."

Taylor approached the table slowly and the man extended his hand. When he wrapped his fingers around hers, the warmth of his skin was strangely comforting. She had expected to feel cold or an electric shock or something else strange. The sleeves of his shirt extended to the base of his palms and she wanted to feel the material between her fingers, but she looked at his face instead and had to remember to breathe.

"It's good to meet you at last, Taylor," he said while shaking her hand. "You can call me, Yezeel."

"Good to meet you too, Yezeel."

As he squeezed her hand, Taylor forced herself to smile and waited for him to release his grip. She did not have the strength to escape his grasp. After the brief physical contact, Yezeel sat at the table again, and her mind recovered enough from the shock to fill with questions.

"I don't want this to get cold," he said after eating a spoonful of oatmeal. "It's probably better warm."

She never expected to talk about such mundane topics with a giant man, an alien. The situation was so strange, Taylor forced herself to act normal and get her own breakfast. Oatmeal seemed like the appropriate choice.

"I thought the machines referred to you as female," Taylor said. "Sorry if that's rude. Are you the one who brought us here?"

"I'm not the only one who helped you get here," he said while watching her at the microwave. As he continued speaking, she could feel his eyes on her back. "But you can consider me as your host. I have to warn you though. I won't answer all of your questions, and probably not the most important ones. I'll wait for Freddy to explain things."

"How am I not surprised," she said and instantly regretted her sarcastic tone. "That didn't come out right. It's just that we've heard the machines say that so often. We appreciate your help by letting us stay here."

"Don't mention it," the man said, laughing. "I understand your impatience. Our visit to Bodn will help alleviate it, temporarily at least."

"So you came to show us the planet?" she asked while walking back to the table. She had difficulty deciding which question to ask next. While walking the short distance, Taylor told herself to remain calm and make only glances at him, so he would not catch her staring.

"I wanted to meet you all in person," he answered while she sat across from him, "and it seemed fitting for me to give you a tour of your new home."

Taylor scooped a spoonful of oatmeal and paused before lifting it to her mouth, suddenly feeling extremely self-conscious. She did not want an alien, human or otherwise, to see her chewing. In the following silence, she planned to eat breakfast quickly and then excuse herself to get the others.

"How has your stay been?" he asked. "After your ordeal on Earth, I was hoping you could have a break."

"It's been the most relaxing time of my life," she said, smiling at the realization. "Your robots have taken really good care of us. Yesterday, you probably know, they performed some kind of sonic scan to eliminate parasites from our systems, and this morning, I feel better than I can remember. I miss my mother though."

Taylor suddenly felt like a child talking to an authority figure. Yezeel's physical size and authoritative tone made her feel much younger and ignorant, as an innocent child. His presence also melted her inclination to conceal her true feelings. She had not intended to mention her mother.

"I am happy to help you all," he answered. "I expect you to feel a little distrustful of me for bringing you here without an explanation. I would very much like to hear your hypothesis of why?"

"The Earth is not ready for our inventions, perhaps?"

"*Your* invention," he said with a tone of correction. "Don't be so modest, continue."

"Maybe your people don't think the people of Earth are ready for it? Holy shit, that sounds stupid, saying it out loud. Okay, pretend you didn't hear that. I don't know why."

His following laugh, deep and reverberating, seemed to vibrate her entire frame. She smiled but felt a little embarrassed. *Is he laughing at me?* She felt stupid for swearing.

"I'm not laughing at what you said. You don't hold back, do you? Freddy said you were like that."

"So that's obviously not it," Taylor said, fighting the urge to ask if he learned English just for them, and then to explain his relationship to Freddy. Several other questions fought for the next place in line, but she had to focus on one topic at a time. She wanted to know his assessment of her hypothesis if it contained any truth. "What does my invention have to do with it?"

"It's part of the story, and that's another question for Freddy." He stopped laughing and looked directly into her eyes. "Without our interventions, none of you would have survived. There are other creatures involved who don't want your new technology on Earth."

"What creatures?"

"You and I are creatures," he said, and his smile returned. "I think you should get the rest of your friends. We are going to have fun for the next few days."

"Okay. I'll go get them," Taylor said and imagined herself as a child in school, dismissed by her teacher.

While she walked away from the dining table with her bowl of oatmeal, she had to focus on each step and disobey the great urge to look back. Before leaving the room, she wanted to confirm the man's existence one more time, but she did not look back. Her short experience with Yezeel seemed like a dream. She imagined returning with the others to an empty room.

"Cesar," Taylor said after knocking hard on his door. "You need to get up. One of our hosts wants to meet everyone."

The door opened almost immediately. As expected, Cesar was already awake, probably reading a book before getting Dominga for breakfast.

"You said, *one of our hosts*?"

"Yes," she said, after scooping the rest of her breakfast into her mouth. "It's a giant man. Well, tall at least. I'd say over 8 feet."

"A man?" Cesar said, more to himself than Taylor. He stepped into the hallway and closed his door. "Let's get everyone and go as a group. Did he tell you anything?"

As they walked from door to door, spreading the news, Taylor told Cesar about her encounter. In just a few minutes, all of the adults had gathered in the hallway. Taylor glanced at her watch, twenty minutes after six. About twenty minutes had passed since she met Yezeel.

They left the children asleep in their rooms, and walked as a group to the dining hall, Taylor leading the way. To help prepare them for the meeting, Taylor gave a brief description of the man. Surprisingly, no one asked any questions, and Taylor wondered if everyone felt as she had and needed time to purge from their minds the expectation to see an alien creature. She still expected them to feel surprised.

As they approached the entrance, Taylor held her breath, afraid to find the room devoid of the giant black man. When she saw him standing at the table waiting for them, she exhaled a long sigh of relief. He held both hands in front of him, clasped together, his lips stretched into a welcoming smile. Taylor led the group to the table, a few meters away from the giant man. Cesar stepped next to her, but the rest of the group stopped behind her.

"Yezeel," Taylor said after realizing he was waiting for her to speak. "This is everyone, except for the children. They are still asleep. Do I need to introduce anyone?"

"No thank you, Taylor," he answered, glancing at her. "I know all of your identities. It is my pleasure to meet everyone."

"Thank you for helping us," Cesar said sincerely, and Taylor wondered if he had practiced those words. His accent was a bit less pronounced.

"Again," he said with a slight nod of his head. "It is my pleasure to help you. I know you all have questions, so why don't I answer the most obvious ones. I am a human, but you would call me a different race, and yes, humans exist outside of Earth."

"You have all been allowed to come for Freddy's sake, but I will let him decide to tell you more when he arrives. Bodn, the planet we will explore for the next few days, can be your home if you wish, or you are free to return to Earth. Consider this station only as a temporary abode. Once you have established a settlement on Bodn, you cannot return to the station, but our machines will always be at your disposal."

"We are giving ownership of Bodn to Freddy, including the responsibility to protect its inhabitants. There are dangerous creatures in this universe of ours, and we are training Freddy to deal with them."

THIRTY-NINE

Josef

Gordon Booth turned his attention to one of the computers built into the desk. As he worked the communication boards, Josef heard controlled breathing and hoped it was a sign that he'd recognized Joseph's irritation.

Twenty seconds later, the larger screen on the wall flickered to life, showing a view of a desert horizon through the windshield of a car. The sunrise in New Mexico reminded him of his time in the Sahara, and then of the previous day, when Freddy Carlson had successfully eluded them for the third time.

Gordon grasped one of the microphones on the table, a different one than he'd used to communicate with Agent Phillips. He pressed the button before speaking.

"Alois, are you listening? Please wear your glasses."

Josef experienced a brief disorientation as the screen showed Alois transferring the glasses to cover his eyes. The view on the screen, through the glasses, quickly switched from the horizon to the dashboard, then to the ceiling of the car, and returned finally to the horizon.

Before answering, Alois looked into the rear-view mirror, which showed only half of his head. Josef immediately recognized the dark brown eyes, but the glasses and military hat effectively obscured his identity. Melissa, the girl from the store who had interacted with Freddy Carlson, would never recognize Alois if she met him in non-military attire or saw him in the media.

"I'm here," Alois said into the rear-view mirror, emotionless. "We are waiting for the signal to visit the girl."

"Good," Gordon said, glancing at Josef for further instruction. Josef just nodded. "We're just waiting for General Franks to get here."

"Okay," Alois answered, looking away from the mirror.

Josef saw the sun in the upper right of the screen and an unobstructed view of the horizon. Although not technically the same, the sagebrush, desert junipers, and cacti reminded him again of Libya.

"The speakers are tickling my ears," Alois said. "Is there anything I can do about that? It is kind of distracting."

"Then they were inserted improperly," Gordon said with some irritation. "You should not feel them. Tapping your ears might help, but you might just have to deal with it. I suggest you concentrate on writing notes in your notebook during the interrogation. That will help distract you and give Melissa the impression that everything is not being recorded electronically. Remember to keep your phone close. The speakers in your ears have a range of about a meter."

"Got it," Alois said.

Josef heard the door to the room open. Without turning, he listened as General Franks walked into the room and approached them. Josef glanced at him and nodded then turned back to the screen.

"Stand by and we'll contact you shortly," Gordon said, then made two clicks with the mouse on the table. He turned to the men standing behind him. "He can't hear us anymore."

"Where is Lieutenant Hinckley?"

Josef turned to face the general. He smiled politely before speaking. "There's been a change of plan."

"What change of plan?" the older man asked.

Josef detected irritation in his tone already. He broke eye contact and turned to Agent Booth. "Gordon discovered something last night. I'll let him tell you."

"We discovered the identity of the pilot."

"Who is it?" General Franks asked, his tone becoming curious.

"He's not Freddy Carlson," Agent Booth said with the correct amount of sincerity and surprise as if the information had actually shocked him. "But I'm not authorized to reveal his identity, yet."

"I see," General Franks said, squinting and looking down. "And you met early to discuss it without me?"

"Yes, we did," Josef said, feeling irritated again. "Last night, Gordon acquired the intel and I want to minimize exposure. But I will tell you, the pilot works for Max Garner and it was his company that developed the vehicle, with help from Taylor Evans and the pilot. Unfortunately, we still don't know how the vehicle works."

"So," the general said slowly. "Where does that leave us?"

"After today," Josef began, "we'll no longer require your resources."

"So, you still can't find Max and his people?" the general asked. "And this pilot escaped us again, and you don't need my help? That doesn't make any sense."

"Because you are working with limited information," Gordon interjected. "We understand your frustration, but this is a very sensitive issue."

"What am I supposed to tell my people?" the general said to his cousin, his anger rising. "Your failures have made us look like incompetents."

"Tell your people that we are regrouping," Josef said, wanting to return General Frank's attention to him. "We have failed at nothing. We've been gathering intelligence. The regulars can think this is all a training exercise, but tell your people we are creating a specialized task force to deal with the issue. Terrawatch is the key. Max Garner has betrayed his family for a girl of no blood."

"The Garners," General Franks scoffed. "The rumor is they stopped Henry Garner from becoming the Secretary of the Treasury because of Max, but I think they just decided to keep Geithner. That's what Erik Garner thinks at least."

"It's almost 0830," Gordon Booth said. "We should get started. We're still hoping to learn something useful from the incident in New Mexico."

Gordon pushed the button on the microphone and leaned forward. As he spoke, Josef stepped to the left of the man, leaving the general on the right. He wanted to continue monitoring General Franks' disposition. He still seemed too disturbed by the new information.

"Phillips, deliver the chief to the interrogation room then wait for the signal to begin the questioning." Gordon released the button and turned to General Franks at his right. "Agent Phillips doesn't know about what happened in New Mexico, or that we'll be visiting the store attendant at the same time."

"I know how this works," General Franks barked.

While they waited for the Mountainair Police Chief to enter the interrogation room, Gordon Booth removed a piece of paper from his pocket and spread it on the table, his list of questions for the session. The chief wore the same police uniform as the day before when they had mistakenly tranquilized him instead of Freddy. In the interrogation room, he carried his wide-brimmed hat and set it on the stainless steel table. Instead of sitting, he stood and paced. The wide-angle lens in the ceiling captured the entire room. The chief glanced upward a few times without looking directly into the hidden camera.

"He looks worried," Josef said.

"He should be," Booth responded. "He woke up on a military base and doesn't know where he is or how he got there."

"Let's begin," Josef said and tried to imagine how he would feel in the same situation. That little mental exercise would help him understand the man better.

"Time to start, Phillips," Booth said while looking at his piece of paper, and then clicking the button on the microphone. "We want him to think he's in trouble. Here's your first question: Why does he think we took him for questioning?"

"Got it," Agent Phillips answered, and the door to the interrogation room opened.

The Central Intelligence agent let the door close, then stepped into the center of the small room. From the angle of the camera, Josef could not see their faces clearly, only that the chief was much taller than Agent Phillips. Josef inhaled in preparation to speak, but Gordon Booth spoke first.

"I'm switching to Phillip's view," he said, then after a brief pause, tapped on the keyboard in front of him and the screen changed viewpoints from the camera in the ceiling to the camera in Phillip's glasses.

"Please have a seat," Agent Phillips said politely, but with confidence.

"I'd prefer to stand," he answered defiantly, looking down at the man with anger in his eyes.

"If you want this experience to end favorably," Agent Phillips answered with the same amount of intensity in his voice as Josef saw in the police chief's blue eyes, "you will sit down and comply with my requests."

The Chief inhaled through his nostrils and complied slowly and silently. Agent Phillips sat on the other side of the man, and the view changed to a more horizontal position, instead of an upward angle. The Mountainair police chief looked into the camera, and Josef felt as though he had actually made eye contact with the man. Did camera operators on a movie set feel the same, he wondered. He was suddenly jealous of the camera operators who watched his wife for several hours a day.

"Chief Collins," the CIA agent began. "Why are you here, do you think?"

"That's my question for you," the chief said with irritation. He drew a deep breath and spoke more calmly. "It's related to what happened yesterday."

"Good. What happened yesterday."

"You tell me to detain this guy in town," he answered, gritting his teeth. "Then I wake up on some military base as a prisoner."

Gordon leaned forward and spoke into the microphone. "Tell him he's not a prisoner, then make him give you the details."

"You're not a prisoner," Agent Phillips said, "but you need to give me more details."

"Yesterday afternoon," the chief said, "you guys called the station and told us to visit a consignment store in town. I complied immediately and met a young man meeting your description buying a hat. I made him stay in the store until you arrived, then someone shot me in the neck and I don't remember anything else."

"He's excluding something," Josef said and Gordon nodded.

"Get a more detailed description," Gordon instructed.

"Don't play this game with us," Agent Phillips said. "You know we need more information. What happened when you arrived? Did the target try to get away? Did he say anything to you?"

"I'm kind of tired," Chief Collins responded. "So excuse me for not answering all of your *unasked questions*. When I got there, he was finishing the transaction. He did not try to get away and seemed like in a good mood."

"That's better. What did he say to you?"

"Well, I blocked the entrance first thing. I don't remember the exact words I said, but I let him know that he was not going anywhere. Then he tried to convince me that he would do whatever I said."

Chief Collins drew a deep breath and looked more relaxed, then snorted.

"It's funny. He seemed more worried about me than his situation."

"Did you believe him?"

"Yes, I did." He glanced at his hands on the table and then his eyes narrowed as though making a sudden realization. "I've seen a lot of people try to worm their way out of things, saying what they thought I wanted to hear, but this guy was different. I believed him. It was very strange."

"Did he say he would surrender himself?"

"No," he said, looking to his left, attempting to remember the specifics. "If I remember correctly, he just said he would do whatever

I told him to do, and I believed him."

"How long did you wait in the store before the soldiers arrived?"

Chief Collins looked to his right and paused for a moment.

"I think about ten minutes."

"And you just waited with him and Melissa Cook until the soldiers arrived? What else did you talk about?"

"I really don't remember," he said defensively. "Nothing important enough to remember."

Josef grabbed the microphone.

"I think he's hiding something. Tell him that the girl remembers what you all talked about."

"The girl told us what you talked about. Try to remember."

Chief Collins squinted and squirmed in his seat as though physically uncomfortable. Josef thought he looked more than just uncomfortable. He also looked confused. Before answering, Chief Collins cleared his throat.

"He said that he needed something from the store across the street, and I..."

"You what?"

"Okay," he began and stared directly into Agent Phillips' eyes, challenging the Central Intelligence officer to accuse him of lying. Josef felt as if the man was looking directly at him through the video display again. "I did not intend to withhold this, but he asked me to buy something for him and he would stay in the store...and that's what I did."

"You left him in the store because you trusted him. Right?" Agent Phillips asked, pretending to already know the information. For just a moment, Josef worried the interrogator would reveal his surprise. "Did he tell you he would stay?"

"He must have. I know it sounds stupid," he said like a scolded child. "It's not a very clear memory. What did Melissa say?"

"You know I can't reveal that," the agent said. "Please explain what your *unclear memory* means."

Chief Collins drew a deep breath and sighed.

"I remember leaving him on his own, but the memory feels like a dream. That's the only way I can describe it. At the time, I felt good about the decision, mostly."

Gordon Booth pushed the button on the microphone and told Agent Phillips to discuss what happened when the soldiers arrived. Then Josef, Gordon, and the general mostly listened. In Josef's opinion, the interrogator deftly extracted the remainder of his story, what they already knew. Chief Collins returned to the shop, then the soldiers arrived, and then Major Summers entered the store. He remembered only leaving the store with the Major and then getting shot in the neck with a dart.

At the end of the interrogation, Agent Phillips asked the police chief to think hard about why he wanted to help the man in the store more than his country. Chief Collins sat alone in the interrogation room while they discussed what to do next.

"That's how my memory feels," Booth said, staring at the screen, "when we reviewed the video last night. I thought we were looking at the Freddy impostor."

"I know," Josef answered, not wanting to repeat their conversation of the previous night after they had reviewed all of the video footage. "Let the chief simmer while we visit the girl. We need to know what he told her if anything."

Booth stretched his arms, then spoke into the other microphone.

"Alois, we're ready. You can initiate contact."

FORTY

Josef

Alois's view from the vehicle switched again from the horizon to the rearview mirror. He extended his thumb up for Josef to see, and then he turned to his companion in the passenger's seat.

"It's time to go," he said.

"Got it," said his companion, another man wearing the same military uniform, the same hat and glasses.

Alois looked forward while starting the car and pulling away from the side of the road. For the next three minutes, Josef, Gordon, and General Franks watched as Alois and his companion drove through Mountainair, New Mexico. When they turned on Roosevelt Avenue, they passed the other CIA agent on the side of the road, the one responsible for assuring the girl did not leave her home. Alois made eye contact with the man in the driver's seat then quickly looked away.

"Your destination is on the left," the Google navigation program said with a female voice.

"There's her car," said the man in the passenger seat, pointing to the two-door blue hatchback. "A 2001 Ford Focus."

Josef noticed the old stucco walls, grey and dirty, the rotting shingles on the low roof. In stark contrast, the new white doors and new windows did not help the old structure look any more appealing. A newer home was on the left of her home and appeared as part of the same property. Neither home had much of a yard, only dry dirt with a few scattered weeds. Josef wondered if the girl did not care about the appearance of her home, or if her financial situation prevented her from making improvements.

Alois parked in front of the home, next to an ornamental chain link gate. Two wooden posts supported the metal gate and a sign hung on the right post with "BEWARE OF DOG" printed in bold red letters. When the barking began, Alois looked quickly from the sign to a small wooden dog house on the right of the home where a large Rottweiler had appeared and approached the car. The animal stopped a few meters away and continued to bark.

"Here we go," Alois said, chuckling and looking from the dog to the door handle. "I hope that chain keeps the dog away."

"Shut up, Foley," a female voice yelled. "Get over here."

Before stepping out of the car, Alois looked to the front door to the short blond girl in the doorway. She glanced at the men and then turned to her dog. The animal continued to bark and showed no sign of obedience.

"Good morning, madam," Alois yelled, holding the car door as a potential shield.

"Use ma'am instead of madam," Gordon Booth said into the microphone.

Alois nodded in acknowledgment and the view moved up and down slightly.

"I was wondering when I'd be getting a visit like this," the girl said while running to her dog, leaving the door to her home open. She stroked the animal's head with one hand while grasping the chain with the other. The dog stopped barking but began growling and pulling the girl towards Alois. The short but stocky girl had to use all of her strength to keep the dog from pulling her forward. "Stop, Foley! Stop! That's a good boy."

While Alois walked tentatively toward her, Josef heard the car doors close and then the other man appeared on the edge of the screen, in Alois' peripheral vision. The girl stayed crouched on the ground, holding the dog who had stopped growling and seemed to enjoy the girl's strokes on its head.

"Good morning, ma'am," Alois said, looking from the dog to the girl's face. "You're Melissa Cook, right? I'm Captain Foster and this is Captain Bryant."

"That's me," she said with her back to them.

"Sorry to cause you such trouble. That's a beautiful dog, by the way. I've always wanted a Rottweiler."

"Yeah. They're great dogs."

The girl stood and began pulling the creature toward its dilapidated home. The animal resisted at first, so she pulled harder and managed only to change its direction. She had to use both hands to finally get the animal moving away and when she released the chain, momentum propelled the dog forward. She watched as the dog entered its home, turned around, and lay on the floor.

"Can we talk with you for a few minutes?" Alois asked. "It's about what happened yesterday."

"I expected as much. You can go inside. I'll meet you in a minute." She turned to the dog. "Good boy, Foley. Thanks for protecting me, but these guys are friends."

As Alois and his companion walked to the front door and entered the home, Josef could hear Melissa talking to the dog, out of their view. Josef suddenly wished he could trade places with his special assistant. Fieldwork was more fun than spending time in the control rooms.

"It's nicer than outside," the other man said after they entered the home. The screen quickly adjusted to the lower light levels, and the control room darkened a bit. As Alois inspected the living room, Josef heard the dog whine in the background as a final protest.

The view on the screen revealed a large living room with a checkered fabric sofa, a wooden rocking chair, a large-screen television, a stereo, and several pictures on the walls and on the coffee table. He stopped inspecting the home interior when the girl appeared in the doorway. Josef suddenly felt as though they were watching a movie, and then he thought of Lise, his wife.

"Ask about the photograph," Gordon instructed. "The one on the TV. Get her talking about her parents and maybe the town. Be as friendly as you can."

"While we talk," Alois began, taking a small notebook in his left hand with a pen in his right. "I'm going to take notes."

While the interrogators and the girl became better acquainted, Josef reassessed his goals. Although he doubted Freddy would have told the girl anything important, Josef hoped she could help them find Freddy and the vehicle. He also wanted to discover who or what had helped the young man. Freddy Carlson could not possibly have single-handedly thwarted all of their attempts at capturing him.

After each of their failures, Josef had expected to feel frustration. But instead, his excitement kept climbing to new levels. The Freddy Carlson case had transformed into a much greater challenge than his assignment in Libya. Josef enjoyed the chase and especially how his superiors had chosen him. He now had to rely on intelligence and cunning rather than their nearly unlimited resources.

In his updates to his superiors, Josef had focused on what they had learned from each encounter. Only after his latest report of losing Freddy's location, did they seem less than satisfied by his progress. Josef did not let their reaction upset him. He would only find success by extracting information from their past experiences and devising better plans.

In Portland, he had witnessed first-hand the young man's abilities when the soldiers had just let him escape, a feat facilitated only by some form of telepathy. Freddy's recent record already indicated that ability and the extensive psychological evaluations of the soldiers had also helped confirm his suspicions. The soldiers could not accurately describe their experiences except with the help of mind-altering drugs. They had given conflicting testimonies, as though each had experienced the situation entirely differently. One in particular caught his attention. Josef would never forget Major Summers' statement about fighting a giant silverback gorilla.

Josef had based his strategy in Norway on a flawed assumption, he'd concluded afterward. Since Freddy had seemed to barely escape their grasp in Portland, Josef had mistakenly assumed they would succeed with more troops and resources. The footage showing Freddy's collapse in Bergen suggested complete exhaustion. But Josef now wondered if that was just an act, another illusion.

Only in New Mexico did Josef learn that Freddy could transfer illusions through larger distances and possibly even through video. He remembered distinctly thinking they had caught Freddy instead of the police chief. Josef would not underestimate Freddy again, or whoever had assisted him.

If the girl did not help him locate Freddy, Josef planned to interrogate his friends in custody, the web developer from Portland, Oregon, and the retired botany professor from Seattle, Washington. He considered capturing his other friend from Portland, Brian Jacobsen but decided for the present to continue maintaining close surveillance in case Freddy attempted to make contact.

"Yeah," Melissa said with a smile. "I have a sweet setup here. The owners know they wouldn't get any money from this if I left."

"That makes sense," Alois said. He nodded slightly and the view on the monitor moved correspondingly. "Mountainair doesn't seem like a good market for renters."

"She's ready to talk about yesterday," Gordon said during the pause. "Ask an open-ended question and let's see what she willingly offers us."

The view shifted toward the coffee table as Alois took a sip of his tea, gaining time to decide on a suitable question. So far, Josef was pleased with the performance of both men. The other interrogator employed a more intimidating personality, which helped the girl to feel more comfortable with Alois. She seemed to sincerely like him.

"So you know why we're here," Alois said after returning the cup to the coffee table. He put the notebook in front of his face and held his pen ready to write.

"I was wondering when you'd get to that," she said then paused. As expected, the girl responded to the uncomfortable silence by continuing. "I just want you to know that before yesterday, I'd never seen that guy before. He just came into the shop."

"Don't worry, Melissa. We're not accusing you of anything. We know you were just a victim of circumstance."

"Yes, exactly," she said with relief. "So, this guy comes in and starts looking for a hat."

"Was anyone with him?"

"I saw him park on the street in a really nice car, a BMW. The windows were really dark. I noticed that first thing. I suppose someone else could have been inside with him, but I got the impression that he was all by himself."

"What gave you that impression?"

"Hmm," Melissa said, then leaned back on the loveseat and put her right foot under her thigh. The view shifted to her exposed leg for a millisecond longer than Josef thought appropriate. "He didn't seem to be in a hurry."

"So he was looking for a hat?"

"Yeah," she said and her eyes widened a little bit.

"Did he say why?"

"No," she answered.

Alois took another long sip of his tea.

"She's lying," Booth said after turning to Josef. "Should Alois challenge her about that?"

"Let's see how he handles it," Josef said.

Booth turned back to the screen, and they waited for Alois to finish his sip of tea. Josef glanced at the general who had remained quiet for the entire morning. The older man looked content to let the intelligence agents direct the show.

Alois wrote in his notebook, making sure to look directly at the paper so his audience could see his words.

She's hiding something.

"Did you ask why he was buying a hat?"

"No," she said, then quickly continued. "But I helped him pick one out. He bought it and that's when Chief Collins came in and blocked the entrance."

As Alois continued to get the girl's account of what had happened, including the description of the hat, Josef wondered about the reason for his purchase. The two main reasons for buying a hat seemed equally likely. The practical purpose of keeping sunlight from one's head could indicate a plan to remain in the area, or another sunny location. Josef doubted Freddy would stay in the area where they knew he had visited. He also could have wanted the hat as a disguise. But from her description of the hat, Josef expected Freddy to purchase other complementary clothing, something he had failed to do at the shop. Otherwise, the hat would make him look more conspicuous.

The girl mentioned how the chief had left Freddy in the store with her, and then gave an accurate account of the encounter with Major Summers. She expressed confusion about why the chief had left the store instead of Freddy. Josef remembered watching her on the video from the major's camera and had wondered if she knew they recorded the incident.

Melissa then began telling her account of what happened after the soldiers had tranquilized Chief Collins. Josef's heart rate accelerated. In his peripheral vision, he noticed Booth sitting forward in his seat.

"It was like the movies," Melissa said. "The chief fell to the ground, and then all these soldiers surrounded him. I thought they were going to come into the shop and get Freddy, but they all just stayed outside."

"So he told you his name was Freddy?"

Melissa looked shocked, her eyes wide.

"That's not his name?"

"It's okay to call him that," Alois said. "What happened next?"

"Freddy and I watched the soldiers try to get into the BMW with the chief's keys. That was so weird." Melissa paused and laughed uncomfortably, looking suddenly confused. She took a sip of her tea. "We were watching them try to get into the car, and then..."

"And then what?" the other interrogator asked impatiently.

The girl squirmed in her seat and put the mug on the coffee table. During the short wait, Josef recalled when he had given the orders to leave the BMW and get Freddy while he was still unconscious. At the time, the decision to get the car later seemed logical.

"I remember the soldiers leaving our view and then Freddy just getting in his car and leaving. Seems like I'm forgetting something."

"That's okay," Alois said with a glance at his companion. "Our minds are fragile sometimes, especially in stressful situations. Did he just leave without saying anything?"

"He wished me luck. I remember that."

"That was it?"

"That was it. After the soldiers captured the chief, it was pretty uneventful." Melissa yawned, then squinted as though confused. "I did have a strange dream last night."

"I'm sure you did," Alois said, smiling. "About what?"

"I was in the store with my boss and the chief," she began, looking down at her legs. "Freddy was outside with the soldiers, and then a huge gorilla came from behind us and killed my boss."

Melissa laughed uncomfortably. Alois wrote in his notebook.

What next?

"How did the dream make her feel?" Josef asked into the microphone.

"How did the dream make you feel?" Alois asked.

"So you're a psychologist now?" she asked and laughed uncomfortably. "Just kidding. I didn't remember the dream until just now. It was scary. I just remember feeling scared."

"Scared for who?" Josef asked and Alois repeated the question.

"For myself and..." she paused, then cleared her throat.

"And for Freddy?" Alois asked.

"Yes, and for Freddy," she said apologetically. "Listen, this guy came into the store, bought a hat, and was very nice. I had no reason to dislike him, but I'm not trying to hide anything. He didn't tell me where he was going, just that he needed a hat. He said he wasn't from the desert. I got the impression that he needed it for his stay here, a tourist thing."

Feels legitimate. Anything else?

After writing the note, Alois put the notebook down, along with the pen. He pulled a small card from his shirt pocket.

"Wrap it up," Josef said after grabbing the microphone.

"If he tries to contact you," Alois said and extended the card toward her. "Please contact me. Will you do that?"

"Of course," she said, then exhaled. "Is there anything else?"

Alois turned to his companion who shook his head.

"I'm good," the man said.

"Thank you for your time this morning, ma'am," Alois said appreciatively, but then his tone transformed into a warning. "This is very sensitive information. Do not discuss our conversation or this event with anyone, not even Chief Collins. If he attempts to discuss it with you, inform us immediately."

FORTY-ONE

Taylor

"**P**oor guy," Taylor said, standing at the entrance of the cockpit. She waved at Mark who stood in the hangar with his wife and sons. They were standing next to Sadi, her girls, and Yezeel who made them all look like a group of children. The giant black man turned his head toward her, so Taylor looked away before their eyes met. Ever since meeting him that morning, she had difficulty keeping her eyes off the man. Taylor had never seen such a beautiful person.

"Susan knows Mark wants to come," Taylor continued after looking away from the window. "At least he got to come on one of the test flights."

"His excuse was reasonable," Simon answered. He was standing next to her at the jet entrance. "At least two people should stay with the kids, but it's like I've always said."

"I know," Taylor interrupted. "They can do whatever they want with us, at any time."

"Yeah, so it doesn't matter if anyone stays or not."

After Simon went to his seat, Taylor entered the cockpit and sat in the pilot's chair. She plucked the startup checklist from the pouch on the left of the chair and started following the items. When she energized the engines, the quiet hum in her bones caused chills to pulse through her body, and her lips stretched into a wide smile.

The jet's enhancement had made the engines noticeably more powerful and stable. Taylor wished they could take off that minute, but she had to wait for Sadi to say goodbye to her girls, for everyone to board the plane and get strapped into their seats, and for the machines to load all of their supplies.

"Seems more fitting for Mark to pilot the jet with you, like when we arrived," Cesar said after sitting in the copilot's seat. "Seems like the appropriate action."

"I can't believe we're doing this," she said. "Doesn't feel real. It's even more unreal than what we've experienced so far."

"I agree."

"We're flying to an alien planet with an alien," she began, glancing through the window and wondering if she could see Yezeel, but he was probably still standing with Mark. Conversation was replacing her impatience to begin their journey. "I wonder if this is how the pilgrims felt while crossing the Atlantic to the Americas."

"We are in a better position," Cesar said. "We're in excellent health and have everything we could need. I kind of feel unworthy of the advantage."

"Yeah," she sneered. "We probably don't have to worry about the indigenous population killing us."

"Or conquering them."

"Good point."

"I don't suppose you're going to use their new autopilot program?" Cesar asked.

"What's the fun of that?" Taylor looked forward and smiled.

—※—

Ten minutes later, Taylor flew their spacecraft slowly through the giant landing bay doors and began their journey to Bodn. She felt tempted to turn the jet around so they could view the station, as they had done on their test flights. The station was huge and beautiful, a large disk floating in the blackness of space, partly illuminated by the brilliant light of Dzalm. Yes, she found the planet more beautiful, with the cloud cover, the blue and green oceans, and the white-tipped mountains, but she had enjoyed seeing where they had lived for the past few weeks. On their return trip, she looked forward to seeing it again.

After their test flights, they had flown all around the orbiting station. She had first noticed the lack of windows or large openings. Most of the surface was composed of a solid material resembling a mixture of stone and metal. She had seen many structures, which probably acted as detectors of one sort or another.

She still remembered her surprise at its enormity and realized that they only had access to a small portion. Taylor had tried avoiding suspicious thoughts, but Simon had vocalized them for her.

They're hiding something from us.

They had discussed other possible sources of concern. Cesar had said that the station probably had other landing bays and plenty of space for other creatures to occupy. Taylor doubted that possibility though. She saw no evidence of activity from outside the station, and especially no other spacecraft traffic.

The station's resources, water and air recycling, waste treatment, air circulation, power generation and distribution, all probably required an exponential portion of the station's volume. Taylor had had only one concern though. How many people, or other creatures had passed through the station for a purpose similar to theirs? She could not imagine someone building such a structure just for them. In the end, Taylor decided to avoid paranoid thoughts and focus on their care and lack of mistreatment.

While watching the clouds below them, Taylor made a sudden realization. Their sonic treatment the previous day had left her with much less concern about their predicament. Her thought process now seemed much clearer and less cluttered.

After meeting Yezeel, Taylor could not stop wondering about him.

Although she lacked direct evidence to support her suspicion, she had assumed he knew her thoughts. He reminded Taylor of how Freddy could answer their unasked questions.

Taylor wanted to ask Cesar or Sadi if they shared the same questions about Yezeel. Did he arrive on the station from some sort of spacecraft, or did he just live on another part of the station and had been watching them the entire time? If she gained the courage and the appropriate situation, she preferred to ask Yezeel directly. Never before had Taylor spent so much time premeditating to speak with someone. She usually spoke to people as soon as she wanted to know something.

Approaching the cloud cover reminded Taylor of her first test flight with Max and then of his current state. She wished his recovery would accelerate, and tried to remain hopeful but secretly wondered if he could recover. Even after his treatments with the disgusting flower and the sonic purge, he still acted subdued and distracted by disturbing thoughts. She had noticed an improvement in his condition though, so she attempted to concentrate on that positive observation. Maybe he just needed time. She would add that question to her list for Yezeel.

For the first part of their descent, they accelerated toward Bodn with no apparent gravity, and Taylor could use some of her conscious thoughts on subjects other than flying the craft. She and Cesar talked about what they wanted to do on the planet's surface. But when she began decelerating, all other thoughts fled to the back of her mind. Survival for herself and the group rose to the top of her priorities. She liked the responsibility for their safety. It helped her concentrate.

"ETA at your coordinates in approximately five minutes, Yezeel," Cesar said into his headset.

After announcing the remaining flight time, Taylor and Cesar stopped their conversation and watched the approaching surface of Bodn. She descended, the jet positioned horizontally with respect to the planet's surface. When she noticed the rivers flowing from the mountains, eighty kilometers ahead, she began decelerating vertically and flying forward. The number of visible mountain peaks slowly decreased with their elevation, leaving only the closest peak in view, the upper half covered with snow.

Their final destination lay across a valley on the closest mountainside, and Taylor shifted her gaze between the map program and the view from the window. The screen showed a grid contour map overlaid on the land with their destination shown as an X at the base of some tall cliffs. While flying across the large valley, she glanced several times at the land but focused mostly on their destination. Dzalm was behind them, about thirty degrees above the horizon, and climbing.

"We're here," Taylor announced after bringing the spacecraft to a slow stop, fifty meters above a meadow surrounded by trees. "We'll be on the ground soon."

Taylor was too impatient to land the jet manually, deciding to relinquish control and click on the landing program. While the computer lowered the jet to the ground, the view of the tall cliff ahead disappeared behind the trees, tall evergreens similar to ones on Earth. They looked different somehow, and she was excited to inspect them closely. She wanted to stand on solid ground again, touch the trees, and look up at the sky. All other desires vanished.

"I'm getting out of here," Taylor said once the jet landed peacefully on the ground. She placed her headset on the seat and stopped at the entrance of the cockpit to speak to the passengers. "Time to see this place!"

FORTY-TWO

Freddy

After escorting him over the brink of total oblivion, the woman from the plane showed Freddy how to recompose himself and reconnect with the corporeal world. He had embraced a new reality, his former dread, and was ready for the next phase of his existence. When he merged with a new body and then opened a new pair of human eyes, the sensation of light was a rebirth.

Through the murky liquid, Freddy gazed at the machine standing on the other side of his crystal container. He remembered the same machines on his first visit to the orbiting space station. Without motion, it initiated the draining process and Freddy felt the water level quickly drain below the level of his head. He waited patiently for the draining process to complete, then expelled the liquid from his lungs, coughing at the end of the procedure to eliminate the last remaining fluid.

Physical sensation flooded his awareness, liquid evaporating from his skin and hair, wetness in his nose, the grating under his bare feet. After the glass enclosure slid from his sight, Freddy looked down at himself, at the replica of the body that had died under the Sahara on Earth, the vehicle of his former life. He remembered seeing his body through the eyes of the child, then wondered about its state of decay.

The thought was more interesting than disturbing.

"Welcome back, Mr. Carlson," the machine said audibly.

"How are my friends doing?" he asked, not feeling the need to thank it. No creature controlled the machine. It was just following its creature interaction protocol code. "When will they begin the cleansing procedure?"

"They are in good health and disposition. They are having breakfast now. We will escort them to the location next."

"Good," Freddy answered, wiping the liquid from his hair and stretching. His new adult body felt strong and invigorating. "I plan to watch them but would like to get some clothes, and take a shower."

"Of course," it said and began floating away, maneuvering around all of the containers, which stored the other bodies.

While following the machine, Freddy recalled his first visit to the station, seeing all of the interesting creatures on display and then meeting Dod for the first time. That memory led to his next encounter with Dod, as the bird deep under the Sahara, his final guide on Earth as a regular human.

He enjoyed the sensation of walking barefoot on the cold stone floor while hugging his arms across his chest to fight the chill from his wet body. Every sensation felt so amazing, he wanted to experience more. He would have difficulty waiting until the next day to watch Dod join his friends on their trip to the planet, acting as Yezeel. After exiting the large display room, the machine led Freddy through some dark hallways to a wooden door.

"This is your room for your stay here," the machine said, moving to the right side of the door. "The screens on the wall will show you whatever part of the station you desire. If you would like, I can stay and help you."

"No," Freddy said, wrapping his fingers around the metal door handle. "I can figure it out."

"Of course," the machine said, then began floating away.

When Freddy opened the door, he did not expect to see a replica of his room at Mr. Smith's residence. His bed stood directly inside, next to his dresser. An unexpected flood of emotions almost overpowered him, bringing tears to his eyes. While dressing himself and then sitting on his bed, Freddy reviewed his plans for the immediate future and reminded himself how to manage physical emotions again. At the next possible opportunity, he planned to visit his former boss.

FORTY-THREE

Taylor

Taylor exited the jet first and then Simon. While waiting for everyone to join them in the meadow, she inspected the plants, mostly wildflowers and grass which did not look particularly alien, then the trees from a distance, and finally looked up at the cloudy sky. Dzalm shined briefly through a break in the clouds then disappeared again. The fluffy white clouds looked the same from below as from above, and just like they had on Earth, inaccessible.

Yezeel was the last to join them, and Taylor stopped inspecting her surroundings to watch the tall black man duck as he exited the jet. Once on the ground, he inhaled deeply and then looked at the group.

"Welcome to Bodn," he said, extending his left hand to the sky and looking at every member of the group with his light grey eyes. "I can imagine how you feel. Solid ground feels good under your feet, eh?"

"Yes it does," Cesar answered.

"It feels like I've needed this," Dominga said, "mentally."

"Me too," Gerald said, staring at his feet.

Taylor and Sadi turned from Yezeel to look at Gerald, the man who rarely spoke. She wondered if Bodn would have a therapeutic effect on him and Max. She definitely felt better standing on solid ground, surrounded by flowers and trees. She wanted to see the evergreens more closely but waited to see what Yezeel, their guide, would do next.

A group of birds suddenly flew from the trees on the other side of the jet and all of the humans watched them fly overhead. Taylor thought they looked like birds she might see on Earth, the size of starlings with blue feathers and dark grey breasts. After they disappeared into the other side of the meadow, Yezeel recaptured the group's attention when he began walking in the birds' direction.

"Let me show you where you'll be staying," he said. "I've prepared a temporary dwelling for you until you can make places of your own."

As the group followed Yezeel on a path through the trees, no one spoke. Taylor quickly examined the tree bark of the nearest trees and was surprised when nothing looked particularly abnormal. She had expected to encounter totally different flora and fauna than she had known on Earth. She thought suddenly of Gerda, then felt guilty for escaping without her and Franklin. Gerda would have probably noticed the subtle differences in the vegetation. She would have loved the experience more than any of them.

During their walk through the trees, Taylor thought of the forest they had left in Canada, except they had landed in the place during spring, and not late fall. She was excited to experience spring again without suffering another wet winter in the northwestern United States.

"Welcome to your temporary residence," Yezeel said when he stopped at an enormous opening at the base of a high cliff wall. "This is the main entrance into the complex, but for safety purposes, there are other entrances. There are more than enough spaces for everyone to call their own. I have also left the equipment used in its construction, so you can build more."

"You built all of this for us?" Taylor asked, suspicious again. She stepped to the opening in the rock and looked at the ceiling, five to six meters above her head. "This is amazing."

"You'd be surprised how easy things can be when you have the energy and tools you need." Yezeel walked past her to the large wooden doors inside the short entrance tunnel. "It's especially useful when you can build machines to do all the work for you."

"So there's a smaller door in the door," Simon said, walking past Taylor and stopping at the double doors. Taylor thought Simon looked so small, standing before the huge walls of wood.

"The larger doors are for equipment and supplies," Yezeel said. "The smaller door is for human traffic."

When Yezeel opened the smaller door, Taylor expected to see darkness, but she saw a bright interior instead. Yezeel entered first. Simon followed, then the rest. Once inside, Taylor noticed two machines, similar in appearance to the ones on the station, but about twice the size and they seemed a little dangerous. They hovered silently above the smooth floor on either side of the entrance. After walking past the machines, Taylor inspected the large interior, which reminded her of the landing bay in the orbiting station. She looked at the ceiling, the same height as the main entrance, and noticed the same lights as on the station.

The rectangular room extended about five meters into the cliff and ten more meters on either side of the main doors. A column of rock about two meters thick was near the middle of the room. *Must be load-bearing*, Taylor thought. She could see several entrances carved into the left and right walls.

"Is that some kind of drilling equipment?" Cesar asked, pointing to the large machines ahead of them.

"Yes," Yezeel answered with a glance at the machinery, and Taylor heard his deep voice echo in the chamber. "I'm leaving them here for your use."

"You are too kind, Yezeel," Dominga said, then turned to Sadi who stood next to her. "Helen and Daryn are going to have fun here."

"Let me give you a brief tour," Yezeel answered with a smile. "But I don't want to spend much time here. You'll get plenty of that later. We came to explore this entire world. I think you'll appreciate a hike up the mountain."

At the end of the tour, Taylor felt mentally drained. Yezeel had shown them power generators, the plumbing and sewer system, a communal kitchen, and a few of the rooms, including one for recreation. Each room had a separate bathroom with a simple shower and toilet just like their rooms on the station. Cesar asked most of the questions, mostly about plumbing. Taylor could have spent all day listening to Yezeel explain how everything worked, but he quickly exited the habitation rooms and led them into another large cavern.

"Can anyone remember what these are called?" he asked after walking ahead of the group to a wooden fence.

Two large creatures stood on the other side, eating some sort of plant in a trough. Two smaller animals stood behind them. The larger animals watched the group of humans with curiosity while the two smaller ones walked away to the other side of the pen. Yezeel reached over the fence and affectionately rubbed the closest one on the head. It made a low growling noise. Each had a horn like a rhinoceros, and they looked like cows but with thinner bodies.

"Are they called fult?" Taylor asked, remembering the machines showing pictures to her and the children.

"Yes," Yezeel said, continuing to stroke the creature's head. "You've been eating their milk products. They stay mostly in here for protection from predators. If you open those doors over there, they can go outside. When the young get old enough, you might want to return them to their herd in the valley and replace them with two new mothers. I'll leave that up to you."

Simon, Cesar, and Sadi walked to the fence and took turns stroking their heads. The young ones stayed behind their mothers during the exchange. At some future time, Taylor might consider touching one of them, but for the present, she would pretend the smell did not bother her.

"Let's go on a hike," Yezeel said a few minutes later, then led them outside.

Taylor inhaled the fresh air again in deep gulps, glad to leave the fult pen. She liked eating the cheese but preferred not to see its source. Cesar would probably welcome the experience to milk and care for them.

While they walked on a path in front of the cliff, Taylor reflected briefly on the benefits of a more natural economic system, where people built society by following their individual interests. Taylor had little interest in caring for animals, but she hoped to contribute by developing their technology. Statistically, one of the others was more likely inclined to deal with animals. She was also excited to see the kind of society they could build, especially with the assistance of advanced technology. She loved the concept of building machines to perform the less-enjoyable tasks.

They walked past the main entrance, and then fifty meters farther, they reached a cliff wall, the highest one so far. Before following the trail away from it and into the forest, she looked up to appreciate its height.

"How high do you think the cliff is?" Taylor asked Max.

"Pretty high," he answered with just a single glance upward.

He was walking behind her, followed by Simon at the very end of the line. Due to the width of the trail, they had to walk single file. Taylor chose to walk near the end, hoping to enjoy the experience without feeling obligated to converse with Yezeel. She also wanted to help keep Max talking instead of just thinking. If they let him, he would get lost in his thoughts and spiral into a strange depression. Sadi was doing the same thing with Gerald in front of her.

"Reminds me of the Tetons," Simon said. "That was a fun trip."

"You mean exhausting," Max replied, his lips stretching into a barely recognizable smile.

"Those are in Wyoming, right?" Taylor asked.

"Yes," Simon answered after waiting a moment for Max to respond. "Several years ago, we went hiking there with some people in the company. We hired local guides to help us reach the Grand Teton summit, but when we got to the rough part, someone thought it wasn't a good idea anymore."

"We got close enough," Max said, laughing quietly. "And I was just agreeing with our guide who didn't like the look of the weather."

"Still," Simon replied with mock regret. "I was ready to do it."

"So, Max didn't want to get rained on?"

"That would have been a great article," Max answered, glancing at Taylor. "Terrawatch CEO leads his employees to their death after ignoring the advice of professional mountaineer guides."

"Did Mark go on that trip with you?"

"Yes," Max answered. "And he agreed with me."

"Sure he did," Taylor responded, hoping to goad him further.

"Maybe we'll find a good peak to climb here," he said, keeping his eyes on the trail.

—✳—

For the next hour, Yezeel silently led the way, and the rest of the group conversed quietly with their closest neighbors. Simon and Taylor continued in their attempt to keep Max in conversation while they followed Yezeel up the mountain. After entering the forest, the trail led downward for a bit, and they had to cross a wide stream by jumping on big rocks spaced evenly across it.

Taylor knew the machines had built the trail, and had most likely placed the rocks so they would not have to get soaked in the knee-deep water, or swept away by it. Once safely on the other side, Taylor rubbed her hands in the freezing water and then wondered if they would see the glaciers that had produced it.

After the stream, the trail led up a steep incline to the top of a ridge. Taylor had to use her hands to climb up a few rocky places. She enjoyed the exercise but wondered why the machines had not carved steps as they had elsewhere on the trail. Yezeel paused at the top of the ridge and waited quietly for the rest of the group to join him. Taylor was surprised to see the big man breathing deeply from exertion. During her short time with Yezeel, she had begun to think of him as invulnerable.

"Feels good to get the heart pumping," he said in between breaths. "Makes me feel alive."

"Are we going to any specific destination?" Dominga asked, breathing harder than anyone else.

"I wanted to show you a good view of the mountains and valley," he said after a long inhale. "I know you saw it from the jet, but I think you'll appreciate the view and the journey. Let's rest here until you are all ready to go. It's a nice little clearing, isn't it?"

"It's beautiful. This is fun. I haven't been hiking in a long time." Sadi stood while resting her hand on a tree. She was staring at the bark next to her hand, peering closely. "Ooh, there's ants on this tree. Looks like ones on Earth, but maybe larger antenna."

"There's lots of different species on Bodn, as on Earth," Yezeel answered.

FORTY-FOUR

Taylor

"These ants aren't poisonous are they?" Sadi asked, removing her hand from the dark brown bark.

Yezeel stepped next to Sadi, and Taylor thought she noticed Sadi stiffen as if nervous. The giant man bent over slightly and stared closely at the tree, farther away than Taylor considered sufficient to see the little creatures. *He must have amazing vision*, Taylor thought.

"Some species of ant can inject poison but not these ones. They don't seem to have any injectors, although a bite might cause irritation. Bodn has dangerous creatures, but so does Earth. I'm sure you'll all have an enjoyable time of discovery here."

"I should have spent more time in the wilderness," Dominga said. "This is refreshing, although I am feeling my age. That is for sure."

Yezeel turned from the tree to smile at the beautiful older woman. Unlike Sadi, Dominga showed no evidence of intimidation. That look reminded Taylor of Dominga's stories about meeting foreign dignitaries. Some of her dark brown hair, usually confined neatly behind her head, had escaped and lay across her moist forehead. During the brief pause, she brushed it away.

"When Freddy arrives, maybe he can help improve that situation."

Yezeel was speaking with more solemnity than usual, looking intensely at the woman, then turned away from the group to where the trail led. "Let's continue."

Dominga and Cesar shared a brief quizzical look but said nothing. Everyone took their same positions in line, Cesar behind Yezeel with Dominga behind him, followed by Gerald, Sadi, Taylor, Max, and Simon. After several minutes, Taylor let the distance between her and Sadi widen. She wanted to keep their conversation separate from the others. Yezeel could most likely still hear them, Taylor assumed but might become distracted.

"What do you think he meant?" she asked quietly, turning to face Max and Simon.

"You mean by *improving her situation*?" Simon asked.

"Yes, specifically her age situation."

Taylor simultaneously feared and hoped for Yezeel to respond from the front of the line. On a more conscious level, she preferred to hear speculation from her friends rather than more concrete information from Yezeel. When she made eye contact with Max, he looked away, so she returned her gaze to the ground while waiting for one of them to respond.

"I don't know what the hell to think anymore," Simon said with a tone of comical frustration. "I'm just glad to have solid ground under my feet again."

"That's a good attitude," Taylor said and laughed.

For the next thirty minutes, they climbed higher into the mountain. The temperature dropped, but not enough to cause Taylor any discomfort. Dzalm shined down through the trees, warming her while the cool wind helped to dry the sweat from her body and clothes. Although Taylor experienced the effects of physical exertion, she did not feel drained of energy. She could not remember ever feeling better physically.

When she heard the loud, deep screech from above, everyone stopped walking, even Yezeel. All eyes turned to view the sky, through the trees, searching for the source of the sound. Taylor only noticed the clouds. Their slow movement made the forest canopy appear to move.

"What was that?" Gerald asked.

"Hmm," Yezeel said calmly after stopping and turning to the sky. He paused as if deciding to reveal something. "Let's go see. We're almost to our destination."

They heard the noise two more times before the trail exited the trees. The sound sent a chill to her core, despite the warmth from physical exertion. The trail ended at the bottom of a steep rocky incline where they waited for Yezeel to continue. Taylor looked up at the nearly vertical cliff and gulped. She did not fear heights but felt intimidated by the vertical wall of rock.

"Whatever is making those noises," Gerald said, pointing up the cliff, "is up there."

"Yes," Yezeel said dismissively. "We might have some creatures watching us, but you'll be safe with me. The view is worth the effort."

"We're climbing this?" Dominga asked, more afraid of the climb than the source of the screeching.

"There are plenty of handholds," he answered. "Even the way down is safe. It looks worse than it is."

"Don't worry, Dominga," Simon said from the end of the line. "I'm pulling up the rear. If you fall, I'll catch you."

"Well then, I don't have any worries," she said, smiling.

"Follow me," Yezeel said after a laugh and stepping to the nearest crevice, a large crack in the rock. He began climbing. "If I fall, Simon, don't try to catch me."

"Consider it done," Simon said.

Cesar followed Yezeel up the rock crevice and Dominga followed him without hesitation. They heard the loud screech once, at the beginning of the climb, but only the sound of light wind for the remainder of the journey. The climb required twenty minutes and Taylor came to agree with Yezeel's initial assessment. She experienced no difficulty finding secure handholds and footholds. Although concerned about the return descent, Taylor decided to worry about that later.

"Oh my God," Dominga said after disappearing from Taylor's view at the top. The older woman finished speaking after several seconds of heavy breathing. "We're not climbing that, are we?"

"No," Yezeel said and laughed, also breathing hard.

"Wow," Taylor said after reaching the top and stepping away from the cliff edge. "What a view!"

While waiting for Max and Simon to reach the top, Taylor enjoyed the wind on her face and the view of the valley. They stood on a rock ledge five meters deep and stretching maybe forty meters to the left and right, with a vertical cliff at their backs. To the right of the cliff, they had an awesome view of the closest peak looming above them with the mountain range disappearing into the horizon.

"Humans are programmed for this," Yezeel said, turning away from the valley to glance at everyone. "We can have a better view from the sky, but we can't fully appreciate it until we climb to get here."

"And stand on it," Simon said, solemnly. "And connect to it."

"This is amazing," Cesar said.

"Awesome," said Sadi.

For the next several seconds, no one spoke. Taylor attempted to clear her mind of all thought and let the view fill her consciousness. She inhaled deeply through her nostrils and exhaled through her mouth and enjoyed the sound of the wind, the cool air on her face. When the screeching began again, Taylor jolted, as if awakening from a pleasant dream by a splash of cold water.

Taylor looked upward to the source of the noise. A hundred meters above them, two large birds shot from the cliff like a pair of missiles. They soon flew in opposite directions, gliding away from each other and then beginning to converge again.

"Solka," Yezeel said, his deep voice contrasting with the high-pitched sound of the birds. "This is another treat I was hoping to show you."

"They look like our size," Simon said.

"Bigger," Taylor said, staring at the circling birds. Even at their great height, she could see their immense size. "The machines showed me and the kids some videos of them.”

"They're the top predator in this area," Yezeel said. "No pun intended."

"Is it me," Dominga asked, "or are they dropping in altitude?"

As if in answer to her question, one of the birds began a dive, staying a few meters away from the cliff wall. The bird descended at nearly eighty degrees, Taylor guessed, from her right. Yezeel stepped into the bird's path, separating the group from the creature. After a moment, Taylor remembered to breathe.

"It's just testing us," Yezeel said as the bird continued its descent toward them. "Stand your ground and try not to look frightened."

The bird screeched again, just before abandoning the dive, and then shot away from them across the other side of the rock wall, maybe ten meters above their heads. The noise hurt Taylor's ears. As she watched it fly away, the rush of wind from its wings blew her hair away from her face.

"Here comes the other one," Yezeel said. "Gerald, it won't hurt you. Just stand still."

During the first assault, Gerald had stepped to the other side of the group only to find himself in the same position as Yezeel. Taylor gazed at the sky again, where Yezeel watched, and saw the second bird in a similar dive from the other direction. The sight hypnotized her temporarily, but she quickly found the strength to look away, and then she noticed Gerald, frozen in fear.

Sadi took a single step toward him and then stopped as though afraid to continue moving. Right before the bird abandoned the dive, Gerald extended both hands over his head to protect himself. When the second bird screeched, Taylor thought her eardrums would burst. As the wind rushed around them, she heard a heavy thud behind her, and then a noise that sent chills down her spine, giant claws scraping against stone. The first bird had landed, the male.

"They're deciding if they want to eat us, or throw us over the cliff," Yezeel said as though relaying a triviality.

Taylor turned around to see the giant Solka standing a few meters away from Yezeel, and then she heard another thud on the other side of her as the second bird landed. It stood a few meters away from Gerald. Taylor stared at the second one with a mixture of fascination and dread. She could see its giant curved beak about half of a meter above Gerald's head. The creature resembled a grey hawk with small black stripes extending from its head to the tip of its wings.

"Gerald," Sadi whispered. "You should join the rest of us."

Gerald stood perfectly still. Taylor thought he looked paralyzed.

"Yes, Gerald," Yezeel said from behind Taylor. "Walk slowly backward to me."

Gerald still failed to move, not even when the bird extended both wings and took two hops toward him, then two hops back to its original position. The creature flapped its giant wings, causing a rush of wind, then screeched again, its beak opened wide.

"Okay," Yezeel said calmly. "Everyone step against the wall and stay still. I'm going to help Gerald. Move slowly."

While Taylor and the rest of the group stepped backward against the cliff wall, the birds began squawking at each other. They sounded like crows, Taylor thought. With her back against the cold stone, Taylor watched as Yezeel reached Gerald's side and grasped his shoulder with his giant black hand. Yezeel extended his other hand toward the bird, palm up. Only then did Taylor notice that the black man towered over the creature.

"This is the female," Yezeel explained to Gerald, loud enough for everyone to hear. "After I calm her down, they'll leave us. Stay here."

Yezeel left Gerald's side and slowly approached the bird. As the distance between them decreased, the bird began stepping backward and flapping her wings. The male bird behind them squawked when Yezeel stood within arm's reach of the female.

Taylor thought she heard Yezeel say something to the creature, but could not resolve the words. After he finished speaking, the bird folded its wings and bowed as a sign of submission. In utter astonishment, Taylor watched as the giant creature allowed Yezeel to stroke its great head.

FORTY-FIVE

Helen

After Helen's mother and the other adults departed in the spacecraft, the children spent much of the day, as usual, with the machines in the observatory. Helen, Daryn, and the boys watched the spacecraft deliver her mother and the rest of the refugees to the mountains. Daryn and especially the boys wanted to continue watching, but the machines said they would enjoy hearing about the visit from the participants more than watching them. Helen agreed. She felt like a spy watching the adults and disliked feeling jealous for not getting to accompany them.

After her mother had departed, Helen was excited to spend time without parental guidance, thinking she would have more freedom. But Susan immediately took Sadi's place as a watchful parent. After their experiences together, Susan and Mark seemed like an aunt and uncle. Susan treated them kindly, however firmly, and immersed herself in the role of mother while Sadi explored Bodn.

Helen and Daryn soon discovered how strong of a grip the woman held over her children. Helen felt sorry for Susan's oldest boy, Harvey. He had more homework, had to wake earlier, and always had to eat everything on his plate. Sadi gave Helen and Daryn more freedom.

Sadi would scold her girls only if they slept too long, and they had to at least try a little bit of everything, not eat everything.

Harvey told the girls something they already knew, something he thought was a secret. His mother did not want to stay on the planet and just wanted to go home. Although the boys missed their grandparents, they wanted to stay more than anything, and so did their father. Helen and Daryn promised not to reveal what they knew.

"Susan, do you think they'll come back tomorrow?" Helen asked while chewing the last bite of her roll, enjoying the cold butter on her tongue. "You made great bread, by the way."

"Try not to talk with your mouth full, Helen," Susan said, failing to hide her irritation at having to repeat herself and for Helen using her first name. "I told you. They were planning to spend three days and two nights there. If the plan changes, I will tell you."

"Well, I don't know," Helen answered, swallowing. "You adults don't tell us everything."

Susan, Mark, and their youngest son, George, sat on the other side of the table from the three older children, where Helen sat between Harvey and Daryn. Helen turned from the woman to view the room and half-full table. The dining hall seemed so empty without everyone else present. Helen enjoyed the extra emptiness.

"Can we go to the observatory now?" Harvey asked while scraping his plate and scooping the last of his mashed potatoes on his spoon.

"The girls can go," his mother answered with a stern look at the three children. "But you should wait for your brother."

"Okay, Mom."

"We can all wait," Daryn said. She had finished eating before everyone else, even the adults. "Thank you for dinner, Mrs. Salmon."

Helen sighed audibly and considered kicking the older girl's foot but stopped herself after noticing a movement in her peripheral vision. She looked away from her glass of juice and noticed Miss Poofie enter the room. The machine was hovering toward the dining table. Susan and her husband followed her gaze, and then the other children turned. Helen glanced at Susan and noticed her eyes grow wider.

Poor Susan, Helen thought. *Miss Poofie's not gonna hurt her.*

"Anything wrong?" Mark asked the machine before it reached the table.

"Sadi wants to connect with you," Miss Poofie answered.

"Hi, Mom," Helen said in excitement as the machine stopped on the other side of the table from her, behind Mark.

"Hi, Honey," Sadi answered, her voice projecting clearly from the machine. "Is Mark or Susan around? I want to speak with them."

"We're here," Mark said, smiling. He placed his fork gently on his plate and the metallic sound filled the room. "We're just finishing dinner."

"Hi, everyone!" she said. "Gerald and I are coming back for the night."

"Is anything wrong?" Susan asked.

"Nothing's wrong at all," she answered and Helen heard excitement in her mother's voice. "I'm going to take the girls tomorrow morning for the rest of the tour. It's been fun. We'll see you in about thirty minutes."

"Who's flying the jet?" Mark asked in confusion.

"Are you flying it, Mom?"

Sadi laughed.

"Yeah right. No, it's on autopilot and the machines are going to bring us in."

"What's the planet like?" Daryn asked.

"We'll tell you all about it when we arrive. See you soon."

"Sadi has cut the connection," Miss Poofie said.

—※—

Helen and the other children waited at the entrance to the hangar for the spaceship to arrive. Through the large windows, they watched as the bay doors opened and the spaceship floated gently inside and landed softly on the floor. When the entrance began to slide open, Helen ran through ahead of the other children while Mark and Susan walked.

Sadi emerged from the spaceship first, followed by Gerald. The man was smiling, reminding Helen of how much her mother liked him. Helen liked him too but did not know how she felt about them as a couple. She did not like the idea of having a father figure and was determined to call him Gerald, never *Dad*.

When she noticed the excitement in her mother's eyes, she forgot about Gerald. Sadi looked at her daughter, then Daryn, and her smile stretched to her ears. Before speaking, she took a deep breath.

"Hi, dears," she said before descending the ladder. "It's great to be out of that thing, and breathe fresher air."

"Hi, Mom," Helen said.

"Hi, Sadi," said Daryn.

"Hello, Salmon family," she said, placing one arm around each girl and pulling them to her side. Helen immediately noticed the sharp scent of smoke on her mother's clothes.

"Welcome back, Sadi and Gerald," Mark said, stepping to Gerald's side and grabbing his shoulder. "You've got to tell us what it's like down there."

"We'll tell you everything," Sadi answered. "But first, let's go sit down and get something to drink. I'm thirsty."

"Are you hungry?" Susan asked.

"No, we just ate," Gerald said, looking at the kids. "Yezeel made us dinner over a fire!"

Helen thought he was trying a little too hard to sound excited.

"You guys go to the lounge," Susan said. "I'll go get something to drink. Juice?"

"Anything cold would be great," Gerald said.

While waiting for Susan to return, they walked to the nearest lounge and arranged the wooden furniture in a circle with a small table in the middle. All the chairs and tables on the station, available to the refugees, were made from different kinds of wood, all harvested from Bodn. Helen and the other children chose to sit in rocking chairs, their favorite seats, while the adults sat in simple chairs with small cushions. After they arranged the furniture, Susan arrived, carrying a tray with several glasses and a pitcher full of ice and red juice.

"Thanks, Susan," Gerald said after she placed the tray on the table. He stood from his seat and poured two drinks. He handed one to Sadi, then looked to the rest of the group. "Anyone else?"

"We're all good," Helen said impatiently, turning to her mother. "Okay, why did you change your mind?"

"I didn't know what to expect," she said, then took a drink. "So, I didn't want to bring you girls until I knew it was safe."

"Safe huh," said Susan. "Flying to an alien planet, guided by an alien we know nothing about."

"It's all crazy, I know," Sadi answered with a sarcastic chuckle.

Helen noticed the insincerity in her mother's tone, an attempt to agree with Susan, she guessed. She wanted to interrupt and remind them about their fortunate situation, but she kept her mouth closed. Why were they always so worried about everything? Yezeel and his machines had done nothing to hurt them, quite the opposite.

"It's like we're on a train," Gerald said suddenly and Helen wondered what he meant. Everyone waited for him to continue.

"I feel the same," Mark said, breaking the sudden silence. "So, what happened down there?"

"We landed at the base of some mountains, at the bottom of a cliff. They made an extensive home for us there, carved in the rock." Sadi spoke quickly, then sipped her drink. "A temporary home for those who plan to stay. It was amazing!"

"We get to live in a cave? That's so cool." Helen turned to Daryn, expecting to see the same excitement she felt. But her adopted sister looked at Sadi with wide eyes. "Doesn't that sound fun, Daryn?"

"I don't want to go in a cave," Daryn said. "What if it falls on us in an earthquake?"

"A bodnquake," Helen corrected and laughed, then turned to her mother. "We don't have to worry about that. Right?"

"I doubt it," Sadi said, making eye contact with each girl. "It was very well-made and didn't feel like a cave at all. It felt a lot like this place, actually."

While her mother answered all of Mark's next questions about the cave home, Helen fidgeted with her fingers and rocked loudly in her chair. She hoped her mother had an exciting story, rather than just a description of their new home. She had spent so much time in the observatory studying the planet and wanted to hear a first-hand experience. When Sadi began talking about their hike, Helen slowed her rocking frequency.

"We saw birds!" Sadi said excitedly, looking at Susan. "Most of them looked just like birds on Earth. I didn't expect to enjoy seeing them so much."

"All the birds weren't amazing to see," Gerald interrupted, the second time he had spoken since the strange statement about the trains.

"Maybe you should tell that part, Gerald," Sadi said with a smile.

Gerald took a drink of juice and then cleared his throat before speaking. He attempted to smile, but Helen thought it looked fake.

"Yezeel took us on a hike," he began. "It was fun at first, actually, kind of therapeutic. At the end, we climbed up a cliff."

"Did Dominga climb the cliff too?" Susan asked.

Helen stopped rocking and leaned forward.

"We all did," he answered. "It wasn't dangerous until we reached the top. Two huge birds, Solka, I think they were called, tried to scare us off. They lived higher above and didn't like other predators in their territory, I suppose. At first, they just flew over our heads but eventually landed, a male on one side of us and a female right by me."

"Were you scared?" asked the youngest boy, George.

Gerald turned to the child and stared at him for a moment. He was considering the question as though he did not know the answer, Helen thought.

"I thought it was going to rip me apart," Gerald said finally, then looked at the floor. "Yezeel saved us."

"Yezeel actually went up to the bird," Sadi continued, "and the thing let him pet it, one of the most amazing things I've ever seen."

—※—

That night, Helen fell asleep thinking of the Solka story, imagining herself on the cliff with her mother and their friends. At first, she stood in Gerald's place, facing the giant creature while its wings stretched wide. They slowly folded around her little body, enveloping her in a world of darkness. Helen could still hear her mother speaking to their friends, but she did not seem to remember her daughter. They were all laughing and talking, quite oblivious to Helen's disappearance.

The sound of adult conversation reminded Helen of a party at her home on Earth, lying in bed and listening to her mother and her friends talking. She remembered wondering how she would feel as an adult, and if she would ever invite her friends to play games and talk at her own home. After listening for a while, she forgot about the bird wings folded around her. Then she was back on Earth, in bed with warm blankets covering her.

She heard three knocks on their front door.

Helen listened as the door opened and her mother said a familiar name, *Freddy*. A few seconds after the door closed, she heard the sound of footsteps up the stairs. When someone began turning the doorknob to her room, she pulled the covers over her head and heard the quiet swish of air as the door swung open. Although she did not fear Freddy, he reminded her of a horrible place, a dark hotel room with a monster. As the blankets were pulled away from her face, she held her breath.

"Helen," Freddy said. His blond hair looked longer and messier than she remembered. "Do you want to see the party?"

She nodded and noticed a warm light in his eyes.

Helen grasped his extended hand. After he helped her sit up, she swung her legs to the floor. He led her to the door and then to the top of the stairs. Helen could hear her uncle Brian singing and playing his guitar. She wanted to run down the stairs, but she allowed Freddy to lead her by the hand.

When they reached the bottom of the stairs, Helen saw the crowded living room. Her mother turned first, smiling silently. When the other people in the room turned to her, Helen looked at the ground, feeling suddenly bashful.

Brian stopped singing. He continued to play softly, filling the room with music. When she finally saw him, he stopped and placed the guitar on the floor. He stood, held out his arms for her, and Helen ran into them.

FORTY-SIX

Freddy

Freddy stood in the observation room, watching the jet deliver Gerald, Sadi, Daryn, Helen, and the Salmon family to Bodn. He knew Sadi would be able to convince Susan to return with them to Bodn. Yezeel and the others were waiting for them, and then they would all continue the tour of the planet. Yezeel planned to show them the South Pole first then some tropical islands. He was planning to tell them that when they returned to the station, Freddy would explain the situation.

Watching the spacecraft glide smoothly through the void of space reminded Freddy of flying the BMW and of his life on Earth. The memory caused a mixture of emotions. He was excited to fly the convertible on Earth again, but he dreaded the tasks required to heal Sadi. Not only would she have to endure further trauma, but he might lose even more of his humanity.

"You will soon have a visitor," the machine said while gliding silently into the room. Since no creature sat at the controls, only a guidance program, Freddy had not sensed the machine's presence.

"What visitor?"

"Be on your guard," the machine said. "Where would you like to have the meeting?"

"Let's go to the gardens," Freddy said without hesitation or concern. "Prepare seating and some coffee."

Not knowing the identity of his guest seemed like a gift wrapped in lustrous mystery. On his walk to the gardens, Freddy wondered who would enter the gardens to join him. A friend? An enemy? Both? Although he did not know who would visit him, Freddy knew who had made the invitation. The woman from the plane, his new friend, had invited another creature to the station, probably to test him. Freddy had expected more lessons, ever since she had charged him with the protection of Bodn and its inhabitants.

Freddy entered the gardens and looked up at the milky glass dome, twenty meters above him. An intense radiation above the glass provided light and heat to the various grasses, bushes, flowers, and medium-sized trees. The light was currently positioned directly overhead, but Freddy could choose any position to simulate any time of the day. Noon was as good of a time as any. Since waking on the station, Freddy had visited the gardens three times already. He felt peace there, a temporary substitute for Bodn or Earth.

While walking down the stone pathway to the middle of the large room, he enjoyed the radiation on his face and arms, the cool breeze, and the sound of songbirds. The machines had placed a small wooden table in the gazebo with two black metal chairs on either side. Four stone pillars, four meters high, supported a flat roof of long metal strips, creating a pleasant shadow for the table and chairs. On his last visit, he had positioned the metal strips to allow half of the light above to pass. Before sitting, Freddy took a deep breath and let a small amount of adrenaline enter his bloodstream to prepare him for a potentially dangerous encounter.

"We will be escorting the guest shortly," the machine said while setting the vacuum flask of hot coffee in the middle of the table, then two white ceramic mugs on either side. "Do you require anything else?"

"No," Freddy said.

He expected the machine to leave, but it remained in place, perfectly still. For the next few seconds, the corporeal world seemed to stop and then the machine began vibrating like a plucked rubber band. Freddy stared curiously at it and then noticed the similar vibration of his surroundings. The gazebo pillars and garden vibrated at the same frequency. Freddy extended his hand in front of his face. His hand was the only steady object in view.

"He's on the way," the machine said as though nothing abnormal was happening. While gliding away, the machine continued vibrating along with the rest of the world.

While staring at his steady hand against the vibrating background, Freddy considered the situation, the illusion. The approaching creature had created a seamless blending of background and corporeal. Although Freddy did not yet know how to restore his true senses, the creative manipulation of his reality intrigued him. He had not previously considered that avenue of disruption and wondered what else his new guest could accomplish, could teach him.

"Nice trick," Freddy said to himself while pouring some black coffee into his mug. He held the vibrating liquid to his lips and inhaled the steam through his nostrils, relishing the scent. "I hope you like freshly brewed coffee."

Shortly after the machine had disappeared down the trail, Freddy noticed the top of a human head above the bushes, a head covered in blond, nearly white hair. The person walked along the stone trail toward the gazebo, alone. The world was still vibrating, everything except for Freddy and the guest who would soon enter full view.

When the man walked into the open area in front of the gazebo, he saw Freddy and then stopped. The vibration also suddenly stopped, and Freddy found himself looking at a replica of his own body. When he saw the familiar pair of lips stretch into a wide grin, he remembered seeing the same sight countless times in the mirror.

And then Freddy began seeing the world through the eyes of his guest. He could see the same human body from two different viewpoints, one sitting under the Gazebo and one standing on the trail. Freddy smiled in return, showing no surprise and pretending to have expected the situation.

His replica wore the same clothing, a simple grey shirt and blue pants composed of the same cloth. When the guest continued walking, his smile vanished.

"Welcome," Freddy said while placing his mug on the table and then standing. He felt a brief temptation to introduce himself, reveal his name. "Sit with me, and have a drink."

The guest did not respond until he entered the shade.

"English?" he asked incredulously, a final penetrating stare at his host before sitting. "Thank you for the invitation. Yes, I will try some."

"You're welcome," Freddy said while pouring the liquid.

"We remember you, the thief."

His guest said the word, *thief*, in a tone of praise and not an accusation. He sat in the chair on the other side of the table. While placing the mug on the table, Freddy stared into the same brown eyes he had seen his entire life in the mirror. The situation reminded Freddy of a game. The objective was to determine the identity of his guest while simultaneously concealing his ignorance. He also had to play with an interesting distraction, playing against himself.

"I'm glad you remember me," Freddy said after sitting again. "But I'm confused. What have I stolen, exactly?"

"That's a strange question. Why do you want me to say it?"

"It would give me pleasure."

"I see your friends," his guest said after taking a drink. "But they are not here in your garden? We are above them somewhere, if I am not mistaken."

"That's correct."

"The place resembles Earth, but it's not," his guest continued, and Freddy knew the stranger was seeing Bodn through the eyes of his friends. "I congratulate you for capturing some ripe ones. But you can't keep them, you know. We are too many."

"They are free to leave," Freddy answered, feeling perfectly calm.

"If you return them, we can wipe the slate. They can have their previous lives. Everything will return to steady-state."

"They are not mine to return."

"Of course not," he answered with a grin.

The Freddy across the table looked pleased.

"This conversation must bore you," Freddy said. "Let's play a game."

"Excellent," his guest answered. After a sip of coffee, he leaned over the table, staring at Freddy with wide brown eyes, each pair of liquid orbs his own reflection.

FORTY-SEVEN

Thomas

Thomas parked his 1990 Toyota Land Cruiser in the driveway, and left the vehicle running while he finished listening to the Rush Limbaugh show on 107.3 FM. He liked listening to the radio and usually avoided silence. All of the noise from his life suffocated Thomas and needed replacement. His only solution, a permanent escape, seemed too far from his reach. He had several obligations, children, a wife, and a mortgage.

Rush Limbaugh was talking about the latest news from the Soviet Union and taking calls from his listeners. Thomas often fantasized about calling the show and talking to his radio idol.

"It's just what you've been saying, Rush," the caller said. "The liberals are having another Gorbasm. But if Reagan hadn't kept up the pressure, I shudder to think about the kind of position that lunatic, Gorbachev, would be in now. If the liberals were in charge of this country, we'd already be in World War III."

For the next few minutes, Thomas listened to the rants of Rush and his adoring fans until the downpour subsided enough for him to reach the front door without getting soaked. The current situation at his work and the possible actions inside his home both competed for his attention. After arriving at his front door, he grabbed the door-knob then took a deep breath, and attempted to make the mental transition from rational adults to wife and kids.

"I'm home," he said, hanging his jacket on the coat rack next to the door and then slipping off his shoes. He walked into the kitchen and saw his wife leaning against the counter next to the stove.

"Hi, Thomas," she said. "After you eat, Alex needs help with his homework. I made spaghetti for dinner, and everyone ate it, if you can believe that. Oh, it's cold. I'll heat it up."

After eating dinner and helping his son with homework, Thomas said they should take a break and finish in the morning. He wanted to watch the latest episode of Seinfeld. Jerry and the other actors on the show always made him laugh and helped him survive work until Thursday night without losing his sanity. He worked at the Coca-Cola plant in Roanoke, Virginia. After becoming an executive, he had mistakenly expected his stress levels to decrease, but they had only increased.

While watching the show that night with his oldest son, the episode became his new favorite. In the episode, George Costanza thought he had a heart attack, but his doctor said he just needed a tonsillectomy. While trying to decide whether to follow his doctor's advice for surgery, Thomas's favorite character, Kramer, convinced George to visit his holistic healer friend. In the scene when they visited the healer, Thomas watched from the edge of his seat.

Holistic Healer: *What month were you born in?*

George: *April.*

Holistic Healer: *You should have been born in August. Your parents would have been well-advised to wait.*

George: *Really?*

Holistic Healer: *Do you use hot water in the shower?*

George: *Yes.*

Holistic Healer: *Stop using it.*

George: *Okay.*

Kramer: *I'm off hot water.*

Holistic Healer: *Kramer tells me that you are interested in an alternative to surgery.*

George: *Yes. Yes, I am.*

As usual, Thomas recorded the show to watch later and see what humor he had not initially caught. He often appreciated the show more during the second and third viewing, another reason for loving it so much. Later that night, Thomas cleaned the kitchen with his wife then rewound the VHS cassette and watched the holistic healer part again with her. She pretended to laugh with him, and he pretended not to notice.

Thomas lay in bed that night with a million thoughts swirling in his mind, every late report from his employees, every homework question from his son, every comment by Rush Limbaugh, every joke from Seinfeld. After only a few minutes, his subconscious self won the battle for control and he fell into dreams. He only remembered one dream, a disturbing one. He was in the holistic healer's home with Jerry Seinfeld and Kramer and when they addressed him, they did not call him George. They called him Freddy.

Friday and Saturday passed quickly. They visited his parents in Bedford and then went to church with them in Lynchburg to hear a sermon by Jerry Falwell. The experience was almost euphoric, seeing a political and religious celebrity mixed with the adrenaline rush from an enthusiastic crowd. Although Thomas remembered none of the information from the sermon, he left the mega-church with a negative impression of homosexuals and atheistic Soviets.

Several weeks passed, each one becoming a blur in his memory. Every day at work seemed the same, and every weekend left him feeling stressed about the kids' performance in school and their futures. After the first few days of June had passed, Thomas awoke one morning and tried to remember where the time had gone. The memory of his life seemed like the memory of a movie.

The anticipation of a single future event kept Thomas from losing his patience with life—the NBA playoffs between the LA Lakers and the Chicago Bulls. The names of Scotty Pippen, Magic Johnson, and Michael Jordan entered almost every conversation at work, continually reminding him of the upcoming event. He often imagined his co-workers and friends as zombies, constantly attacking each other with repetitive comments about the playoffs. All of the sports talk became a distraction from the feeling that he was on a trail to nowhere.

Thomas and his family went to his friend's home to watch the last two games of the playoffs. While he and his friend watched the games, their wives talked and their children played together. During the fourth quarter of the final game, Thomas sat on the edge of his seat even after the Bulls had pulled into the lead. For some vague reason, he disliked Magic Johnson and wanted to see someone beat him. After the Bulls eventually won, Thomas felt as though he could claim some of the victory.

"So, what the hell are we supposed to do until next season?" his friend asked at the start of the after-game commentary. "Are you still taking the family to Hawaii this summer?"

"That's her plan," Thomas said, gulping his Coors. "I don't think of it so much as a vacation but as a ten thousand dollar present that evaporates after two weeks."

"Come on, Thomas," his friend said sarcastically. "You're buying memories that last a lifetime! Ha! What kind of vacation would you prefer?"

"One where we don't have to come back."

"There you go again...pun intended." His friend paused to laugh at his little joke. "You can't escape life. It's all we got."

"I just can't shake this feeling," Thomas said. "I need something different."

"Like what?"

"I don't know. Maybe I just need to escape civilization." Thomas paused to stare at the chips and salsa in front of him. "Something far away. I've heard Greenland is an amazing place to visit."

"Greenland," his friend said in exasperation. "You can count me out. I hate the cold."

Thomas continued talking, more to himself than to his friend.

"We could go next year, but that's too far away. I don't think I can make it until then."

"Why don't we do an overnighter somewhere?"

"How about next weekend?"

FORTY-EIGHT

Thomas

The Friday night before his camping trip, clouds began filling the sky. On his way home from work, Thomas vowed to continue with his plan no matter what the weather did to them. He desperately needed to get away. The thought of canceling or postponing the trip caused extreme anxiety. A wet and cold night on the hard ground seemed preferable to another night in his warm bed, surrounded by civilization.

After dinner, Thomas excitedly prepared all of his gear, then watched the news with his wife before going to bed. The meteorologist, a beautiful blond woman, said the weekend had a ten percent chance of rain.

"Does that mean I have a ten percent chance of seeing you tomorrow night?" his wife asked with sarcasm. "Then I wouldn't have to take the kids to church by myself."

Thomas half-expected her to say she hoped it would rain on him. For the entire week, she had attempted to make him feel guilty for leaving her and the kids. But he would not make the mistake of addressing her frustration directly. She was probably looking for a confrontation.

That night, Thomas dreamed of a fire consuming the forest while he watched from inside a tent. He woke in the early morning darkness with the beautiful firelight of the dream filling his memory. Before getting out of bed to leave for the trip, he planned to whisper goodbye to his wife, but she was only pretending to sleep. Saying something might provoke an argument, so he kept quiet.

Before the sun rose that morning, Thomas and his friend began their drive to the Lake Sherwood Recreation Area in the Monongahela National Forest. For most of the drive, dark clouds filled the sky and showered the windshield with a light mist. But his worst fear never materialized. The drizzle never transformed into a downpour, forcing them to return home.

They parked just after sunrise, still dark from the cloudy skies, and walked along a damp trail. Thomas inhaled the cool air deeply through his nose and felt as though nature was flowing through him. He enjoyed the sound of dirt and sticks under his feet, and even the wet mist hitting his face. Their conversation about nature and the NBA playoffs distracted him from work and the problems of his life.

Thirty minutes later, they found a suitable camping spot far away from the main trail. They set up their tents under a thick forest canopy, then left their gear and hiked back to the lake for some fishing. Thomas did not mind the mist, but the water drops hitting his neck from the wet trees began to annoy him.

"Stay away, rain," Thomas said, "until I catch a couple."

While they fished, the skies cleared a little and Thomas stopped worrying so much about the rain. The sun occasionally appeared, its intense heat reminding him of the summer, but the dark clouds prevented them from getting too warm. The experience was significantly reducing his stress, and he had only to keep his mind from wandering forward to Monday to the start of another work week.

Later that evening, they returned to camp with two fish apiece, cleaned and ready to cook. When Thomas began searching for firewood, he wondered if they could find anything dry enough to burn. He almost quit in frustration, until an hour later when they finally succeeded in building a self-sustaining fire.

"That was close," his friend said. "I was getting ready for a sushi dinner."

They finished dinner at six-thirty and decided to go on a small hike while there was still daylight. The hike helped relax his muscles and Thomas felt as if he could walk forever. They walked mostly in silence until they heard thunder in the distance.

"We'd better get back," his friend said.

When they returned to camp, the raindrops had grown larger, so Thomas began throwing all of their wood on the remnants of the fire. The rain signified an early end to their evening. Thomas did not want to spend more time in his tent than absolutely necessary, preferring to sit around the campfire and stare into the flames for as long as possible. Staring into a fire and fishing defined camping for him.

"We need to build this up, so it survives the rain."

"I'm getting out of this, Thomas," his friend said. "That's probably enough wood."

Thomas threw more wood into the fire and then disappeared inside his tent. While zipping the entrance closed, he watched the dancing firelight through the fabric. He removed his wet clothes and attempted to get comfortable in his sleeping bag.

Sounds from the world outside of his tent consumed his attention. The quiet forest had transformed into a place of noise. Nature was forcing him to listen to the slapping of raindrops on leaves and his plastic tent, the hiss of water on hot coals, the crackle of sparks.

He readjusted his position several times to minimize the rocks and uneven ground under his shoulders and hips. After a long time of squirming, he looked at his watch and groaned in disappointment. It was not even ten o'clock. Only forty minutes had passed since climbing into his sleeping bag. The time had seemed like several hours.

Another uncomfortable hour passed and seemed like an eternity. Although the rain had stopped, the outside sounded the same, as all of the water in the trees continued falling to the ground. The noise added to his state of discomfort and became a major distraction from sleep. Thomas could no longer distinguish the sounds. The raindrops sounded just like the sparks from the fire, and he imagined the forest burning all around them.

"Eleven-fucking-thirty?" Thomas whispered after inspecting his watch for the third time in forty minutes. "That's it!"

In the darkness of his tent, he searched angrily for his flashlight and then got dressed with the light beam aimed at the ceiling. When he entered the wet night, he noticed the red coals under the charred logs. The small cavern of coals seemed to contain the only light in the world.

While rebuilding the fire, large water drops fell on his hat and neck. He searched for wood with his little flashlight and cursed quietly when making too much noise, not wanting to wake his friend. Twenty minutes later and after much frustration, Thomas had re-stored the fire to its previous intensity, and the sparks finally became louder than the water drops hitting the forest floor.

Everything was wet, so he had to stand, leaving him physically tired but still wide awake. While waiting and hoping for drowsiness to over-come him, Thomas fed the nearby branches to the fire and enjoyed watching the water sizzle away from the wood. As the firelight dimin-ished, the forest around their camp seemed to shrink, transforming into a cave of crackling embers.

Before the fire died, Thomas had to travel farther to find more fire-wood. For more than half the time he spent away from camp, he shined his flashlight into the trees, searching for wild animals. He kept imagining a wolf or bear was waiting for him in the darkness, and he felt better only when the light revealed an empty, wet forest.

After returning from his third search for firewood, Thomas had a strange vision. He imagined seeing himself, from a distance, standing by the fire and staring into the flames, his face and chest illuminated. Strangely, the mental image reminded him of people staring mind-lessly at small rectangular objects in their hands.

"Strange," he whispered to himself. "What are they holding?"

Snap!

Before Thomas could look away from the fire, his heartbeat became painfully fast. He raised his head to peer into the dark forest, searching for the source of the noise, and had to wait for his eyes to adjust to the dark. His imagination quickly produced two equally frightening possibilities, a hungry bear or a psychotic human killer standing just out of eyesight. He shined his flashlight into the forest and found nothing. While listening for any other sounds, Thomas concentrated on breathing deeply. He needed almost two full minutes for his heartbeat to relax.

Thomas kept his attention on the fire, focusing on the hottest coals, and saw the people again in his mind, multitudes of people staring at rectangular objects in their hands. He could not identify the objects but noticed the flat surfaces shining into their faces. Thomas felt as though he was seeing a world of aliens and not people on Earth.

"Where am I?" Thomas whispered, suddenly feeling lost and alone. The heat from the fire began burning his knees, so he stepped back a little. When he glanced away from the fire, nothing seemed to exist beyond the circle of illuminated trees, and his friend's tent seemed empty. "Only the fire looks real."

After returning his attention to the red and orange coals, Thomas remembered his dream of being on the *Seinfeld* show when they had called him Freddy. While staring into the coals, he entered the dream again.

"Freddy," the holistic healer had said. "Kramer tells me that you are interested in an alternative to surgery."

"Yes," he remembered saying. "Yes, I am."

"I think we can help you."

Snap. Snap. Snap.

The snap of broken twigs nearly made Thomas turn from the fire. Fear threatened to break his concentration, but then the image of a young man with blond, almost white hair materialized in his mind, and Thomas finally recognized the home in his imagination. His dream had not taken place in the holistic healer's home from the *Seinfeld* show, but from a more familiar place where an old man lived. The old man had three guests, a beautiful woman with dark blue eyes and her two young daughters.

Snap.

A low growl suddenly filled the world, then a white polar bear stepped into the circle of trees, illuminated by the firelight. The giant beast stood on its hind legs and raised its arms. It roared threateningly, saliva dripping from bone-white teeth. Thomas looked calmly into the polar bear's eyes, and the beast froze in place. The crackling of the fire died and the water stopped falling from the trees, leaving the forest in silence. Freddy stood, extended his right hand, and felt the creature's claws. They were sharp.

—※—

"You're new at this, aren't you?" the guest said from across the table under the gazebo.

"I don't know," Freddy said with a grin. His life as Thomas had become just a memory. "You tell me."

"You have help," the guest said. "Don't tell me. I'll figure it out."

"I'm sure you will," Freddy said. "Now it's my turn."

"No," the guest said loudly, extending his index finger vertically in the air and making Freddy pause. "We can play another game if you want after I show you something first."

FORTY-NINE

Freddy

After hearing three knocks on a metal door, Freddy opened his eyes and stared at a ceiling of polished aluminum. His small cabin had no windows, but cool air was blowing on his face from a vent in the ceiling. He sat up and a single blanket slid from his chest. On the opposite side of the small room, he noticed a desk with a lamp, an opened laptop, and a stack of papers.

"What is it?" Freddy asked after getting off his bunk and opening the door. A soldier stood in the hallway.

Freddy had not intended to do or say anything. He was not in control of the body, but he could feel its physical and emotional sensations. While waiting for the soldier to answer him, Freddy looked down the hallway and noticed the absence of windows. Then he saw the pipes running along the ceiling.

"The captain requests your presence in his quarters."

"Thank you," Freddy heard himself say in another man's voice. "I'll be there."

The soldier shut the door, and Freddy got dressed in an officer's uniform. Before exiting the cabin, he looked into the mirror and rubbed his eyes.

"What's going on?" he asked, sighing.

Freddy immediately recognized the tall man in the mirror. The one charged with finding him on Earth, Josef Brunner, was staring back at him.

While walking through the hallways, Josef was thinking about his wife and how much he wanted to see the sky again. He hated living on a submarine—the novelty had worn off after the first day. After reaching the captain's cabin, he knocked on the door. He was suddenly angry at his superiors for how much trouble they had cost him and the world. Would he see his wife and children again?

"I am partially to blame," he said while shaking his head.

"Come in, Herr Brunner," the captain said with impatience.

Josef did not blame the man for his anger and pretended to ignore the insolence. Freddy could feel the prevailing stress from everyone on the submarine. All of the enlisted men and officers worried for their lives, for family and friends. The world seemed dangerous.

The captain's quarters consisted of a large office with a door to his private chambers in the back wall. The captain sat at his desk with two men opposite him, a laptop in front of each man. When Josef entered, the two men on either side of the captain stood. They were the captain's two most trusted men, the weapons officer and the executive officer.

"What's going on?" Josef asked while taking a seat across from the captain.

"We were wondering if you could tell us," he said and turned his laptop so Josef could see the screen.

Josef immediately recognized the central Chinese news station from Beijing. Although he could not translate the Mandarin words fast enough, he understood many of them. While the Chinese anchorman spoke, the corner of the screen showed a city in ruin, smoke rising from demolished buildings, and people searching through rubble for survivors. The screen then showed American fighter jets flying away from the scene.

"The Chinese have declared war, and they're sending a delegation to the Russians and Iranians," the captain said. "What can you tell us about this?"

"What can I tell you?" Josef said without looking away from the screen. "This is the first I've heard of it."

"Is this the beginning of some secret operation?" the man asked, slapping his right hand on the table. "Morale is borderline already. I don't know how we can tell the crew about this."

While waiting for Josef to respond, Freddy focused on the captain's eyes and emotions. The man's anger and frustration were screaming at him. After several seconds, Freddy realized that the captain's face had become perfectly still. He even seemed to stop breathing.

The scene seemed like a display at a museum with Freddy seeing through the eyes of a statue. He could move Josef's eyes, he soon discovered, and looked away from the captain. In his peripheral vision, he noticed a shadow cast against the wall by some invisible light source, and then a man emerged from the shadow.

The man had straight black hair falling just below the shoulders, a stark contrast to his pale face. He dressed in a long white silk shirt, embroidered with gold and silver thread. A band of woven beige fabric encircled his head, holding the strands of his hair neatly away from his face.

"It's clear, Mr. Carlson," he said with a sharp accent, walking behind the captain where Freddy could see him more clearly. "It's clear that you are no threat to us. We will ultimately succeed in restoring your friends to Earth. So, as a gesture of sportsmanship, I'm allowing you the honor of making a key decision for the game back on Earth."

"What key decision?" Freddy asked, using Josef's lips.

"First, let me get you up-to-date," the man said, smiling and stepping to the other side of the captain. He touched the top of the computer monitor and the image on the screen changed. Russian troops surrounded the Kremlin. "Three years ago, the Chinese betrayed their pact with the royal families and backed a socialist faction in Russia. They succeeded in restoring the Russian Federation to communist control."

He tapped the top of the screen and the scene became a video of the night sky, full of shooting stars with a small explosion preceding each trail of light. Freddy wanted to move his head closer to the screen, but he only had control of Josef's eyes and mouth.

"Over the next two years," the man continued, "there was a secret war for control of space. In the end, the Russians and Chinese managed to destroy most of the Western military satellites and install their own. Then they showed that they could destroy nearly any aircraft threatening them, including what the space agencies attempted to send. They could even damage aircraft carriers. Only the submarine fleet could evade their orbiting weapons."

"The future sounds truly frightening," Freddy said, feeling detached from the situation. "What decision do I get to make?"

"I think you're all caught up," the man with black hair said, then tapped the screen. The scene returned to the Chinese news station. "Now for your regularly scheduled program."

The man disappeared, and life returned to the captain's eyes.

"My superiors knew nothing about this," Josef said, no longer under Freddy's control. "We're not working with the Chinese anymore, and they eliminated the royal bloodline in Russia."

"So this is the deliberate start of a war?" the captain asked. "You should have never let that much money get into Asia."

Josef blinked and then Freddy was staring at the aluminum ceiling in Josef's cabin again.

The room was quiet and the laptop screen on the desk provided the only light. For the next several minutes, Josef lay on his back and stared at the ceiling, the frustration of insomnia consuming his thoughts.

The quiet room reminded Freddy of another scene where two twins under a gazebo sipped coffee. They were sitting in silence and enjoying the plants, the breeze, and the artificial sunlight. Freddy was tempted to flee the dark submarine cabin and return his attention to the garden, but the stranger was forcing him, somehow, to view the future world through Josef Brunner's eyes.

A loud and prolonged buzz made Josef jump in surprise. Then more silence, but his pulse had already doubled. Then another buzz.

Knock. Knock.

"Yes," Josef said while opening the door.

An enlisted man stood in the hallway. He stiffened, then saluted.

"Your presence is required in the captain's room. It is urgent, sir. He ordered me to bring you in your present attire."

The man led Josef quickly through the narrow hallways, then opened the captain's door without knocking. After Josef entered the room, the sailor quietly shut the door and walked away.

The captain was seated and talking on the phone. Josef looked at the officer standing beside the captain, the second in command, and the only other man present. He was holding both hands behind his back. He glanced at Josef, nodded, then returned his attention to the captain. Freddy noticed perspiration on his forehead.

"That's what I'm fucking telling you," the captain said into the phone receiver, almost screaming. "But you will act like it is a drill. Now get your shit together. The launch window closes in twenty goddamned minutes. Prepare both fucking trajectories!"

The captain slammed the phone on the receiver.

"Shit!" he said to the phone before looking up at Josef.

"What's going on?" Josef asked. "It's not time to test the dog pack."

"They're going to obliterate Los Angeles and Portland as payback for Hangzhou. Two ICBMs are in the sky now."

"But what about–" Josef began.

"We don't know how, but they disabled our defensive capabilities," the other officer said. "We're the last line of defense, the closest at least, but we only have one dog pack."

"So we have to choose?" Josef asked, hiding the panic suddenly threatening to choke him.

"You have to choose," the captain said. "General Olsen said it was your call."

While Josef's heart raced, the men stared at him and waited. After a few seconds, Freddy noticed that all background noise had stopped and so did the hearts of all three men in the room. A shadow appeared in the wall behind the captain and transformed into the man with black hair again.

"I am sorry, Freddy," the man said, frowning and shaking his head with fake sorrow. His black hair swung in the air over his shoulders. "But this is the future we have planned, and you will be the one to make this choice."

Freddy quickly scanned the room with Josef's eyes then looked back at the man with black hair. Seeing and not breathing was strange. He felt tempted again to leave and return to the garden, but curiosity was now the only force keeping him there, in the office deep under the ocean.

"Should be an easy decision," the man continued. "L.A. has so many more people. Millions more. On the other hand, L.A. is full of debauchery, a lot more than Portland. Believe me, a lot more! You might be doing the world a favor to let them destroy Los Angeles."

"Of course," he continued as if just thinking of another point. He touched his chin with a thumb and index finger. "Sadi ends up returning to Portland with her girls and brother, so you couldn't let them destroy Portland. But sacrificing millions of more people just to save a few friends might be a little immoral."

The man with black hair vanished and the men in Freddy's vision returned to life. He waited several seconds for Josef to answer the two navy officers, but then he realized what was happening. Freddy controlled the body now.

"So what are your orders, Herr Brunner?" the captain asked, making no effort to hide his emotions. His frustration and anger were partly directed at Josef.

"Los Angeles has more people," Freddy said, not expecting to use a German accent. "But both cities have strategic value, Portland possibly more."

"They're not planning an invasion, sir," the second-in-command spoke before the captain could. "They don't dare send their navy across the Pacific. They are sending a message, nothing more."

"I need some time to think," Freddy said. "I will return in five minutes."

Both men looked at each other and then watched Josef exit the room. Freddy could feel their eyes on his back. Once in the hallway, he attempted to breathe and regain control of his racing heart. The horrible consequences of nuclear war prevented clear thought. He imagined two nuclear blasts vaporizing millions of people, erasing his childhood friends, Sadi and Brian, and Helen and Daryn.

The experience was too real, the narrative too convincing. Josef and the other men on the submarine behaved just like real living creatures, feeling real emotions, fear, panic, and anxiety. In comparison, his life in Roanoke, Virginia, had seemed like a dream, a low-budget movie. The man with black hair had much more control over the background than Freddy could have imagined.

"Future events can only be planned," Freddy said, knowing the man with black hair could hear him. "They cannot be known with such certainty."

Freddy needed physical exertion to help him think, so he started reviewing the information on a short walk, searching for clues. Something about the story did not feel right. The narrative seemed to lack harmony, but he needed more time to determine the reason for his feelings.

Freddy wandered through the narrow hallways for five minutes. He passed several men who glanced curiously at his sleeping attire. After ten minutes, Freddy knew he had to return and hoped to make a final decision before reaching the captain's office.

On his walk back, he thought of his lonely journey into space and leaving Earth far behind him. The view of Earth from so far away had looked so peaceful and the memory suddenly restored his peace of mind. That experience contrasted sharply with the future scenario presented to him. While wrapping his fingers around the door handle, the story unraveled.

"What is your decision?" the captain asked after Josef entered the room. His anger had vanished, replaced by panic.

"It is all a lie," Freddy said with a sigh. He no longer saw the captain but the man with black hair. "Do whatever you want."

Freddy placed his cup of coffee on the table and stared at the body of his twin. It lay face down on the table, quite still.

PART V

AWAKEN

When born again
Forget what's forgot
And look within

FIFTY

Brian

"Good night, Brian," his aunt said, struggling with her use of English. She rose from the couch and stretched. "For me, too late."

"Good night, Aunt Mina," Brian said.

After Freddy had left him alone in Bergen, Norway, Brian rented a car and drove north to a city he could not pronounce where his aunt and uncle lived. To his relief, they'd acted overjoyed to see him, even after learning of his status as an illegal alien. Brian had prepared to tell them a partially true story if necessary, but they had declined to ask for more details. That was another relief. Inventing a credible but false story had seemed beyond his capability. His sister could have devised one easily.

Brian stood from the couch and hugged his aunt, appreciating how solid she was for an older woman. He had definitely inherited his height and muscle mass from the Jacobsen side of the family. He usually had to give weak hugs to older people. His uncle had already retired for the night, politely declining the offer to watch the movie with them. After returning to the couch, Brian yawned and grabbed the remote control.

To remind him of home in the Northwestern United States, he chose to watch the movie *Coraline*. The movie also reminded him of earlier that year when he had taken his niece, Helen, to see the movie in the theater. After two nights with his aunt and uncle, anxiety from his experience in Bergen had partially dissipated, leaving Brian with a feeling of homesickness, which related more to his sister and nieces than any geographical location.

Before pressing play, Brian yawned and stared at the television screen at the still image of Coraline holding a dowsing rod. The illuminated screen and flickering light of the fireplace helped keep the darkness and cold of night away. The soft background noise of crackling fire and screaming wind helped him relax.

When Coraline first met the other mother, a witch disguised as a creepy version of her real mother, Brian began struggling with drowsiness. But he was enjoying the experience, so he fought to stay awake and watch the whole movie. During the mouse circus of Mr. Bobinsky, Brian heard a small knock on the front door.

While leaving the movie playing, Brian stood from the couch and walked to the front door to meet the visitor. For some unknown reason, he was not worried about who might be waiting for him. Since he seemed to have bad luck with unplanned visitors lately, he thought that his lack of worry was strange. After opening the door and looking outside, Brian failed to notice the messy-haired blond child walk into the home and continue toward the bedroom his aunt and uncle had let him use.

While shivering from the cold air, Brian stared at the BMW parked on the street and noticed the streetlights reflecting off its dark windows. He shut the door a few seconds later and then returned to the living room to finish the movie. Ten minutes after pressing play, he fell asleep.

In one of his dreams, Brian played his guitar and sang a song for a group of friends at Sadi's home. In the middle of the song, the crowd parted and Helen appeared. She looked at him curiously and then started running toward him. As she ran into his arms, the impact jolted him awake.

The fire had died, leaving only a soft red glow from the coals. Brian opened his eyes and stared at the television screen for a few seconds. The movie had ended, but a short introductory sequence continued to play where the evil witch was sewing the Coraline doll to a peaceful melody. After noticing movement on the loveseat where his aunt had sat, Brian turned and saw a child sitting there.

"Hello?" he whispered, rubbing the sleep from his eyes. When his sight returned, the child with messy-white hair was still there.

"Don't be afraid, Brian," the child said. "I am Freddy and I'll explain everything later. I'm going to sleep for a little while longer, but we need to go in the morning. When they wake up, say goodbye to your aunt and uncle. I'll see you later."

"Wha..." Brian began.

"Shhh." The child pressed a small index finger to his lips. "Go back to sleep."

—※—

At seven o'clock in the morning, Brian opened his eyes and looked at his watch. The window still showed darkness outside, but a light from the dining room made the living room a little bit brighter. From the noise, his aunt was probably making breakfast.

Brian took a deep breath, sat up, and then looked at the empty loveseat where the child from his strange dream had sat. For some reason, his memory of the encounter did not feel like a dream. He distinctly remembered the child identifying himself as Freddy, and although Brian had not known Freddy at that age, his physical attributes were consistent. His rational mind tried to reject the information, but the memory seemed undeniably real. After all of his other recent experiences with Freddy, Brian could not easily discredit the strange situation.

"Good morning, Brian," said a small voice. The child walked into the living room and stood in front of the loveseat. He was looking at

Brian's chin, not his eyes. "I know this is very disconcerting, but I will explain after we leave. Pretend that I'm not here. Your aunt and uncle won't notice me, so don't worry about introducing me. Try to act normal."

Brian just stared at the child through half-open eyes. All thought had disappeared from his mind. Before he could think of how to respond, his aunt appeared, blocking the light from the dining room. Brian paused for a few seconds before turning to her.

"Breakfast is ready," she said with a smile. "Hungry?"

"Uh, yes," Brian stammered. "Thank you. I'll be right in."

"Morten is at work already," she said before walking away. She did not even glance at the child.

Brian washed his hands, rinsed his mouth, and then entered the dining room. He found the child sitting at the table, eating eggs and a biscuit. While they ate, his aunt talked only with Brian and did not seem to notice the young boy sitting with them. After quickly eating his breakfast, Freddy left the table with his dishes and placed them quietly in the sink. A few seconds later, the front door creaked open and closed softly.

Brian turned to his aunt and smiled. She showed no signs of noticing the noise. Less than a minute later, they heard three solid knocks on the front door.

While Brian wondered what to do, his aunt placed her fork on her plate and stood calmly from the table, showing no signs of concern for such an early visitor. She walked from the room, opened the front door, and spoke in Norwegian to a man with a deep voice. Brian remained at the table and listened. Before he thought to join her, he heard the door close.

His aunt returned to the dining room entrance and stared at Brian with a little sadness in her eyes. She stood with her arms folded, recovering from the cold.

"Your friend waits outside," she said with a frown. "He says you need to leave."

Twenty minutes later, Brian stood at the passenger door of the

BMW, a duffel bag in one hand and his guitar in the other. He had already said a final goodbye to his aunt, but she remained on the front porch with her arms folded for warmth. Brian held his guitar in the air as a substitute for a wave, then took a final look at the quaint Norwegian home. He hoped to burn the image in his memory, the lush green vegetation, the roof of red ceramic tiles.

"Hi," the child said as Brian closed the passenger door. "We need to visit New York City. I'll explain everything on the way."

The boy looked so small in the driver's seat. He could not even see over the dashboard, and Brian wondered how he could see to drive and fly. When the boy turned to face him, Brian realized the situation—Freddy the child was blind.

FIFTY-ONE

Freddy

Freddy the child parked at the closed gate of a cemetery in Portland, Oregon. Before leaving the warm interior of the BMW and entering the cold night, Freddy rubbed his eyes. They were dry. After losing his ability to see, he had used his other senses so much he often forgot to blink. Keeping his eyes closed seemed too forced, especially when concentrating on other sensory input. He was not complaining though. The calm of physical blindness helped him concentrate and might help him endure the next hour.

Freddy did not need physical sight anyway. He had full access to the probe and could sense every aspect of the earth for several miles in all three dimensions. After successfully passing through the cave under the Sahara, the woman from the plane had given him ownership of the probe.

He would require the extra help, she had claimed. Only after his encounter with the creature in the garden had Freddy understood his need for assistance. He needed help to remain hidden while on Earth. Traveling as a child would only fool the human creatures in the corporeal world, not a shark of the background.

When the cold October wind hit his small body, Freddy shivered and pulled the fleece jacket hood over his head. After shutting the door to the BMW, he began walking on the narrow cemetery road. From high above the trees, the probe scanned the area, its sensors penetrating the earth for several meters, revealing the coffins resting there. While walking on the road, Freddy scanned many of the bodies, all lying on their backs with arms folded across their chests. The sight reminded Freddy of horror movies. Instead of fear, however, he shook his head and chuckled at the ridiculous scenario of dead bodies returning to life. His smile disappeared after recognizing the first dead child.

Breathing hard, Freddy stopped the scan and quickly returned the sensors' view to the surface. He hugged his chest more tightly and decided to continue the search by scanning the headstones for the name, Jacob Jacobsen.

The probe required only a moment to find the headstone. From high above, Freddy watched as his child body left the road and walked across the grass toward the small grave. He stopped and crouched so he could touch the name with his small fingers. The cold headstone caused his heart to race and his breathing to accelerate. With his hand on the engraving, he imagined the name glowing.

Jacob Elias Jacobsen

January 2005 – November 2008

Rest in Peace

Freddy read the inscription out loud. The sound of his small voice seemed to help extract the plan from his mind to the corporeal world. Until that moment, the plan had only existed in his imagination. Now he wondered if his next actions were immoral. The night was suddenly much colder.

Freddy wanted to continue with the plan but wondered if he could muster the emotional strength to begin the necessary steps. For the first time since passing through the tunnel, Freddy was afraid, not for himself, but for Sadi's possible reaction to the gift he wanted to give. Even if assured of success, could Sadi heal from the trauma?

As the wet grass soaked into his small knees, Freddy looked through other eyes at Sadi sitting across a fire. She and the others were listening to Dominga tell a story. Sadi did not notice Yezeel looking at her. He and Freddy knew the torment of her dreams and wanted to assist in her healing.

While the flames performed their chaotic dance for the refugees, one of his favorite childhood cartoons, *Invader Zim,* burst to life in Freddy's imagination. Some creature was inviting Freddy to play another game in the background, one specifically designed to arouse his curiosity. Unlike the creature from the garden who had crashed the new world around him like a wave, this new creature dangled the scene before Freddy and waited. The situation reminded him of standing at the edge of a pool. He had only to reorient himself and let gravity pull him into the cartoon world.

—※—

"I know you're spying on me, Dib," Zim said from across the yard between their houses. He leaned out of his window with a small fist raised in the air. "Come over and I'll show your pathetic human brain how your planet will end. Ha ha ha ha."

Zim disappeared from his window, and Freddy leaned outside of his window. A full moon devoid of features hovered in the purple sky while black clouds flowed past like a river. Freddy held his right hand in the air, wiggling his thumb and three fingers. His cartoon hand looked cute.

For the next little while, Freddy forgot about the headstone below his face.

"My master wants to show you something," a little robot said cheerfully as Freddy approached Zim's front door. Tall yard gnomes with coned hats stood motionless on either side of the walkway and followed Freddy's movement with their eyes. "Do you want to see my pig?"

"No," Freddy said with fake irritation. He enjoyed playing the part correctly. "Keep your ugly alien pig away from me."

Zim's little robot servant, Gir, led Freddy into Zim's house, and the door shut automatically behind them. He followed Gir through the mock human living room, past the robot parents standing motionless against the wall, and then down a long hallway. Gir opened a door at the end of the hallway and pointed to the large toilet.

"My master's waiting in the lower levels," Gir said. "I'm gonna play with my pig."

Freddy walked to the toilet, jumped inside, and then the world spun around him and disappeared. When he could see again, he stood in a huge underground laboratory, surrounded by grey walls and bright purple machines. Freddy turned around and noticed Zim standing before several large screens on the high wall. Zim had bright green skin, large pink eyes, and an intense sneer.

"There's only one reason why I've allowed you into my super-secret base," Zim said, then turned to face the screens on the wall. A keyboard floated toward Zim attached to a large flexible tube, which connected to the wall under the largest screen.

"I've been here before," Freddy said flatly.

"Shut up," Zim yelled with a high-pitched squeal. He began pounding the keyboard with both tiny hands. "The reason, foolish human, is to show you your doom. You've been a worthy adversary, so you have earned the right to attend the premiere."

"Whatever, Zim," Freddy said, trying to sound condescending. "Just show me your stupid plan so I can go home and do something, not stupid."

The largest screen in the center flashed with blue light, then a white box appeared with cartoon bees flying in and out of a small entrance. The lid floated away to reveal a swarm of bees dancing on a honeycomb.

"The honey bee," Zim began and turned to Freddy. "Pollinating the flowers, making delicious honey only to be stolen by their horrible human slave masters. What if the bees were just a little bit smarter? I wonder what would happen then? Ha ha ha ha."

While the bees danced on the honeycomb like teenagers at a disco, a beaker containing black liquid descended from the ceiling, connected by another tube. The liquid almost spilled when Zim grasped it in his little hand. He extended the beaker above his head and the liquid splashed on the computer screen.

"Behold," Zim said with a malevolent snicker. "The smart virus! After I inject my first lucky victim, he'll infect all of his friends, and their friends, until every bee is infected. After the bees are smart, they'll realize how stupid they've been to help you humans, and then they'll go into hiding."

"Why not just make a dumb virus for humans?"

"Ha ha ha ha ha," Zim laughed wildly. "Make humans dumber? That's impossible!"

On the giant screen, the image changed to a bee strapped to a surgical table. A syringe suddenly appeared and injected the bee. The little creature struggled in pain for a moment, then became still. Zim typed on the keyboard and the straps loosened. When the bee realized he was free, he buzzed in anger, spitting at the syringe. Then he flew out of a window and into the night.

While Zim laughed hysterically, Freddy paused to appreciate the setting. He remembered the creature who was playing as Zim. She had also played the part of a raven in the cave, providing companionship in that lonely place. His old friend had come to the rescue again.

Before Freddy could think how to respond, two separate flex tubes with giant robot fingers grabbed him from two sides. They lifted him into the air, pulling his cartoon body so that he stretched in both directions. Although feeling no pain, Freddy began struggling.

"Let me go, Zim," he said after ascending halfway to the ceiling. "What are you going to do? Kill me?"

"Oh, I'm not going to kill you, dear human," Zim said while spinning in his levitating chair and rising to look at him, eye to eye. "I wanted to drill something into your stupid human brain."

"Let me go," Freddy said while struggling. "Your words are meaningless to me. Besides, I am looking forward to seeing your pathetic plan fail."

"You humans," Zim began while floating backward, away from Freddy. "You humans take everything so seriously. Horrible things happen, then people recover. Yes, I'm going to destroy humanity. Blah, blah, blah. Why don't you just try to have fun? Make a game of it. You really don't need my amazing powers of destruction. Your miserable human genes are already leading you down the path of doom!"

The arms began squeezing next, and Freddy's body began to get thinner. Eventually, his head exploded and Freddy was looking at the headstone in the corporeal world again.

—※—

After his experience in the cartoon world of his childhood fantasy, Freddy felt better. At some point in the future, he would have to repay Dod for the kindness. He also understood Dod's advice and would try to enjoy the next experience.

The probe had descended until it hovered five meters above the headstone. Before initiating the necessary steps, Freddy inhaled deeply. He slid his tiny fingers across the inscription one last time.

"Let's get you out of here," Freddy whispered, and the cold wind suddenly became colder.

He stood and walked a meter behind the headstone and then waited for the vibrations to start. His human ears could not hear most of the frequencies, but what he could hear intensified until the ground in front of the headstone began to ripple. The ground waves grew larger until the grass ripped apart in several places and the grave site became a fluidized bed of rippling dirt and grass. Freddy could feel the movement from where he stood, but the ground did not rip apart under his feet.

After seventy seconds of intense vibration, the top of a small wooden coffin rose from the ground. After ten more seconds, the coffin had risen to the top and appeared to float on a pool of dirt. The vibrations abruptly stopped and Freddy stood motionless for a while, staring at the box. The next minute seemed like an hour.

When he took a couple of steps forward, he could not see the head-stone anymore. The heavy stone slab had sunk into the earth.

FIFTY-TWO

Audrie

Audrie locked her apartment door after returning from work, pausing a moment to stare at the deadbolt. Locks now reminded her of the incident two weeks ago at the psychiatric hospital with her brother. Many things now reminded her of Max, and also of Freddy Carlson. Although the young man was several years her junior, she could not stop thinking of him and especially their last moments together. She often dreamed of seeing him again, and some of her dreams even included sexual encounters.

After securing the door, she followed her usual routine of preparing dinner and catching up on email. Since she had no plans that evening, she dressed in her usual sleeping attire, shorts and a silk shirt. If she accidentally fell asleep while reading, she would at least be comfortable.

After dinner, she sat on the couch with a laptop computer. She read with the fire crackling and providing an extra splash of warmth and light. While in the middle of her first article, someone knocked on the door.

Her heart rate immediately accelerated. The person at the door had bypassed the normal routine and somehow had entered the building without the permission of the guards. They should have notified her. Before standing from the couch, she set the laptop away from her and considered calling security. But when the person knocked again, she decided to speak to them through the locked door first.

"Who's there?"

"My name is Brian Jacobsen," said a deep male voice. "Freddy sent me. I'm Sadi Jacobsen's brother."

Before responding, Audrie assessed the threat potential. She was expecting the intelligence agents watching her to attempt some kind of subterfuge, to gain more information about her involvement with Max's rescue. The man on the other side of the door was either telling the truth or an intelligence agent, and Audrie did not know which situation caused more alarm.

"How did you get up here?"

"Don't worry," he said after a short pause. "Security doesn't know I'm here. To tell you the truth, I really don't know how I got past them. They just let me in and did not ask any questions."

Definitely an agent, she thought but then doubted they would invent such a stupid story.

Audrie unlocked the door and opened it just wide enough to see into the hallway. She immediately looked upward at the tall man. In her peripheral vision, she thought a child with white hair stood next to him, but no one was there, just the man with dark brown hair and deep blue eyes.

"What do you want?"

"Freddy sent me," he said. "He'll be coming later. I can explain in more detail."

Brian extended both hands in the air, attempting to show peaceful intentions, and her concerns mysteriously melted. Audrie disliked her sudden emotional shift but could not change how she felt. She had to remind herself of the dangers of letting a formidable man into her apartment. Although she had training dealing with threatening people, he looked too strong for her to handle. A warning voice inside her head said to proceed cautiously. Even if he was telling the truth, someone might overhear their conversation.

"Come in," she said, opening the door just wide enough for him to enter and then leading him to a chair by the sofa. She folded her arms after remembering she was not wearing a bra. "Please have a seat while I get in something more appropriate for company."

Audrie closed her laptop on the couch and then left the room. After slipping into a robe, she grabbed one of her pistols, a nine-millimeter Heckler-Koch. She considered hiding the weapon but decided to let him see it. When she entered the room again, she watched his eyes instantly fall to the weapon. She resumed her position on the couch and faced him.

"I know how to use this," she said and placed the pistol in her lap. "Please don't try anything, because I don't want to use it."

"I am who I say I am," he answered, looking her fearlessly in the eyes. His deep voice seemed to resonate inside her chest. "Freddy told me to tell you the last thing he said to you, and then you would believe me."

"And what was that?" she asked, hoping to portray a relaxed disbelief. She had heard Freddy's last words in several dreams.

"He asked," Brian began, then looked to his right, as if listening to someone, "if you would remember him."

Audrie sat back against the cushion and stared at her guest. All of the emotions from that incredible evening rushed back to her. She could never forget the almost magical experience of meeting Freddy and his friends and then coordinating an infiltration of a military installation. Hearing him speak Freddy's last words to her seemed to fill the quiet apartment with electricity.

From his body language alone, Audrie had already believed Brian. She did not know any agent who could act so well for another agent. Every gesture, facial expression, and intonation declared sincerity. She admired Brian Jacobsen's features, dark blue eyes and hair, pale skin. His blue jeans and a black canvas jacket covered a broad and muscular frame. She felt a natural attraction to him and wondered if his sister possessed the same physical beauty.

"I believe you," she said, suddenly feeling like a rude host. "Can I get you something to drink? You look tired."

"I don't need anything, thanks. Freddy and I got back from Norway just after midnight, and we've been waiting around all day for you to get home."

"Why didn't he come with you?"

"He needed to do something first," Brian said and shifted his weight in the seat, getting more comfortable. "But don't ask me what. He wouldn't tell me."

"So what are you doing here?" she asked. "Why me? Does he want me to do something?"

"I'll just say it," he said and sighed. "He's offered to send us to where they went, your brother and my sister."

"To another planet?" she asked, squinting.

"Yep," he said as if the answer was not astonishing. "Through some portal or something."

For several seconds, Audrie and Brian stared into each other's eyes. Only the quiet crackle of the fire filled the room. For the first time since waking from the psychiatric hospital, Audrie thought she might see her brother again.

"My brother's head of security, Simon Thatcher," Audrie began, breaking the silence, "told me about escaping Earth and going to another world. But I didn't believe him until I met Freddy."

"Freddy said that we can come back."

"But probably not Max," Audrie said and sighed. "I don't know what to think about any of this. My world is not the same anymore. Tell me what you know. Start with how you know Freddy."

"Sadi and I met Freddy in high school," Brian began after taking a deep breath. "He was a foster kid who moved into the neighborhood and we let him hang out with us. I felt sorry for the kid and so did Sadi. He came from a messed-up situation. He didn't have any friends and there was something different about him. He was super smart, and he was also in love with Sadi."

"That was nice of you," she said and wondered if Freddy still felt the same about his sister.

"Sadi went to college," he continued. "Then I graduated high school and moved out with my friends. We kind of lost contact with him. He came back into the scene a few months ago, and all this happened."

"Simon said that Freddy rescued your sister's daughter from kidnappers. How did he do that?"

"He tried explaining it to me, but I don't understand it," Brian said and shook his head. "Freddy says there's this place called the background, where we go when we sleep or daydream. For most people, the background's like watching a movie or something."

"Wait a minute," she said, wondering suddenly if Freddy could enter her dreams. "So you're saying our dreams take place in this *background*?"

"I think so."

"Sorry for the interruption."

"So, Freddy can do whatever he wants there. Some alien creature taught him how to influence people, kind of from behind. He can make people see things that aren't there, feel what people are feeling. He did some serious shit in Bergen."

"Bergen, Norway?"

"Yep," he said, taking a deep breath. "We just got back."

"Okay, what happened in Bergen?"

"Well, it started in Portland after Freddy showed up at my apartment. The military tried to get us, and we thought we escaped, then they tried shooting us out of the sky. The explosion knocked us both out. When I came around, we were in space and I could see the whole Earth. It was the coolest thing I'd ever seen. Too bad I was scared shitless."

To suppress her astonishment, Audrie concentrated on breathing. She wanted to appear calm and in control of her emotions, especially for Brian. Her instinct to impress a strong and charismatic male had become an annoying distraction.

"Then we went to Bergen, Norway. Freddy said he wanted to hide me at my aunt and uncle's home while he went and did something on his own. But the military tracked us there too. American special forces joined the Norwegian military and surrounded our hotel. There were helicopters and everything. I thought we were fucked, sorry."

"Don't worry about it," she said, smiling at his language. "How did you get out of that?"

"It was crazy. We disguised ourselves as soldiers, went outside and then Freddy made everyone blind, even me. But it was too much for him and he fainted, from exhaustion probably. The soldiers jumped us and were holding us on the ground, so I didn't see what happened next. The alien must have come and paralyzed everyone somehow. All I remember was an explosion that threw everyone to the ground. I carried Freddy to his flying car and she took him away. The next thing I knew, it was morning and I was in the hotel room as if nothing had happened, except Freddy wasn't there and neither were the soldiers."

"So," Audrie began, hoping to pause the story. Before she let Brian continue, she needed to assimilate the information. She had to choose from her many questions, choose what she wanted to know the most. "The alien was a female? What did she look like?"

"It looked just like my niece, Helen." His eyes suddenly became moist with tears, and he tried blinking them away. "Sorry. She looked just like Helen, but that was an illusion."

"What did she say to you?" Audrie asked, ignoring his emotions. Curiosity prevented her from breathing.

Brian sighed and rubbed his eyes. They were red, but no tears fell.

"I can't remember exactly, but she said that she needed to clean up the mess, and something about Freddy being in training."

"Training for what?"

"I don't know," Brian said with a hint of irritation. When he continued, his tone became apathetic. "I went to my aunt and uncle's for a few days until Freddy came back and we came here. He did not tell me what he did afterward, or what he's doing tonight."

"I apologize for the interrogation," Audrie said. "It's just my training. You've had some very traumatic experiences."

"It's okay," Brian said and smiled sincerely. "I just want to see my sister and niece again. They've been through worse shit than me. You probably want to see your brother too."

"Yes," she answered. Before she could stop herself, Audrie revealed what was on her mind, unfiltered. "I used to blame Max for all of this. Betraying the family. Betraying the world. I know it's not his fault, and I do want to see him again. I feel like the traitor now."

"What do you mean?" Brian asked. "Betraying the world and family?"

"I'm really not supposed to talk about this with people outside of the family."

Brian narrowed his dark blue eyes in preparation for more questions, so Audrie continued before he could ask them. She could not stop herself.

"I mean, I come from a privileged group of families who are working to keep the world from falling apart, and that means we have to work on improvement projects. Max doesn't believe in it, and I always just assumed he lacked vision and was selfish. Now I know he's just doing what he thinks is best."

In her former estimation, Max had always acted like a child. That thought suddenly reminded her of something Director Flanagan had said. *My little grandchildren know what's most important in life and they didn't need college for that.* Audrie smiled at the memory and would consider the idea later on her own. For the present, she wanted to control the conversation.

"But can we really go to another planet? Do you trust Freddy?"

"I don't have a choice," Brian confessed. "I do trust him, though."

"The background is an interesting concept," she said, her analytical mind replacing emotion. "Does that mean we're all connected to it?"

"It makes my head hurt just thinking about it." Brian laughed, a deep resonating sound. "Come to think of it, Freddy did say something like that. My sister would understand better. Hey, I have a question for you."

"Yes," she said, still digesting the idea of being connected to some kind of inter-dimensional space. The concept frightened her. She wondered what else might exist in such a place.

"What happened after you helped rescue Max and Gerald?" he asked, his eyes narrowing. "I mean, why didn't they arrest you or something?"

"I was there to visit my brother," Audrie said, smiling mischievously. "Freddy and his friends followed me."

"Why did they believe that? I don't understand."

"Even if they suspected me of complicity," she began, "they know Freddy has extraordinary abilities. They would just think he had controlled me somehow and I was not aware. My connections also offer further protection."

"Lucky for you," Brian said.

"I am very fortunate."

Audrie felt overwhelmed by all of the information and she knew she had to take a break. She got a bottle of red wine, poured some for both of them, and they continued conversing as the alcohol helped ease their tension. While her subconscious mind digested the information, she decided to become better acquainted with her guest. She had decided to go on the journey with him.

She told him about her work and family, and a short summary of her life. When she asked about his life, he spoke first of his music career and how he felt guilty for leaving his bandmates. When he talked about his sister, Audrie felt envy and regret. She recalled an enjoyable childhood with Max, and then the choice to follow her father's life, which ultimately caused her to resent Max.

"I've decided to go," she said during a lull in the conversation. "When can we leave?"

"Tonight, after Freddy returns," he answered, seeming pleasantly surprised. "He said we should take something to sleep. The flight is about twenty hours."

"Twenty hours?" she asked, incredulously. "In the BMW? What if we need to relieve ourselves?"

"The car does have something we can use," he said. "But Freddy said he can give us something to help us sleep, so we can sleep for most of the way."

"Then we should not be drinking," she said and rose from the couch, the gun in her left hand. "If you'll excuse me, I'm going to use the restroom now, get the process started."

"Good idea," he said.

Brian took one last sip of wine and placed the glass on the table. When Audrie returned from the bathroom, she found him standing at the fireplace, looking at a framed picture on the mantle.

"A skier, eh?" he asked. "Where was this?"

"The Alps with some friends."

While they discussed the details of the journey, her excitement began to replace the trauma generated by the incredible information. Of course, she wanted to see her brother again, and Freddy. She also wanted to experience space flight, something she had never even imagined. Brian assured her of their safety, but the risk of death seemed like an insignificant price for such an amazing experience. Even if she died on the way, Audrie would probably not regret the decision to go.

"I'm going to pack some of my things. Is there anything specific I need to bring?"

"Freddy said I didn't need anything," Brian began, "but I brought some clothes, a razor, some bathroom stuff."

"Okay, I'll go pack some supplies of my own," she said and turned away from him. She could feel him watching her leave. "I'll return in a few minutes."

Audrie put some clothes in a leather travel bag, a pair of shoes, her toothbrush, toothpaste, deodorant, and some implements for her hair. During the process, she began thinking more concretely about the trip. She could not access her money, which would probably be useless, but she packed five hundred dollars in cash anyway. She would depend totally on Freddy and his friends.

For just a moment, the thought of depending on poor people was too degrading, and she reconsidered her decision. Then she felt stupid for thinking like that when none of her privileged friends would ever have such an awesome opportunity. She got to see her brother again and travel through space to another planet. She was thinking too much like her father, and needed to think more like Max.

While closing her bag, Audrie heard three knocks on her apartment door. She stopped breathing and listened to Brian rise from the couch and walk across her apartment. Without saying any words that she could hear, Brian opened the door. After it closed, she drew her first breath. She was suddenly afraid to leave the room and see the new visitor.

"Get a hold of yourself," she whispered. "You're Audrie Garner."

While walking the short distance to the living room, she felt dizzy and had to stop and rest against the wall. She closed her eyes, drew a deep breath, and after a few seconds, she felt a little better.

But after opening her eyes again, the apartment seemed different somehow. Everything looked familiar, but Audrie felt as if she was seeing her home for the first time. As calmly as possible, she rejoined her two guests in the living room.

"Hello, Audrie," said a voice she remembered from her dreams. "I apologize for the intrusion. Please have a seat."

Freddy Carlson looked exactly as Audrie remembered from the psychiatric hospital, but his brown eyes seemed distant. When she turned to Brian, he gave her the same impression. Although they stood together, just four meters away, Audrie felt as if a soccer field separated them.

She opened her mouth to return the greeting, *Hello Freddy,* but after failing to say anything, she shut her mouth to avoid looking like an idiot. Brian quickly stepped to her side and grabbed her shoulder, then guided her to the couch.

"Are you okay, Audrie?" he asked.

"I don't know," she answered. Brian seemed like the only real object in the room. She held onto his arm for a moment. Physical contact helped make Audrie feel more solid.

"This is a lot of disturbing information to process," Freddy interjected, joining them on the couch. Brian returned to his previous position opposite Audrie. Freddy continued speaking and she turned to him. "You just accepted the proposal to leave your home planet, solar system, and now I'm reminding you of the traumatic experience of rescuing your brother."

"I think you're right," she said, grateful for the justification, even though the explanation seemed inadequate.

"Are you ready to go?" Freddy asked.

"I think so," she said.

"Do you trust me, Audrie?" Freddy asked.

"Yes."

"Then here," he said and sat beside her. She noticed a glass of pink liquid in his hand, which she had not noticed previously. "Drink this. It will help you relax on the flight. Just ask Brian. The escape can be quite unnerving."

"Okay, but I need to call my replacement at work." Audrie paused and took the glass. She broke eye contact with Freddy and stared at the sloshing liquid. Her mouth was suddenly dry. "I need to tell him that I'm going on a trip."

"I am sure they can figure out what to do without you," Freddy said quietly, soothingly. "If you do not give notification, they are likely to think you were kidnapped or something happened out of your control. That will be better for when you return."

Freddy turned to Brian.

"Go get her things."

Audrie put the glass to her lips and drained all of the liquid in two gulps, a slight sweetness remaining on her tongue. In just a few seconds, her vision blurred again and the dizziness returned, stronger than before. Despite the vertigo, her body was beginning to relax, but she had to spend more effort keeping herself erect on the couch.

When the room began to swirl around her, she had to lie down. She watched Brian return with her bag and give it to Freddy. Then Freddy said something to her, but she did not understand the words.

Audrie closed her eyes for a moment, and when she opened them again, Brian was carrying her through her apartment door. And then they were in the parking facility, approaching the BMW. She felt Brian gently lay her in the passenger seat and listened as her seatbelts clicked into place. She no longer had the energy to open her eyes.

—✳—

Audrie awoke slowly from a long sleep, feeling stiff and groggy while listening to music. At first, the music seemed distant but the sounds eventually grew louder and more distinct until she recognized the instrument, a guitar.

Although the memory was blurry, she remembered being carried from her apartment and placed into the BMW. She remembered Brian knocking on her apartment door and then Freddy appearing. After opening her eyes and noticing the star-filled sky through the car windows, Audrie gasped. She turned to the window behind her and saw Earth and the moon, both fully illuminated by the sun. Her home was the size of a fist held at arm's length.

"Good morning, Audrie," Brian said while continuing to play his guitar. "The computer says we'll be at our destination in about ten hours. I have to tell you that I'm a little nervous. I've never been this far away from home."

FIFTY-THREE

Brian

"Welcome, Audrie and Brian," a familiar male voice said through the speakers. "We will take control of the BMW and bring you in safely. I'll meet you in the landing area."

They glanced at each other silently and then returned their attention to the giant space station through the front window. In his peripheral vision, the bright horizon of a planet was just visible through the passenger window. With so many distractions, Brian required another second to realize who had spoken to them. It was Freddy.

Brian remembered Freddy explaining his dual existence as both the child and as the adult. At the time, Brian had not fully appreciated the implications of the information. Only after recognizing the adult voice of Freddy, did Brian understand that he also lived on the station.

"That was Freddy," Brian said, taking a deep breath and attempting to hide his shock. "I think."

"Sounded like him to me," Audrie said more confidently. "So he's been here the whole time. Amazing."

Brian was still recovering from the experience of traveling through the tunnel of absolute darkness to explain the full situation to Audrie. At one point, they were traveling faster than any rational human should travel and less than a minute later, they were peacefully hovering above a new planet. Then the space station had appeared.

The female voice before the black tunnel still rang in his memory, *cover your eyes*, and then the brilliant flash of light, shining bright red through the blood in his hands.

During their journey through space, Brian chose not to tell Audrie the whole story about what had happened at her apartment. At the time, Brian wondered if learning about Freddy's child and adult bodies would overwhelm her since he'd felt that way about the information. She thought the experience of seeing Freddy had been an illusion, that Freddy had manipulated what he called the background to give the appearance of his presence when he was actually far away.

But after becoming better acquainted with her, Brian felt confident in her capacity to accept the truth. He had considered telling her but then decided to let Freddy explain the complete story. If necessary, Brian would apologize later.

When he had told Audrie about his experiences with Freddy in Portland and Norway, she had questioned him without emotion, showing no surprise or astonishment. She had shown particular curiosity at how Freddy had accomplished everything. Her method of extracting the information had reminded Brian of a police detective, thorough and emotionally detached.

She lost her patience with Brian only once on the trip when he failed to provide a satisfactory explanation to one of her many questions. Her reaction had not bothered him though. Brian refused to let people damage his mood.

"You'll have to wait for Freddy to explain it," he'd said with a calm smile, careful not to provoke further frustration.

The more Brian interacted with Audrie, the more he liked her. She acted similarly to his sister and showed interest in more than just what existed in her life. He had learned quickly how Audrie liked to take control of the conversation. He did not mind and enjoyed the break. Although he liked meeting new people, Brian usually had to make all the effort. He had also learned not to worry about hurting her feelings. Her self-confidence and self-esteem seemed impenetrable.

After learning the basics of each other's lives, she had asked for his opinion on some current events, but his blatant ignorance shocked her. When she asked why he didn't care about what was happening in the world, he told her what he told Sadi. She did not understand what the Black Sabbath quote meant.

The world is full of kings and queens, who blind your eyes and steal your dreams.

—※—

"They better have a toilet on this thing," Audrie said, pulling Brian from his internal reflection.

Brian turned to her, laughing softly in agreement. At one point during their long journey through the solar system, Audrie needed to urinate, so Brian played his guitar and looked out the window to give her the most possible privacy. He remembered feeling impressed by her attitude about the incident. She had made no apology and showed no sign of embarrassment.

"I could use one right about now," Brian said. He had needed to empty his bladder before then but had not yet reached the point of desperation. After Earth had become just another bright light, traveling in space had lost its novelty and sense of adventure. "I'm more excited to see Sadi and the girls."

A huge door began sliding open on the space station, and they floated inside like a ship on an invisible ocean. As they landed, Brian felt acutely anxious to escape the car and stretch his legs. He chuckled while considering the situation.

"What are you laughing about?" Audrie asked, staring through the front window.

"You'd think I would be more curious about this place," he began, laughing again, "but I just want to get out of the car."

The BWM descended smoothly to the floor and landed almost imperceptibly. During the process, they quietly inspected their new environment just beyond the windows. Brian first noticed the flat, smooth floor, which looked like multicolored marble, the different colors swirling together. A soft light shined down from the ceiling and the low light level was peaceful.

"I just realized," Audrie said suddenly, breaking the silence. "It feels almost therapeutic to see something other than the stars. Traveling in the void of space was like a drain on my soul like it was sucking all of my energy. I didn't notice it until now."

"There he is," Brian said, pointing through his side window at Freddy who stood a few meters away from the car, smiling and waiting patiently. His old friend looked the same as when Brian last saw him. He also looked like a stranger. His blond hair was just as messy, but his clothes fit him perfectly and he looked good in them.

Brian never remembered Freddy wearing flattering clothing, but now it was different. Freddy wore loose-fitting pants of some thick-stringed beige material, and a long sleeve shirt, smoother material than the pants and dark blue. The material of his shirt and pants reminded Brian of linen.

As Brian waved, he realized the main reason why Freddy looked so different. His old friend appeared extremely relaxed and confident. He wore a natural smile, not forced.

"I suppose it's safe to get out," Audrie said, putting her hand on the door handle.

They exited together, but before turning his attention to Freddy, Brian admired the floor again. It looked like polished stone. He resisted the urge to slide his fingers across the smooth surface.

"Oh my god, Freddy," Brian said while stretching. "I can feel every one of the hundred bazillion miles we just traveled."

"I cannot tell you how good it is to see you through these eyes, Brian."

Freddy stepped forward and threw his arms around Brian.

When his old friend hugged him, Brian was shocked and hesitated a short moment before returning the gesture. During their entire friendship, they had never embraced. He always seemed to avoid physical contact, even shaking hands. Brian also expected Freddy to feel frail. He was thinner and smaller than Brian, but he felt solid. During their physical contact, Brian wondered if the person before him was an impostor.

"It's me, I promise," Freddy said and laughed.

After releasing Brian, he stepped toward Audrie who had come to stand next to them. He grabbed Audrie's hand and shoulder in a single motion.

"I am so glad you decided to come, Audrie. I bet you are excited to see your brother."

While waiting for Audrie to respond, Brian was confused by her body language. The woman appeared intimidated by Freddy which seemed abnormal for her. From what Brian had learned, Audrie held an important position and often met with very influential people. Maybe she felt something other than simple intimidation.

Hmm! Brian would have to think about that more later.

"Thank you, Freddy," she said after he released her hand. "Sorry, but this is such a strange situation."

"Yes, it is." Freddy smiled then turned and began walking away from them. "Follow me. I will show you to your rooms. Everything you might need is at your disposal."

Audrie turned to Brian with confusion in her eyes. She did not move.

"Where is Max?"

"And Sadi?" Brian asked, suddenly wondering why they were not present.

When Freddy failed to stop or turn in their direction, they started following him.

"They're not here yet," Freddy said. "They're visiting Bodn, the planet below us, and they don't yet know of your arrival. They don't even know that you will be visiting. Come on, we have important things to discuss before they return."

—✳—

After Freddy showed them to their rooms, he left and promised to return in an hour. He wanted to give them some time to recuperate from their journey. He also said that their brains needed time to assimilate all of the new information, especially their new environment.

Brian spent the first few minutes alone in his apartment, shocked to discover his room with the same layout as the one on Earth. He placed his guitar gently on the bed, pausing before he released the instrument. *This is so weird*, he thought. His acute feeling of disorientation lasted for several minutes, even after using the toilet, which he promised never to take for granted again.

While washing his hands, he stared at the swirling water almost as if in a trance. He didn't know how to spend the remainder of the time, so he left his room and knocked on Audrie's door.

"Hey," he said. "I kind of don't want to be alone. This is just too weird."

"Come on in," she said and stood out of his way. "Is your apartment the same as the one where you live? As you can see, mine is."

"Almost exactly the same," he answered and laughed. "Actually, it's nicer, and there's some clothes for me too, just my size."

"I was just about to take a shower," Audrie said, closing the door behind him. "But I don't mind the company. You're right. This is very strange. I won't take long."

While waiting for her to shower and get dressed, he discovered the window curtains.

FIFTY-FOUR

Brian

After noticing the curtains on the far wall, he felt instantly curious, along with some dread, about what he would see on the other side. He imagined strange creatures with fangs and claws, ready to jump at him. Taking a deep breath, he parted the curtains and had to shield his eyes from the light. There was a window with an amazing view of the planet in full daylight. The view became an instant reminder of their location.

"Wow!"

For the next few minutes, he just stared at the glass. The planet filled his view in all directions. As he looked at all of the clouds, land masses, and bodies of water, he wondered about his sister, Helen, and Daryn. According to Freddy, they were down there somewhere. *What are they doing*, he wondered. He hoped they were having fun. Sadi and the girls deserved it.

While thinking about his sister and nieces on the planet's surface, he began to wonder more about what Freddy wanted to tell them. He hoped to discuss the subject with Audrie before Freddy returned.

When Audrie exited the bathroom, she was wearing only a towel and some of her blond hair had fallen over her shoulders, wet and a little darker than usual. For a moment, Brian held his breath at seeing so much of her skin. He already appreciated her physical appearance, but he suddenly wanted to touch her.

This one's not for you, buddy. She'd make you watch the news.

She smiled and then turned to the window, her eyes opening wide. Instead of continuing to her bedroom, she joined him. Brian forced himself to focus on her brown eyes, which suddenly reminded him of a hawk.

"They're down there somewhere," he said, turning back to the window.

"This must be a monitor screen," she said after looking more closely. "Pretty advanced. Hmm. A window would be too risky."

She touched the screen with her index finger and the view responded by shifting a little bit. Audrie glanced at Brian in alarm then swiped her fingers as she would on a touchscreen, and they suddenly appeared closer to the planet. In his peripheral vision, Brian noticed her bare arm, right next to his face. Her wet skin seemed to shine in the light and he almost forgot about the planet.

"Very interesting," Audrie said, then stepped back from the window. "I'll go get dressed and we can talk a little before Freddy gets here."

While waiting for her, Brian's heart rate returned to normal.

"Looks good," Brian said after she opened the door to her room. He was referring to her clothes.

"Not really my style but comfortable." Audrie wore pants similar to what Freddy had worn, just a different color, peach. Her long-sleeved shirt looked the same. She sat next to him on the couch. "I was thinking about the situation while getting dressed."

"And?"

"I don't want to speculate about what Freddy wants to discuss. We'll probably just end up scaring ourselves. We should probably just prepare to be shocked. What do you think, Brian?"

"Sounds good to me," he said. "As long as I get to see Sadi and the girls."

When Freddy arrived, he knocked on Audrie's door and then showed no surprise to find both of them. Before entering, he stepped aside and a tall mechanical thing hovered within view. Audrie jolted, her eyes flying wide open. She grabbed Brian's shoulder.

The machine did not resemble any form of organic life Brian knew. It had two appendages extending toward the ground, like legs but hovered smoothly above the floor. Several other appendages extended from a central mass of tubes, rings, rods, and other shapes. Some of the appendages resembled hands but with three robot fingers arranged in a circle.

"No need for alarm," Freddy said, chuckling. "This is one of my helpers here. Your niece, Helen, has affectionately named this one, Miss Poofie. I wanted you to see one, so it will not frighten you in the future."

"Miss Poofie?" Audrie asked incredulously. She released Brian's shoulder, acting as if her nervous reaction never happened. She stepped closer to the doorway and began inspecting the machine. "How in the world did she come up with that name?"

"You will have to ask her, I'm afraid," Freddy said then turned to the machine. "You can leave now."

He closed the door and everyone got comfortable in the living room. Brian and Audrie sat on the couch while Freddy chose the loveseat opposite them. Brian thought his old friend looked calm and relaxed, as though on a benign social call. Audrie was probably worried about what they would learn, but Brian could not imagine Freddy saying anything disturbing. So far, he had only helped them.

Before beginning the conversation, Freddy took a deep breath.

"You will better understand what is happening," he began and paused briefly, "if you think of this as a game. Every creature is part of another creature's game."

"What do you mean by *creature*?" Audrie asked.

"I mean everyone," he said. "We are all just creatures in different bodies. Even what you might call an alien is just another creature. Some creatures are bigger than others, and I do not mean physically bigger. For lack of better words, some have more *attention capacity*." Freddy shook his head and took another deep breath. "But I do not want to get into all the details now. That conversation would never end. You have a lot of time to figure all that out."

"I'm not sure I understand," Audrie said.

"Let me start over. You are here, because things got a little messy back on Earth. But the creatures in charge of that realm want you back. They want everyone back, all of our friends, and me. Another creature prepared all of this, the station we are on now, the planet we are orbiting. She put us all on the path that led us here. We are part of her game now, and we must play it."

"Wait a second," Audrie said, standing. While continuing, she walked to the window. "The creature in charge of this place caused everything to happen? Can we help you stop her?"

"We cannot stop her," Freddy said with wide eyes, and Brian wondered if he was challenging Audrie to argue. "Even if I wanted to stop her, I could not. She is more skilled than I am, probably more skilled than the creatures who claim Earth as their territory. For the present, we need her help to protect us from them."

"All I know," Brian said, turning to Audrie, "is that they tried to hurt my sister. They took your brother and Gerald and hurt them. Right, Freddy?"

"But," Audrie interjected, still looking at Freddy. "You're also saying that this creature put us in this predicament?"

"She orchestrated all of this to train me. So you could say that I am to blame."

"None of this is your fault," Brian said, not wanting Audrie angry at him.

"She has given me ownership of Bodn, the planet below us. She wants me here, and I want my friends here with me. This is what I wanted to discuss. I want to explain why staying here would be to your benefit. Can we talk about that first? Afterward, I will answer your other questions if they are still important to you."

"Alright," Audrie said, returning to the couch. "Why would we want to stay here?"

"We can fix your genetic code," he said flatly. "We will erase the death program and make you much less susceptible to creatures who want to feed off you. You can finally escape Earth and live a life for yourselves."

Audrie didn't answer. She was staring at Freddy, her mouth slightly open. For Brian, the information was overwhelming, and he no longer worried about Audrie's reaction. Maybe he had misunderstood.

Can he make us immortal?

"There's more," Freddy continued, addressing Brian. "I am giving Sadi a gift, but I need to know your opinion first because you know her best. I plan to bring Jacob back, Sadi's son."

"You want to what?" Brian asked, still trying to process his first statement.

"You and your sister were my first friends," Freddy said and smiled as if reliving fond memories. "When Jacob died, part of Sadi died with him. This is the best gift I can give her. My new friend will help me find Jacob and restore his life. But I do not know how to approach Sadi. Should I tell her first? I would like to include her in the process, but the experience might be too traumatic."

"I don't like this," Audrie said, standing and taking a step away from them. "It feels unnatural, evil."

"They corrupted your natural genetic code long ago, Audrie." Freddy's smile disappeared. "You have also been conditioned to react this way. Think of the fix to your genetic code as a restoration to a higher state. I offer that choice to you, but I am returning Sadi's son whether you like it or not."

FIFTY-FIVE

Taylor

"Is everyone ready?" Taylor asked, standing at the entrance of the cockpit. She looked at the kids in the front rows and acted like she was trying to find troublemakers. The children liked to sit together, the boys on the left and the girls on the right. "Got your seatbelts on?"

"Yes, captain!" they said in unison, except for the youngest boy who spoke last.

"Good," she said sternly. "We're taking off now."

Taylor smiled at the adults and then joined Cesar in the cockpit.

"We haven't all been on this thing together since our arrival," Cesar said while she strapped herself into the copilot's chair. "Remember how the journey felt like a dream?"

"Well, I vividly remember how sick we all were of being cooped up together for so long. I broke my tension on Simon a little too hard, I'm afraid." Taylor laughed and spoke more quietly. "I thought Simon was going to actually slap me at a couple points."

"I think you were the only one who thought that was funny," Cesar said, his lips curving into a wide smile but hiding his teeth. "It is a good memory though, now."

"I amused myself," she answered. "That's all that matters."

Taylor swiveled around to see if Simon had heard them. He was out of her eyesight. Before returning her attention to the front window, she noticed Yezeel's light grey eyes focused on her from the back row, his broad shoulders towering over Mark and Susan in front of him. Taylor gulped and nodded. As usual, Taylor felt self-conscious under his gaze. Although she despised people who made her feel that way, the giant man was too polite and considerate to dislike or resent.

When Cesar brought the engines to life, the jet seemed to transform into a living thing, a predator. Taylor often imagined the spacecraft breathing softly, ready to attack. She loved that part of the process, the awakening. She loved take-off almost as much, shooting into the sky like a rocket, pressed into her seat. She suddenly forgot about those grey eyes set in a black face.

"You ready?" he asked.

"Let's do it."

Cesar tapped the screen in front of him, and ten seconds later, the spacecraft began the ascent. The thrust started almost imperceptibly and increased steadily until the ocean in front of them had disappeared below their view. For the next forty seconds, Taylor watched the scene until they ascended above the fluffy white cumulus clouds.

"Not much to do for a pilot," Cesar said and released his hold of the armrests. "Tap a button and initiate a preprogrammed launch sequence."

"We'll have to take this thing out again later." Taylor grasped Cesar on the shoulder. "We'll have some fun. It'll be strange to see Freddy. What do you think he'll tell us?"

Taylor had been waiting for a good opportunity to discuss the situation with Cesar, privately. They had plenty of time to talk on the thirty-minute trip back to the station.

"I don't know," Cesar said. "I hope he found Franklin and Gerda, and maybe even brought them, but that might be too much to hope for."

Before responding, Taylor watched the largest satellite of Bodn reveal itself on the horizon. She remembered the Salmon family arriving on the planet and Yezeel showing them the three natural satellites, all much smaller than the moon of Earth. The outer two satellites appeared as fast-moving stars and only the closest one could be identified as a physical object.

"If he hasn't found them," Taylor said without turning, "maybe we can help in the search and rescue. I wish I could have gone to the psychiatric hospital with them for Gerald and Max. I need to get my mother anyway. Can you imagine her response when I tell her about all of this? I might have to drug her. Got any more of what we used on the FBI guy?"

When Cesar failed to react as Taylor had hoped, she chuckled to herself. He was facing forward, lost in his thoughts. Taylor wondered what he was thinking. *Probably his daughter.*

"You're way too optimistic, Taylor," Cesar said finally. "It's too dangerous to return right now, or anytime soon. Freddy barely got us out of there. Dominga and I might be stuck here for a long time. It's probably easier for you to think like that since you're young than for an old man like me."

"True," she said, not knowing what to say. She wanted to shake him, remind him of their exciting situation and what opportunities they had. "Just think about all the people who've been uprooted in history. They had no choice but to move forward, make the best of the situation. It's true that I would have chosen this on my own, but we will have an amazing time here. Trust me."

"But you don't have a daughter, Taylor. Even if we can go back, she won't want to come here. I've already lost my sons, and now her. Doroteo doesn't want to leave either."

"Too bad you've only got Dominga and me," Taylor said sarcastically. "Sorry. I didn't mean that." Clichés suddenly began materializing in her mind. *Look on the bright side! Stay positive! Don't give up!* Taylor pursed her lips together tightly to prevent any of those annoying phrases from escaping into the air.

"Don't worry about it, Taylor," he said while staring at the darkening sky. "I shouldn't complain. At least my daughter's alive, and I feel great, especially after that parasite treatment. How have you felt?"

"I've never felt better," Taylor said, glad for the change of subject. "It's no wonder doctors aren't taught about parasites anymore. There'd be a lot less sick people buying medicine."

Cesar finally turned to look at her. When he smiled, Taylor knew he had forgiven her for the sarcastic remark. She could not relax if her words had upset him. Taylor had come to consider his opinion as highly as her mother's, and even more than Gerald's. The situation suddenly seemed like a contest for her respect and the comparison made Taylor smile to herself.

"Did you notice how Susan stopped complaining to Mark?" he asked quietly. "I think she might be feeling better about staying. Improved health might have something to do with it."

"I haven't talked to her about it, but I thought I overheard them say something about bringing her parents."

Stars filled the sky now and Taylor finally saw the outline of the orbiting station, illuminated from behind by the intense light of Dzalm. From their distance, the station looked like a small disk. When they got close enough to see the massive landing bay doors, the station would fill their entire view.

"Well," he said after a deep breath. "Maybe Freddy thinks it's safe to make a trip back to Earth to get some people."

Taylor held her right hand in the air, fingers crossed.

They flew the remainder of the way to the station in silence. Taylor reviewed her conversations with everyone about whether they planned to stay or return to Earth when it was safe. She knew Sadi was planning to stay on Bodn with her girls. Sadi planned to ask her brother but didn't know if he would want to come. He loved his life on Earth, mostly because of his band. He loved Helen more though, and if he chose to come, she would be the deciding factor.

Mark felt the same as Taylor and preferred a new life away from Earth. He was excited for the new experience and the opportunity to help build a society from scratch. But more than that, he wanted his children to experience a life with more personal freedom, a life away from a toxic environment and dangerous people. So far, all of the children had shown only excitement about their new lives. Taylor often found herself fantasizing about growing up in their situation.

Although Dominga had grown to love everyone, she would go wherever Cesar went. Taylor did not even need to ask. Simon had claimed not to care. He would go wherever Max went, but Taylor secretly thought he preferred to stay. When she had asked Gerald and Max, they showed no excitement about the situation and seemed noncommittal. Their lack of emotion and motivation always made her sad, and then angry about what had happened to them. She didn't know how to deal with them and hoped Freddy would have the answers.

Just like the Wizard of Oz, she thought, snickering. *Everyone's hoping Freddy will grant their wishes.*

While watching the station fill in their view, Taylor reviewed her decision to stay on Bodn. For the present, she had no real choice, since returning to Earth was not an option. The authorities would either apprehend her or she would live in fear of being caught for the remainder of her life. Although she had struggled through the mental process, the decision was quick. She preferred to start a new life with people she respected, and so far, she loved interacting with everyone. She did not know Freddy well, but she trusted Sadi, and she trusted Freddy.

The only deciding factor was her mother. More than anyone else, Taylor wanted her mother to join them. Given the choice, Taylor knew she would accept the opportunity, even if it frightened her. But would Taylor stay if they could not contact her? That seemed too unlikely, so she would not consider it, yet. Too much time had passed since they had talked last, and her mother was probably physically sick from worry. If not for her mother, Taylor secretly hoped Freddy would just tell everyone they could not return to Earth, and that would be the final answer.

Her experiences on Bodn had become a confirmation of her decision to stay. After visiting their residence in the mountains and seeing the Solka, Yezeel had taken them to several other places, tropical islands, a desert, a rain forest, and the North Pole. It was her best vacation ever. Not even her trip to Hawaii with her brother could compare. She wanted to return to Bodn as soon as possible.

In addition to the opportunity of colonizing Bodn, Taylor loved having access to real information and not having to worry so much about corrupt sources. Most everything they had already learned was verifiable. She did not just have to trust the source.

Taylor had especially enjoyed watching the kids have fun learning about the world and had participated with them. At their current rate of mental development, they would catch up to her in just a few years. They would not have to waste so much time taking pointless classes. Although those thoughts compounded her anger and resentment of the past, Taylor felt no jealousy at all, just happy for the children. She had enjoyed watching them and was content to assist in the learning process, both intellectually and emotionally.

For the first time in her life, Taylor had seriously considered the possibility of having children. On Earth, she had never allowed herself the luxury of those thoughts. She had always considered children as a burden, something which would limit or eliminate future opportunities.

While on Bodn, Taylor had entertained the possibility of having a child with Max, without telling him of course, and only if he returned to his previous mental state. The current Max seemed unable to care for a child or her. In the society she imagined creating, Taylor did not need a man to help her raise a child. They would be living, at first, in a group setting and would depend on each other.

Taylor ultimately decided not to worry about the situation and just accept whatever the future held for her. Even if Max did return to Earth, she would still stay on Bodn. She had grown to enjoy his company enough to entertain romantic thoughts, but she felt confident that the right opportunity would appear in the future, either with him or someone else.

As the landing bay doors opened and they floated inside the station, Taylor imagined meeting Freddy again. In her imagination, he was the classical concept of a god, living in the sky, watching over humanity. Maybe in the real world, the gods lived in orbiting space stations. Taylor smiled uncomfortably at the thought.

—※—

"Mom," Helen yelled from the cabin. The children were standing by the window, looking out at the landing bay. "It's Uncle Brian. It's Uncle Brian, Mom!"

Taylor stepped from the entrance of the cockpit to stand behind the girls then looked over their heads to see Freddy. He was standing by a man and a woman a few meters away from them. She immediately recognized the woman, Max's sister, the one who had interrogated her in Brazil and taken her to jail. She thought the man looked familiar, then suddenly recognized the similarity to Sadi. While making the connection, Sadi stepped to her side and covered her mouth with her right hand, her eyes glistening with tears.

"Oh, my God," Sadi said while placing her hands on Helen's shoulders. "That is your uncle, isn't it?"

"Hey, Max," Taylor said as Sadi and her girls stepped to the exit door. "Your sister, Audrie, is standing outside too."

"What?" he asked, squinting in confusion. "Audrie?"

After she exited the jet, Taylor watched Sadi run into her brother's open arms. As he pressed her head into his chest, her tears flowed generously down her cheeks. Helen stood next to her uncle with her hand on his elbow. Brian released his sister and plucked Helen from the ground like she weighed the same as a doll. While looking at him, Taylor suddenly felt self-conscious about her appearance.

Wow! He's cute.

Max and Audrie approached each other more cautiously. As Audrie threw her arms around him, Taylor noticed a mutual but fleeting hesitation. When Taylor saw the tears falling from Max's eyes, she felt her own eyes getting moist.

Taylor stood next to Cesar and Dominga and the rest of the group who were patiently waiting for the emotional reunions to finish. When she turned away from the scene for a moment, she found Daryn standing next to the Salmon boys and their parents. Dominga stepped to her side and hugged her with one arm. Taylor suddenly felt pity for the poor little thing. She looked confused, not sure if she should join her adopted family.

"Daryn," Brian said, and Taylor turned to see him walking toward the girl. He carried Helen with him but set her down when he arrived within arm's reach. He bent down and hugged her, and Daryn's arms slowly wrapped around him. "How are you, you beautiful girl? I was so worried about you."

While Taylor wiped tears from her own eyes, she turned and noticed Yezeel standing away from the group. While watching the reunion, he and Freddy had the same expression, a serene and closed-mouth smile. They reminded Taylor of parents watching their kids do something cute.

When Cesar began walking toward Freddy, Taylor glanced at Dominga who acknowledged her with wide eyes. As he approached, Taylor's heart rate accelerated, and she felt as if they were all watching a television program interrupted by an urgent message from President Obama. She remembered watching President Bush tell the nation about the invasion of Iraq, the event that ultimately led to the death of her brother.

"It's great to see you, Freddy," Cesar said, extending his hand. "When did you arrive?"

Freddy smiled wide, showing perfectly straight white teeth. He grasped Cesar's hand and put his other arm around the old man who looked shocked by the sudden affection. "It is so good to see you too, Cesar. I have been here for a while, but I will tell you all about the journey some other time."

In Taylor's peripheral vision, she noticed Sadi leave her brother's side and stop at Cesar's right. Freddy turned to her and grabbed her with both arms then pulled her tightly to him. Even from where she stood with Dominga, Taylor could see that the woman was getting squished.

"I'm glad you're finally safe, Sadi," he said, quickly releasing her. "You and the girls."

"Thank you for bringing Brian," she said.

The rest of the group, except for Yezeel, stepped closer to Freddy and soon formed a semi-circle around him.

"Before we got here, Brian and I had some fun together back on Earth," Freddy said, turning to Brian. Taylor thought he looked completely comfortable as the center of attention. "I think you will enjoy hearing him tell you all about it."

"It wasn't fun at the time," Brian said, laughing and wiping his eyes. He stood a meter away, one hand on Helen's shoulder while still holding Daryn. He looked down at Helen. "Maybe I'll tell one of the stories before bed tonight."

"So what's the news, Freddy?" Cesar asked. "Did you find Franklin, Gerda, and Bill Smith? How's Doroteo?"

"They are all fine, actually," he said and his lips relaxed a bit. The smile remained, but Taylor thought he seemed ready to tell them something serious. "I have some important information to share with you, but I think you should recover from the journey first. Take some time to clean up, rest a bit, and get something to eat. I will meet you in the dining area at noon. How does that sound?"

—※—

Two and a half hours later, Taylor and the rest of the group met Freddy and Yezeel at the large dining table where they had first met after arriving at the station. Both men were waiting for them, sitting at the table with half-eaten plates of salad and glasses of water.

As Freddy began explaining the requirements to stay on Bodn, Taylor experienced a rollercoaster of emotions—excitement, dread, confusion. After learning about the requirement to upgrade their genetic code, Taylor felt nothing initially. Even though she had understood his words, the information seemed impossible to comprehend. Cesar was the first to recover enough to respond. He expressed disbelief, exactly how she felt.

When she noticed the serious look in Freddy's eyes, Taylor felt the kind of dread she imagined might accompany a cancer diagnosis. After he explained how his genetic code had been modified, Taylor began to feel a little better about the prospect. And when he explained how it was the only way to cure Max and Gerald, most of her other concerns vanished. In the end, she felt as though she had just won the lottery.

But not everyone felt the same. A glance at the other refugees suggested fear, anxiety, and incomprehension.

"I know this is a lot to think about, and you'll want to talk through this," Freddy said and stood from the table. "Brian and Audrie have had more time to think about this, so I would suggest you start by asking for their thoughts. He smiled at everyone, and then he and Yezeel turned and walked from the room.

FIFTY-SIX

Freddy

"**I**'m ready," Freddy said as he stared at the small corpse. But he did not feel ready.

The body of Sadi's dead son was lying on a large stone slab, perpendicular to Freddy with the head to the right. The stone slab connected seamlessly to the wall and stretched to both ends of the room, about ten meters in length. The dark stone surface looked as cold as the dead child, Freddy thought. The body's unceremonious placement on the slab seemed inappropriate for something Sadi had loved so dearly.

A large box sat on the bench to the right of the corpse, an incubator crafted from an ivory-like, semi-transparent material, measuring one and a half meters in length, and half a meter in height and width. Freddy could see a small human body inside, overlaid with a real-time temperature map from red to blue. He could also see the interior of the body, including blood flow and a pumping heart.

The movement of the blood and heart, and the slight shifting of the temperature map added another dimension of life, a stark contrast to the corpse on the left of the box. Each artery pulsated with the heartbeat, reminding Freddy of a fast-forward view of people entering a subway train. The room was quiet, except for a soft bubbling noise from inside the box. The sound reminded Freddy of a fish tank.

After the probe delivered the body to the station, Freddy covered it in a new white cloth, leaving only the head exposed. While wrapping the tiny body, the corpse had seemed too delicate to touch, and he feared it might fall apart. In the graveyard, he remembered feeling afraid to see the body. Now it was just another object, a machine that had once served a purpose and stopped working.

For the past several minutes, he'd stared at its small face and imagined it filled with life, smiling, crying, laughing. Grey eyelids now covered sunken eyes, and the dark brown hair contrasted sharply with the pale skin, a lifeless grey, cold and thin. The nose and closed mouth looked too small as if they had shrunk after death.

"I understand," Freddy whispered in response to his friend's silent message. "We'll follow you."

A strong black hand grasped Freddy's right shoulder. The fingers squeezed and felt like another kind of gravity, pressing him slightly harder to the stone floor and causing him to feel even more connected to the orbiting station. In his fragile emotional state, physical contact with another creature provided comfort and peace. Freddy needed that.

Anxious anticipation for his next task reminded him of his experience in the tunnel under the Sahara. At least now, he did not have to make the journey alone. He was also a little excited for the experience, another lesson in his new state of existence.

In his peripheral vision, Freddy noticed Yezeel turning his head slightly toward him. Then he heard a click from the box on the bench. Without any noticeable command or action, his friend from the plane had initiated the open sequence of the incubator box. Freddy turned from the corpse and watched as the end of the incubator opened and a tray began sliding toward the left, carrying the body of the small boy. When out of the box, the overlays disappeared.

Like the corpse, the animated body was covered by a cloth with only the head exposed. Its head rested on a small pillow in a crescent-shaped piece of polished metal, which extended above the ears. The child appeared asleep, the same length as the corpse and with the same dark hair but no other resemblance. When the movement of the incubator stopped, Freddy felt the presence of another creature.

I'm going with you, a new voice said. *Just for the fun of it, and not because you need any help.*

Although the voice seemed to originate from his left, Freddy knew the sound existed only in his imagination and not as air compression waves. He imagined turning and then he saw his friend, Dod, standing beside him, a young man in his early twenties, short and skinny with light brown hair and dark eyes. A baseball cap sat on his head with *Cubs* written on the front. Except for the hat, he dressed as a young man from the early twentieth century, baggy striped trousers, a long-sleeve white shirt, and a dark brown vest.

"Thanks for the Zim episode," Freddy said. "I needed that."

No problem, pal.

Yezeel's giant hand suddenly entered his field of vision again, returning Freddy's attention to the top of the incubator. Yezeel touched a glowing green circle on the surface and a line replaced it. The line length represented the head cradle's level of neural network suppression protecting the child's brain.

If the level of suppression decreased enough, creatures from the background would feel its oscillations and attempt to synchronize with it, fighting to experience the body. Although Freddy understood what would happen, he had not yet experienced the effect. Yezeel touched the top of the line and slid his finger down, cutting the length in half. Freddy felt the complex electric field weaken around the boy's head.

Can you feel the oscillations yet?

Freddy turned to the child's head resting on the cradle. *Yes. It is strong.* While focusing on the brain, he imagined its innumerable clusters of neurons as stars in a galaxy with invisible plasma currents connecting them. It was intricate and beautiful and reminded Freddy of staring at the Milky Way on his journey to Mercury. He suddenly felt the urge to resonate with the neural network and then remembered that other creatures would also.

There's still sufficient suppression, Dod said in answer to his silent concern. *Until we find Jacob, we won't allow anything to resonate with it.*

Yezeel used his finger to return the line to its original length, and Freddy immediately felt the absence of the neural network. The room was suddenly quieter and emptier. The familiar sensation reminded Freddy of waking from a daydream.

Can you feel the oscillations from the dead? Dod asked after Yezeel had withdrawn his finger from the screen. *It's very weak but still present.*

"I did not even think to try," Freddy said. He turned his attention to the corpse and then closed his eyes for extra focus. Eliminating visual input helped him sense what remained of the neural network inside the corpse's skull. "The signature feels like a match, just weaker. Too many connections are broken, I suppose."

The body is beyond repair, Dod said. *Although resonance is impossible, the weak neural network will keep attracting untethered creatures until all the lights are extinguished. Jacob should be there too, still trying to find his way back.*

Freddy recalled his lesson on creature interactions with the corporeal world. Dod used the word *tethered* to describe creatures connected to the corporeal world through resonance with neural networks, and *untethered* to describe creatures not resonating with a neural network and thus disconnected from the corporeal world. Tethered creatures were much easier to isolate in the background. Freddy needed only to detect its neural network, or signature, in the corporeal world and then he could recreate it in the background unless a higher-capacity creature was somehow concealing it.

Are you ready to find him?

"Yes," Freddy said and glanced upward at Yezeel's head. The giant man stood still while looking down at the animated child's body.

Freddy had enjoyed experiencing the world from Yezeel's point of view. Before controlling the giant body, Freddy had often wondered how tall people felt. But standing taller than everyone was no longer as appealing. He was satisfied with the body the woman from the plane had prepared for him.

To interact with an untethered creature like Jacob, Dod began, *we need to join what he's created for himself, usually what he remembers most fondly. Before seeking another vessel, untethered creatures will build a safe place. They fear releasing their former lives. Where do you think Jacob would feel safest?*

"At his home," Freddy said.

Show me.

FIFTY-SEVEN

Freddy

"I suppose we should knock first," Freddy said. He stood with Dod on the front porch of Sadi's home in Portland. While raising his fist, he glanced at Dod and noticed the man's new clothing. Dod had the same face, hair, and hat but wore smooth blue jeans and a long-sleeve blue shirt with horizontal black stripes. Freddy was still taller.

"What's the plan?" Dod asked.

"Let's just go inside and see if we can find him."

"Doesn't sound like much of a plan," Dod said, looking at Freddy with the eyes of a teacher disappointed in his student. "He won't be alone and we also don't want to scare him."

"Good point," Freddy said and nodded. "I'll be your son and you're bringing me to play with him. That'll be an excuse at least."

"Alright," he said. "That's better than what you didn't have."

Freddy transformed into a child, a younger version than the one that had remained on Earth, the size of a four-year-old. Although he could have chosen any appearance, Freddy preferred the younger version of himself.

"I'm ready, Father," he said, glancing up at Dod. He raised his tiny fist into the air and knocked three times. After waiting for several seconds and not hearing any movement inside the house, Dod grasped the doorknob and twisted. Freddy felt no surprise when the door opened. He had imagined an unlocked door.

"Anybody home?" Dod asked loudly. He entered first, followed by Freddy who suddenly felt like an obedient child. After shutting the door, they paused, listening for any sign of life. "This is how you remember it last?"

"Yes," Freddy answered. He walked into the living room and stared at the couch where he remembered Helen sitting and playing the video game, *Mario-Kart*. "This is exactly how I left it, without the people of course."

"I'm not feeling it," Dod said. "The place would probably look more like Jacob remembers it. Let's look anyway, just to make sure, but his signature does not feel a part of this place."

Freddy walked up the stairs and searched every room. During the search, he recalled his experiences in the home, arriving with Brian to visit Sadi and show her the spider in the crystal. Although the memory was now pleasant, he knew the experience had been more awkward.

After walking through the final room upstairs, Freddy sensed conflicting emotions in the atmosphere of the home, Sadi's horror from Helen's abduction, then her relief after arriving home with Helen and her new daughter, Daryn. Perhaps his associations with the home were interfering with the search. Freddy descended the stairs and saw Dod sitting on the couch.

"No luck?" his friend asked.

"You're right," Freddy said, hopping onto the loveseat next to the couch and his feet barely reaching the edge. "He's not a part of this. Do you think I need to recreate it exactly as he remembers it?"

"That's not necessary," Dod answered, looking around the room. "No one experiences the same thing as another. There's got to be another place he feels safe, someplace that feels like home. A park or something?"

"Hmm," Freddy said. "Maybe they lived somewhere else before

here. I didn't think of that until now."

"Go find out. I'll wait."

To acquire the information needed to find Jacob, Freddy decided to seek Brian instead of Sadi. He wanted to limit interaction with Sadi until after he retrieved her son. Further contact with her might result in the conclusion that restoring Jacob would overwhelm her. He initially disregarded the concern, thinking he could fix any issue that might arise. But overconfidence seemed like a real and potent danger, despite his nearly limitless options.

Besides, he did not need Sadi. Brian could provide the required information. Freddy was sure of that. He would locate Brian in the corporeal world first, then find him in the background, an easier method than directly locating a tethered creature in the background. He had originally planned to perform the restoration himself, but he was relieved now to have Dod's assistance. The woman from the plane, standing beside him as Yezeel, had offered only to play the role of guard in the task, should he and Dod get trapped somehow by another creature. If Freddy knew he could rely on her additional assistance, he would not learn or grow as much.

Freddy sensed Brian's signature from their location, but just a little too faintly. Signatures in the corporeal world cast distinct wave patterns through the aether and decayed by the inverse square law as electromagnetic radiation and sound. With a sufficiently strong source signal, Freddy could resonate with Brian and influence Brian's interpretation of his sensory input.

Neural networks that were integrated with corporeal bodies translated sensory input into information creatures could utilize, what Dod called *background information*. Words translated to concepts and ideas. Radiation on the retina translated to shapes, colors, and contrast. Emotions translated to a complicated mixture of abstract concepts. The information usually represented a specific memory set or a mixture of memory and abstract associations, stored in the background and accessed directly by the creature. Higher-capacity creatures often influenced the flow of information from other creatures by suggestion, or directly if the target creature lacked the capacity to stop them, or through subconscious permission.

From all of the shielding on the station, Brian's signature was too weak, so Freddy decided to use a separate neural network rather than leave his present locations. Each of the helper machines contained a specialized set of neural networks for use by Freddy, Dod, or any other creature the woman from the plane might allow. Freddy referred to them as *access points*.

He began oscillation with the nearest machine, Old-One-Eye. The machine moved quietly through the passageways toward Brian's location. Freddy quickly coupled with him and then waited. Before riding along with Brian in the background, Freddy paused to experience his current conversation with Sadi. He preferred not to think of it as eavesdropping.

Freddy had abandoned any feeling of guilt for eavesdropping on people. He usually disengaged from the conversation when he thought the participants would want privacy. Freddy made a conscious effort to avoid Sadi's feelings and focus solely on Brian who was telling her about their encounter with the military in Norway. Brian was hurrying through that part of the story, more excited to talk about their aunt and uncle.

Like all tethered creatures, Brian oscillated with his neural network and received input from the corporeal world, and then acted based on that information. But that consumed only part of his capacity. He still existed in the background and continued to subconsciously create different storylines there, influenced largely by the most recent information he had received from the corporeal world. Brian had only a fractured memory of what he was imagining. Larger-capacity creatures, Freddy and Dod, could oscillate simultaneously with multiple neural networks while also consciously controlling the background. Freddy had easily existed as Yezeel, as the adult on the station, and as the child on Earth.

Most creatures preferred interaction with the corporeal world, not only for the direct generation of background information, but also for stability, and especially for social interaction. In the background, lower-capacity creatures found interaction with other creatures difficult and fleeting, depending mostly on their capacity to focus. Sensory input from the corporeal world forced creatures to dwell longer during the flow of information. In the background, creatures made modifications at will, usually resulting in abandoning social contact when any contention arose.

Other creatures acted as parasites to the tethered ones, consuming some of the information flow from the corporeal world, usually tainting the information in the process. They caused a similar impact as barnacles on the bottom of a boat. While attempting to restore Jacob to the corporeal world, Freddy expected to encounter parasitic creatures, or something more belligerent.

To join Brian in the background, Freddy had to focus first on the entire signature, the resonance of the neural network and the creature. The experience reminded Freddy of singing the lyrics to a song and feeling the vibrations of the instruments. Only then Freddy could identify the creature itself and join the setting it had created. He needed more practice joining a creature directly in the background without going through the corporeal world. That required copying its signature.

Freddy joined Brian in his daydream by walking down the main aisle of a dark theater. After reaching the front row, he paused to look at the band performing on the stage just a few meters away. He instantly recognized Brian at the microphone, holding his guitar, but Freddy discovered that the creature on the stage was not real. The band members were just lifeless actors, performing the music like broken-record robots. Brian was not on stage.

"Where are you, Brian?" he whispered.

When he turned to inspect the audience, Freddy was surprised to encounter a theater full of mannequins, all wearing new clothes with price tags still attached as if they belonged in Target or Walmart. They were sitting in the seats, motionless and facing the stage. After spending some time inspecting them, Freddy located a mannequin in the middle of the third row who resembled Brian. Freddy walked past the other mannequins in the row until he reached the empty seat next to Brian the mannequin.

"A great concert," Freddy said after sitting. "These guys are awesome."

Brian the mannequin tried his best to act the part and stare forward motionlessly. But after a moment, he slowly turned his head to face Freddy. When the head finally stopped rotating, Brian was still wearing the same frozen expression. Smiling politely, Freddy waited until his plastic lips stretched into a smile. The rest of his face remained frozen.

"Ah yes, of course," Freddy said, turning away and facing the stage again. "You would not be here if you disagreed." Freddy acted like a polite audience member and spoke quietly. He could feel Brian's desire to remain a silent mannequin.

"Brian," Freddy whispered. "You should take me to Sadi's old place sometime. I'd like to see where she used to live."

FIFTY-EIGHT

Freddy

Freddy stood on a sidewalk under a cloudy sky, facing a beige duplex and Brian at his side. The front door was a cheap white thing with scratch marks by the handle. The doormat had WELCOME displayed in black rubber letters. From outside, Brian remembered those two details the most.

Freddy watched Brian's next memory from just inside the front door. A young Helen was playing with a doll on the floor, messy blond hair barely contained by two short pigtails. Sadi sat at the kitchen table with an open book, attempting to read while a young Jacob pulled on her leg. Neither of them showed any sign of noticing him.

After Brian entered through the front door, Helen's blue eyes and mouth opened wide, a mixture of surprise and joy. She ran into his arms, smiling as she squeezed his cheeks with both hands. Brian's memory was so pleasant, Freddy wanted to watch it again, but he had to focus on finding Jacob. He could replay the memory anytime in the future. Now it was his memory too.

He still needed Brian to show him the rest of the interior, so he made Sadi, Helen, and Jacob disappear, and then Brian led him through the rest of the tiny habitation. Once satisfied with his impression of the place, Freddy sent Brian back to his concert in the theater, then stayed in the empty duplex.

Then he heard four quick knocks on the front door.

"Took you long enough," Dod said, smiling wide.

"I know."

"Don't forget to be the child," Dod said while entering the duplex. "He's close. Can you feel him?"

Freddy returned his attention to the corporeal world, to the corpse lying on the slab. He now understood the situation more fully. The decaying neural network still pulsated but was broken and fragmented. Although creatures could not fully oscillate with it anymore, Freddy could feel Jacob desperately attempting to restore the connection, even despite the silence of the body. Jacob's background signature was strong, and Freddy felt the distinct difference between an untethered creature and one still oscillating with a neural network.

He suddenly felt sorry for Jacob. He remembered the horror of the tunnel under the Sahara when he cut his own connection to the corporeal world and dove alone into the abyss. At least Jacob did not have to find his way out again.

"So that's Jacob," Freddy said and looked up at his pretend father.

"Let's go meet him."

After shutting the door, Freddy turned to face the living room with Dod. Standing next to the adult figure helped Freddy feel even more like a child, and he kept having to remind himself of his disguise. As he had already learned several times, creatures could easily get lost in the background. They often forgot about the illusion.

"So, we'll meet him once we complete the structure?"

"Yes," Dod said. "You've got the spatial dimensions. Now you need to recreate the emotional connections."

Freddy focused his attention back on Jacob's signature and its complex emotional aspect. After significant struggle, he was finally able to isolate some emotional information from the end of Jacob's childhood. He remembered playing with his older sister Helen, and then crying when she would steal his toys and make him beg her to return them. The borrowed memories made Freddy smile but also want to cry.

The duplex suddenly felt like home.

—※—

"Hi, Jacob," Dod said, turning to the stairs at the far left of the room.

Freddy followed his gaze and saw a dark-haired child at the base of the stairs, narrow slits for eyes, surprised by the two new characters in his home. In his right hand, the boy clutched a worn blanket, light blue and frayed at the edges. The tattered blanket hung loosely at his side, the fabric dragging on the floor.

"Who are you?" the child asked, his tone a strange mixture of confidence and fear.

"We're from down the street," Dod said. "Just moved in. Is your mother here?"

"Mom's not here."

"She wanted me to bring my son for a play date. This is Freddy."

"Hi," Freddy said, quickly raising his hand and then letting it fall back to his side.

"Hi," Jacob said. He remained motionless and his eyes were still only half-open.

"Why don't you two go upstairs and play?" Dod asked, looking from Freddy to Jacob. "I'll stay here until your mother returns."

Without waiting for a response, Dod turned and walked to the couch. Freddy and Jacob watched as he sat down, plucked a magazine from the coffee table, and then pretended to read.

When Freddy turned and looked into Jacob's blue eyes, he felt a strong impression. Jacob did not like them in his home and was wondering how to get rid of them. But Freddy felt another source too. The impression did not only originate from the child. Another creature wanted them gone.

Freddy smiled sweetly as if he didn't notice the other creature's signature, then he quickly re-examined the setting. When Jacob had appeared, he changed the interior of the duplex a little. At first, Freddy did not immediately recognize the specific changes or anything unusual other than more detail.

From his viewpoint near the door, Freddy could see the entire living room and also the kitchen area on the right of the stairs. The wooden chairs around the dining table were all pushed to the edge, neat and evenly spaced. Nothing sat on top of the counter or table that he could see, although the angle of his view prevented him from seeing their surfaces. The entire area showed little evidence of use, nothing to indicate that a child lived there.

A clean home probably helps him remember his mother.

Then the stairs captured his attention. Toys were placed on the sides of each step, forming two parallel lines up the stairs. Most of the toys were shiny plastic automobiles of different models and colors, although *Bakugan* toys in their spherical configurations occupied some of the positions.

A stuffed animal sat facing forward on the left side of the top step, a black and white panda bear, soft and fuzzy. When Freddy focused on the panda's face, he noticed the eyes looking at him. The mouth was smiling but the eyes were not happy.

"I like panda bears," Freddy said, pointing to the top step. "What's his name?"

Jacob turned and looked at the top step.

"Panda," he said, then pressed the blanket against his neck.

When Jacob faced Freddy again, the frayed edges of the blue blanket became more distinct, and Freddy noticed that the blanket was glowing faintly. While focusing on the blue of the material, Jacob's signature felt more potent to Freddy. The sensation confirmed his suspicion. The blue blanket represented the neural network. For Jacob, it was the neural network. Freddy especially noticed the boy's tight grip on the fabric.

"Can I see Panda?" Freddy asked while walking toward the stairs. Jacob stepped aside to let him pass.

He had initially planned to gain Jacob's trust and then lead him to the new body. But after locking onto the signature of the decaying neural network, Freddy knew Jacob would stay until the blanket no longer pulsated, not even if Jacob trusted them.

Before guiding Jacob to his new neural network, Freddy would need to isolate him from the other creatures, the parasites who wanted a piece of his next life. Freddy began climbing the steps and then stopped when the panda bear was within his reach.

"Hi, Panda," he said, still smiling sweetly. "You're so cute. I just want to squish you."

Jacob bypassed the formality of running up the stairs and just appeared on the top step instead. Before Freddy could reach for the stuffed animal, Jacob grabbed the angry little creature with his left hand.

"I got you," he said, the blanket still clutched in his right hand.

Jacob glared at Freddy who was smiling and pretending not to notice the anger directed at him. After focusing on the bear again, Freddy could not stop himself from laughing. The bear's mouth had transformed into a frown, and Freddy imagined Sadi wondering why her son loved such an angry bear.

"I won't let him hurt you," Jacob said, hugging the bear tightly.

"I just wanted to hug him," Freddy said, not laughing anymore and acting hurt.

When speaking, Jacob looked at Freddy but addressed the bear.

"I know," Jacob said, confident but slightly afraid. "This isn't one of your games, is it? No? Good. I didn't think so. Yes, I want them to leave too."

Freddy paused to focus on the ugly signature of the creature in Jacob's hand. After sending it away, he planned to purge his memory of the vile little thing. The lower-capacity creature could not contend with them, but it could call for aid and delay the process, maybe even ruin it. Freddy appreciated its grasp on the child and decided to force a confrontation to begin the next phase of the operation.

Freddy turned to Yezeel in the corporeal world.

"It is time," Freddy said calmly, but he could feel the perspiration on his forehead. Before refocusing on the scene with Jacob, he felt a single drop of sweat sliding down his right temple.

Freddy sighed and returned to the duplex.

"Okay," he said to Jacob. "We'll leave in just a few minutes. I'm sorry for bothering you."

Instead of replying, Jacob pulled the blanket up to his neck again and then looked in panic at the fabric. Freddy felt sorry for Jacob for what was about to happen, and he had to remind himself of the end result and not the despair Jacob would soon feel. He followed the boy's gaze and watched as the dim light of the blanket faded. The process of disintegration accelerated, and the fabric began to stretch and then slowly fall apart.

Jacob dropped the bear and grasped the blanket with both hands, scrunching it up into a ball and hugging it to his chest. When he began crying, his fear, despair, and panic became a thick emotional fog, filling the interior of the duplex.

"No, no, no," he whimpered.

As the fog continued to thicken, Freddy turned his attention to the bear. He extended his right hand, intending to grab it, but a snake shot toward his face from the panda bear's fluffy white stuffing. Without flinching, Freddy caught the wiggling creature in his outstretched hand. The snake struggled and opened its mouth, revealing white fangs. While Freddy held it close to his face, liquid dripped from the fang tips.

Preventing the creature's escape or transformation into something else did not require a significant amount of focus, Freddy realized. After a moment, he extended the creature to Jacob.

"*This* was hiding inside Panda," Freddy said, glancing at the stuffed animal now lying on the floor at the top of the stairs. The face of the bear had returned to its happy, smiling condition. He turned back to Jacob and shook the snake. "*This* is not your friend."

With tears in his eyes, Jacob looked at the snake in Freddy's tight grasp. He showed no sign of fear, or understanding even, only confusion. After a moment, a piece of the blanket broke away from the rest and fell to the floor, then another, and another. With each piece that escaped the boy's grasp, the duplex became darker, then a new light burst to life in the living room.

"What's happening?" Jacob asked as more of the fabric fell to the floor. He held onto scraps of decayed blanket, useless and no longer blue but an ugly brown.

While gripping the disintegrating fabric, Jacob used his arms and shoulders to wipe the tears from his cheeks. He looked away from the snake in Freddy's hand, his eyes wide with desperation. His face was illuminated by the strong light suddenly shining from the living room.

"Mom," Jacob yelled, stepping down the stairs.

Dod was standing at the bottom, blocking the way. After taking three steps, Jacob stopped and stared at the living room which was filled with a blinding white light. During the pause, Freddy could feel the creature wiggling in his tight grasp.

"I'll take that," Dod said, extending his hand in the air. The snake suddenly flew from Freddy's grasp and landed in Dod's hand, writhing and hissing. "It's time to show Jacob what you brought him."

"My mom's outside," Jacob said while running down the stairs. He no longer showed any interest in the snake. "I need to see Mom!"

Dod turned and walked with the snake into the living room, then disappeared in the intense white light. Freddy joined Jacob at the bottom of the stairs, using his right hand to shield his eyes. White light surrounded his hand. Behind him, he felt an empty darkness.

Freddy could not see Dod anymore, only the child in front of him and the floor directly around their feet. Together, they walked toward the light. When they could see Dod again, he was facing them with the door at his back, the snake writhing in his tight grasp. Brilliant white light shined from the small window in the door, just above Dod's head.

"Jacob," a woman said softly from behind Dod.

Freddy felt Sadi's signature outside the door, indistinguishable from the woman he knew. When she called her son's name, the sound was like the strike of a crystal bell. The pure, high-pitched tone filled the world.

He suddenly realized what the light represented. It was the intensity of a mother's love for her child. The light was blinding. Then Freddy remembered his first encounter with Sadi, his nearly overwhelming infatuation. The memory threatened to destroy his concentration.

"I'm outside, Jacob," Sadi said. "Come on. I want to see you. Come outside, into the light. I miss my sweet baby!"

Freddy paused to analyze the signature of the creature speaking to them from the light. Although he learned quickly it was not Sadi, he also learned that the voice was actually a group of creatures speaking in unison.

In horror, Freddy realized the truth. They were too much for him to handle alone. Just keeping the door between them was requiring too much of his attention.

Strangely, Freddy wanted to forget about the door, release his grasp of it, and join the creatures on the other side. They promised him an existence free from all negative influence, free from obligation and pain. The temptation suddenly paralyzed him.

"I'll keep the door together," Dod said, restoring Freddy to the present. "It's time to show Jacob what we have for him."

Dod attempted to smile, but Freddy noticed the strain on his face. A long vein ran from his forehead to the top of his right eye, a raging river just under the skin. Freddy shook his head, closed his eyes, and transferred the responsibility for the door to Dod.

He noticed the body of Yezeel who stood next to him in the corporeal world, black lips stretching into a wide smile. In his grey eyes, Freddy saw the woman from the plane. She would not let him fail.

While Jacob stared at the light, wondering desperately how to get past Dod, Freddy suddenly felt calm. He remembered the plan. Freddy the child reached behind his back and produced a new blanket, identical to Jacob's original one. The beautiful material glowed with a deep blue light, warming Freddy's face, hands, and arms.

"Jacob," Freddy said, extending the blanket in his hand. "I have a present for you."

The child turned, tears in his eyes. After glancing at Freddy, he stared at the blanket, the blue light illuminating his face. As the desperation in his eyes faded, the serpent writhed in Dod's grasp and fell to the floor. It slithered on the ground toward Freddy, opening its mouth and exposing its fangs. While calmly watching the snake, Freddy crushed its head under his foot.

Jacob extended his hands, dropping the decayed material to the ground, and pulled the new blanket to his chest. While hugging the blanket, he closed his eyes.

—※—

In the corporeal world, Freddy laid his hand on the forehead of the sleeping child, feeling as if he were a father touching his son for the first time. The warm head under his hand brought tears to his eyes. When Freddy looked at the corpse on the left. Another crescent-shaped piece of metal was lying over the forehead.

Well done, said the woman from the plane.

Freddy wanted to thank Dod, but he was gone.

FIFTY-NINE

Christine

After finishing her last class that morning, Christine walked to her job at the clothing store on Mississippi Avenue. During the short walk, she enjoyed listening to the rain hitting her waterproof jacket. While passing the café where she and Franklin had met during his escape, she was reminded of the thrill she had experienced helping him. As usual, she needed another thrill, so she was saving money for another snowboarding trip to Mount Hood. Until she heard from Franklin, a good snowboarding trip would have to suffice.

Only after Franklin had escaped did Christine understand its full significance. They had broken the law and helped a fugitive escape the clutches of evil government agents. She had no regrets, though, and wondered if she would have made the same decision to help him, given more time to think about the implications. As usual, being absorbed in her thoughts helped work pass quickly.

For the entire first week after helping Franklin, Christine had waited for him to call her, or a visit from the police or FBI. To her disappointment, neither had occurred. She had devised an excellent cover story to tell the authorities and had even practiced it in front of a mirror and then for her sister, Francis. During the second week, she began to worry more for Franklin and wondered if she would ever see him again.

The situation made no sense. Her escape plan had worked perfectly. Even Francis and Franklin's friends had all believed in its success. The people following Franklin had not even continued their pursuit. They had just remained in their car. The situation only made sense if Franklin had been captured.

Franklin would have called even if he was afraid of the risk. The guy had displayed an obvious physical attraction to her. She wanted to think he had escaped and abandoned the idea of contacting her. But her gut instinct told a different story and would not let her forget about him.

Christine would have to begin an investigation of her own. Her conscience refused to let her think of anything else. While studying at the kitchen table later that night, she broached the subject with her sister.

"What do you think happened to Franklin?" she asked, placing her pencil on the table. As Francis read a book, Christine stared at her dark blond hair falling over the edge of the couch.

"No news is good news," she answered without turning.

"Do you really think he got away?"

"Yes," she said while turning a page. "There's nothing we can do about it anyway."

From her tone, Christine suspected a fake disinterest.

"Nothing huh? He would have called."

"He probably just forgot your number," Francis said.

"Yeah, right," Christine said, but she felt a small twinge of doubt. Franklin could have been lying when he claimed to remember her phone number. "You saw how he looked at me. My number was burned in his brain."

"Try to forget about him." Francis was talking like a loving sister, protective. "Your mind associates Franklin with a thrill and you're only interested because of that. He's not your type. You like guys who will go skydiving with you. Franklin was nice, but I can't see him doing things like that."

"Don't major in psychology, Francis," Christine said and laughed. "Following that logic, I would also be interested in his friend, Screwdriver."

"Uh-huh."

"If I wanted to find him," Christine said, "any ideas where to start?"

"Not a good idea," Francis answered and turned to face her sister. She let the book close over her thumb. "I'd like to keep the FBI from knocking on our door. There is no way to find him anyway."

"I know," Christine said despondently and turned her attention to her textbook about early childhood development. Francis had said a key phrase, *no way to find him,* a challenge and additional motivation to begin an investigation. In her peripheral vision, Christine saw her sister staring suspiciously. After a few seconds, Francis turned to her book again and they spent the rest of the evening studying quietly.

After Francis fell asleep that night, Christine quietly opened the back door of their apartment and stepped onto the patio. The shock of cold water under her feet erased the fatigue from her long day. She checked for anyone watching, then walked barefoot across the wet grass, cold rain falling on her head and soaking into her shirt. She had to pass three other apartments before getting to the back of Franklin's. The occupants of two apartments were watching television and the other was dark. No one saw her.

Christine put her face to the glass of the sliding door and cupped her hands to see better. Looking into the empty apartment was strange, exciting almost. Light from an open microwave illuminated the kitchen and dining area. Christine turned from the glass and searched the patio. On that first surveillance mission, she had not expected to find anything specific. Franklin kept nothing outside. She needed to find a way inside, even if she had to break the glass. Tomorrow, she would look for a glass cutter.

Before leaving the patio, she grabbed the sliding door handle to see if it moved at all. Instead of breaking the glass, maybe she could bring something to pry it open. To her surprise, the door slid open without any resistance.

"What the hell," she whispered, looking at the other apartments. She was suddenly afraid of being seen. "Is this some sort of trap?"

After pausing for a few short breaths, Christine reminded herself to replace paranoid thoughts with the more realistic scenario. In his haste, Franklin had simply forgotten to lock the back door. No one had seen her, and no one was waiting for her to enter the apartment.

She quietly slid the door closed behind her and then walked to the living room where they had reviewed her escape plan. The light from the microwave failed to illuminate the place enough for a proper investigation. She had not considered the possibility of entering, so she did not bring a flashlight. She considered returning to her apartment then decided to just turn on the light. No one in the apartment complex knew of Franklin's absence and the watchers were long gone. She could live with the possibility of Francis finding her, which was the most probable consequence.

Christine quickly searched the living room for clues, then the kitchen. Looking under cushions and in drawers reminded her of *Scooby Doo*, her favorite cartoon. As a child, she had spent countless hours watching Scooby and his friends solve crimes and mysteries. She had always fantasized about being a private investigator. In the end, she chose a more realistic career, as a teacher because she also loved children.

After failing to find anything useful in the living room or kitchen, Christine turned off the lights then entered Franklin's bedroom. She tried looking at the scene from the perspective of someone who did not know what had happened. They would probably think the occupant had left in a hurry. The covers lay all twisted on the bed, with some empty folders scattered on top, including two torn books about programming. Christine noticed the absence of pillows and felt an odd relief, imagining Franklin at least had those.

She went to Franklin's clothing dresser and switched on the lamp sitting there. Most of the drawers were open, some more than others.

Franklin had left a few clothes, grey socks that had once been white, old tee shirts, and pants. One drawer had several envelopes, mostly junk mail. She quickly shuffled through them and found a dollar bill. She put the money in the back pocket of her shorts and then felt like a thief.

"Yeah, I'd make a great burglar," she whispered.

Franklin kept several business cards in his top drawer. After inspecting each card, she would set it on the dresser. Most came from local businesses, including one punch card from a café she liked. After placing the punch card in her pocket, she found a card from a lawyer's office, Foster and Fowler. A phone number was handwritten on the back. While reading the information on the front, an excited chill coursed through her.

She put the card in her pocket and continued searching, but she failed to find anything else that might help her find Franklin. Only the business card seemed like a real lead. After school the next day, Christine planned to investigate the Law Firm of Foster and Fowler.

When Christine returned to her apartment, she found Francis facing away from her, still in bed. She stared at her sister's dark blond hair for a few seconds, wishing she had the same color, and then she went to her own bed. After walking through the cold rain, snuggling under the covers felt amazing.

Falling asleep required more than an hour. The experience of breaking into a dark apartment consumed all of her thoughts. She finally lost consciousness while considering the logistics of working as a seventh-grade teacher during the day and private investigator during the night.

SIXTY

Christine

After work the next evening, Christine grabbed the business card and then performed a search on the internet. She first entered the term, *foster and fowler law firm*, and found just basic business information. The company seemed to have no specialty other than small business issues. Then she entered Gerald Foster's name since the business card was his. At the first link, she felt a sense of dread.

The article summarized a local court case and appeared on a small independent news site from Seattle. The author focused on Gerald Foster embarrassing the FBI when he had exposed their attempt to entrap his client. Christine did not fully understand, but she guessed that this Gerald Foster had made dangerous enemies who could have somehow found interest in Franklin.

While reading the article again, Christine assumed that some kind of connection existed between Franklin and the law firm, and maybe even that specific case. Had they hired Franklin to handle something computer-related? She doubted that Franklin could afford their legal assistance. Or maybe he had read about the court case and contacted Gerald Foster with questions about the illegal activities of other friends. Whatever the specific connection, Christine knew she would have to contact Gerald Foster.

"What are you reading?" Francis asked.

"Just surfing the internet," Christine said. While reading the article, she had failed to notice her sister's approach.

"You specifically searched for a..." Francis paused and bent closer to the screen, "Gerald Foster. Who's that?"

"Long story," Christine said, smiling wide and knowing Francis could not see her face. "You know how one thing leads to another. I was reading one thing, and that led to another, then another, and another. I could explain everything, but you probably have things to do."

"Yes," Francis said and walked to the refrigerator. "No need to explain further. I know how your distorted mind works."

Christine waited for Francis to leave the kitchen with her bowl of cereal, then she opened a new *Microsoft Word* document and began typing a letter to Gerald Foster at his law firm address. Christine had to act more discreetly and not let her sister see the letter. She had considered the option of calling Gerald but did not want to make any traceable connection. Instead, she would mark the return address with Franklin's apartment number and ask for a response by mail.

—※—

The next day began like any other. Christine awoke early for a run, in the rain, then attended her morning classes at the Portland Community College, Cascade Campus. After class, she walked to her job at the clothing store. Business was slow during the rainy season and Christine usually had some time to study.

While sitting at the cash register reading a textbook, a man and a little boy entered the shop. The man had thick dark hair with a beard and the boy had curly white hair. They looked like an odd pair, and Christine failed to recognize any family resemblance.

The man did not even seem to be paying any attention to the boy. The man looked potentially dangerous and Christine felt an instant attraction to him even though he exceeded her age by maybe twenty years. Her rational self ignored the impulse and listened to what Francis would say.

You're not attracted to him. You're attracted to danger.

"Hi, little guy," Christine said after leaving her seat at the cash register. "What's your name?"

"Freddy," he said in a sweet voice.

Christine bent down and put her hands on his small shoulders. While looking into his eyes, she felt a strange sensation. Although he had much blonder hair than hers, his face seemed like a younger version of her own, and looking into his brown eyes was like looking into a mirror. Then suddenly, Christine's life quickly replayed in her mind, from the present to her first encounter with Franklin.

In the next instant, she was standing and the dark-haired man was talking to her.

"Something for my girlfriend," he said. "Maybe a jacket."

While waiting for Christine to respond, the man looked at her, squinting as if concerned about her mental state. For some reason, she had been thinking about a small white-haired boy. Then she remembered asking if the man needed any help.

"Do you know her size?" Christine asked, smiling and pretending the pause never happened. She had to abandon the effort of remembering the child to better focus on her only customer. "A jacket for rain or snow?"

She was accustomed to helping men purchase clothes for their girlfriends or wives, and she enjoyed helping men more than women. They usually let her make the choices and she had a good track record. Only one man had ever returned what she chose for them.

Two minutes later, the man made his purchase decision. While taking one of their more expensive jackets to the cash register, Christine felt his eyes on her butt. He paid for the jacket with cash, thanked her for the suggestion then left without looking back.

While watching him walk away from the shop, she attempted to remember the entire encounter. The memory seemed incomplete for some reason, especially when he first entered the shop. And then after he left her view, the whole encounter seemed like a dream. Only the transaction history in the cash register proved his visit to the store.

She walked home after work, enjoying the lack of rain and feeling hungry. The short walk assisted with her mental transition from work to home and more studying. She ate dinner with a textbook and a computer.

"I'm bored," Christine said after swallowing a mouthful of leftover spaghetti. "Want to go do anything?"

"I need to study," Francis said from the couch.

"Well, I'm taking advantage of the good weather," she said while staring at the back of her sister's head. "I'm going on a walk."

"Have fun."

While walking past all of the shops and restaurants on Mississippi Avenue, Christine enjoyed mingling with the crowds, composed mostly of young people of nearly every ethnicity. She passed two older men smoking pipe tobacco and enjoyed the scent in the air. She spent some time in a comic book store, searching for a new mystery to read. Back on the street, Christine heard someone call her name.

"Hi, Kiel," she said after turning and recognizing a good friend from one of her classes. She quickly scanned her friend's appearance to see if she could guess his plans for the evening. He wore a dark red ski hat covered with white snowflakes and pulled just above his light blue eyes. She liked the colorful composition of his clothes, dark blue jacket and black polyester pants with light purple stripes. She especially liked how his tight pants glistened in the lights and accentuated the shape of his legs.

"Let me guess," she began. "You're meeting some friends for a drink?"

"Kind of," he said and laughed. "Please come with me. I'm meeting my brother-in-law and need someone to add a little spice."

"That sounds perfect," she said. "I needed to get out. I was working on our English paper, but my brain felt fried. So, your brother-in-law huh? Is there anything I should know about him?"

"Nah," he said then grabbed her hand and started pulling her down the street. He released his hold after she had gained enough momentum. "But with you there, he probably won't talk about having sex with my sister."

"Well, then I'm extra glad you ran into me."

They had to walk only one block before arriving at the restaurant. Kiel pulled her through the crowded entrance and found the table with his brother-in-law. He was sitting in the closest booth to the entrance and had a view of the street through a large window. Christine ordered a lemon drop on the rocks while the two men ordered a beer and some fries. She enjoyed the conversation and fries, but she thought they had made her favorite drink a little too sweet.

As a fun way to get better acquainted with Kiel's brother-in-law, Christine tried guessing some details about the man's life. Although she only made one correct guess, she was proud of herself for noticing the clue, which helped identify his profession, as a programmer. On the palm of the man's hand was written a messy string of computer code.

"I thought of the solution to a problem and didn't want to forget it," he said after she released his hand. "I had a pen, just no paper."

Seeing the computer code reminded her of Franklin, but she wanted to postpone thoughts of that investigation. She wanted to enjoy the moment and forget about work and everything else. A few minutes later, Kiel complained about how fast college tuition had risen in the past few years. His brother-in-law thought the rate would stop rising, but Kiel and Christine disagreed.

"I don't think..." she said, then stopped after noticing the two people walking past the restaurant, a white-haired little boy and the man who had purchased the jacket from her earlier that evening.

The child looked strangely familiar, but she did not remember seeing him with the man. Christine leaned closer to the window to see them more clearly before they left her view. At first, she failed to notice anything suspicious about the pair, but then she noticed how the boy did not walk beside the man. He walked behind him. Without realizing the reason, she shivered from a sudden chill.

"I need to go," she said and stood from the table. "Sorry, Kiel, but I need to talk to someone who just walked by. It was good to meet you, James."

Christine threw some cash on the table then left the restaurant and immediately saw the man and child walking up the street. She kept a good distance between them and avoided looking at their backs directly for too long. She remembered how people can often feel others looking at them. After watching them for a while, she wondered if the man even knew the child was following him.

As they walked farther away from the shopping area, the number of people on the street decreased. Christine feared the man might turn and recognize her, so she crossed the street and continued walking in the same direction. When they turned down the street where she and Francis lived, her heart rate accelerated. She suddenly felt glad for the dark of night and the shadow of the trees.

The man and child reached her apartment complex, then without pausing, stepped onto the grass and walked around the back, out of her sight.

"What are you doing?" she whispered and then ran to the other side of the complex. She stopped when the back of the apartments came into her view. She saw the man but not the child.

The man walked casually, seemingly unafraid of any tenant noticing him. He walked onto the patio at the back of Franklin's apartment and seemed surprised to find the door unlocked, reminding her of the same experience. After he opened the door and disappeared inside, the kitchen light illuminated.

When the man left her view, Christine felt brave enough to approach Franklin's patio. She stepped to the sliding glass door, the side concealed by the blinds, and watched the man search the apartment. While he searched through all of the shelves and drawers, Christine thought he acted more at ease than she had. He walked down the short hallway to the bedroom, leaving her view again.

While waiting, Christine glanced behind her every few seconds, afraid someone might see her. When the man reappeared in the kitchen, she knew he meant to exit the building the same way he had come. In sudden panic, she turned and ran away to the side of the apartment, opposite the way they had come. With her back against the wall, her heart beat painfully hard and she gasped for breath. She peeked around the edge of the wall and was relieved to see the man retracing his steps toward the other side of the building.

"What are you doing?"

Christine jumped in fright at the sound of her sister's voice and cupped her hands over her mouth to prevent a scream, and to muffle another bout of heavy breathing. When she saw Francis standing in the grass next to her, she put her fingers to her lips.

"Quiet! He might hear you," she whispered. "A man broke into Franklin's apartment. I was watching him."

"What?" her sister asked in confusion and stepped slowly to the edge of the building. Francis looked for a few seconds then turned back to Christine. "I don't see anybody."

"I know. He just left," Christine whispered and walked toward the front of the building. Francis followed her until they could see down the street where she had come. While holding onto her sister's shoulder, Christine pointed to the man walking away. "That's him, but there was a child with him too."

"This doesn't make any sense," Francis said, anger tainting her voice. "Why do I get the impression that you caused this?"

Christine ignored her sister and walked into the front of the complex and then toward the sidewalk. She considered following the man but decided against the idea. She would most likely follow him to his car and watch him drive away. That would just increase the chance of him seeing her. Francis needed an explanation anyway.

"Let's go inside and I'll explain everything," Christine said and smiled wide, challenging Francis to make another accusation. During the short walk, her heart rate and breathing returned to a more tolerable level.

"Okay," Francis said once they had closed and locked their front door. "Tell me what's going on."

"I need a drink first."

Although she could still taste the lemon from her drink, Christine needed something cold to rehydrate her tongue. During the short interval, she decided to tell her sister as much of the truth as possible while making herself look like the victim. They sat on opposite ends of the couch. Christine sat on her right leg, her glass of cold water in both hands.

"So that guy came into the shop today," Christine began, then paused as the sudden memory of the child interrupted her thoughts. "He was alone, I think, but he looked dangerous for some reason. I really can't say why."

"What do you mean? *You think he was alone.*" Francis spoke with a tone of disbelief. "Was he or not?"

"Yes, he was alone. I helped pick a jacket for his girlfriend, then he left and I forgot about him until he walked by the restaurant. I ran into Kiel on my walk and he invited me to a drink with his brother-in-law."

"Okay," Francis said and rubbed her eyes. "So you saw him in the restaurant?"

"No, he was just walking by." Christine took another drink. "It was strange. A little boy was walking behind him like he was following or something. I'm not even sure the man knew the boy was there."

"Did he see you?"

"No, I just followed him as he walked to our place." Christine paused after realizing that Francis refused to ask about the strange child or acknowledge his existence in her story. "The child disappeared after they walked to the back. He must have been only eight or so. It was like he wasn't even there."

"So you followed this man to Franklin's apartment?"

Before responding, Christine suddenly imagined the white-haired child walking behind Francis. She squinted and shook her head. She did not see the little boy with her eyes, only in her imagination. Francis was about to say something, so Christine continued before her sister could interrupt.

"After he went inside and turned on the light, I walked to the patio and watched him. He just looked around for a few minutes then left, and then you scared the shit out of me!"

"And that's it? You didn't do anything else?"

"It happened just like I told you," Christine said, trying to act offended. "Why don't you believe me?"

"Because things don't just happen to you, Christine," she said and smiled wryly. "You tend to make things happen. But, it's a good sign that he didn't come here, I think."

"What do you mean?"

"Well, if it was the cops or FBI or something, they would have just gotten a key from Mr. Johnson. Only a criminal would sneak in the back. It's probably a good sign he didn't come to us."

A warning bell began ringing in her mind. The man suddenly seemed even more dangerous than she had first thought. His visit to the shop now seemed like a highly improbable coincidence. Before she could stop herself, Christine revealed her thoughts.

"Probably not a good sign that he just happened to visit my work."

For one long second, the sisters stared silently at each other.

"At least he went away," Christine said.

SIXTY-ONE

Helen

When Helen heard the noise, she opened her eyes and sat up in bed. While listening for the sound again, she turned to face the view screen. Bright stars filled the top half of the screen, illuminating her room while pretty clouds floated above the nighttime surface of Bodn. As usual, the view filled her with peace. She often fell asleep watching the stars grow brighter and the clouds grow darker. She planned to try and sleep again, but she heard the noise again, two quick knocks on the door.

Before the visitors announced their identity, Helen experienced a moment of internal reflection. Before the parasite treatment, she would have felt instant fear and panic to hear knocking in the middle of the night. But now, her instinct was to make a calm assessment of the situation. If someone had wanted to harm her, they would not have knocked. Besides, she had complete trust in the safety of the station. *It's probably Daryn*, she thought. For the first few weeks on the station, Daryn would occasionally visit during the night and request to sleep with her.

"It's Freddy," said the voice outside her door. "I would like to talk to you for a few minutes. Can I come in?"

"Okay," she said and then watched the door begin to open.

As light from the hallway flooded the room, her eyes closed halfway shut while adjusting to the brighter light level. Helen could see only Freddy's silhouette, but she immediately recognized him. She smiled and pushed herself up higher in bed.

Since their return from Bodn the previous day, she had wanted to talk to him. She had so many questions and they suddenly began filling her mind. Why did he look so different? Did he know how Jen was doing on Earth? How had he arrived at the station when her uncle had used the BMW and they still had the jet? Why was her mother so concerned about the opportunity to get an upgrade to their bodies?

Freddy entered her room alone and then shut the door. He stood still and smiled.

"Hi, Freddy," she said.

"Hi, sweet girl," he said. "Sorry to interrupt your sleep."

"It's okay," she said, rubbing her eyes.

"I wanted to talk to you for a bit, then I have something to show you."

Helen opened her mouth to ask a question, then stopped herself and clamped her lips shut again. Speaking would only delay the information he had to share. She took a deep breath and waited, forgetting that it was her turn to speak. Freddy stared at her for a moment then walked to the view screen. He stood there silently, looking at the beautiful scene.

"Do you know what a water hammer is?" he asked, still facing the screen.

"No."

"When water flows through pipes, it has a certain momentum. Do you know what momentum is?"

"Movement," she said, remembering their physics lessons from the machines. "Momentum is moving mass."

"Very good," he said and turned to her. Light from the screen illuminated half of his face. "Water hammer refers to the sudden loss of momentum of water flowing through pipes. If water is flowing and someone closes a valve too quickly, the momentum changes too fast and can damage the pipes and hurt the person shutting the valve. Stopping the flow of water can be very dangerous."

"Okay," Helen said, her eyes narrowing. "You want me to shut a valve?"

"I use that as an example," he said, smiling again. "When a woman has a child, the brain incorporates the child into almost every aspect of her thoughts. Think of it as creating new pathways and her thoughts are like water flowing through them. Do you see the analogy?"

"So when my mom had me, I became a big part of her life?" Helen asked. She enjoyed thinking that way. "I'm the water flowing through Mom's brain!"

"And it also happened to your mother when she had Jacob," Freddy said, "your brother."

Helen frowned and squinted again. She did not like thinking about Jacob. Horrible images and feelings accompanied his memory. Sometimes her brother's dead body haunted her dreams, and even worse nightmares of her mother crying again. Rather than let memories of her brother's death fill her thoughts, Helen decided to speak and fill the physical silence.

"So, when he died," she began before the thought had fully formed. "So, when he died, it was like a water hammer in her brain?"

"Yes, very good."

"Does that mean Mom's broken?"

"In a way, yes," Freddy admitted without trying to sugarcoat the information. "And it happened again when you were taken from the mall."

"Can you help her?" Helen asked, desperation in her voice. She imagined her mother as a homeless person on the side of the street, covered by dirty blankets. Ever since Freddy had rescued her, she had assumed he could fix anything. But now, she began to doubt.

"Yes," he said and turned to the window again. "I thought of a way, and you can help. Will you help me?"

"Yes!" she said, inhaling deeply. Her faith in him was fully restored.

"Come with me."

Freddy turned from the window and walked to the door. He held the door open for her, closed it softly, and began walking down the hallway. Helen followed right behind him.

With each step, her excitement grew and she thought about when Freddy had rescued them from Mr. Smith's house and then drove them to the hospital. While walking in silence, barefoot on the cool floor, she wondered briefly how Mr. Smith was doing and then remembered how much she missed him. With so many thoughts running through her mind, the walk seemed like a dream.

They passed her mother's room, then Daryn's, then Brian's, then Audrie's, and stopped at the first unoccupied room in the long hallway. Freddy stopped at the side of the door so that Helen was standing in front of it. She looked up at him, planning to ask a question.

"You're brother's asleep in this room," Freddy said. "Jacob."

"But Jacob's dead," Helen said, her mouth remaining open.

She began to feel panic, confusion, and shock, his words repeating in her mind in a loop. *He would never lie to me*, she thought. Then she forgot to breathe and then wondered if she would ever breathe again.

Freddy put a warm hand on her shoulder.

"Take a deep breath, Helen. Just go and see. I'm keeping him asleep, so you won't wake him." He opened the door and entered the room, then stepped aside and held the door for her.

While taking several deep breaths, Helen waited for her eyes to adjust to the lower light level. She stared into the dark room until she located the bed. She first saw a lump under the covers, then the pale skin of a small face, dark hair covering a forehead, closed eyelids. She walked to the foot of the bed and stared down at her brother. For several seconds, memories of Jacob flooded her mind. She walked to the side of the bed and felt a strong urge to touch his forehead.

"Go ahead," Freddy said, suddenly standing at her side. She looked up at him, her lips stretched into a wide smile. "He won't wake up until your mother can see him."

When Helen placed her hand on the child's warm forehead, she felt his life force, strong and steady. Chills raced through her core and goosebumps formed on her arms and neck. As the small toddler breathed, she noticed the rise and fall of the covers. For a few seconds, she imagined herself leading Jacob by the hand to her mother, their mother. Then she remembered Freddy's plan. Her mother should be the one to wake him.

"Before we get your mother," Freddy said, "I want you to make a decision. Should we get Brian too?"

"Yes," Helen said without having to consider each option.

She felt another strong urge to run from the room and wake her uncle, but she did not want to leave Jacob's side. After a short pause, she removed her hand from Jacob's forehead, drew a deep breath, and then ran from the room. Not waiting to see if Freddy was following her, Helen ran to Brian's door and opened it.

"Uncle Brian," she said quietly. She quickly reached his bed and began shaking him. "It's Helen. I want to show you something."

"What?" he said, turning to face her and opening his eyes. Before continuing, he pulled himself up and looked at his niece. He smiled and laughed. "Well, hello there, Helen. What's going on? It's not morning is it?"

She wanted to tell him about her brother but then wondered if he would believe her.

"Just come with me and you'll see." She led him by the hand past Audrie's room and into Jacob's room. Without waiting, she released his hand and ran to the side of the bed. "Look, look! Freddy brought him back to life!"

Brian stopped at the foot of the bed and then turned to face Freddy. Why didn't he join her at the side of the bed, closer to Jacob? Then an old memory temporarily erased Uncle Brian from her thoughts. She bent over the sleeping child and placed her lips a centimeter above his. After closing her eyes, Helen inhaled deeply, *stealing his air*, as she used to say.

"Yep," she said after standing erect again. She felt like a detective identifying a mysterious substance. "It's Jacob. Just as I remember him."

Helen stepped to her uncle and grabbed his hand. The action seemed to restore him to life, but he was not smiling and the look in his eyes frightened her. His eyes reminded her of light reflecting off black tar or oil.

"How can it be?" he asked, staring at the child on the bed.

"It's him," Helen said, not understanding his disbelief when the evidence was right before him. "It's Jacob."

Brian allowed Helen to pull him closer. As she pulled his hand to Jacob's head, he resisted but not enough to stop her. "You won't wake him up. Freddy's keeping him asleep until Mom can come."

Brian touched the top of Jacob's head and then took a deep breath. He stood silent for several seconds.

"You did it," he said, addressing Freddy but looking at the sleeping child. "I didn't know what to think when you told me. How is Sadi going to take this?"

"I'm preparing her now," Freddy said from behind them. "Helen should be the one to show her, and she thought it would be a good idea for you to be here too. I know it will be traumatic."

"But not like a water hammer," Helen said, turning to her uncle, then Freddy. She did not understand what he meant by *preparing* her mother. "Right, Freddy? There's no water hammer when water starts flowing?"

"That's correct," he said.

At the moment, nothing else mattered to Helen. She imagined her mother feeling only joy when she saw Jacob. She wanted to run and get her mother who would instantly recognize her son. *Why were adults so worried about everything?* Another shadow suddenly appeared in the doorway behind Freddy, the woman who had arrived with her Uncle. Helen forgot her name.

"What's going on?" she asked then stepped to Freddy's side and focused on the bed. "Oh, my God! Is that?"

"Yes," Freddy said with only a glance at the woman. Helen thought he looked as if he had expected her. "Let's go get your mom, Helen.

But you'll have to wake her up gently. She's having a very bad dream."

"How do you know she's having a bad dream?" Brian asked.

"I just know," he said, then extended his hand. "Come on, Helen."

When they arrived at Sadi's room, Freddy paused and placed his hand on Helen's shoulder.

"You and Brian go in," he said. "Your mother's nightmare is about Jacob, so be gentle. You can tell her about Jacob or just show her, whatever you think is best."

"I'll be gentle," Helen said, then quietly opened the door. She entered first and Uncle Brian followed, but Freddy and Audrie waited outside. When Freddy closed the door behind them and Helen saw her mom on the bed, she understood why Freddy had wanted only her and Brian there. It was a family responsibility.

Helen stopped at the bedside and stared at her mother's face. The cool stone floor under her bare feet reminded her that she was the one awake. She noticed the muscle spasms in her mother's cheeks, the sweat glistening on her forehead. Helen wanted to touch her, rescue her from the nightmares.

"Wake up, Mom," Helen whispered. "Freddy brought Jacob back."

Helen spoke so softly, that she knew her mother could not hear. She wanted to know how speaking the words felt, and after they had escaped her lips, she knew she could not say them to her mother. Helen would bring her to Jacob and show her. She grasped her softly by the shoulder, then spoke loud enough for her to hear.

"Wake up, Mom. It's Helen."

Her mother shook her head as if refusing to wake. Helen squeezed her shoulder and repeated the request. When her eyes opened, they were filled with tears.

"Helen?" she asked and glanced at the view screen behind her. After sitting up, she wiped her eyes. "Is anything wrong?"

"Nothing's wrong, Mom. Come with me. Don't ask why, just come." Helen stepped away from the bed and extended her hand. When their hands clasped together, Helen felt another burst of excitement. She had to take a deep breath.

"Hi, Sadi," Uncle Brian said from his position halfway to the door. "It's Brian. Don't speak, just come."

When he opened the door, light spilled into the room and Helen began pulling her mom toward the entrance, then leading her into the hallway. Freddy and Audrie stood a few meters away from the door. Freddy had a close-mouthed smile and the woman just seemed curious. Helen only cared enough to look at them to avoid a collision. When her mother glanced in their direction, Helen noticed the other woman looking at the floor.

"Follow me," Helen said while opening the door to her brother's room. She ran to the bed and stood at his side, her mother walking slowly behind her. "It's Jacob. Freddy brought him back!"

When Helen turned around, she found her mother standing in the middle of the room, frozen in place. She stood so still, Helen thought time had stopped. She felt tempted to say something but decided just to wait instead. *Mom just needs time to process.*

Helen looked past her mother and noticed Freddy standing in the doorway. He opened his eyes wide and nodded at her. Helen understood that look. *She* had the responsibility to help her mother. During her silent exchange with Freddy, Brian had walked to the other side of the bed. He was focused on Jacob instead of his sister.

"It's okay, Mom," Helen said, taking two steps away from the bed, but the horror in her mother's eyes stopped her. "It's really him. I smelled him."

"This is a dream," her mother said suddenly. "It's only a dream."

It's not a dream, Helen wanted to say but knew mere words would fail to convince her. She walked the remainder of the way and grabbed her mother's hand.

"Does this feel like a dream, Mom?"

"It's a dream," she repeated, tears flowing down her cheeks and Helen suddenly felt her own eyes getting all wet. "When will this end? Jacob's not really there. He's gone."

"Just let me show you," Helen said and pulled her mother forward, using all of her strength. After a few seconds, they stood together at the bedside. She attempted to pull her mother's hand further but lacked the strength, so she released her hand and gently removed the covers away from the sleeping child. Helen immediately recognized the blue blanket Jacob was holding to his chest.

"Freddy," Helen said, turning to the door and grasping her mother's hand again. "Can you wake him up now?"

"Okay, go ahead," Freddy said from the doorway.

With her other hand, Helen grasped Jacob by the shoulder and gently shook him.

"Jacob, time to wake up. It's Helen and Mom and Uncle Brian!"

When her brother opened his eyes, Helen heard sharp intakes of breath from her uncle and mother, and time suddenly began moving slowly like clouds in the sky. Jacob smiled wide then held both hands in the air, dropping the blue blanket on the bed. When Sadi pulled him into her arms, Helen noticed even more tears sliding down her cheeks. For several seconds, silence filled the room. No one seemed to be breathing.

"How is this possible?" Sadi asked while Jacob continued to hold her. "Is it really Jacob?"

Her brother reminded Helen of a baby monkey attached to its mother. Although she wanted to hold him too, she wished the moment would never end. She rested her hand on Jacob's leg.

"We have identified him correctly," Freddy said. "Trust me. That is your son!"

SIXTY-TWO

Christine

Francis went to bed and Christine searched their DVD collection for something to watch. After the strange and disconcerting events of the day, she needed to relax, fill her mind with more light-hearted material. She picked *The Wedding Singer* and almost finished watching the movie, but then fell asleep on the couch when the main character met Billy Idol on the airplane.

The dream began with a white-haired child stepping between her and the television set. He extended his hand silently and pulled her from the couch. When his little fingers wrapped around hers, his tight grasp reminded Christine of a confident adult.

The little boy released her hand, and she followed him through their front door and into the bright sunlight. The child quickly disappeared from her view and memory, replaced by a hot summer sun.

As Christine walked to the restaurant to meet her friend, Franklin, the sun burned her exposed shoulders with no wind or shade to offer relief. The walk seemed longer than usual too, and she almost abandoned the effort. She entered the restaurant finally, feeling instant relief from the heat, and found Franklin sitting in a booth by the front window with a glass of beer in front of him. He smiled and then nodded silently to her chair.

He had already ordered her drink, a lemon drop on the rocks, which sat on the table next to his beer. The glass was covered in beads of precipitation. Before taking her first sip, she grasped the glass with both hands and closed her eyes.

Her entire world was suddenly sweet and sour on her tongue, and then cold liquid sliding down her parched throat. Christine enjoyed the sensation so much, she kept her eyes closed for what seemed like a lifetime. When she opened her eyes again, two cops were walking into the restaurant, angry eyes and pursed lips.

"There he is," one of the cops said, a huge black man with arms thick as Christine's thighs.

His partner, a red-haired man with a freckled face and neck, stepped to the table. He had the same muscular physique and stood a little taller than his partner. He asked Franklin to confirm his first and last name, then ordered him to get up from the table and leave the restaurant with them. In horror and confusion, Christine watched the cops pull Franklin away from the table.

"I didn't do anything," Franklin said as they escorted him onto the sidewalk.

Christine followed.

Once outside, the red-haired man shoved Franklin against the restaurant window and told him repeatedly to stop struggling, but Franklin was only struggling to breathe. The man held Franklin against the wall with his forearm, restricting his air supply. People on the street began to gather around the scene with Christine standing between the crowd and the cops.

Christine just stood there, not knowing what to do, and then she noticed the gun sticking from the other cop's hip, easily within her reach. She needed only to grab the gun, and then she could stop them from hurting Franklin.

The rest of the scene suddenly became blurry. Only the gun existed clearly in her view. She began reaching for the weapon but stopped herself and hugged both arms tightly against her breasts. The temptation to take the weapon was almost overpowering. If Christine took the gun, she could easily force the policemen to stop. She decided to worry later about the repercussions.

She never got the chance.

First, all of the light disappeared, then the sound of Franklin's struggle, then the smell of humans and food from the restaurant, then all other sensory stimulation. After some time in the new darkness, Christine heard waves crashing on a beach in front of her. She inhaled the salty air and enjoyed the gentle breeze.

Christine was sitting in a beach chair in the darkness, cool sand under her bare feet and the drink from the restaurant in her hand. Sometime later, a crescent moon began rising above the ocean. While watching the moon rise higher, Christine felt extremely comfortable and wished the scene would never end.

Am I dreaming? This is definitely a dream.

Was she always this aware in her dreams and just never remembered when she awoke? The possibility seemed likely. She could not fathom why, but the answer suddenly seemed insignificant. As she sipped her drink, a voice interrupted her thoughts. Someone was sitting next to her, hidden in the dark.

"It is beautiful," a male voice said. "People have looked out to sea since the beginning. To the sea and sky. They represent the unknown future. We see our imaginations there."

Christine enjoyed listening to the man and knew that he sat next to her. He spoke as a military commander who was talking gently to a civilian. But when she turned to face him, Christine saw nothing. Only the sea and the moon directly in front of her were visible. She could not even see her legs or the glass in her hand. Before responding, she faced forward again.

"Thanks for bringing me here, whoever you are. I've never felt so relaxed."

"You are welcome, Christine," the man answered. "I wanted to talk to you for a while and present a proposition. Take your time though. I can come back later."

"Now's fine," she said. "Who are you?"

"My identity is not important, but you will meet me later," he said. "Just know that I am helping Franklin and his friends. I am here to ask if you want to participate in his rescue. The control system has him."

"Rescue?"

"Yes," he said. "I cannot promise success, but I am fairly confident. There is always the possibility of some danger."

"Why me?" she asked. The specific kind of danger seemed less significant than the reason for her participation.

"Because I can see you are concerned about him," the man said, laughing softly. "And I know you stuck your neck out to help him. You are also a decent person and like to have a little fun. I was planning to rescue him on my own, but when I found you, I thought of an alternative plan."

"Are you the one who bought the jacket from me today?" she asked, anxious for the first time since the restaurant.

"No," he said. "I was using him to find Franklin, but I found you instead. He is an FBI agent who helped Franklin in the past. I sent him home."

"Using him?" she asked. "Now you're going to use me?"

"That is just one angle," he answered. "From my perspective, I am using you. From your perspective, you will be helping Franklin."

"I can live with that," she said, laughing. Her anxiety melted, and she was excited. "What's the plan?"

"Well," he said. "We still need to find him, but I know where to get that information."

Christine liked the idea of working with the man to find Franklin. After writing the letter to that lawyer, the enormity of the task had almost overwhelmed her. Sharing the burden would help her relax.

"What will happen when I wake up?" she asked, hoping to remember the beauty of the moon's reflection on the waves.

"Your memories of this place will feel like a dream," he said. "Without my help, you would only remember images and your general impression, which I have intended to be peaceful."

"Is this a real place, or just in my mind?"

"It is not a physical place," he said. "It is real though. Some call it the background. I preferred to explain the situation here, rather than in the physical world. That might disturb you too much."

Christine paused to remember his original proposition before she had changed the direction of the conversation. The scene was too relaxing and kept distracting her.

"Sorry," she said. "I'll shut up. Continue with your explanation."

"Most of Franklin's friends have left Earth and went to another place, but Franklin was not one of them. I suspect the authorities are holding him hostage, waiting to see if we will attempt another rescue."

Christine brought the cold glass to her lips and sipped the tangy liquid, hoping to halt the barrage of questions flooding her mind. All of her questions had combined into one nebulous ball of confusion.

"So they are expecting us?" Christine asked after swallowing. Rescuing Franklin seemed more important than the possibility of leaving Earth. She made a mental note to ask about that topic later.

"Try not to worry," he answered. "They should be expecting something, but not you."

"Sounds like you have a plan on how to deal with that."

"Yes and I will show you later, but we will focus on locating him first." The man paused for her to assimilate the information. "Now, about leaving Earth. They went to a new world, named Bodn. Once we retrieve Franklin, I will attempt to persuade him to go there as well, for however long he wants, or at least until I can fix the situation here."

"Okay," she said, not sure how to respond. Another question materialized. "Let's go back to what you said about the control system. Are you talking about something like the Matrix movie, where everything's an illusion?"

"No," he said. "The directors of society fund movies like *The Matrix* mostly for misdirection, and to frighten the population from thinking too closely about the world. The world you see is real, but it is much different than what you believe. Take this experience as an example. You were taught that dreams occur only in the brain."

"Okay," she said, not sure what to say, "so what do we do first?"

"There is one more thing you need to know," he said and paused as if unsure how to continue. "I need to prepare you before we meet. I initially wanted to present an illusion, so you would not be disturbed, but I need all of my concentration."

"You're not an alien are you?"

"No," he said, sighing. "You will see me as a little boy."

"With white hair?" she asked, suddenly remembering the boy following the intimidating man.

"Yes, a blind child," he said, and Christine thought she heard a tone of satisfaction. "I'll leave you here for a while and when you wake, you'll see me."

Christine suddenly felt alone and knew, somehow, that the man had vanished. She sat on the beach for a long time, enjoying the sound of the waves and the rising of the moon in the black sky. While sipping her drink, she let the conversation replay in her mind.

She woke at midnight on the couch, the DVD main menu on the television screen lighting the apartment. Even with her eyes open, Christine could still see the moon and ocean in her imagination. The memory seemed surreal, like any other dream, and she wondered if the conversation had taken place only in her mind or if Franklin's friends had actually gone to another planet. Either way did not seem to matter. Christine still felt at peace.

When the child with white hair stepped in front of the television set, she sat up quickly and stared at him, all thoughts coming to a stop. She lacked the programming of how to react when dreams and reality combined.

"I am from the beach and the name is Freddy," he said, extending his little hand. "It is good to meet you, Christine."

She grasped his hand, and he helped her stand. The warmth and strength of his small fingers relieved her sudden disorientation.

"You should go to bed," he said, nodding toward her bedroom. "We will talk more in the morning. And do not worry about your sister. I will not let her see me.”

Before shutting the door behind her, she stopped and looked down at him.

“Good night, Christine.”

“Okay.”

SIXTY-THREE

Christine

Christine woke up the next morning to the sound of a metal spatula scraping a pan. Francis was making breakfast. After smelling the scrambled eggs, she remembered the man on the beach, and then the dream of Franklin in the restaurant. At the thought of the white-haired child, her pulse accelerated.

She jumped from the bed and had to wait a few seconds until the vertigo passed. Could she really have seen the child in her apartment? Her rational mind rejected the thought, but her desire to see the boy urged her to hurry into the kitchen.

When Christine saw the boy with white hair in the kitchen with her sister, she looked at him with a mixture of relief and disbelief. The boy was sitting in a chair next to the table, facing her with closed eyes. His blind stare sent a chill through her heart. He placed a tiny index finger to his lips.

"Wow," Francis said after Christine slid to a stop on the linoleum floor in her slippers. "Why in such a hurry?"

"Shhh," the child said. "I can talk, but it would make my job easier if you did not talk to me."

"Good morning," Christine said, her gaze still on the child. "I mean, no rush, just hungry."

Francis glanced at the table.

"What are you looking at?"

"Oh, nothing," Christine said after turning to her sister and wondering why Francis still did not see the child in front of her. "Any of those eggs for me?"

Before Christine and her sister sat down at the table, the child moved to the living room. During breakfast, she avoided looking at him and attempted to concentrate on Francis. Her sister talked mostly about her classes that day and her plans for the weekend, which strangely did not include Christine. To her additional surprise, Francis neglected to mention the man who broke into Franklin's apartment the night before. Shortly afterward, Francis left for school.

"I know you have many questions," the child said once the front door closed. "But we are going to Bellingham, Washington. There will be plenty of time to talk on the way."

"Do you think Franklin is there?"

"No, but there is a lady there who might know where he is."

"How are we going to get there?" she asked, squinting. "I don't have a car, and we can't take Francis' truck without her getting suspicious."

"I have a car," he said. "You will like it, and you can drive as fast as you want. You can skip your classes and you do not have to work until Sunday."

When Christine saw the silver sports sedan parked on the street, she stopped walking and just stared. The model was visible on the back, Lexus GS430. The beautiful car suddenly became her new dream vehicle, replacing a four-wheel drive jeep. While shivering in the cold morning air, the child handed her the keys and explained the situation. A member of their group had gone to the new world and left her car for his use.

"She will not even miss it," he said after closing the door and sitting in the passenger seat. "She is from a very wealthy family."

"Poor thing," Christine said and felt difficulty concentrating on anything other than the car. "Hey, shouldn't you put your seatbelt on?"

"Nope," he said. "I won't let you get in an accident."

When the powerful engine began to hum, so did her bones. The energy transferred to her bloodstream and eliminated the last of the morning grogginess.

—※—

For the first few minutes of driving, she navigated slowly through the morning traffic to Rosa Parks Way and then to the I-5 entrance, paranoid of damaging the expensive car despite what the child had said. While accelerating to highway speeds, she wished there were no cars in front of her, so she could ram the gas pedal to the floor.

"The traffic should clear once we get north of Battleground," he said, his lips curving into a wide smile. "I am looking forward to the pleasure you will get out of this."

As the child predicted, the traffic thinned and Christine accelerated to 115 km per hour, then 130. She would have continued accelerating, but fear of getting a ticket stopped her. Then she remembered the child had responded to her thoughts before she had revealed them.

"Can you read my thoughts?"

"Yes," he said and tried to sound apologetic. "I can do a lot of things. Try not to worry about getting a ticket."

"You did hide yourself from my sister."

"There is a highway patrolman in a few miles, but he will not even notice you."

"Okay," she said, not thinking of a reason to distrust him. She smiled at the thought of breaking the law. She pushed the gas pedal until they hit 140 km per hour, then straightened her arms to keep better control of the steering wheel. "Wahoo!"

As they passed the patrolman on the side of the road, Christine kept her gaze straight ahead. Shortly afterward, she looked in the rearview mirror, relieved when she didn't see the flashing police lights, but then a little disappointed for losing the chance to outrun the police. For the next several minutes, she slowly accelerated until they came to 240 km per hour. Passing all of the cars at that speed helped her concentrate, surprisingly, on their conversation.

As they passed more police vehicles and all the other cars on the road, Christine gained a level of audacity she never thought possible. She no longer weaved within the traffic lines. She passed all of her fellow travelers through every space she could find, wearing a smile the whole time. The child even looked like he was enjoying the ride.

During the two-hour drive, Christine mostly listened as the child answered all of her questions. The story of his transformation and then the death of his body caused the most shock, even more than the child abduction or their near capture in Canada. When he explained the rescue at the psychiatric hospital, all doubt in his abilities vanished, and she fully expected to see Franklin again.

At the end of the story, however, the world made less sense than before and she felt like a child. She understood on a superficial level, just not the significance or all of the possible implications. The information would eventually make sense, she hoped, and then she would reach a new equilibrium with reality. The thrill of the drive was helping her swallow all of the disturbing details. Christine expected an anxiety attack later, but until then, she planned to just enjoy the experience.

"Good, she is home," the child said after they took the exit for Bellingham. "I am going to stay hidden and guide your conversation. Just ask whatever comes to your mind. At some point, I might need to review her memories, so do not be surprised if she gets a little distracted."

"Got it," Christine said, surprised at how easily she accepted his incredible plans.

They drove quickly through the city and reached the woman's home in five minutes. An old woman with short grey hair, blue eyes, and a short pointy nose answered the door on the third knock. She briefly looked up at Christine and then quickly scanned the area for anyone else. When her gaze passed above the child, she showed no sign of seeing him.

"Yes, hello?"

"Hi, I'm Christine Morozov from Portland," she said confidently. "I'm the one who helped Franklin get out of town."

The woman stared at Christine for a moment and her narrow eyes opened wider. She stepped to the side.

"Please come in," she said and scanned her yard and the street again. Her eyes rested a moment on the car.

"Thank you."

After Christine and the child entered the warm house, the humid air and smell of plants reminded her of a greenhouse. The woman closed the door, locked the knob and deadbolt.

"Christine Morozov?" the woman asked and made no indication of leading her new guest further into her home.

"Yes." She remembered the child's instructions to say whatever came to her mind. Instead of asking a question, she felt inclined just to wait.

"Why are you here?"

"I'm looking for Franklin," she said. "He said he would call and let me know his status. But I haven't heard anything."

"How did you find me?"

"I broke into his apartment and found your address," she said and had to suppress the urge to laugh. She usually had to prepare mentally and emotionally to tell a believable lie, but she felt no moral responsibility and no need to act convincingly. She felt as though she was reading a script.

"He didn't mention you," she said, looking at her suspiciously. "Franklin doesn't have any friends who would drive a car like yours."

"It's my parents' car," she said without thinking and having fun discovering the next line in the script. "Listen, I know you're suspicious. I would be too. Do you think we can sit down and talk? I can tell you anything you want to know. It was a long drive from Portland. I am one of Franklin's friends and I'm worried about him."

Without responding, the old woman turned and led her to the couch in her living room. Christine sat facing the front window while the old woman sat in a loveseat next to a piano. The boy sat quietly next to Christine. He leaned back against the cushions, closed his eyes, and appeared to concentrate on breathing deeply.

While waiting for the woman to speak, Christine glanced at the dark green plants all over the room and then at the pictures on the piano showing a young family. Thick curtains blocked all of the natural light from outside, but a light in the ceiling kept the room artificially bright, and a fan provided a gentle airflow. The atmosphere seemed ideal for the plants. Christine enjoyed the vegetation's humid scent.

"When I last saw Franklin," the woman said sternly, "a SWAT team broke into his apartment and pinned us to the floor."

"Oh, my God!" Christine said and paused for her feeling of shock to subside. "So they took him?"

"They took both of us," she said and shuddered. "So you can understand why I'm a little anxious to speak to you."

"I understand," she answered sincerely. "So what happened?"

"My questions first," she said abruptly, reminding Christine of her professors at school. "How exactly did you help Franklin get out of Portland? That's not something the average citizen would do."

"That's true," Christine said, feeling a hint of pride.

While Christine retold the escape story, the old woman seemed to relax. She never smiled but nodded several times in understanding and possible satisfaction. Her initial suspicious attitude seemed to transform into one of admiration. Christine tried her best to sound grateful for the success, rather than proud or smug.

"That's quite the story, Christine," she said and her lips almost curved into a smile. "For some reason, I believe you. Please call me Gerda."

"So where did they take you, Gerda?" Christine asked, reading from the script again.

"They told us they were taking us to the police station, but the SWAT team transferred us to another vehicle and we drove blindfolded to some military base. It felt like a long drive, but I couldn't be sure. I haven't seen Franklin since we got there."

"Why did they let you go?"

"I think they only needed one of us," she said and fought the urge to cry. "They questioned me for a long time then kept us overnight. They drove me back home blindfolded without Franklin."

"What did you tell them?" Christine felt uncomfortable asking the old woman anything, which might make her cry.

"I told them everything I know," she said as if confessing a horrible crime. "I was so scared. I shouldn't have said anything, but they seemed to know almost everything already."

"I would have done the same," Christine said. Although reading from the script, Christine probably would have done the same, she realized with a shudder. "Sounds like you don't know where they took you, being blindfolded. Do you think Franklin is still at the same place?"

"I've been wondering about that," she said, then took a deep breath. She wiped the tears from her eyes before they could slide down her cheeks. "It seemed like a large facility with special accommodations for long-term prisoners. They separated us and kept me in an isolated cell. I saw a couple other prisoners there too. That's the only reason why I think he's still there."

"Why did you say they only needed one of you?"

"I've been thinking," she said, recovering from her emotions. "I think it's a trap for Franklin's friend, Freddy."

"Who's Freddy?" Christine asked with an accidental glance at the child sitting next to her.

"What did Franklin tell you?" Gerda asked, her eyes transforming into thin slits again.

"Enough, but he didn't give any names, just that you could go to another planet."

Speaking about traveling to other planets seemed inconsistent with such a casual tone. She felt like a horrible actress and wished she could try that line again.

"He's the key to this whole thing," Gerda said. "I don't know how to describe him, but I think he's the one they want. My best guess is that it's a trap. I'm just hoping everyone else escaped, especially Sadi. She has two young girls and they've already suffered terribly."

"So you don't know what happened to them?"

"The last I heard was that another member of our group was taken into custody," she said.

"The lawyer?" Christine interrupted.

"Yes, but I don't know what happened to him. Franklin shut down the website that we all used for communication."

The old woman suddenly stopped talking and seemed to lose focus, staring through Christine and not at her. Then her eyes began moving randomly at an unnaturally fast rate.

"I am replaying the ride she and Franklin took," the child said, speaking for the first time since entering the house. "They traveled south, ooh, and you are going to like this. They went underground, some base I think. That is where we are going next."

Christine gulped. Then Gerda blinked and rubbed her eyes.

"Are you okay?"

"Just a little dizzy," Gerda said. "That's all."

"Sorry to bring all this up again," Christine said, feeling sincere empathy for the older woman. "But at least you're safe, and it looks like you've got a nice family who probably needs you around. Are those your grandkids?"

"Yes, with my son and daughter-in-law."

"Do they live nearby?"

They spent the next twenty minutes talking about their personal lives. Even though she could have conducted the conversation on her own, Christine just read from the script and enjoyed the ride as a passenger actress. During the conversation, the older woman visibly relaxed and even smiled a few times.

After learning of Christine's status as a student, she showed a more animated interest in her career plans, asking many questions about Christine's motives and goals. At the end of her visit, Christine felt a strong emotional connection to the woman, most likely due to sharing a traumatic experience and having a common goal.

"I should be going," Christine said, suddenly knowing how Freddy intended to give the woman hope and a sense of closure. "For some reason, I feel better about things and think Franklin's going to be okay. It's just a feeling I have."

"I do too," Gerda said, sighing. "While we were talking, I was thinking about Freddy. He's not the kind of person to abandon his friends."

"From what Franklin told me, he would have a plan."

PART VI

CONTRABAND

Get too close

And incinerate

In the atmos

SIXTY-FOUR

Taylor

After returning from their trip to Bodn and learning about the requirements to live there, Taylor returned to her room, stretched, and then lay in her bed for a short rest. She was sore from hiking and just wanted to lie down for a few minutes. Her soft bed felt amazing though, so the short rest turned into a nap, filled with dreams of returning to Bodn and living there indefinitely.

Freddy met Taylor and the rest of the group after dinner for more discussion about the future. When he arrived without Yezeel, Taylor wondered about his relationship with those who had given him responsibility for the situation. She imagined herself in his position, interacting directly with aliens, and much preferred interacting with Freddy. He seemed comfortable with his role, but Taylor felt sorry for him.

Freddy started the discussion by referring to their transformation as a restoration to the original human configuration. While trying to understand the meaning of his words, Taylor suddenly wondered what kind of trauma he had suffered. His new confidence must have cost a high price.

"The original human configuration?" Taylor asked.

"It is how we were before ancient creatures hijacked it," Freddy said. "Bodn will be what Earth used to be, what it could be. I have made the transformation. This body is not indestructible because nothing is indestructible, but the aging sequence has been removed, among other things."

"So," Cesar interjected. "We'll live forever? Will I be young again?"

"Developmentally young," Freddy said, nodding in agreement. "I suggest to view this *requirement* as more like a bonus for staying here. Among the more obvious benefits, you will also have a much greater sensitivity to reality and will not be easily deceived."

"How is all of this possible?" Cesar asked, shaking his head. "It's very difficult to believe, but I know that before arriving here, all of this seemed impossible. So what happened so long ago?"

"That story is quite extensive," Freddy said. "But the purpose is easy to explain. Human lifetimes were limited to keep us from realizing what was happening and escaping. Before we begin to really understand the world, our lives end and we have to start all over again. To make matters worse, our minds are muddled with so much contradictory information, we automatically reject the truth, even if we could live much longer. Think of Earth as a great recycling center."

"For what purpose?" Cesar asked.

"Some creatures steal from your experience," Freddy said with a frown. "You are not prepared to understand the process yet, but there are creatures who can taint your pleasures, enhance your suffering and frustration. They consume experience like how you enjoy helping a child learn or talking with a friend, or learning, or suffering."

"You can think of them as vampires, but I call them parasites. After the reconfiguration, these parasites cannot attach themselves to you. You will enjoy life more fully, think more clearly. This history of humanity is guarded and stored in records on Earth, but we can talk about that at another time after I understand it more."

"Why would they guard this information?" Susan asked. "That doesn't make any sense."

"Information is key to controlling a creature," Freddy said, turning to Susan and smiling warmly. "We base all of our decisions on information."

Freddy said good night to everyone and then let them discuss the situation privately. At the end of their internal discussion, an hour later, no one had a negative opinion of the requirement, not even Susan. Only Gerald and Max continued to express disbelief. But everyone had plenty of time to consider the situation and did not need to make an immediate commitment.

"Not that we have much of a choice anyway," Taylor said.

Taylor thought the choice was easy. How could anyone reject the offer of immortality? Maybe someone super-depressed. Taylor had always wondered why people aged. Physical bodies had the capacity to heal and regenerate themselves. Why could the human body not live forever? The death code had seemed intentional. For Taylor, Freddy's explanation seemed plausible.

Only Audrie expressed a desire to return home since she had come only to see her brother. If Max stayed, she might want to return someday, but she needed more time to make such a commitment. In Taylor's opinion, Audrie was still suffering from information overload and would need more time to process her new reality.

"What if they take you in for questioning?" Cesar asked.

"They don't know anything about my involvement," she said without any trace of concern. "They'll leave me alone. Even if they did suspect anything, I could provide no useful information. I have no idea where this is and they lack the resources to travel here anyway."

Before going to bed that night, Taylor still felt as if she had just won the lottery. But instead of the lottery being just a scam, as they were on Earth, her prize was real.

She had difficulty sleeping. The more she thought of the reconfiguration, the more excited she felt. Like everyone else, she had required some time to accept the incredible news. Taylor was accustomed to accepting the old axiom, *if it seems too good to be true, it probably is*. But after considering everything that had happened, she decided to follow another piece of ancient advice, *don't look a gift horse in the mouth*, especially if you could ride the horse into eternity.

After a night of vivid dreams, Taylor awoke the next morning with the vague memory of flying in the jet and eluding frightening aliens. But the dreams were not nightmares. She remembered easily outmaneuvering them and having fun.

The next morning, Taylor was not the first to arrive in the dining area. When she saw Sadi, Daryn, and Helen sitting at the long table, she did not immediately notice the third little person on Sadi's lap. But when her mind finally processed the sensory input, she stopped halfway to the table. She turned to the child and just stared, squinting in confusion.

"Good morning, Taylor," Sadi said and all of the children turned to look at her. They were all smiling, especially the youngest one. "It's going to be hard to believe, but this is my son, Jacob. Freddy brought him back to life last night."

"Hi," the little boy said from his mother's lap. "I'm, Jacob. I'm three. What's your name?"

"Taylor," she answered, noticing the boy's resemblance to his mother, dark blue eyes and dark brown hair. *Your son who died?* She paused in confusion and did not know what else to say.

"I died and Mom's friend rescued me," he said solemnly but smiling. "But it was just like a dream. Right, Mom?"

"That's right," Sadi said and bumped him on her knee. "Maybe it's best not to think about it."

"Freddy rescued him from a snake," Helen said excitedly. "It was one of those parasites, pretending to be his friend. Freddy said Jacob's the original human configration."

"Configuration," Daryn corrected.

"Thank you, girls," Sadi said. "Sit with us, Taylor. I know it's difficult to take in."

"Everything's like that lately," she said without looking away from the beautiful child.

As Taylor walked the rest of the way to the table, she felt compelled to break eye contact with the boy and focus on the girls. Jacob was looking at her quizzically as if deciding to talk again or remain silent. The life in his eyes seemed much older than just three or four years.

"I've been up all night, just looking at him sleeping," Sadi said after Taylor sat across from her, next to Daryn. Taylor hugged the young girl affectionately with one arm while Sadi continued. "Freddy prepared a new body for Jacob and then found him in the background. I didn't believe it at first, but it really is him."

Sadi wiped dark hair from the boy's forehead and then looked into Taylor's eyes.

"That's so strange to say out loud."

"Well," she said after a deep breath. Eye contact with the older woman suddenly helped Taylor feel better about the situation, at least enough to manage a smile. "It's pretty strange to hear someone say, that's for sure. But, I can't imagine how strange it must be for you! Who else knows about him?"

"Uncle Brian and his friend were there when I woke up," Jacob answered without looking away. The boy suddenly slid from his mother's lap and walked around the table, stopping next to Taylor. Everyone just watched until he lifted his arms into the air.

"You want me to hold you?" Taylor asked, standing from the table. Her heart began beating more rapidly. *Why am I so nervous?* She grabbed him under the arms, then propped him onto her hip. He wasn't heavy, but his significant weight made him even more real. "It's good to meet you," she said, feeling strange to speak so formally.

"I'm real," he said. "Do you believe me?"

Taylor laughed unintentionally and felt the skin on her face stretch as she smiled.

"Yes, I believe you're real."

She hugged him, enjoying the sensation of his small hands on her back. When she looked at Sadi, the woman's beautiful blue eyes were saturated with tears.

"I still can't believe it," she said, rubbing her eyes. "Sorry. I'm a wreck."

Jacob seemed pleased with Taylor's belief in him and ran back to his mother after returning to the floor. As she watched Sadi lift him onto her lap, Taylor felt chills course through her body again. She was imagining being in Sadi's position when she saw Jacob for the first time.

How the hell is she coping with this?

Taylor intentionally let Sadi take the lead in the conversation, afraid to say anything that might cause an emotional outburst. Sadi was obviously in a very fragile emotional state and might have an anxiety attack since she probably already had one that morning.

She and Sadi talked a little, but they mostly just watched the interaction between the girls and their little brother. When Helen would mention certain events from the past, Taylor was surprised at how vividly the boy remembered everything. Taylor could not remember much before the age of three. Jacob could remember when Sadi was nursing him.

Because he has an upgraded body?

After observing the boy's interactions, Taylor was even more excited about the possibility of making the transformation or reconfiguration. She had already made the mental decision to accept Freddy's proposal, but before seeing Jacob, the option had only existed in her imagination. Now she had what looked like a perfect example of the possibility.

From what she could see, the little boy looked physically perfect. Taylor did not notice a single flaw. Jacob had soft, blemish-free skin, and the plump, well-proportioned figure of a toddler. Taylor had particularly noticed his graceful walk. He reminded her of a ballet dancer walking onto a stage.

Daryn showed interest in the time Jacob spent between dying and rebirth, and asked Jacob to tell Taylor everything that he could remember about being dead. After he repeated how the experience had felt like a dream, Helen got impatient and hijacked the story. She wanted the opportunity to tell Taylor anyway, and Jacob didn't seem to mind. He watched his older sister with obvious admiration.

Helen excitedly told how Jacob had lived in their old home and was just playing with toys, and how his only friend was a stuffed panda bear who talked without moving his lips and played games with him. While explaining how Freddy had pretended to be a child with his father, Helen stood from her chair and leaned over the table.

"You were afraid of them, right?" she asked her brother but without waiting for an answer. "The panda bear was telling you that Freddy wanted to hurt you. But then an evil snake jumped from inside your friend and Freddy crushed its head under his foot."

Helen turned to Taylor.

"The blue blankie he used to have disintegrated in his dream, and Freddy brought out a shiny new one. Then he woke up."

"It's more fun when Jacob tells it," Daryn said with disappointment.

Jacob was nodding vigorously while looking at Helen and Daryn. His evident excitement reminded Taylor of when her older brother would let her tag along with him and his friends. She had felt special, one of the older kids.

SIXTY-FIVE

Christine

While driving away from Gerda's house, Christine turned to Freddy. "You've got to tell me how you did that. Maybe you could try to explain again?"

"The deeper level *of how* is too complicated for an oral explanation, but I can try to explain the higher level. Think of it like a computer program. If you examine the programming language code, you can determine how the program works. If you examine the machine language, you can get the same information, but it will be much more difficult to comprehend." Freddy spoke while facing the dashboard. "Have you ever daydreamed?"

"Yes," Christine said. "All the time, but I don't ever remember them. You called it the background?"

"Some creatures in the physical world have more awareness of the background than others. It started slowly for me. At first, I could feel what others were feeling. I only understood later that I was in the background with them, getting the information they were sending."

"My awareness grew slowly until I could manipulate what others were experiencing there, basically making their daydreams appear as the physical world. They think they are doing something, but it is just what I imagined for them. Then I learned how to utilize multiple neural networks in the physical world, nearly simultaneously. For example, right now I am talking to you and watching us from the probe."

"That's what happened in the cave, right?" she asked, not wanting to discuss the probe. She disliked the idea of an alien probe watching them, even if it was Freddy. She preferred what she could see with her physical eyes. "You said it was horrible."

"On one level," he said. "It is very disconcerting being aware of so much. Most creatures could not survive the load, but I am getting used to it."

"I'm sorry," she said, trying her best to understand. "I'm glad you're letting me help you, although I don't think you need my help."

"It gives me pleasure," he said and turned to her with his sightless eyes. "I get to experience what you do. I enjoyed the car ride here."

"Yeah, me too."

"Remember to take the south ramp," he said then started laughing. He turned to the dashboard again. "You know, I just realized something. It is kind of funny, and I do not feel embarrassed to tell you, like I would have."

"What's so funny?" she asked.

"I am pretty sure that I have developed a crush on you."

"Really?" she asked and wondered if she would hurt his feelings. Her question seemed to make him laugh harder. Despite her concern, she thought his laugh was cute.

"Do not worry," he said. "It is not sexual and you will not hurt my feelings. I am experiencing life as a prepubescent boy and you are a beautiful girl. When you become a teacher, you will probably get this a lot."

"Believe me," she said while accelerating onto I-5 southbound, her lips stretching into a wide smile. "I already have."

Christine drove even faster than she had on their trip to Bellingham and they reached the small town of Elma, Washington, in just over an hour. She had so much fun driving that she almost forgot about the next task, the one more dangerous than visiting a harmless old college professor. To help sustain her optimism, she concentrated on driving and positive thoughts—her trust in the boy and his extraordinary abilities, and the possibility of rescuing Franklin.

Before they arrived at the Satsop nuclear power plant, Freddy told her to slow to a normal speed, saying he needed some time to assess the situation. While hitting the brake pedal, she remembered, regrettably, her programmed fear of authorities.

"So the nuclear power plant was never completed?" she asked.

"That is the official story," he said with his eyes closed and facing forward. "According to Wikipedia, the plans were abandoned when the government failed to secure more funding and they turned it into a private business park. It is the perfect cover for an underground network. Franklin is there, I know for certain, but I need to determine the risk."

"What kind of risk do you expect?"

During the following pause, chills coursed through her core. She used the time to brush hair from her right cheek and throw it over her shoulder.

"There are other creatures who can do what I can do, and they are looking for me," he continued calmly as if the possibility failed to concern him. "If I did not have the probe, I would be more worried. And they are not expecting a young mother and her son. They are also unaware of my adult body dying."

"Why do you keep referring to creatures? Are they aliens or other humans like you?"

"A creature is just what I call a living entity," he said, opening his sightless eyes and looking at her. "When your physical body dies, you live on, but after losing your human form, would you still call yourself a human?"

Christine wanted to ask about their true form and what happened after death but decided to focus on their objective. She was not ready to hear the answers, she realized with a shudder. Instead of responding, she drove until they reached Satsop Business Park and the incomplete nuclear power plant. Before arriving at their destination, the cloudy sky cast the first raindrops of the day. She set the windshield wipers on the lowest setting.

She followed the child's instructions and parked on the side of the street in front of the power plant. The office and other industrial buildings looked so small next to the large cooling towers. In her mind, the giant structures suddenly represented the size of their task, and she wondered if she should just drive away and let the child handle the situation alone.

"It should be fine," Freddy said, breaking the silence. He grasped her forearm with his tiny hand as an offer of comfort. "I am going to tell you my plan, but be prepared for me to modify it along the way since I cannot predict everything. As I explained before, most of it will be happening in the background."

"I understand," Christine said, laughing nervously, "sort of."

Freddy paused for several seconds as though considering new information. While listening to the tiny raindrops hitting the windshield, she suddenly appreciated the warm and dry environment of the car, a haven from the physical world.

"It will be pretty simple," he began and smiled. "We will be meeting intelligence agents who are posing as employees of a private company, but they run the underground detention facility and are contracted by the CIA. They do not know who Franklin is, or why he is in their custody. They do not know much actually. I suspect there is some sort of trap laid if anyone tries to rescue him, and these men also do not know about that."

"How do you know all of this?" she asked, then sighed. "Never mind. I don't need to know."

"No problem," Freddy said then continued as if uninterrupted. "No one will see me and they will think you are another agent who has come to take Franklin. There will be a couple other agents with you."

"Will I look like myself?" she asked.

"They will see you as a man, but you will still just see yourself." He cleared his throat. "You will be a man wearing professional business attire and your name is Gordon Booth. They will know your name, because you are very high up in the ranks, but not your face."

"Why won't you be Booth?" she said, not needing an answer. "This plan really doesn't need me."

"That may be true," he answered without apology. "But without you, the task would be much harder, so I appreciate the help and it is nice not to do this alone. You wanted to help rescue Franklin anyway, and he will appreciate it. It is also fun giving you the opportunity."

"Well, I'm glad to help," she said and shivered. "When do we start?"

"Put these on," he said while reaching to the floor and retrieving a pair of black gloves. "We do not want your fingerprints all over everything. Good, now turn on the car."

After starting the engine, she noticed the leg of an adult male in the passenger seat where Freddy had sat. She jolted in surprise at seeing the man's face but his warm smile quickly calmed her. She looked behind her and saw another man in the back seat.

Both of the men had tan skin, short dark hair, and looked like brothers. Their eyes were so dark, Christine could not differentiate the pupils from the irises. After noticing their faces and the dark suits, Christine noticed their muscle mass and then gulped.

"These guys will provide the intimidation factor," the man in the passenger seat said in a deep voice. "The story's also more believable, sir, if you have more manpower to secure the prisoner. We'll start when you feel ready."

Christine breathed deeply through her nostrils for several seconds. Although her rational mind claimed that the men existed only in her imagination, she felt more confident in their company. The man in the back seat grabbed Christine by her shoulder. His grip was strong and very real.

"You've got this, sir."

"This is pretty convincing," Christine said after the man released her shoulder. "It's going to be like at Gerda's house, right? I'll just know what to do?"

"Yes, sir."

"Sir, huh?" Christine licked her lips. "I could get used to that."

She pulled onto the road and turned the way they had come and then drove to the parking lot of another office building. The place felt right. The surroundings also looked strangely familiar, as though she had already seen the area from an aerial view. She drove to the back of the building and then parked next to the only other car, a black sedan.

Without any hesitation, Christine turned the engine off, exited the vehicle, and looked at the entrance, a glass door. The light mist on her face felt comforting. As she walked to the door, her two escorts followed silently and then waited for her to take the next action. She sneered after reading the business name on the glass, *EnergiLab Communications.*

So this is what a fake business looks like.

Pushing the call button on the side of the door seemed like the right action to take. She waited ten seconds before hearing a response.

"Who are you?" a man asked through the speakers, slightly annoyed. "This is not an entrance."

"We're here for one of your guests," Christine said confidently. She heard her female voice but knew they heard a man speak. "You are not expecting us."

"We'll be right there," said the man.

While waiting for someone to appear in the empty hallway behind the door, Christine noticed the thickness of the glass. "Bulletproof," said one of the men behind her.

A man in a blue suit appeared in the hallway, walking casually toward the entrance. He had brown hair, combed straight back, and held a mug in his hand. After reaching the glass, he took a drink.

"Identity please."

For the first time since her escorts had appeared, Christine hesitated to follow her instincts. She slowly reached into her back pocket and found a leather wallet there. Having the thick object in her pocket felt strange. She removed an official-looking security badge and paused to look at the picture of a stocky man. He had hair like a rug and light grey eyes. She lifted the badge to the glass and the man with the mug glanced at it, then opened the door.

"Hello, sir," the man said while Christine returned the badge to her wallet, and then to her pocket. "We were not notified of your arrival, but our computer system's been giving us problems."

"Don't worry about it," Christine said. "Are you going to let us in, or what?"

SIXTY-SIX

Taylor

After Taylor left her room that morning, Sadi's brother went to everyone's rooms and told them about Jacob's arrival. He wanted to prevent his sister from having to retell the whole story again, multiple times. When Brian entered the dining hall and told them what he had done, Taylor scolded herself for not doing the same. *Too engrossed in all of this*, she thought while watching Brian pluck the child from the ground and then sit by his sister.

Taylor had experienced an instant attraction to Brian and quickly realized that his physical appearance was not the sole reason for her reaction. He seemed to emanate a genuine charisma, and Taylor looked forward to getting better acquainted. While watching him interact with his nieces and nephew, she appreciated his consideration and affection.

She did not get the opportunity to talk with Brian. Everyone except for Audrie arrived in the dining hall a few minutes later. Taylor enjoyed watching their reactions, especially Jacob's. He showed no awkwardness as the object of so much attention. He remained sitting on his uncle's lap and saying hi to everyone.

As Taylor had expected, Dominga took control of the situation.

She politely suggested that everyone give Sadi and the boy some space and refrain from asking too many questions. "We have plenty of time to get to know him," she explained, and then despite her own suggestions, she was the first one who requested to hold him. Taylor suppressed a laugh.

Susan's reaction surprised Taylor. She had feared that the woman would show fear and distrust. But when she introduced herself to Jacob, she bent down, put her hands on his shoulders, then burst into tears while hugging him.

Everyone acted extremely pleased while introducing themselves to the little guy, everyone except for Max and Gerald. Max stood on the other side of the table and spoke like an emotionless robot. "Hi, I'm Max."

As Gerald introduced himself, he only glanced at the boy and then focused on Sadi.

"I'm very happy for you, Sadi."

Both of the men seemed afraid, Taylor thought. As usual, their behavior made her feel sad, but she tried to ignore it and focus on happier things. She let Jacob, Sadi, and the children consume most of her attention.

When the children took Jacob to see the observatory, most of the adults followed, including Audrie who had arrived later. Max and Gerald stayed in the dining hall, and Simon who had probably stayed to talk with Max.

Taylor admired Simon's tenacity. She had quit trying to discuss anything with Max and Gerald. "I'm fine," they always said. Taylor forgot about them while in the observatory. The adults talked and watched the children play together and show the planet to Jacob.

So far, Freddy had failed to join the group, probably to allow them to continue their private discussions and adjust to Jacob's arrival. Taylor had difficulty comprehending their predicament. An entire lifetime had seemed to fit inside the past few days.

After touring their new home on Bodn, they returned to the station, discovered two new guests, and were offered immortality. Then that morning, they had witnessed an even larger miracle than their escape from Earth, the raising of the dead. And if Freddy was correct about reincarnation, every birth was also the raising of the dead.

"Our situation hasn't changed," Taylor said in the middle of an argument between Susan and Mark. The adults sat in wooden chairs in a semicircle, several meters away from the observatory window in the floor. "We have only two choices."

When Taylor had interrupted, Susan shot an angry look in her direction, frustration in her wide eyes. Susan wanted her husband to admit that, despite his hospitality, Freddy could be lying to them.

Taylor tried to speak calmly. "We either wait and see if returning to Earth is even an option, or we decide to stay here and go through with this transformation."

"That's true," Dominga said, coming to Taylor's aid. "If Freddy, or they," she looked at Susan with a nod, "wanted to do something to us, they could at any point. We all know this."

"After seeing Jacob, though, I have another question." Taylor did not care as much as Dominga about keeping the peace. She just wanted to keep the conversation in a productive direction. She turned to Sadi at her right. "Jacob got a new body. Is that what's going to happen to us? I don't even want to think about it, but we'd be crazy to reject his offer."

"Freddy was saying something about inhalation," Audrie said. Before speaking, the woman had sat quietly watching the children play. "Do you remember, Brian?"

"Something like that," Brian said. "He kind of lost me while telling us about it. But I know he didn't say anything about getting a new body."

"We were not in a good position to concentrate on what he was saying," Audrie said and laughed. "At the time, I was just trying to wrap my head around all of this, but now I'm sure he was talking about the transformation. We would need to inhale something. It would go to our brain and all of our cells and then something about shedding the unwanted genetic code."

"Well that makes me feel a lot better," Taylor said with thick sarcasm. She shook her head in disbelief. "I just love inhaling things."

"I'm sure that Freddy will explain the details to us," Cesar said.

"Whatever the process requires, I'm going through with it," Sadi said suddenly and everyone looked at her, except for the children. "I'm staying here. I can't let Jacob live forever and watch me die. The girls are doing it too."

While speaking, Sadi watched her daughters and son who were leaning into the viewscreen and pointing. Taylor followed her gaze and waited for someone else to speak. In those few seconds of silence, she thought of another reason to stay—Sadi and her family.

Taylor would help Sadi build a new society for the children. After hearing the new information, inhaling something sounded much better than replacing her body. She did not like the thought of seeing her former body, lifeless on a table. The vivid mental image gave her the chills.

One of the machines informed the group that it would prepare dinner that night and to expect Freddy's company. When they arrived, Sadi was the first to greet him. "Thanks again for returning Jacob to me," she said while hugging him. Sadi had spent all day with Taylor and the others in the observatory, so she had not seen Freddy until then.

"You saved me," Jacob said while extending his arms into the air. Freddy picked him up and the motion reminded Taylor of when Brian had also held the boy. The child seemed weightless in his arms.

"It was fun," Freddy said, smiling. While holding the child, he turned to the whole group. "While we eat, I can answer your questions."

Freddy explained the reconfiguration in more detail while they ate. As usual, he answered their questions before Taylor had prepared to ask them. At the beginning of his explanation, she kept glancing at Gerald and Max. They were watching Jacob with a strange concern in their eyes. But as Freddy talked, she forgot about them. In the end, she felt better about the situation.

"Jacob got a new body only because his old one was beyond repair," Freddy said in answer to Sadi's question. "For the rest of you, we will reconfigure your DNA. There is just one more thing I want to discuss, the control creatures from Earth. They want you back and consider you all as stolen property. Before the reconfiguration, I am afraid they will attempt to recover you, even if it means killing you to do it. They are now aware of what is going on. When we were all on Earth, it was just the human authorities. So going back to Earth before your reconfiguration would be very dangerous."

That night, after Taylor had gone to bed, she had trouble falling asleep. She kept imagining herself inhaling a thick fog from Freddy and then waking up and seeing the world differently. Never worrying about death again would change many of her views. There were so many implications to living forever. She fell asleep only after she failed to think of any more. It required over an hour.

At midnight, she woke up from a nightmare. While lying in bed, the memory of the dream dissipated but left her with a feeling of hopelessness. Taylor got out of bed, turned on the lamp at her bedside, and left to use the restroom.

Before returning to bed, she watched the view screen for a few minutes. She appreciated the contrast between the dark clouds covering Bodn and the star-filled sky above the horizon. She found the brightest star in her view and wondered if she had ever seen that particular one from Earth. She got a drink of water and then returned to bed.

She fell asleep quickly.

In the morning, Taylor awoke with the clear memory of another dream. For several minutes, she just lay in bed and let the dream replay in her mind. She wanted to convince herself of its artificiality, but she knew something real had occurred in the dream. Some real creature had appeared and delivered a message. "Return to Earth and we'll let you have your life back. You and all of your friends. If you return, you can have whatever you want."

The creature had taken the form of an ancient man with black hair, but she knew he was not a typical human. She remembered him vividly. In her dream, he'd held a beautiful wooden cane, ebony with a gold handle. He wore loose clothing made from some kind of fine linen, so white the material had seemed to shine. But more than his clothing, his face was burned in her memory, pale skin, dark eyes, and blood-red lips, all framed by long black hair that fell just past his shoulders, held in place with a silver string around his forehead. His eyes were so dark, she could not distinguish the pupils from the irises.

"Sorry," she'd said, "but I'm not going back. I like it here."

Before answering, he had just looked at her, motionless for several seconds. "I can see that you will not be dissuaded," he said with a smile. "I admire your resolve, Taylor. You will not hear the offer again."

After waking, she took a shower, got dressed then went to the dining hall as usual, the dream consuming nearly every thought. When she arrived, she was surprised to find Cesar and Dominga there, sitting side by side near the end of the table. They were deep in discussion and did not immediately see her. Even though they spoke in Spanish, Taylor knew something was wrong. Dominga did not look happy, and Taylor noticed the wrinkles in the corners of her eyes. After a few steps, they looked in her direction. Cesar's eyes grew wide and Dominga attempted to smile politely.

"What's wrong?" Taylor asked while walking toward them.

"Good morning, dear," Dominga said. "We want to know about your night."

"I had a weird dream."

"A man with black hair?" Cesar asked. "Saying it was safe to go back home?"

"Yes," Taylor said, gulping and coming to a stop.

"He said everything would be normal again?"

"You had it too?"

"Yes," Cesar said. "The same man visited us."

"Do you think it was real?" she asked, then saw the answer in their dark eyes. They reminded her of the man from the dream.

"We think so," Dominga said. "We can't all have the same dream and it not be real? What did you tell the man?"

"That I was staying here." Taylor sat next to Dominga. "It was a very brief meeting, then it ended, but I've been thinking about it ever since I woke up. What did you tell him?"

"I didn't know how to answer," Cesar said, looking worried about her reaction. "He said I could return to Mexico and live near my daughter and the authorities wouldn't try to stop me."

"He said that Freddy could confirm it," Dominga interjected, "if we didn't believe him."

"But I haven't heard Freddy say anything about this," Taylor said, glancing at Cesar's plate of scrambled eggs. She had lost all desire for food.

"We haven't either," Cesar said.

"If it was true, would you go back?"

"I think so," Cesar said. "I'm not young anymore."

She looked from Cesar to Dominga, squinting in disbelief, confusion, and a little anger. "But you could be young again. You'd give up all of this? I don't understand. Freddy said we could go back to Earth and get friends and family. I'm sure you could convince your daughter to come."

"The man said it was a one-time offer," Cesar said, shaking his head, "and he won't let us bring anyone back."

"But he didn't say that to me," Taylor said. "We didn't have the same dream after all."

"What if the man knew you wouldn't change your mind?" Cesar asked. "I wouldn't dare try to change your mind."

Taylor laughed weakly through pursed lips but was unable to smile. "Well don't make any decision yet," she said in exasperation. "We need to talk to Freddy, see what he has to say. I trust him a hell of a lot more than some strange man in a dream."

"No need to get upset, dear," Dominga said soothingly.

Taylor opened her mouth to argue further, but the older woman's warm smile suddenly reminded Taylor of her mother. Dominga put a hand on her shoulder.

"That's exactly what we were going to do," she said. "Wait for Freddy."

SIXTY-SEVEN

Christine

The man inside the CIA front company held the door as Christine and her two escorts entered. When she noticed the gun under his suit coat, she gulped and required extra mental effort to look away from the weapon. After the door clicked closed, he led them silently down the bright hallway and through another bullet-proof glass door, into a small office area. At the entrance, the office looked like an ordinary business with a reception desk, a pair of conference rooms, and several workspaces, but after the man led them inside and past a few cubicles, she could see a large open space and no other people.

A tall woman appeared in an open office door near the wall. She was thin and maybe fifty years of age, wearing a grey pantsuit with an open jacket over a white blouse. Hanging from her blouse pocket was a thick stainless steel pen, which looked out of place. She glanced at the man who had opened the door and then at Christine.

"Officer Booth," she said in sudden recognition, her dark eyes opening wide in surprise. "It's an honor to have you here. Welcome to the facility. I'm Director Turner."

"Yes, thank you," Christine said quickly and without extending his hand. "Good to meet you."

"He's here for one of the guests," the man said quickly. He took another drink and then set the mug on the nearest desk.

"We're here for FH1," Christine said.

"No problem," the woman said with some hesitation, as though she had forgotten the appropriate response. "Do you have the work order so I can attach it to the check-out paperwork?"

"No, but I will sign whatever you require," Christine said impatiently. "He's seen my ID, and you know who I am."

"Of course, sir," she said with a short nod. "We'll go get him."

"While we wait," Christine said, "I'd like to see your surveillance system."

The man and woman exchanged a wide-eyed glance.

"I've got someone working on that now," the woman said apologetically. "It's been giving us problems."

"I'd still like to see," Christine said.

"Right this way," said the man who had led them inside. He walked to a closed door next to the director's office. After turning the knob and revealing the dark interior, he stepped into the entrance. "Russ, we've got company."

Instead of waiting, Christine walked into the room and noticed a man sitting at a console, several monitors facing him, all showing still images. The man turned and stood, but Christine ignored him. In her peripheral vision, she noticed her two escorts and the director enter the room. They watched silently as Christine inspected the screens.

Only one of the images showed a person, sitting at a laptop and motionless. Christine also noticed several views of the outside and the parking lot where she had parked. The Lexus was not there, so the cameras began malfunctioning before they had arrived, which would explain the man's surprise at seeing them.

On the wall to her left, Christine found several rows of smaller screens. Some of the screens on the top row were turned on and showed the interior of a cell while all of the other screens were off. She counted five cells, each containing a single man. Most were lying on a cot, reading, or sleeping.

So, they only have five inmates.

She soon identified Franklin looking at the ceiling, frozen in time. While staring at his face for a few seconds, the director's voice startled her.

"I will get the check-out papers for you to sign, sir, and I'll inform my staff below to bring FH1 up." Before leaving the room, the woman turned to the man at the console. "Russel, answer all of his questions."

Christine glanced at the director and then returned her attention to the console. She began worrying less about her next line and was focusing on her emotional response. "Why is there no live video?"

"We're having technical difficulties," the man said after the director left the room. "The system died earlier and when I rebooted it, none of the video feed was live. So far, I can't find the root cause. I was about to call for help."

"Have you noticed anything else malfunctioning?" Christine asked casually, resisting the urge to show her anger. Seeing Franklin in the cell made her angry at whoever put him there. But she felt sorry for the man. Although nervous, he seemed nice, so she decided to save her displeasure for the director.

"I'm in charge of the surveillance equipment, sir." The man spoke as if talking to a military leader. "We've had no reports of any other system issues."

"Good," she said, then noticed that the director had returned.

"I've got the papers," the director said, and Christine knew the woman intended to disrupt the conversation and divert attention from their technical problems.

The woman handed two pieces of paper and a pen to Christine. She took the pen but just held the tip at the signature line without writing anything. She felt the urge to write something other than her name.

"Go ahead," whispered one of her escorts who was suddenly standing close to her. When Christine turned to him, she noticed his devious smile. "Give them a piece of your mind. They'll only see what we want them to see."

While staring at him, Christine squinted and tilted her head slightly to the side. "Hmm."

Instead of writing her name, she wrote two other words.

Fuck you!

"That'll do," said the man next to her, appreciatively.

Christine handed the papers to the director.

"Thanks," the director said without looking at them. "They should be bringing him up any minute."

Christine felt her cell phone begin to vibrate in her back pocket. But it felt strange, almost as if she was only remembering the sensation. Ignoring the strangeness, she retrieved the phone and stared at the screen. Francis was calling.

"I've got to take this," she said and walked out of the room. She tried to tap the accept button and nothing happened. Then she noticed the gloves on her hands and wondered how she could have forgotten them. After finding a cubicle, she removed one glove and sat in a swivel chair. "Hi, Francis. What's up?"

"Just wondering where you are," her sister said casually. "I'm home and was going to make dinner. Will you be here? You don't have to work, right?"

"I don't have to work but don't know when I'll be home." She sighed and felt herself relax. "I'm in the library."

"Let me guess," Francis said with thick sarcasm. "It's Friday afternoon, so it's definitely for one of your classes and wouldn't have anything to do with finding a certain someone."

"Ha ha," Christine said, clamping her mouth with her hand to quiet her sudden burst of laughter. The situation felt so ridiculous and she must have needed to externalize the emotion. "You know me too well. Listen, I've got to go. I'll see you later tonight."

"Have fun," her sister said.

"I'm having a blast," she said and wanted to laugh more. If Francis had known her sister's location and activity, she would have had an anxiety attack.

Before returning to the group, Christine pulled the glove back over her hand and drew two deep breaths. She needed to prepare mentally for the next part of the script.

After leaving the isolation and safety of the cubicle, she was disappointed to find an empty office area instead of Franklin. The door to the surveillance room was closed and she heard talking from inside the director's office. She entered the office to find the director sitting at a large desk, talking on the phone. Christine's two escorts stood on either side of the entrance like intimidating guards. The director looked nervous under their gaze.

SIXTY-EIGHT

Gerald

Gerald was having another typical dream, hiding from dangerous predators in a city of perpetual darkness. He spent much of his time alone, looking for somewhere to hide, but sometimes he would find Max in a hiding place and have to find another one.

He often awoke when a frightening creature found him, and then he would just stare at the view screen until returning to sleep. On a typical night, he would lose consciousness as the face of a woman slowly emerged from a fog, her eyes closed. He never got to see her eyes open and feared that he might.

Two hours before Dzalm would have peeked over the horizon, Gerald jolted from a deep sleep, his dream quickly vanishing from memory, thankfully. After his heartbeat returned to a normal tempo, he heard movement in the hallway, and then voices.

He crept silently from bed and walked to the door to determine what they were saying and who was speaking. After touching his ear to the door, he just listened. Although he failed to catch any words, he recognized Sadi's voice and what sounded like one of the children. Boy or girl, he could not tell. *Daryn probably had a bad dream*, he thought.

Sadi's voice often evoked sadness and his reaction was getting worse, especially after visiting Bodn. He was afraid to approach the subject of physical intimacy, didn't know how to touch her anymore, not even a brief grasp of her shoulder. There were so many times he wanted to put an arm around her, or just hold her hand. When she spoke, her soft lips taunted him.

Gerald felt unworthy of her affection, and damaged. Memories from his time at the psychiatric hospital haunted him during every waking hour, especially how he had killed the dog, how he had raped that poor woman and then ripped her apart. At least he thought he remembered doing those things. He remembered the anger more than anything, anger at the aliens who had put him in that position. Hate had burned a part of his brain, blinded him, and made part of him numb. The aliens had watched like medical students observing a surgeon cut into someone on a table.

The murders were just a drug-induced dream, like his encounter with the talking bird in the desert. The aliens or the doctors at the hospital had somehow implanted the memory in his head. Gerald wanted to think that. Before they had visited Bodn, he had still partially believed it. But as the memories slipped further into the past, he no longer could convince himself of their artificiality. No dreams could be that vivid.

Before visiting Bodn, he had quit the treatments with the flower. They helped minimize his daydreaming episodes, but he could not bring himself to breathe the scent anymore. The sweet smell of blueberry and cloves began to sicken him.

Gerald's thoughts returned to the present when the footsteps on the other side of the door stopped. Another door opened and closed softly, then silence. Before returning to his bed, Gerald waited a few more seconds to make sure nothing else was happening. He took a deep breath and was about to turn, but he no longer felt alone in his room. To his right, he noticed the open bathroom door and remembered closing it before going to bed. He could see nothing beyond the door frame, only darkness.

He felt a sudden disorientation as if the bathroom was a square hole in the ground and he was standing on a vertical wall, looking down into it. Gravity began pulling him toward the bathroom, but he remained motionless somehow. He grasped the door handle for support against the sudden vertigo.

While staring into the dark bathroom, Gerald thought he saw movement, something shifting in the dark. Chills quickly raced through his inner core, beginning in his gut and spreading to his chest and back. Some creature stood just beyond the light, and Gerald could feel its eyes inspecting him. He prepared to run into the hallway, enter the light. Then he heard a voice.

Calm yourself, Gerald, a raspy voice whispered in Gerald's mind. *If you fear too loudly, they will become suspicious. We can't hurt you.*

"Who are you?" Gerald asked, thinking the voice sounded familiar and feeling slightly less frightened. An adult male spoke to him, a man about his age. He squinted, trying to see into the bathroom.

Gravity kept pulling him toward it.

"Step into the light so I can see you."

We don't want to deceive more than necessary, the voice said. *We're not really here.*

"What do you mean, not really here?"

We are like what Freddy has become, the voice said, and then Gerald saw the outline of a man. *We feel your thoughts and your questions before you ask them. We make you believe things are, when they are not.*

So you don't exist, Gerald thought, feeling a bit of relief. He began turning slowly toward his bed again, but the room spun so that he kept facing the bathroom. He had to squeeze the door handle harder to remain standing.

Don't do that, the voice said impatiently. *We exist, just not here. We are here to give you a warning. Freddy has crossed a dangerous line, forcing our intervention.*

"What dangerous line?"

He won't be distracted for too long. The outline of the man disappeared. *So we must be brief. He has violated the natural order and re-*

stored the dead to life. The dead are a poison to the world.

Gerald felt as though he'd just watched a horror movie. He imagined a zombie crawling from a grave, rotting flesh covered in a nice new suit. In the absence of noise, the man's outline became visible again, standing inside the bathroom, motionless and arms held at his side. When the man's right hand moved to his mouth, Gerald jolted in surprise.

Go back to sleep and I'll contact you later.

—※—

Gerald opened his eyes to the sound of knocking on his door. He was lying in bed and could see his apartment in the low light of early morning. He turned from the window and looked at the bathroom door. The bathroom door was closed, but his encounter with the man was still fresh in his memory.

"Gerald," said the voice from the hallway. "It's Brian. I need to talk to you."

"Just a moment," Gerald said, rubbing his eyes. He sat up and looked out the window. Dzalm would soon rise over the horizon and he would have to either shut the curtains or change the view to keep the star from blinding him. While Gerald walked to the door, he saw the man's outline in his peripheral vision, the man who had stood in the bathroom. Gerald ignored the temptation to look.

"Good morning, Gerald," Brian said, excitement in his eyes. He stood in the hallway with Max's sister at his left. She nodded almost imperceptibly. "I'm telling everyone, so they don't all ask my sister the same questions."

"Okay," Gerald said, seeing the shadow of a man superimposed over Max's sister. "What's going on?"

"Freddy brought her son back," he said, shaking his head but with a smile. "I know how that sounds, believe me, but I was there. He rescued him from wherever he was and created a new body for him. That's pretty much all I know. We're going to see them in the dining hall in about ten minutes."

While listening to the news, his mouth and throat lost nearly all moisture, leaving him almost unable to swallow. He tried to smile but knew it looked forced. After hearing about Sadi's son, and what Freddy had done, the vision of the man in his bathroom felt more real than ever.

Gerald agreed to accompany them, said goodbye, and then shut the door. When he heard the people gathering in the hallway several minutes later, he took a deep breath, opened the door, and then joined them.

He walked silently at the end of the group on their way to the dining hall, behind Max and Simon. Brian was already there with Taylor, Sadi, her girls, and her son. While everyone introduced themselves to the child, Gerald faced the floor, his heart racing. He concentrated on smiling and pretending to patiently wait for his turn to meet the child.

He attempted to forget about the man from his bathroom—the man hiding in the periphery. He existed only in Gerald's imagination, like so many other things.

When Gerald knew he could no longer just stare at the floor, he stepped forward, smiled at the child then quickly introduced himself. He attempted to turn his attention to Sadi, but he made eye contact with the boy and stopped breathing.

The young boy smiled sweetly, too sweetly, and Gerald gulped. The smile reminded him of the beautiful flower in his room and its sickeningly sweet scent. He swallowed, then turned to Sadi and said something that he instantly forgot.

While everyone talked, Gerald ate breakfast and attempted to forget about how Jacob's smile had disturbed him. He also tried remembering what he had said to Sadi and hoped it was appropriate for the situation. He felt like an insensitive ass. The old Gerald would have shown genuine pleasure in his friend's joy, especially a woman he had come to love, and especially for something so miraculous as Jacob's return from the dead. He should have been a part of the celebration, but he couldn't even bring himself to look at her son.

The dead are a poison to the world.

The voice originated from Gerald's left, but it failed to surprise him. The shadow man was now sitting at his side and staring at him. Gerald tried to ignore the voice, refusing to turn and verify that only Simon sat there.

When all of the adults suddenly stopped talking, Gerald turned his attention to the children who were talking about all of the things they wanted to show Jacob.

Sometime later, Gerald could not tell how long, everyone else rose from the table to follow the children to the observatory. As usual, Gerald walked at the end of the group. When the group turned down a different hallway, he continued walking straight. No one seemed to notice his absence.

SIXTY-NINE

Christine

"What happened when you tried the manual override?" the woman at the desk asked. While listening to the receiver, she stared at the empty chairs in front of her desk. "I see. Thank you. We'll be right down."

"Is there a problem?" Christine asked.

"My apologies, sir," the woman said. She reminded Christine of a child caught breaking some rule then forced to confess. "Apparently, there's a security feature I was unaware of. Some of our guests require a bio-confirmation of ID for check-out. To retrieve FH1, the control system requires a higher security clearance than the guards. I'm afraid you'll have to come below with us."

"Great," Christine said sarcastically. "A tour would be nice, I suppose."

"I'll take you down myself," the woman said. "Again, I apologize for the inconvenience, Mr. Booth. I wish we would have been informed of this security feature."

Christine silently waited as the director stood and walked away from her desk. She walked past them and turned left outside of her office. Christine followed with her two escorts close behind her. As she walked past the man who had opened the entrance doors for them, she thought he looked relieved to see their departure. He did not follow them.

The director led them into the large open area behind the cubicles. While following her, Christine noticed the floor. Large squares of thin, cheap carpeting covered the ground, identical to the flooring in the office area. After stopping in the middle of the room, the director retrieved the pen from her blouse pocket and clicked it with her right thumb.

"This is our guest entrance," she explained as the floor split open. Two door flaps began lifting, perfectly hidden by the seams between the tiles. "We have two other service entrances for equipment and such, but this is large enough for most travel."

As the entrance continued to open, Christine felt a growing panic. Until that point, she had been almost excited, but the thought of going below filled her with a strong sense of foreboding. The hole in the floor seemed to represent a one-way journey, like death. Every instinct urged her to run away.

The entrance suddenly seemed like a trap and reminded her of a recent nightmare, visiting Francis in prison. In the dream, the prison guards did not let her leave.

When the doors stopped moving, Christine heard a soft clank of metal hitting metal. She jolted in surprise.

When the director began descending the wide stairs, Christine stood motionless and her eyes opened wide. Less than a second later, a strong hand grasped her shoulder, reminding her of when she had first encountered her two escorts. Although she knew his hand existed only in her imagination, it was warm and offered comfort.

"I won't let anything happen to you," the man whispered in her ear. "Just breathe. If it's a trap and they try to take you or harm you, I will destroy them and this place."

His message gave Christine the chills but provided her with enough courage to take the first steps down the stairs. On the descent, she reconsidered her opinion of Freddy. So far, she had only seen his polite and friendly side, which could have just been an act. She hardly knew him, she realized. His threat revealed an angry, dangerous side. She did not want to see what he could do when anger motivated him. She did not want to anger him either.

So far, Christine had trusted in her emotions, and Freddy had already shown the ability to create emotions, or at least influence them. Did her emotions exist only in her imagination? In reality, Christine had no escorts. She was entering an underground prison facility with people who could incarcerate her. What if Freddy's abilities failed to work underground? What if the CIA had some kind of protective shield down there?

Before more concerns and fears completely consumed her courage, Christine decided to continue trusting the child known as Freddy. So far, he had not hurt her and had brought her to Franklin's location. He had also let her drive a fancy car as fast as she dared without police interruption. That alone had earned her loyalty.

They descended maybe four meters in elevation and entered a short hallway that had what looked like an elevator at the end. The director led them quietly through the hallway and then she pressed her thumb on a glass pad on an illuminated panel. The elevator door slid open and the director stepped to the side to allow Christine and her two escorts to walk in front of her.

"We're excited about the expansion," the director said while the doors closed. "The new additions to the business park will make our work here much easier to hide from the public."

"Yes," Christine said, curious to hear what would escape her lips. "We've been waiting too long for the production and storage facility to be fully functional. I hope we made the right choice in the director."

"You did, sir," the woman said confidently.

Christine felt the elevator stop and then the door slid open to reveal a wide circular tunnel with cement walls. LED lights on either side of the walkway provided just enough light to see the path but kept the ceiling in darkness, giving Christine the impression of a mine shaft.

When the elevator doors closed and they all exited, Christine felt completely isolated from the outside world. She could almost feel the weight of the earth on the other side of the walls.

"Here's how this will work," the director said. She pointed to the end of the tunnel, to a set of doors with another glowing control panel. "That's the entrance over there. It's sort of like a loadlock chamber. We'll enter one at a time and it will require a fingerprint scan. Once your identity is confirmed in the database, the other doors will open. Don't worry, I'll show you. Follow me."

Christine's eyes flew wide open and her heart began racing painfully fast. They could not scan her fingerprints. She would go to jail for sure. In horror and panic, Christine stared at the end of the tunnel, at the steel doors there. They truly represented the end.

In just fifteen meters, they would know the deception. Her predicament suddenly seemed impossible to overcome, but she started following the director anyway, her doom feeling more certain with every step. Freddy could only create illusions. Sure, they worked on people, but illusions could not fool a fingerprint scanner. That required an actual finger.

For the third time since the rescue operation had begun, a reassuring hand grasped her shoulder. The man directly behind her whispered in her ear. "When the director enters the chamber, follow her. She won't see you and you'll get in with her fingerprints. Stop worrying and try to have fun. This is a piece of cake!"

How long would it have taken me to think of that?

When they reached the end of the tunnel, Christine had almost completely recovered from her panic. Shaking her head, she laughed at herself and felt a new respect for Freddy.

"Just push this green triangle and the doors will open," the director said while following her instructions. The door slid open slowly, revealing a square room with cement walls. "FH1 should be waiting for us on the other side."

Before the stainless steel door closed, Christine slipped into the entrance chamber with the director. They stood silently, facing another stainless steel door. Christine breathed calmly and stood still while a female computer voice gave instructions.

"You will see the outline of a hand on the wall to your right," it said. "Place your right hand inside."

The director's hand fit nicely inside the outline of a much larger hand. When the black screen turned green, the door in front of them opened. They both exited. The director stepped away from the entrance and turned to face it, while Christine inspected their new surroundings.

A large open area with a cement floor lay before her, ending at a glass wall with a large revolving door in the center. The door immediately drew her attention. A control panel was mounted on the wall next to it, similar to the ones at the elevators. She initially stared blankly at the glass until she recognized what lay beyond it. Her heart rate increased again but from excitement instead of fear.

Franklin sat at a table on the other side of the glass. At least Christine thought it was him. He had about the same build. A black hood covered his head, falling just below his nose. His hands were behind his back, probably handcuffed. A surge of empathy hit her. Was he terrified? Or worse, did he feel hopeless? She shuddered at the thought of being in his predicament.

Franklin sat motionless next to a tall, bulky man in a light blue uniform, not military attire as Christine had expected. The man was looking at the director and seemed relaxed. Turning away from him, Christine noticed the side walls of the room. Each had a single door with a glass window at the top, revealing a hallway beyond.

When Christine heard the door open behind her, she turned and was shocked to see a strange man enter. He stood slightly shorter than the director, stocky with thick hair and irritation in his light eyes.

So, that's how they see me, she thought with a scowl. *I've looked better.*

The man quickly inspected the room without showing any sign of noticing Christine. He glanced briefly at the director and then at the glass wall separating them from Franklin and the other guard.

"My two escorts will wait for us in the tunnel," he said sternly, looking at the revolving doors. "There he is. Before we get him, I'd like to see the new security feature in effect."

"You want me to show you how it works?" she asked, squinting and looking confused.

"I ordered this security enhancement," he said, more irritated now, "and I want to see it in effect. Humor me, Director Turner. Let the guard come out first, to show me how it normally works. Then I want to see you try to get FH1 out."

The director walked to the revolving door and spoke into the control panel on the right.

"We want to bring you out first, Thompson, to show how this works."

The guard and Franklin stood to their feet and stepped to the side of the revolving door together. Christine watched as the guard put his hand to the panel, then Director Turner. The computer voice spoke, "Do you wish to initiate checkout?"

"Yes," the director answered.

Christine heard a click and watched as Franklin stepped inside the revolving door and then entered the room with her. She stepped to Franklin's side and pulled him away from the door, not saying anything. Her next urge was to escort Franklin to the entrance chamber door and wait.

"Okay," Booth said. "I want to see you try to get FH1."

Christine led Franklin, holding his upper arm tightly and wondering how they were going to get out of there. But she wasn't worried anymore, just curious. While walking with him, she heard the director speak again into the panel by the revolving door. When she reached the loadlock door with Franklin, he quietly faced the ground, breathing steadily.

"If you can hear me, just nod," she whispered. "It's Christine."

He quickly lifted his head to face her, then slowly nodded.

"I'm with your friend, Freddy," she continued. "We're getting you out of here."

She noticed his body relax, but when they heard the computer's voice, he jumped in surprise.

"Insufficient security clearance," the computer said from behind them.

While still holding onto Franklin's arm, Christine turned to see the director with her hand on the scanner. Another Franklin stood on the other side with his hand also on the scanner.

Booth stepped to the door next and put his hand on the scanner.

"Do you wish to initiate checkout?" the computer voice asked.

"Yes," Booth answered. Ten seconds later, the other Franklin exited—the fake one. Booth grabbed him on the top of the shoulder. "Walk this way."

"Do you wish to see anything else?" the director asked before following them.

"No," he said politely. "Thank you."

After the entrance chamber door opened, Christine and Franklin slipped inside with the director. When the door had closed, the woman drew a deep breath and sighed. "Almost there, Turner," she said to herself then followed the computer instructions to scan her hand. The door opened a few seconds later and the director stepped inside the tunnel with Franklin and Christine following.

Her two escorts were waiting for them and only nodded in acknowledgment when she and Franklin exited the chamber. She expected to see Booth and the other Franklin pass through the chamber next, but the door never opened. When she realized it would not be opening, Christine turned to the director.

For several seconds, Director Turner seemed confused. At first, she looked at Christine without recognition, almost as if staring at a statue. Smiling politely, the woman rubbed her eyes and spent a moment focusing. Afterward, she led them quietly through the short tunnel as if nothing strange had happened.

Their final journey to the surface and then through the office occurred without incident. As they exited the building, the director held the door open for them.

"It was good to meet you, Mr. Booth."

"Thank you, Director," Christine said, smiling politely. "Keep up the good work."

She turned and did not look back.

SEVENTY

Gerald

We will lead you, the voice said from his side. *Freddy is distracted, and we trapped the one who helps him. So we can show what is real.*

Gerald walked alone through dimly lit hallways, barely paying attention to his surroundings and soon feeling lost. After realizing that he stood in an unfamiliar area, he felt a rush of paranoia.

"Won't the machines know where I am?" Gerald asked, looking behind him. When he turned, the shadow standing at his side vanished. His mysterious companion suddenly seemed less menacing, and he was more afraid of the machines than the shadow. He had always thought of them as giant insects with stingers.

We will deal with machines. We're almost there.

Gerald stopped unexpectedly at a three-way intersection, each direction identical to the other. *Prepare yourself,* the voice said. *Don't be afraid. You'll be safe. Now go to the right.* After about twenty meters, he entered a large open area with even higher ceilings than the hallways. The lights above him were so high the circles of plasma appeared as large dots.

The place reminded Gerald of a museum. Enormous crystal containers stood in every direction on short marble stands and were full of silvery grey liquid. At the base of each one, strange symbols were carved into the stone bases, some kind of cursive writing. Behind each one stood another and then another farther back. There seemed to be no end to them. The surface of each one reflected the light, obscuring their contents.

When he noticed the creatures suspended in the silvery liquid, he almost forgot to breathe. A single alien creature occupied each giant container in a murky fluid, which looked like translucent mercury. The creatures ranged from a meter tall to the size of a large giraffe. Most of the light in the room originated from the illuminated crystal walls of the displays.

After Gerald resumed breathing, he realized the creatures showed no sign of life so he stepped to the closest one and touched the glass with his right hand. He expected to feel cold, but the crystal wall was warm. The container stood maybe four times his height with the creature inside at least twice his height.

The liquid obscured most of the creature, but he could see enough to recognize its features. It reminded him of a sasquatch statue he had seen on a trip to Mount St. Helens. Short black hair covered its huge body and the thing might have weighed at least five hundred kilograms, but it seemed weightless in the liquid. The huge face looked intelligent, pensive even.

He looked at the next column and the next and then the next. Each one held a different creature. From what he could tell, most looked like land-based animals, except for two flying creatures with wings and a single sea creature with flippers. When he looked directly at each one, their eyes were closed tight. In his periphery, all of the creatures seemed to be looking at him. After several seconds of inspection, he turned his attention to the base of the closest container, at its inscription. He did not want to look at the creatures anymore.

Did Freddy or his friends intend to put Gerald and his friends inside one of the containers, on display or for some other purpose? Had they killed all of the creatures or put them in suspended animation?

The questions in his mind seemed ridiculous, but they appeared too quickly to reject. His anxiety soon grew as large as the enormous display room.

Keep going to the left. The voice spoke softly, breaking the eerie stillness. The quiet felt oppressive. *Don't look if they disturb you.*

Gerald walked facing the ground, seeing only the pedestals of the giant containers and their elegant inscriptions. He walked through the large area, passing so many containers he lost count until he almost collided with one. After stopping, he stared at the inscription without really seeing it. When he looked just a little upward, he recognized human feet in the murky liquid. He opened his eyes wider so he could see them more clearly.

This is Freddy Carlson. The voice still came from inside his head, but Gerald could also see the shadow standing next to him in the periphery. *Look!*

Gerald attempted to resist the command but eventually looked up at Freddy suspended in the liquid. His eyes were closed and his blond hair shot from his head in all directions. The murky liquid obscured most of his naked body, except for his face. Like every other creature, Gerald did not want to look at Freddy's face for too long. He was afraid Freddy would open his eyes.

"Is this where Freddy goes when he's not with us?"

No. This is his prison. The creature you think is Freddy is not.

"I don't believe it," Gerald whispered, taking two steps backward.

Let us show more.

"This isn't real," Gerald said louder, his voice echoing inside the huge room. "It's a dream."

Truth can be unpleasant. Don't flee from it.

"There's got to be an explanation," he said to himself, closing his eyes and drawing a deep breath. No matter how real everything seemed, Gerald would take control of his thoughts and stop listening to the voices inside his head. Even if he was dreaming, he still needed to determine what to do. Talking was helping him concentrate. "This is just a replica."

Ignore us at your peril.

"How do I get out of here?" he asked himself, turning around the way he had come. "I need to talk with Freddy."

A scream suddenly shook the floor.

Do not ignore us!

Gerald covered his ears protectively. Cringing, he waited for the voice to continue, but the room remained quiet. His former conclusion still felt right. He was either dreaming or hallucinating. While walking, the man's dark outline appeared again in Gerald's peripheral vision.

"No one's there," he said to himself.

A dark doorway suddenly appeared in his path and he stepped into a black abyss. Without wind or any other indication of movement, he began accelerating forward. Euphoria soon replaced his fright and Gerald did not care if he ever entered the world of light or touched ground again. He soon felt weightless.

He stopped abruptly on a thin cloth as if landing face-first on a firefighter's safety net. Then he felt a cold metal table under his back with his arms strapped to his side, unable to move. A light suddenly burst to life above the white cloth, forcing his eyes shut tight.

Through the thin sheet, heat from the sun began to burn his face, and he heard voices from a group of giant birds all around him, including the one that had threatened to eat him at the psychiatric hospital. He recognized individual words but could not understand their meaning. Instead of listening to them talk, he spent all of his energy on avoiding notice, breathing quietly.

While lying still on the table, Gerald dreamed about typing on the computer in his office, except the view through his window was different. Instead of viewing the street and neighboring buildings, he could see the inside of the empty hangar on the station above Bodn.

He focused on the computer screen while typing, but a jumping spider suddenly appeared in front of him. The creature stood on his desk with its two front legs raised in the air, almost as though trying to get his attention. But Gerald was too focused on his work to give an insignificant spider any attention.

—✳—

While staring at the view screen in his room, Gerald tried to remember how he had arrived there. He remembered shutting the door but not opening it. He must have stood in the same position at the view screen for at least five minutes. He remembered watching Dzalm disappear completely behind the horizon, one of the few peaceful experiences he enjoyed lately. The transition from day to night had happened almost imperceptibly. He would need to energize some lights soon if he did not want to stand in darkness, where shadow people might lurk.

Like so much of his time on the station, the day felt like a jigsaw puzzle with only the border completed. Having gaps in his memory should not have concerned him, but this day felt different. Maybe he was just having difficulty accepting what Freddy had done, restoring Sadi's son to life.

Since his friends had rescued him from the psychiatric hospital, almost every day had contained gaps. He clearly remembered that morning and meeting Jacob. Then after leaving his friends, he found Freddy's container in the huge warehouse. Gerald could not deny that he had heard a voice. Something must have guided him to that frightening room. He would not have found it on his own.

After energizing the lights in his room, Gerald felt good about a decision. He needed to discuss the situation with one of his friends, someone he could trust. The situation was overwhelming, impossible to grasp completely. To make matters worse, Gerald felt so tired. Maybe if he got a full night of sleep, he would gain better mental clarity. He would talk to Taylor about the situation in the morning.

Before getting ready for bed, he looked at the flower on his nightstand and considered taking a treatment. That would help clear his mind and probably help him sleep. In preparation for the experience, Gerald drew a deep breath and then paused. He imagined inhaling the sweet fragrance again and the memory almost made him gag, even more than usual.

No, he would just go to sleep and put faith in his friends. But before getting into bed, Gerald closed his bathroom door.

SEVENTY-ONE

Taylor

"As you know, some of us want to visit our relatives and bring them back here," Cesar said. "Now that they know about us, can we still do that? I mean, will you be able to shield us from them?"

Freddy stood at the front of the group in one of the lounges with all of the seats arranged in a semi-circle around him. After breakfast, all of the children had gone to the observatory, leaving the adults to discuss the situation. To Taylor's great relief, Cesar had begun the conversation by declaring that he and Dominga wanted to stay.

"Yes," Freddy answered confidently. "But we will have to plan the trip very carefully."

"For those who want to return," Cesar asked next, "can we trust their agreement?"

"They will uphold their end of the bargain," Freddy said, turning from Cesar and looking at several of them. "But you will just fall back into the recycle loop again. You will never be truly free and live life for yourselves. You can even go back to Earth after upgrading your genetic code if that is what you want. But they will just hunt you if they ever discover what you are."

"Well, I don't believe it, Freddy," Susan said with a sneer. "This doesn't feel right at all. There's got to be something else going on. Did you ever stop to think that you're being fooled too? Why can't we talk to your friend, the one you say is in charge of this place? And where's Yezeel? You say he's not in charge. It's a little suspicious, don't you think?"

"Susan," Freddy said calmly. "As I have explained previously. They have given me the responsibility for all of you, and this place. They want me to solve the issues, and I am trying to keep everyone informed. Like it or not, we are in this together."

In the following silence, Taylor wondered if she would have responded so politely to the woman. Susan seemed to have lost what remained of her sanity after having the dream. Although Taylor understood her anxiety, the woman should trust her friends. Everyone wanted the same thing and had the same concerns.

Taylor felt especially sorry for Mark. Earlier, Susan had aimed her anger at him for not being supportive, for making her stand by herself against everyone. The poor guy had reminded Taylor of a deer in a headlight, unsure how to appease Susan before she ran him over.

If that's what marriage is like, no thank you!

"Well, we're taking the offer and going home. No one can live forever."

The woman stood from her seat and paused to look at Mark. Although Taylor sat across from them, she could see the threat in her eyes. Susan turned away and then walked from the room. Mark took a deep breath and followed her, his eyes on the ground.

"So Earth is a recycle center, and these creatures want us back so they can keep extracting our life force or whatever?" Audrie said after watching Mark exit the room. "I'll accept that, for now. So, what are these things that can talk to us all in a dream? I know many important people who manage things on Earth and I can tell you that they don't know about any of this."

"I am sure they do not," Freddy said. "Although the top directors of the intelligence agencies maintain the artificial history narrative, they are being deceived just like the rest of us were."

Freddy maintained eye contact with Audrie while continuing. "The system is designed to self-perpetuate itself. The elite are just working to strengthen their positions, which naturally suppresses the rest of society. The process maximizes human trauma and stress, giving less resistance to those at the head of the control system."

"So, what are they?" Audrie asked.

"They are creatures just like all of us," he answered, turning and looking at no one in particular. "They are just maximizing their pleasure, just like the rest of us, but some of them can do what I can."

"I don't care what they are, Freddy," Taylor said. "I'm staying. You helped us escape and got us all here, and everything's been going fine so far."

"Thank you, Taylor," Freddy said with a smile. "It was a team effort getting here though."

"This doesn't change my decision," Sadi said. "My girls and I are staying and going through with the change."

"Me too," Brian said.

"I'm not doubting you, Freddy," Simon said. He sat at Taylor's left, separating her from Max and Audrie. "But since they contacted us, doesn't that mean they know where we are? Are we still out of their reach?"

"They know how to reach us without knowing our location.," Freddy said. "Distance is meaningless in the background, but this facility was shielding us from them until now, so this must be another one of my tests, a puzzle for me to solve."

"Are we all just puppets for your lessons?" Max asked, grunting and surprising Taylor with his sardonic tone.

"Puppets?" Freddy asked himself. "I guess so, from her point of view. But she is more concerned about my ability to protect you all."

"Well, I don't trust you to protect us," Max said, losing none of his angry tone. "I don't have anything personal against you, Freddy, but I'm taking their offer."

Taylor's stomach tightened, his angry declaration momentarily distracting her. If not for the additional sense of betrayal, she would have called him a fool. Although Max and Gerald had grown distant from everyone, she still hoped for their recovery and trusted in Freddy's ability to heal them. Max's decision to return home threatened to crush her hope.

"Have you been taking the treatments, Max?" Gerald asked suddenly and Taylor looked at him in surprise. Like Max, this was Gerald's first contribution to the conversation. "They've been helping me. I did one last night, and feel good about staying. Reconfiguration should repair the damage done to us at the hospital."

"It's all in your mind, Gerald," Max said, shaking his head. "We're fine. The treatments haven't helped me."

"Well, if you'll excuse me, I'm going to the bathroom," Gerald said suddenly. While rising from his seat, he smiled at Taylor and the rest of the group then turned to Freddy. "Let me know when we can go through with this transformation."

As Gerald walked from the room, Taylor noticed Freddy watching him suspiciously. She had expected Freddy to say something, but he seemed as surprised as everyone else. He always seemed to know what people were thinking.

Maybe he doesn't know as much as I thought.

"So when can we return to Earth?" Max asked as the door closed behind Gerald. "I suppose after everyone's let you mess with their DNA?"

"Max, what the hell is wrong with you?" Taylor asked, turning toward him. She avoided making eye contact with Audrie who appeared ready to defend her brother. "Are you really going to pass up this opportunity? They really did a number on you at the psychiatric hospital."

"Well, if this is true," Max began calmly, "and Earth is just a big recycle center, then I will be living forever. I still have friends there, and family. If I stay here, aren't I betraying them? Leaving them to deal with our *evil* overlords?"

"We're your friends," Taylor answered, ignoring his sarcastic reference to their enemies. She had considered that same question, so she did not need to think of how to answer. "I'm not betraying anyone. I'm doing what's best for me, and who knows, maybe by going through with this transformation, we'll be in a better position to help our friends back there. Did you consider that, Max?"

"No need to take this personally, Taylor," Max answered. "This has nothing to do with you. I know there are positive aspects to any side of a debate, but I just don't trust that Freddy can protect us."

"We all choose who we want to stand with," Taylor said, attempting to ignore the pain of not factoring into Max's decision to leave. Before continuing, she glanced at Audrie. "Even if I knew this was a sinking ship, I'd still choose to be here."

"It is not an easy decision for any of you," Freddy said, making brief eye contact with Taylor. "But neither is actually returning to Earth. Now that they are aware of us, it will be more difficult to get more people from Earth. It will take some planning. And we also need to discuss the transformation. Who will go first and when? That is what we should discuss."

Taylor felt a distinct impression to trust Freddy. With her racing heart and anger, she had forgotten about him. Taylor closed her mouth tightly, to prevent any more angry outbursts, then drew a deep breath to calm herself. Freddy knew how to handle the situation. They did not have to deal with Max and Susan yet.

The discussion continued for another hour. Taylor let the more exciting topic of reconfiguration distract her from thinking about Max. He made no additional contributions to the discussion. Whenever Audrie spoke, Taylor avoided looking at her.

When Cesar asked Freddy to describe his experience with the reconfiguration, Taylor did not like his answer.

"I experienced something different, something not so pleasant," Freddy said. He refused to give any other details at that time but promised to explain one day. Taylor felt as though he was protecting them from frightening information. But she still trusted him.

Sadi wanted to go through with the reconfiguration first, but Cesar said he did not want her to be the guinea pig. Freddy said the process would be ready in two days. Before then, he claimed to have something requiring his full attention.

At the end of the discussion, Taylor considered going to the observatory, thinking that interaction with the children would help her recover emotionally from Max's coldness. While walking there with Sadi, Cesar, and Dominga, Taylor wondered how long Max had felt such discontent. Maybe if she would have done more to help him, he would have decided to stay.

Instead of listening to the conversation, Taylor attempted to determine the reason for her anxiety. After just a few minutes, she assigned her stress to an emotional attachment to Max. While she had pretended to feel indifferent, Taylor had let herself consider a future with him. Then after his angry outburst, she felt betrayed. He did not feel the same and that hurt.

When she saw the opening to the observatory and heard the children, she changed her mind and decided to spend some time alone in one of her favorite places, the jet. She did not want to run into Max or Audrie.

"I'm going back to my apartment," Taylor said. "I need to use the bathroom and I might take a nap. I'll see you guys later."

Taylor loved the jet and all of the memories associated with it, even her time with Max there. She and Mark had spent their time thinking and talking about all the places they could go in the jet once it was functional and safe. Other than living with Cesar and working on the BMW, living in Brazil had been the happiest time in her life. She did not have to worry about school or money and could just concentrate on what she loved most, creation and solving engineering problems. On her walk to the hangar, she fantasized about building more mechanical things and living on Bodn with everyone, including her mother.

After arriving in the hangar, she noticed that the stairs were lowered and the door to the jet was open. She remembered shutting the doors when they returned from Bodn. *Cesar or Mark must have been here,* she thought, *or one of the machines doing maintenance.*

While climbing the stairs, she heard typing on a keyboard from the cockpit, but as she entered the cabin, the typing stopped, replaced by the sound of movement from the pilot's seat. After coming into view, she found Gerald sitting in the pilot's chair and facing her, his lips stretched into a wide smile.

"Hi, Taylor," he said. "How did the discussion go after I left?"

"Some more arguing with Max," she said, trying to sound indifferent. She entered the cockpit and sat in the copilot's seat. "Why didn't you come back? And what are you doing?"

"I was on my way back to the discussion but didn't feel like arguing anymore. I had an idea, actually."

"Okay," she said, looking at the control panel in front of Gerald and wondering what he'd been typing. The navigation program showed on the main screen. Whatever Gerald had typed was gone. "But what were you doing on the computer?"

"Oh, just trying to familiarize myself with this thing a little," he said and laughed. "I was wondering if you'd teach me and Sadi how to fly? You and Mark enjoy flying, and it might be fun to do with Sadi."

"Flying is fun," Taylor admitted. "After all this time, you're just now thinking about this? I'm happy to teach you, but why now?"

"I've been feeling a little better lately." Gerald turned from her finally and looked at the control panel again. "I've let things slip a little with Sadi and me and need an activity to do with her. I was hoping to do it before she goes through with this reconfiguration. After might be too late."

"Why would it be too late after?"

"Do you think that she'll feel any different afterward?" he asked. "I mean, be a different person?"

"Not according to Freddy," she answered, curious and a little afraid of the possibility.

"Freddy's definitely changed," he said.

"Physically, yes, but he's still the same person," Taylor said, believing her thoughts even more after speaking them. "He's still our friend."

"I hope so," Gerald said, but doubt laced his tone. "So, it's a plan? What about tomorrow for the flying lesson? I wanted to ask you before asking Sadi."

"I guess so," Taylor said, squinting and pausing to evaluate her friend. She had difficulty transitioning to a less despondent version of Gerald. If she could only get Max to take more of the treatments, maybe he would return to his old self, as Gerald had appeared to do.

SEVENTY-TWO

Gerald

Gerald left the group discussion and wandered through the empty hallways, attempting to remember what had just happened. He'd been sitting and listening to the discussion with Freddy then getting up suddenly and leaving. Did he make some sort of excuse to leave? Or did he just leave without saying anything? *I should have done that treatment last night*, he scolded himself.

While lost in thought, Gerald wandered into the hangar and then stopped when he saw the jet and the BMW parked by it. For the next few minutes, he stood and stared at the jet, remembering all of his experiences inside of it, traveling through their solar system, through the portal, and arriving at the station. Gerald imagined a future museum on Bodn where they would put the jet on display for their children.

Everyone would put an item from Earth in the museum, something reminding them of home. Maybe he would make a replica of his office where it all had started for him, with the email from Taylor on permanent display and the spider on the desk. He remembered staring into the spider's eyes and then at the screen after the spider had disappeared. For the next little while, he stared at the computer screen from his memory and wondered how his law partner, Albert, was doing.

"Hi, Gerald," said a female voice from behind him. "What are you doing?"

Before turning to see who had spoken, Gerald realized he was sitting in the pilot's chair in the jet. But he did not remember getting there. After seeing Taylor standing in the entryway, he smiled weakly, needing a moment to process her words and adjust to his new surroundings.

"I don't know," he said slowly. He considered telling her the truth but decided a cover story would probably improve her opinion of him. "I didn't feel like going back to my room, or being around anyone, really, so I came here, a place to sit."

"I like to come here too. I have a lot of good memories in this thing," she said while joining him in the copilot's seat. "I'm so glad you've decided to stay. After Max, I began to have doubts about everyone. I thought it was a no-brainer to stay here. We can't trust those creatures from Earth that offered the pardon. They're desperate to get us back and will probably promise us anything."

"Yes, I definitely want to stay," Gerald answered. Taylor's comments reminded him a little of their conversation with Freddy, which he'd forgotten. He wanted to keep her talking and hopefully hide his ignorance. Also, if she was talking, then he did not have to think of what to say. "Has Max talked to you about wanting to leave?"

"Not at all," she said, turning from the front window and looking at him. "I had no idea he was so fucked up."

In his peripheral vision, he noticed her narrowed eyes. She was looking at him closely, and he was fighting the temptation to look in her direction. She was expecting him to respond, but the next few seconds passed in silence.

"You know what would be fun?" she asked finally after facing forward again.

"What?"

"I can teach you how to fly this," she said. "We can do it tomorrow."

"Are you sure?" he asked. "You're not afraid I'll break it? Or crash?"

"I'll be there," she said, laughing. "I wouldn't just let you take it. Ooh, we can bring Sadi too. It can be a kind of date. What do you think?"

"It sounds fun," Gerald said, surprising himself. His instinct was to reject the offer, but maybe the experience would be therapeutic. "As long as you're there. But what about the reconfiguration?"

"Freddy said that couldn't be for a few more days," she said and stood from her seat. "I've been trying to think about how to pass the time and this would be perfect. Besides, more people need to know how to operate this thing. Will you talk to Sadi about it today?"

"Okay."

"Cool. We'll leave early in the morning," she said and squeezed his shoulder, hard. "I'm gonna get something to eat. Wanna come?"

Gerald imagined her hand on his shoulder as the claw of a giant Solka bird of prey, ready to lift him into the sky. He focused on smiling and acting unconcerned.

"I'll stay here for a little while longer," he said. "Yeah, flying should be fun."

After Taylor released her grip, she exited the jet. From the cockpit window, Gerald watched her walk across the hangar, and the cabin suddenly felt blissfully quiet and peaceful. For the next several minutes, Gerald just sat there, staring out the window and imagining the Solka carrying him to the top of a high cliff, then dropping him into a giant nest full of hungry mouths.

—✳—

After an hour of sitting and daydreaming, Gerald left the jet and walked back to his room. He passed Brian and Audrie in the hallway where all of their rooms were located. They were headed to the dining area and asked if he would meet them there. "Maybe later," he said. He remembered Brian smiling politely and Audrie looking at him curiously.

Once inside his room, he felt safe from having to socially interact with anyone. He took a shower, ate an apple from his refrigerator, then decided to skip dinner. The apple had satisfied him. He poured a glass of juice and set it on the table by his bed, next to the flower. For the next hour, he sipped the juice and read a novel, *The Scarlet Pimpernel*, one of the few books that someone brought. Gerald hoped that reading would help him gather the courage to visit Sadi and ask if she wanted to have flying lessons with him.

A sudden knocking on his door jolted Gerald from the story, and he felt a brief frustration for the interruption. In the book, he'd been enjoying the experience of rescuing the French aristocracy from the guillotine. Then he remembered what he had wanted to ask Sadi.

"It's, Sadi," she said. "Can I come in?"

"Coming," he said, his heart beating fast. He placed the book on the nightstand without marking his location. Before opening the door, he drew a deep breath. "Hi, Sadi."

"Hey," she said, walking past him. "I wanted to talk to you."

She wore a lavender t-shirt and light grey shorts, both made from the fabric that showed the thick strands of thread. Gerald immediately noticed she wasn't wearing a bra and quickly looked away, shutting the door as his heartbeat picked up even more. She took a seat on his couch and casually glanced around his room.

"How are you doing?" she asked. "I was looking for you after the meeting."

"I took a nap, then went on a walk and sat in the jet for a while," he said while sitting on the couch next to her. He required significant effort keeping his gaze level on her face. "I was going to come see you in a while."

"So how are you doing?"

"I'm doing a little better, actually," he said and noticed her dark hair falling over one shoulder, drawing his eyes to her breasts again. She moved her right leg over the other and breathed deeply. He was having difficulty thinking of what to say and how to act.

"That's good," she said, smiling wide. "At the meeting, you seemed a little more like the old Gerald. That was nice."

"It must be so strange having your son again," Gerald said, suddenly thinking of the topic and then wondering if he wanted to hear about the child. He remembered feeling frightened of him.

"Wow, I can smell that flower from here," she said with a glance at the plant. When she looked back at him, her eyes widened. "Yes, very strange. I still keep expecting to wake up and find it all a pleasant dream. But I don't like thinking of that, so I'm just trying to enjoy the time. It's been fun seeing him interact with the girls."

"I can imagine," he said, forcing himself to smile. Before he forgot again, Gerald wanted to ask her the question about the next day. "I was talking to Taylor, and she wants to give us flying lessons tomorrow, in the jet. I thought it sounded fun. Want to do it?"

"A flying lesson, hmm," she said, pursing her lips in thought. "That'd be fun."

Sadi drew a deep breath and then sighed loudly. She stood from her seat and walked to the view screen. Dzalm had already set, but the clouds on the horizon were still illuminated, filling the room with a soft light. While gazing at the screen, she stood to the side and pulled her hair over her shoulder, highlighting the shape of her breasts again. Gerald glanced at them and then quickly returned his attention to the window.

"Are the kids in bed?" Gerald asked from the couch.

"They're having a sleepover in the observatory," she answered without looking at him. "Helen wanted to have a little party for Jacob and all the kids. Taylor is being the chaperone."

Sadi stepped closer to the screen. "There's one of the moons." She turned her attention to Gerald again. "It's beautiful in the light. Come and see."

When he stepped beside her, she grabbed his shoulder and pointed at a spot in the sky. Gerald saw the illuminated satellite, but his heartbeat was too loud to focus on it. Only the warmth of her hand held his attention. In one graceful motion, Sadi turned from the screen and wrapped her other arm around him. As she pulled him close, he felt her breasts against his chest, then her warm lips.

SEVENTY-THREE

Josef

"Franklin Harvey's not there," Gordon Booth said, confusion in his eyes. "Apparently, I came to get him already."

"What do you mean?" Josef Brunner asked.

"I mean," he said and cleared his throat. "They told me that I already came two days ago and took him."

Josef had hoped to gain more personal information about Freddy from his friend, Franklin Harvey. After interrogating Franklin, Josef had planned to visit Gerda Schreiber and question her. But after discovering that Franklin had escaped from the Satsop nuclear facility in Washington, Josef Brunner had to change his plan. He would visit William Smith, Freddy's former employer.

Out of respect, Josef had delayed interrogating the old man, since he was sick and the questioning might be too stressful. But more importantly, Josef could not treat his great uncle as an ordinary suspect.

On the following journey to Portland, Josef spent most of his time consumed in thought about the case. He intentionally did not speak to Gordon Booth about Franklin's escape, hoping the silence would make Gordon worry about his failure to keep him incarcerated, and also worry about Josef's opinion of him. Although Josef did not blame Gordon or the people at the facility, a little psychological pressure might help them devise an effective method for capturing Freddy.

Despite their failure, Josef had learned an important piece of information. Freddy truly cared about his friends and would risk capture to help them. Alternatively, maybe Franklin had information that Freddy did not want to be revealed. Probably both, Josef thought.

While mentally preparing for his visit to William Smith, Josef tried to ignore his growing sense of impotence. Every method to catch Freddy had failed, all of their highly accurate tracking methods and superior military force. As he already knew, all of their methods depended on human participants to correctly interpret sensory information. He needed some sort of robotic asset that could not be psychologically manipulated.

Until he devised a better plan, Josef would not expect to catch Freddy and would focus instead on gathering intelligence, always the first step for an effective plan. Freddy had probably already visited his former employer and bypassed all of the human assets guarding his residence.

Gordon called ahead and arranged for the visit. He spoke directly to William Smith, identifying himself as a Central Intelligence officer who wanted to ask some questions. To Josef's surprise, the old man did not refuse.

"Will I participate in the interrogation?" Gordon asked after his phone call.

"No," Josef answered. "I will talk with him alone."

"Yes, sir," he answered without any hint of disappointment. "Do you want me to bring any backup?"

"No," Josef said quickly. "If Freddy's watching the residence somehow, I don't want him to take more of a defensive attitude. There's probably not much we can do anyway. Just stay alert."

"You think he might be there?" Gordon asked. "There have been no sightings."

"Would you expect any?" Josef asked.

Gordon chose not to answer.

After passing through the front gate of the residence, Gordon stayed in the car while Josef walked to the door. Although a dozen men were already watching the home and had him in their sights, Josef felt completely exposed, a new sensation for him. He had entered Freddy's territory.

A large woman met them at the main entrance, her brown hair in a tight ponytail. "CIA?" she asked. After Josef nodded, she stood aside for him to enter. She looked at him threateningly and he could feel her eyes on his back as she closed the door.

"Please wait here," she said. "I'll go tell him you have arrived."

A few minutes later, the woman returned and led Josef up a flight of stairs and through the open door of William Smith's bedroom. After she shut the door, Josef paused at the entrance to assess the situation. The old man lay on a large hospital bed with the upper half of his body inclined at a twenty-degree angle. A chair sat by the left of the bed with a monitoring machine on the other side. Oxygen tubes extended from his nose. The raspy sound of the man's breathing and the rhythmic clicking of a pump filled the room.

William Smith looked weak but had the eyes of a healthy man. Josef entered the room and stopped two meters from the foot of the bed. He glanced at the book resting on the old man's chest, just long enough to notice the word *astronomy* in the title.

"Hi, Uncle," Josef said, surprising himself. He had not intended to reveal their relationship, and he then felt the need to identify himself. "My name is Josef Brunner."

"I'm sorry," William said, squinting to see the man who had entered his room. "I apologize for not recognizing you. My memory has deteriorated a little, I'm afraid, as my eyesight."

"No need to apologize," Josef said. "My grandmother was your sister, Ingrid Schmidt."

"Ingrid," his uncle said, breathing deeply then exhaling as though savoring a memory. "Brunner, yes. She married a Brunner. I attended her funeral in Austria, over twenty years ago. Did we meet then?"

"I was not able to attend."

"Please, feel free to sit." William raised his hand from the bed and extended it to the chair at his right.

"I would prefer to stand for a few minutes at least," he said. "I've been sitting in a car for a while."

"Of course," William said. "So you are with the CIA?"

"I am not," he said and cleared his throat. "The man who called you is."

"You're here to ask about Freddy. Correct?"

"Yes."

"What do you want to know?"

"I just want to know who he is," Josef answered flatly.

"Before we continue," William said, pausing for a raspy breath. "I just want you to know that I don't have any information that will help you capture him."

"If you had such information, would you tell me?"

"No."

"Then you consider him a friend?"

"Yes," William said.

"Did he visit you recently?"

"He visited me yesterday morning," William said.

"Do you know where he went?"

"Another world."

SEVENTY-FOUR

Josef

Josef spent the next twenty minutes learning how his great uncle had met Freddy Carlson and how their relationship had developed. He learned about the young man's horrid mother and sister, about his disabilities, and then about his friends. When William mentioned their inventions, Josef suspected that the old man was withholding information, but he knew to conceal his suspicions and just let him talk. Toward the end of the discussion, Josef could see the old man losing energy.

"We can stop for a while, Uncle William," Josef said, placing his hand on the older man's shoulder as he coughed. "I apologize for the stress my visit might have caused. Do you think I can have a look at where Freddy used to stay? You left his rooms untouched, you said."

"Feel free," he answered after clearing his throat.

As Josef descended the stairs to the lower level, he began to feel some trepidation, as if he was trespassing and had a moral obligation to turn around. But he kept going and stopped after arriving at the bottom of the stairs, standing at the end of a long hallway. While deciding which closed door to open first, a vivid memory suddenly hijacked his attention, a forgotten memory from his childhood. He stood motionless for over a minute, reliving the experience.

—※—

Instead of practicing the piano after dinner as his governess in-structed, Josef played a game of hide and seek with his older brother. In one of the guest rooms, Josef was hiding inside a closet and could see nothing except for the light from under the door.

When he heard the guest room door open and his brother enter, Josef clamped his mouth shut to keep from laughing and revealing his location. But after his brother had entered the room, he stood still for several seconds, probably listening for movement.

When the door to the room suddenly slammed shut, the loud noise made Josef jump and his heart pound uncomfortably. Then a heavy chain hit the wooden floor and began sliding toward the closet. To re-cover from his sudden fright, Josef required only one deep, quiet breath.

As Josef listened to the loud scraping sound, he decided to open the door instead of having the door open on him. If he opened the door, the game would end and Josef would lose, but it would be on his terms. If Josef let his brother open the door, he would lose to his fear and the game, and there was also the chance his brother would be-come the monster from Josef's imagination.

"Du hast mich erwischt," Josef said, his hand on the doorknob and ready to twist.

But Josef did not open the door. After declaring his resignation, the chain stopped sliding across the floor, and Josef waited during the long silence. For some reason, he did not want to open the door until his brother answered. He wanted his brother to say something, any-thing. Josef held his breath.

—※—

Josef quietly turned the door knob and found himself looking inside

Freddy's bedroom. While standing in the open doorway, he realized there was a gap in his memory. He did not remember walking to the door, only opening it. In the game of hide and seek with his brother, Josef had opened the door and found his brother laughing at him for being afraid of the chain. But now the door opened to an empty room.

The low light of dusk illuminated the room just enough for Josef to see the bed, the computers, microscopes, and other instruments on the tables next to the walls. He turned on the lights then stepped to the bed and inspected the white sheets. They were perfectly smooth and undisturbed as if no one had slept there for years.

When the electric discharge shook the room, Josef jolted. In his peripheral vision, he watched the lights in the ceiling get brighter and then die. He was suddenly paralyzed while listening for another sound. He no longer felt alone.

"Are you in here, Freddy?" he asked, chills coursing through his core. "Show yourself."

No response.

Josef removed his cell phone from his back pocket and activated the camera. In the low light, he extended it forward and started recording. He walked across the room and recorded everything in front of him. At several points, he saw a flash of movement in the corner of the screen, what looked like a moving shadow, but when he moved the camera to catch it, he found nothing. He walked back to the bed and aimed the phone at the covers. When Josef saw what lay on the bed, he froze and could not move.

A small boy lay on top of the covers, curled into the fetal position and breathing softly with his face hidden behind both fists. He had short blond hair, nearly white, and wore faded yellow pajamas with ugly brown stains on them. For nearly a minute, Josef just stared at the sleeping child through his cell phone.

Josef removed the phone to see with his own eyes, but he saw only an empty bed. When he returned to the camera view, the child was no longer asleep. He was sitting on the end of the bed, right in front of the camera lens and looking up. The child was looking through Josef, not at him. When he saw the child this time, he recognized the boy— his son.

Josef stepped back in fright and almost fell to the floor, but he managed to keep the phone aimed at the child. As another test, he removed the phone from between them and his son disappeared.

"Are you doing this, Freddy?" he asked in a whisper, looking around the room. Josef inhaled slowly through his nose and told himself to think rationally. He kept the camera aimed at the ground, afraid to look through it again. "Why are you showing my son?"

No answer.

For the present, Josef would ignore the reason and just accept the child as a hallucination fabricated by Freddy. It was strange though, and contradicted what he had originally intended. Josef had used the camera to see through the illusion, hoping to catch Freddy. Instead, the illusion was projected directly into his mind through the phone. As an opponent, Josef continued to appreciate Freddy's abilities and tactics.

Josef could waste time considering all the possible reasons for Freddy showing his son, or he could just play Freddy's game. He was tired of swimming in an ocean of possibilities, a slave to a powerful current. He felt more secure on dry land.

"I will play your game, Freddy," he whispered.

With some trepidation, Josef aimed his camera at the bed again to see what Freddy wanted to show him. The image of the child immediately returned to his cell phone screen, a perfect replica of his son. The child sat on the bed, looking at the floor as though waiting. When he turned to face Josef, he seemed to look through him again. Josef had never seen him so sad and frightened.

The next few seconds passed quickly, leaving Josef feeling dizzy and disoriented. The screen expanded until his son, the bed, and the wall behind them were the only things he could see. The whole world now was coming through his phone. But he had little time to reorient himself to the situation before the door opened and a woman appeared.

The boy turned from Josef, jumped off the bed, and faced the woman with wide eyes.

Josef was shocked when he recognized the woman. She was his wife. She had plastered her once-beautiful face with cheap makeup and her long blond hair seemed to explode from her head, frizzy, matted, and intentionally arranged that way. Tight blue jeans squeezed large hips and thighs, and a low-cut white shirt accentuated several rolls of belly fat.

"You're going to live somewhere else," she said to their son.

"I will live with someone else?" the boy asked and immediately began hyperventilating. He covered his face with both hands and shook his head slowly, speaking between deep breaths.

"I will be good."

"I promise."

"I cannot stay here?"

"Look at me," Josef's wife said with angry eyes, but she did not wait for the boy to uncover his face. "A woman is waiting for you. She'll take you to people who know how to deal with your problems. You're sucking me dry, leaving nothing left for your sister. She needs my attention now."

His wife did not wait for the young child, their son, to move on his own. She stepped behind him and had to push him out of the room. Tears poured down his cheeks, but grief and shock prevented the boy from wiping them away.

Without choosing to move on his own, Josef felt himself stand from the bed and follow his wife and son into the hallway. While following them toward the stairs, Josef daydreamed about his other life.

He said goodbye to his Great Uncle William, wished him well, and thanked him for allowing the visit. He traveled in a helicopter to Peterson Air Force Base with Gordon Booth. "I need to make a report on what we've learned," Josef heard himself say. Then he spent several hours in a high-altitude jet watching the clouds far below him.

Josef was now standing on a lawn covered with dandelions, watching as a social worker delivered his son to the foster home. When he noticed the foster mother's fake smile and exaggerated affection, an overwhelming anger drove all other thoughts from his mind. But Josef could do nothing to alleviate the fright in his son's eyes. He could only watch.

After the social worker drove away, the foster mother gave his son a quick tour of the small house then put him in a room by himself and shut the door. While standing where the woman had left him, the boy inspected his new room with wide eyes. The room was small and had several cardboard boxes stacked in one corner by his bed. Crayon markings and dirty hand smudges covered the cream-green walls. In contrast to the dirty walls, the thick brown carpet looked freshly vac-uumed. After inspecting the room, his son walked into the closet and shut the door behind him.

Then Josef was standing inside the closet with him, the only light entering from under the door. His son sat in the corner, knees pulled to his chest and counting each deep breath. Frozen and silent, Josef counted with him.

While watching his son and wishing he could help, Josef imagined having a conversation on the phone with his superiors. "I need to dis-cuss the situation with you in person. Yes, I'll meet you at the library." Then he was watching more clouds far below him. When the first white iceberg appeared in his view, he heard a noise from the other side of the closet door. A man had entered the room.

"Where is he?" the man asked in frustration.

"I left him in here," a woman answered. "I know he didn't leave."

"Check the closet."

Josef's son stopped counting and held his breath until the closet door opened. As light flooded the small space, Josef felt his own heart pumping wildly as if the man was looking for him too. His son kept his face hidden.

"Hey, little guy," the man said, attempting to sound friendly. "What are you doing in the closet?"

When Josef's son failed to respond or lift his head, the man sighed impatiently. "Geez kid, we're not going to hurt you."

"Hey," the woman said. "Look at us when we're talking to you."

"This is going to be fun," her husband said when the child failed to move. He turned and walked away. "I'm hungry. This is your problem."

After her husband left the room, the woman reached down and pulled the boy's hands away from his face. Josef's son opened his eyes but kept looking at his knees. Then she squeezed his chin and forced him to look at her.

"It's not our fault your dad left and your mom can't handle you. Now get up. It's time for dinner. I have two sons and they're waiting to meet you."

SEVENTY-FIVE

Taylor

After leaving Gerald in the jet, Taylor walked to the dining area, thinking about their conversation and his strange behavior. In the far corner of her awareness, she felt uneasy about flying with him the next day. His state of mind had seemed to improve, but he was still not the same man she remembered. *Maybe he's just pretending to feel better and thinking that will help*, she thought and smiled. *That's something Gerald would do.*

Everyone had dinner together that night, except for Gerald, Max, Audrie, and Freddy. Taylor was relieved for Max's absence but not Freddy's. She had wanted to talk to him about taking Sadi and Gerald on the flight the next day. Although the activity seemed benign, she wanted Freddy's opinion about its effect on Gerald. Taylor would feel better if he approved. Later that night, if she was still too concerned, she might invite Max. She considered asking Mark but did not want to risk upsetting Susan. She seemed more calm than earlier in the day.

At least Taylor did not have to deal with Max and could have dinner in peace without the fear of a confrontation with him. If she did see him, she did not plan to initiate a conversation.

She sat next to Sadi and Jacob during dinner. The little boy asked many questions, seemingly unrelated. *What was her favorite color? Was she smarter than the average boy? Would she jump in ice water?* While answering all of his questions, she suspected that he just liked talking to her. She enjoyed their short conversations too.

Taylor considered talking to Sadi about the flight lessons but decided to let Gerald initiate that conversation. It was his idea and maybe he had planned a special way of asking her.

As usual, the four other children sat together but seemed more excited than usual. When Taylor was almost done eating, Daryn approached them and asked Sadi if they could have a sleepover with Jacob in the observatory. Before answering, Sadi turned to Susan on the other side of the table.

"What do you think, Susan?"

"I don't know," Susan said and Taylor thought the woman was going to say no.

"I can chaperone," Taylor said, wide eyes and attempting to look innocently impartial.

"I guess," Susan said. "If you're okay with it, Sadi."

After a quick smile at Taylor, Sadi turned to Jacob. "Want to have a sleepover with the others?"

"Oh yes," he said, then turned to his older sister. "In the observatory, on the floor?"

"Yep, and with all the lights off!"

After dinner, Taylor took a shower and brushed her teeth in preparation for the night, possibly a long night. The children were waiting for her to take them to the observatory for their sleepover. Taylor had spent a lot of time with the children on the station and expected a night with little sleep. She remembered having sleepovers with her friends, and the excitement of sleeping in a familiar place where you normally don't sleep. While preparing for the night, she wondered how she would have felt on the station.

Five minutes later, Taylor stood outside the door to Sadi's room with several blankets and a pillow clasped to her chest. The four older kids were waiting impatiently behind her, talking about how much fun they were going to have. When Sadi opened the door, Jacob was standing at her side, a pillow under one arm and two blankets tucked under the other arm.

"Are you ready, Jacob?" Taylor asked.

"Oh yes," he said, quickly joining the other kids in the hallway.

"If you need anything, feel free to wake me up at any time," Sadi said, smiling wide.

"We'll be fine," Taylor said while turning to the kids, "as long as each of you have gone to the bathroom?"

Before she shut the door to her room, Sadi hugged Jacob one last time then told all of the kids to listen to Taylor and do what she said. Taylor told them to follow her and not run ahead. They had plenty of time to have fun together. As they began walking, she heard a sound and saw Gerald open his door. He looked at Taylor as though surprised to see her.

"I'm going to ask Sadi about tomorrow," he said. While passing her, he smiled nervously and raised his eyebrows in a *wish-me-luck* sort of way.

"I'm looking forward to it," Taylor said and continued following the kids. They were not going to wait for her. She took a deep breath and sighed. "Wish me luck."

Before turning the corner, Taylor glanced back as Sadi opened her door and began talking with Gerald, but after returning her attention to the kids, Taylor forgot about them. The anticipation of a long night consumed her thoughts. She could not worry about Gerald. He was on his own.

Taylor attempted to blend into the background and let the kids enjoy the night as if no adult accompanied them. That had been her plan, but Jacob kept her occupied with his questions. And then the other children began asking questions and she spent several hours telling them stories of her childhood. They asked about her brother and she had to tell them what happened, about the war in Iraq, his depression afterward, and his suicide.

To her surprise, she did not become emotional. The children kept her too busy, responding to their reactions and resulting emotions. They asked a lot about war in general and the reasons for it. The conversation became a revelation to Taylor. If their new life was on Bodn, then the affairs on Earth were only a story to them and would not impact their lives.

While explaining, she felt more adamant than ever about the future. She would not let Bodn become another Earth, at least not the human society on Earth. She would help to teach the children how to think for themselves and not let anyone deceive them. Taylor hoped that Freddy was correct and the reconfiguration would help make the children more impervious to psychological manipulation.

Taylor woke up before any of the children and needed to use the restroom. The view screen in the center of the large room provided enough light to see the outline of the children under the jumble of blankets on the floor around her. From the light level, Taylor guessed that Dzalm had not yet risen but would soon.

As Taylor prepared to stand, she noticed the small body cuddled into her back, Jacob. While enjoying the warm sensation, she spent the next few minutes listening to all of the soft breathing around her. She would have a child of her own one day, she decided. The possibility no longer frightened her. The future seemed full of opportunities.

Although Taylor could have returned to sleep, she decided to start her day. She carefully detached herself from Jacob and stood on her feet, careful not to make any noise, then tiptoed over the other children who had all fallen asleep near her. Before leaving the room, she paused at the entrance to see if any of the children had noticed.

Taylor ran into Gerald and Sadi on the way back to her room. As she approached, only Sadi was smiling. Gerald looked a little nervous.

"How was your night?" Sadi asked.

"Not that bad actually," Taylor said and laughed. "The kids talked my ears off. They fell asleep around one in the morning."

"So they should be out for a while," Sadi said, also laughing. "Last night, I told Susan that we would be leaving in the morning, so she'll get the kids while we're out, flying around. I'm kind of excited. This is going to be fun. I promise not to crash."

Taylor had not expected to see them ready so early and felt rushed, wanting more time to assess the situation. She had expected to leave later and wanted to talk with Cesar first, and hopefully convince him to come. Taylor opened her mouth, about to tell them of her plan, but she noticed movement behind them. Freddy was approaching.

"Hey, guys," he said, his lips stretched into a wide smile. "Can I come too?"

"Hi, Freddy," Taylor said, feeling relieved to see him. "Yes, please join us. You obviously know what we're doing."

"Yes," he said and laughed. "And I think it's a great idea."

SEVENTY-SIX

Taylor

Freddy was the last to enter the jet, after Taylor. As she closed the door behind him, he sat in the front seat of the cabin. Taylor enjoyed hearing the click of the seal. The sound always gave her a small feeling of satisfaction and security.

For the first ten minutes, Taylor stood in the cockpit and explained the basic controls and engine placements. Gerald was sitting in the pilot's seat with Sadi next to him as the copilot. They listened intently and seemed to understand everything. Taylor was surprised at the scarcity of their questions and suspected they just wanted to get started.

"Click on the folder named, *Maneuvers*," she said and watched as Gerald opened the folder, revealing a list of files, her flight programs for the jet. "We could fly out manually, but it will be easier to learn the controls when there's nothing around to run into."

"Good idea," Gerald said and chuckled. "Is it the *hangar_exit* file?"

"That's the one," she answered. "Click it, then select *OK* at the prompt."

"Aren't you going to sit down and get buckled up?" he asked after clicking on the file and then hovering the mouse pointer over the *OK* button.

"Only when you start actually managing the controls," she said seriously, keeping her eyes on the computer screen.

Gerald clicked the button and Taylor felt the jet begin to ascend from the floor. The occupants of the cockpit watched through the front window as the jet slowly turned and began moving toward the massive hangar doors. When the jet came within twenty meters from them, they began to slide open. Their view showed a sky full of stars and a narrow strip of oceans on Bodn, illuminated by Dzalm from behind the station.

The flight program oriented the jet so they faced the station while moving away from it. After entering the void of space, the distance between the station and the jet continued to increase, almost too slowly to notice. Despite having plenty of experience already in space, Taylor still felt disoriented while traveling there. Without anything physically connecting them to the station, it just seemed to shrink instead of getting farther away.

While the station blended into the background of space, Taylor explained how to control the engines. After she felt satisfied with their understanding, she told Gerald to stop the exit maneuver and initiate manual control of the spacecraft. He followed her instructions, then she told him to cut the engine power.

"I wasn't expecting that," Sadi said as the jet suddenly became weightless. "I thought it would be a slower transition."

To keep herself from floating away, Taylor held onto the edge of the loadlock seal between the cabin and cockpit. "I just wanted you to feel how quickly the engines respond," she said while suppressing a smile of satisfaction.

"So we're falling toward the planet, right?" Gerald asked, holding onto the seat's armrests. "It doesn't look like we're falling."

"We are falling alright," Taylor said and laughed. "Remember, you can always look at the *Spacetime* screen to see our altitude, trajectory, and the time remaining until the next calculated collision."

"Just over four minutes before we crash into the ocean," Sadi said, looking up at Taylor. "Does that take into account the drag from the atmosphere?"

"Not on the *Spacetime* screen," Taylor said and pointed to another icon on the main screen. "But the *Estimation* folder contains some common calculation programs. Let's get further out and then we can do some maneuvers."

"Okay, Gerald, begin acceleration in the upward direction. Remember, no matter what our orientation is with Bodn, when I say *up*, I will always mean relative to the jet interior. If you accelerate upward until it feels like normal gravity, what would that mean?"

Gerald sat back against his seat and stared forward. He was probably attempting to remember the controls while also listening to her. He grabbed the yoke with both hands. "If it feels like normal gravity, that means our altitude is constant."

"Correct," Taylor said, satisfied, though she had expected a different answer. "We need to accelerate more if we want to move to any higher altitude. So take us up at twice normal gravity. You can always look at the *Spacetime* screen or do what I like to do, try to feel it first and then check to see how close you got."

"Start now?"

"Yes."

When Gerald began acceleration, the hum of the engines replaced the silence, and the jet suddenly felt like a living creature, powerful and ready to run. As the acceleration increased, Taylor released her grasp of the loadlock door between the cockpit and cabin. When they accelerated past normal gravity, the muscles in her legs began tightening to handle the extra load. She loved the sensation of increasing weight and then felt sorry for all of the overweight people back on Earth.

"This feels about twice normal gravity," Gerald said while looking at the computer screen. "I was pretty close. It's almost two and a half times more."

"It's a nice workout," Taylor said, bending her knees a little, then straightening them again. "Let's wait a few minutes until we get about three times as far out."

In less than a minute, the station blended with the background of space and disappeared. Only a sliver of Bodn was visible at the bottom of the front window, but as even more time passed, Bodn had disappeared from their view, leaving only the stars.

Taylor never tired of seeing all the celestial objects: Bodn, its satellites, stars, galaxies, nebulae. If Taylor let herself, she would probably fall into a trance just watching it all. No one spoke during the time. Everyone was enjoying the view.

Taylor loved the feeling of peace. Only the sound of the engines and their breathing filled the interior of the jet, reminding Taylor of their trip to Mercury after Earth had become just another star. She remembered feeling almost totally isolated from humanity, and amazement at the immensity of the universe. When the fatigue began in her legs, she looked at their altitude, fifteen hundred kilometers.

"I guess this is far enough," she said. "Time to play."

After giving Gerald and Sadi some additional instruction, Taylor joined Freddy in the cabin. She buckled herself into the seat and told them to begin testing the controls. They could take turns flying the jet, practicing whatever they wanted. The jet would warn them if any trajectory involved a collision.

Taylor began having fun almost immediately. Having Freddy on the other side of the aisle was also comforting. If they got into some sort of trouble, he could help. She was also excited for Gerald. He would have some good bonding time with Sadi. Taylor was glad for them but recalled her time with Max in the BMW, a bittersweet memory.

While Gerald and Sadi practiced flying, Taylor looked through the window and did not have to intervene. She enjoyed transitioning between weightlessness and acceleration in multiple directions, seeing Bodn suddenly come into view only to disappear a moment later. *No rollercoaster on Earth could compare with this ride*, she thought during the first full rotation of the jet.

"They're doing pretty well," Freddy whispered. He leaned into the aisle toward Taylor and put an index finger over his mouth. "I think they like each other."

"Ya think?" Taylor laughed, suddenly uneasy with Freddy so close.

When he sat back in his seat again, he resumed facing the window. He remained silent for a few more minutes, and Taylor enjoyed looking out the window again. But she jolted when he spoke next.

"I'm doing pretty good," he began while still facing the window. "So far, I've kept you all safe. After all the work you've done, it would be a pity for me to fail, especially for you and Gerald, the ones who started it all. You guys really put everything on the line for the rest of us."

"Yes," she said, a warning suddenly pounding inside her skull like a headache. She forced a smile. "Thanks for all you're doing for us."

Taylor faced her window and concentrated on listening to the conversation between Gerald and Sadi in the cockpit. While Gerald took another turn controlling the jet, Sadi talked about how much Helen would love flying lessons. Daryn was probably too timid for them, but Sadi knew the young girl needed her traumatic past buried beneath additional pleasant experiences. Since arriving at the station, Sadi had already seen amazing growth and thought the young girl had plenty of time to heal, so there was no rush.

Sadi and Gerald suddenly stopped talking.

During the next five seconds, the jet began accelerating toward Bodn, under them, until the seatbelt straps dug into Taylor's shoulders hard enough to hurt. Although her orientation in the jet remained the same, their artificial gravity had flipped. Only the straps prevented her from falling into the ceiling.

"We have a problem," Gerald said loudly. "Taylor, you need to come up here."

"Cut the thrust and then I can get out of my seat."

"That's the problem," he said. "I can't do anything. The main screen just went blank and the controls don't work anymore."

"Give me a second," Taylor said with a glance at Freddy. He was sitting in his seat and calmly looking out the window, not seeming to notice her. Taylor's heart thumped loudly in her chest. "I need to get un-strapped."

Taylor unbuckled one strap, then held onto it as she worked on the others. When the last buckle clicked free, she lost her grip and fell toward the ceiling. Just before impact, she managed to grasp the strap again, cringing as it burned the palm of her right hand.

Ignoring the pain, she quickly got to her feet and began walking unsteadily on the ceiling, heading for the cockpit. To her horror, one of her worst fears was confirmed. The main computer had lost power but for some reason, the engines had failed to follow the reset condition by automatically adjusting to cancel their acceleration.

"Are you guys okay?" she asked while looking at Sadi, nearly at eye level but from upside down. Her dangling ponytail swung close to Taylor's face.

"I didn't do this intentionally," Gerald said. "The jet just took off then all of the computer screens went blank."

Taylor heard a thud from behind her, the sound of someone landing on their feet. She turned and saw Freddy standing on the ceiling with her. He stepped into the cockpit entrance and stopped behind Taylor.

"What seems to be the problem?" he asked, showing no concern.

"The computer shut off," Taylor said, then drew a deep breath to fight the lump of panic in her throat. "I should be able to do a reboot. A flash drive has the backup. It's in that compartment at your right, Sadi. Can you get it for me?"

"Sure." Sadi opened the small compartment and several items fell to the ceiling at Taylor's feet. "Oops, sorry."

"That's fine," Taylor said, feeling dizzy from the inverse gravity. She paused a moment before bending down and grabbing the blue flash drive from the ceiling. "Gerald, put this in the drive port. Okay, good. Now hold down the computer power key."

While Gerald pressed the key with his thumb, Taylor began whispering. "One, two, three, four..." When five seconds passed without any change to the computer screens, her heart seemed to sink into her stomach. The computer should have rebooted.

"How long do I have to hold this down?" Gerald asked.

"I don't understand," Taylor said, her panic growing. "It should have rebooted. Let go and try again."

After five more seconds, the same result happened, nothing. They now had five fewer seconds than before.

"Not rebooting, eh?" Freddy said from behind her. "We knew you'd be prepared for a computer malfunction. What are you going to do next?"

"What are we going to do?" Taylor asked, turning to him. Her confusion was now anger. "We've got to get the fucking computer back up!"

"Quite a dilemma," he said in an appreciative tone and nodded. "You've got only a few minutes more to find the solution before we hit the atmosphere and vaporize."

"This better not be another one of your lessons, Freddy?" Taylor said. Although extremely angry now, she waited with hopeful anticipation for an affirmative answer.

"We're sorry," he said, frowning and shaking his head as though sincerely apologetic. He placed a warm hand on Taylor's shoulder. "But we are not Freddy."

"What?" she asked.

"Try not to panic," he continued, gently squeezing her shoulder. "It will all be over very quickly. By the time we hit the atmosphere, we'll be going fast enough to vaporize in just a few seconds, a very merciful death. And to show our good sportsmanship, we're going with you, down with the ship, so to speak. Then we can guide you back home."

Taylor, Gerald, and Sadi all turned to look at the impostor. Feeling his grasp on her shoulder made Taylor's eyes open wider. Her mind suddenly felt empty, with only the power to observe.

Sadi broke the silence. "Who are you?"

"We are representatives from home," he said. "Your true home, Earth. Did you think we would just let you leave?"

"Where is Freddy?" Sadi asked, calmly. "How can you be Freddy?"

"Freddy's been keeping some secrets from you," he said. "But understandably, considering your limited capacity."

Taylor pulled away from his grasp and stepped closer to the dashboard, between Gerald and Sadi, and above the front window. Her anger was now fear. To catch up with her heart, she began breathing faster.

"We've got a couple of minutes to spare, so let us help you understand," the impostor said. "Like us, Freddy can manage multiple bodies and assimilate their information simultaneously. Currently, he is preoccupied back home, and we trapped the one who helps him, so they don't notice we've borrowed his spare body."

"So you're here to kill us," Sadi said calmly.

"It's gotta be a test," Gerald said, drawing Taylor's attention to his upside-down face. "What can I do?"

"That's a good idea," the impostor answered and nodded in approval. "It will help the time go by more quickly."

Taylor began desperately scavenging for viable solutions but had to reject all of them. Each option required too much time, and even if she thought of a shorter solution, she would have to work on the computer while it was above her head, requiring even more time.

"You couldn't come up with a better plan and kill everyone?" Sadi asked curiously, as though she spoke of a mere board game strategy. "You failed to manipulate us, so you're just going to kill us? Not very creative or elegant."

"It is a beautiful plan," the Freddy impostor said, affronted. "When the rest of your friends learn of your death, they'll beg us to come back."

"You have very high confidence," Sadi said, smiling wryly. "I'll give you that. But after your stolen body *dies*, I will kill your connection to this place."

Instead of responding, the impostor stared at Sadi like a reptile, cocking his head while looking at her. During several seconds of frozen eye contact, Taylor held her breath. Although he appeared identical to Freddy, the impostor suddenly looked like a stranger.

"What do you mean?"

"You don't know?" Sadi asked, sarcastic and smiling as if about to laugh.

"We will keep returning," he said, confused. "You know this."

"We shall see."

The space around Sadi began shimmering like air over a hot road and a wave of nausea quickly spread through Taylor's gut. As her consciousness threatened to expire, the edges of her vision began to turn black.

But after just a few seconds, Taylor's vision returned to normal and her nausea decreased to a tolerable level. Sadi turned to the dashboard, spreading her fingers over its surface and the screens illuminated again. Then she grasped the yoke and stopped their acceleration in just a few seconds.

Before Taylor could readjust completely to weightlessness, Sadi unbuckled herself and pushed herself toward the impostor. While floating toward him, she flipped in the air and landed on the ceiling next to him. He simply watched and did not attempt to stop her as she pulled him by the shoulder into the cabin. With her back to them, Sadi held the impostor suspended in the air, his feet a few centimeters away from the ceiling. He was facing Taylor and Gerald in the cockpit and hung from Sadi's grasp like a stuffed animal.

"Your plan would never find success," the impostor said to Sadi. "You have to know that."

Sadi said nothing.

"You think your lives were unfair," he said, turning to Taylor and Gerald in the cockpit. "We are merciful and let you live in a beautiful world with friends and family. And your pain is only temporary, erased after each cycle."

Chills coursed through Taylor's core. The man's eyes suddenly looked like windows to an alternate universe, a place without light and full of savage creatures, but she could not look away.

In her peripheral vision, Sadi put her hand against the wall, fingers extended again. Before Taylor could comprehend what was happening, the loadlock door separating the cabin from the cockpit slid shut, and she heard the click of the airtight seal.

After the airlock door had shut, effectively cutting eye contact with the impostor, Taylor regained control of herself again. But Gerald sprang to life before she could do anything. He rammed into the door in a futile attempt to break it down.

"Sadi, no!" he yelled, watching through the small window at the top. "There's got to be another way."

"What's happening?" Taylor asked.

"I think she's going to open the door and get sucked out with him," he said in panic, pounding the door with his fist. "How do you open this?"

Taylor turned to the dashboard, preparing to shove herself from the wall toward the controls. But when Gerald yelled again for Sadi to stop, a loud noise burst from the cabin. The panic in his eyes suddenly vanished, replaced by confusion. After pulling him out of her way, Taylor looked in the window but required several seconds to interpret the scene. One of the station's robot machines stood at the open jet door, the fast-approaching Bodn clearly visible.

In contrast to their speed, Freddy's impostor was floating slowly away from the jet, covering his eyes to keep them from bursting. A few seconds later, blood began escaping from under his hands, bright red globules of liquid, which exploded into puffs of red mist.

A brilliant light suddenly appeared between him and the jet—the probe—the light of Dzalm reflecting off its mirror surface. The light nearly blinded her, but she managed to watch as the strings of light from the open end of the probe wrapped themselves around the impostor. Then in a blur of speed, the probe propelled him like a missile toward Bodn. In amazement, Taylor watched as his body shrunk to a small dot and then became a bright flash, a shooting star.

SEVENTY-SEVEN

Josef

Josef stood at the edge of a large floating platform in the Southern Ocean, holding frozen handrails and staring at a choppy sea. As he waited for the transport to the library, the cold wind attempted to steal all of his warmth. Despite the cold, he loved this part of the journey, seeing what very few humans got to see, the giant ice walls of Antarctica. While staring at the impenetrable frozen fortress, Josef daydreamed of a strange woman scolding a frightened little boy—his son.

The white wall on the horizon separated the cloudy sky from the grey water and vanished into a thin line in both directions. Even in the absence of direct sunlight, the wall still seemed to shine. Josef tried imagining the reaction of an ancient whaler, sailing in the treacherous waters and seeing the frozen cliffs. He would have wanted to see what lay beyond them.

Large waves crashed against the platform, spraying him with mist. The platform was larger than a football field and painted white to resemble just another great ice sheet. He could have waited with the other visitors in the warmth of the bunkers below, but he preferred to experience the harsh Antarctic environment alone. It was beautiful and he needed the solitude.

When the submarine surfaced several hundred meters from the platform, Josef thought he was seeing a whale. The submarine rose above the water slowly and approached them as the clouds, moving almost imperceptibly. A few minutes later, an older man and woman joined him at the edge of the platform and they all watched the approaching submarine in silence. Speaking felt like blasphemy to the awesome power of nature and the audacity of humanity for intruding in it.

Josef spent the next forty minutes with the old couple in the passenger cabin of the submarine. The couple sat on a cushioned bench and talked while Josef stood at the thick glass windows on the other side. He never saw much through the glass, but when the submarine slid under the ice shelf and all of the light vanished, he felt as if they had entered an empty universe. He listened to the old couple as they conversed with each other in some African language.

During their journey through the dark channels under the ice, Josef imagined a child standing next to him, a small boy with white hair. If he looked down at his side, Josef almost expected to see the boy. But he just kept looking through the window, waiting for the reappearance of light.

—※—

"Welcome to the library," an old man said from the top of the steps. He spoke with an English accent, and the cold dry air made his white breath as thick as smoke. He nodded politely to the couple as they walked past him. When Josef reached the top, the man grabbed his left shoulder. "Welcome back, Josef. It's a pleasure to see you again."

Josef bowed slightly before answering, keeping eye contact but noticing the iridescent material of his dark blue suit. "The pleasure is mine, Secretary."

They stood above the subglacial river where the submarine had surfaced, in a rectangular cavern carved into the mountain. Josef remembered the dimensions, eleven meters high, thirty-three meters wide, and eleven meters deep. White lights in the ceiling illuminated three open tunnel entrances, allowing the areas between them to remain in partial shadow.

The old man turned to face the wall, waiting silently and allowing Josef to appreciate the scene. The tallest tunnel was in the middle and formed the trunk of an intricate tree carved into the rock. The tree reached the ceiling, and its branches spread across the entire wall. The carving of a three-meter-tall woman stood under the tree to the right of the tunnels. She faced the entrances, her hand extended with an open palm and her lips curved into a serene smile. A man of the same height was carved on the left side of the tunnels, facing Josef with arms folded across his chest. His stone eyes seemed alive.

"When would you like to meet to discuss the case?" Josef asked, breaking the silence. "Now?"

"No, of course not," the man said. "You must be exhausted from your journey. We can meet in the morning after you've had a decent rest."

"Thank you, Secretary."

Josef turned for one more look at the docking station below them. The peaceful sound of flowing water echoed inside the immense ice cavern, adding to the serene atmosphere. Long steel beams extended from the rock wall below him, supporting the dark ceiling against roughly two kilometers of Antarctic ice. The translucent walls simultaneously reflected and absorbed the artificial lights. While staring at them, Josef wondered if any sunlight could penetrate so much ice.

"You know how this works," the man said as he began walking toward the tunnel on the left. "Find an available room, and I will meet you in the morning."

The old man disappeared into the tunnel, leaving Josef alone in the cavern. He had two choices, enter the library through the entrance in the center or find a boarding room through the right, next to the carving of the woman.

While struggling with the decision, Josef imagined his son sitting at a table in a cluttered and dirty kitchen. The child was holding his right hand flat on the table, palm down. The foster mother stood on the other side of the table, next to her older son, who watched Josef's son with a mixture of fear and excitement. He kept glancing between the young child and his father, who held a wooden ruler.

The boy on the other side of the table was squinting in anger at Josef's son. "I told him not to play with it, Dad."

"Is that true, Freddy?"

The child did not look up at the man or answer. He stared at the table, eyes wide with fear. Josef stood like a ghost on the other side of the room, only able to watch. He did not understand why the man called his son, Freddy, but that did not seem to matter. The boy appeared exactly like his son.

"It's very simple, Freddy," the man said, dramatically slapping the ruler against his own palm. "You don't touch other people's things, especially mine."

Josef could hear his son's heartbeat. The fast rhythm matched his own.

"You will obey the rules of the house," the man said, hitting Freddy's fingers with the metal edge of the ruler. The child cried out in pain, attempting to pull his hand away, but the man pinned his wrist to the table. As he raised his hand to strike again, Josef winced. But he felt a small hand grasp his own.

The kitchen setting vanished and Josef was staring at the wall again and the beautiful tree carved into the stone. Tears were running down his cheeks. When he looked down, he saw a child at his side, holding his hand. The child had messy white hair and sunglasses concealing his eyes.

"That's enough," the child said gently. With his other hand, he pointed behind Josef.

Josef turned and saw a shiny metal object rising above the edge of the railing. He wanted to wipe the tears from his eyes, but it came into full view, and he could not move or look away. The object was shaped like a giant bullet with an extremely sharp tip. As it floated toward them, the lights from the cavern reflected off its polished surface, casting light and dancing shadows all over the walls.

The bullet passed Josef at eye level, just a meter away. When it came between him and the middle tunnel entrance, Josef saw long tendrils of light extending from the back, silent and floating in defiance of gravity.

"Who are you?" Josef asked, not looking down but keeping his eyes on the large bullet.

"You know who I am," the child said. He released Josef's hand and began walking toward the tunnel entrance. "Follow the probe or stay here. It is your choice. I don't need you anymore."

Josef did not hesitate or look away. He began following, the fear in his son's eyes still fresh in his mind. "Was that your memory?" he asked. Speaking helped the experience feel more real and less like a dream.

"Yes," the child said as he entered the tunnel. Small lights at the edges of the floor gave just enough illumination to see the walls but kept the ceiling in shadow.

While waiting for the child to speak again, Josef kept his focus on the back of the probe and the lights. He felt like a character in a fairy tale, under the spell of a thousand magic wands. Although he could only follow and observe, he could still gather intelligence.

Pleasant memories of his first visit to the library suddenly flooded his thoughts. He remembered his amazement when he saw for the first time the ornate carvings at the tunnel entrances. Just like that first time and every visit afterward, Josef extended his right hand to the wall and slid his fingers along the perfectly smooth surface. He remembered his father telling him about the library's construction.

"So you moved the records and historical artifacts after the war," the child said, breaking the spell of his memories. "You transferred them from Vatican City."

"How do you know that?" Josef asked, then realized the answer. The child was scanning Josef's memories. They were not randomly appearing in his mind.

"And many are from the library in Alexandria before that."

SEVENTY-EIGHT

Josef

"Why are you appearing to me as a child, Freddy?" Josef asked. "How do I know that any of this is real?"

During the following silence, Josef considered stopping. He needed to prevent Freddy from stealing more classified information. But before he could continue assessing his options, the world disappeared.

Josef was standing in the dark, with soft dirt and decaying leaves under his bare feet.

The peaceful silence succumbed to the sound of trees swaying, then screeches from birds and monkeys, high above him and far away in every direction. When he took his first breath, humid air filled his lungs, and he was assaulted by the scent of thick vegetation.

The growling began soon afterward and Josef froze in terror. A large jungle cat was somewhere in front of him. The deep frequency of its growl vibrated his whole body, and he suddenly understood how the cat's prey felt before being ripped apart. On the left, he thought there was movement, the glint of liquid eyes vanishing into the foliage. He took a step backward.

The screeching of birds and monkeys grew in volume and the cat roared again, then another cat somewhere behind him. The noise soon became overwhelming, and painful to his ears. "This is not real," Josef yelled, but he could not even hear himself.

"But this is real," Freddy said.

The underground world reappeared, and the silence felt like a slap to the face. Sweat covered Josef's body, making the cold air even more penetrating. He shivered.

After seeing his new surroundings, he noticed the probe. It floated at eye level, the sharp tip almost touching his forehead. Josef gulped, standing perfectly still. After drawing breath, he acquired the courage to speak.

"How did we get here?" he asked, looking beyond the probe to his new location, an immense oval cavern.

Freddy stood at the center of a giant compass carved into the stone floor. He was facing North, away from Josef. Tunnel entrances surrounded them, and lights in the ceiling illuminated inscriptions carved above each entrance.

"We walked here," Freddy said from the center of the room. "You can remember it if you try hard enough."

The probe suddenly turned and began floating away from him toward the north entrance. Freddy followed it. With the sharp tip no longer close to his head, Josef felt some relief and also amazement at how the probe maintained a constant height above the floor. But Josef did not like where they were going.

"I could take you on a tour of that west tunnel," Josef said, pointing to his left. Maybe he could stall by engaging Freddy in conversation or distracting him somehow. He hoped security was monitoring the situation and preparing to intervene. "It's the history of my genealogical line and overlaps a little with the world you know."

The child did not even pause and continued following the probe into the north tunnel. Josef suddenly remembered the jungle and the horrible noise again, so he decided to start walking before Freddy sent him there again. The memory made him shudder.

While following the child, he wondered how his superiors would react to his failure to divert Freddy to one of the other tunnels. The north tunnel contained some of their most valuable secrets, those shared by all of the sovereign families.

The other tunnels represented separate, family genealogical lines, the preeminent families of the world. Each tunnel contained the historical records of their family, along with their most precious heirlooms and artifacts. Only the north tunnel had no specific family attachment. The north tunnel contained the artifacts and records of the time before the sovereign families joined together.

The probe floated at the child's pace and Freddy followed in silence, casually as if he felt no danger of apprehension. A few minutes later, a woman and teenage boy walked past them. They did not show any sign of noticing the probe, or Freddy, but the woman greeted Josef with a smile.

"Good day, sir," she said as they passed.

During the next fifteen minutes, they walked through the dark tunnel, passing openings in the walls, entrances to rooms full of displays and lights. Josef remembered visiting many of them on his previous visits to the library. Each display room represented a more distant time than the previous room and Josef felt the same sensation as his first journey through the north tunnel, as though walking backward through time.

When they reached the end of the tunnel and entered the final room, Josef felt a burst of relief as two guards inside the entrance greeted them. They were almost as tall as Josef but with more muscle mass. They looked Italian, wore light blue uniforms, and had military haircuts just barely visible under camouflage hats. One of them recognized Josef and stood at attention with his companion quickly following suit.

"Good evening, Herr Brunner," he said with an Italian accent.

Josef passed them without responding then stopped, his eyes on Freddy. When he turned back to the guards, his relief vanished. Neither man seemed to notice Freddy or the probe. They were only looking at him.

"Good evening, gentlemen," he said, nodding politely then turning away. Josef quickly abandoned his first instinct, asking if they saw the probe. They clearly saw nothing abnormal.

Freddy and the probe paused at the first display case with the tip of the probe against the glass. While the probe remained motionless, Freddy extended his small hand to the glass. The case contained three broken pieces of rock on a black marble pedestal. The pieces of stone inside were part of a large circular stone with a map carved into its broken surface. Like all of the other displays, details about the artifact were written on a plaque below the glass case, evidence supporting the different theories of its age and significance.

After a few seconds, Freddy removed his hand from the glass, then the probe turned and began moving again. Freddy followed it through the large cavern, weaving through the maze of display cases and giant stone support columns. Before following, Josef glanced at the security guards at the entrance. They stood as still as statues.

While walking behind Freddy, Josef attempted to focus on the probe, but he paused several times to look at the contents of some display cases. They passed cases holding intricate jewelry, shiny metal tools, giant skulls resting on random pieces of bone, thin sheets of shiny metal full of beautiful script, and several portraits composed of multi-colored foil.

On the outer wall of the large circular display room, openings revealed glimpses into other rooms full of more displays. As the entrances came into view, Freddy did not even seem to notice, and Josef feared that they were heading toward the exhibit at the back of the room, known simply as, *The Historian*. Josef followed curiously and full of a dread he did not want to acknowledge.

Freddy and the probe stopped at *The Historian* exhibit, a stone statue of a giant man sitting at a desk, which was also carved from stone and extended from the floor as though part of it. The man was facing their direction and staring at an open book made from stained wood, a look of concentration etched into the corners of his eyes. A glittering silver thread circled the man's head and long hair of stone fell over a brilliant blue robe with gold trim. Lights in the ceiling reflected off the torched enamel.

The statue was located in front of a smaller room carved into the wall, a cave within a cave. A glass wall protected the contents of the cave and connected seamlessly to the stone edges around the entrance. Freddy's head was below the stone desk so he could not see the book or the cave behind it. But he was probably using the probe to sense his surroundings, Josef guessed. Or perhaps the glasses were enhancing his senses.

Despite his concern, the beautiful artwork filled Josef with a sense of awe. While looking at the exhibit, he forgot momentarily about Freddy. He looked into the cave behind the statue, made to resemble a primitive habitation, and wondered about the ancient world if the famous historian had actually lived in a cave.

When the probe began moving again over the table and toward the cave entrance, Josef jolted back to full consciousness. The child walked around the statue and met the probe at the glass wall of the cave entrance where a large computer screen stood on a stand. Josef followed and stopped two meters from the probe with Freddy between them.

The glass wall was so clean, Josef had to look closely just to see any light reflection. Behind the glass stood several pedestals with a single book or scroll resting on each polished stone surface.

"You plan to steal something," Josef said accusingly.

"That is a funny word, steal," Freddy said with amusement, swiveling the computer screen, so it was easier for him to reach. "Stealing implies ownership."

The large screen showed the interior of the cave behind the glass, a view from the ceiling. A circle surrounded each stand, and Freddy touched the stand at the very back of the cave. The image quickly expanded and filled the entire screen, showing the book in clear detail. A row of options appeared at the left of the screen. Freddy touched the icon of an open book, and a new image appeared, the first pages of the book.

"This is very user-friendly," Freddy said while quickly turning the pages. The child stared forward, not looking at the screen. Above his head and to the left, the probe hovered completely motionless.

"You're recording everything, aren't you?"

Without answering, Freddy quickly turned the pages and reached the end of the book in a little over a minute. While watching, Josef felt even more helpless and frustrated than before, then he began to grow angry.

"Try to relax, Josef. It is just information." The child spoke while staring at the computer. After clicking on the next book, he began scrolling through the pages, then turned to face Josef again, smiling sweetly. "You have no power here so just accept it and enjoy the experience."

It is just information.

That phrase replayed in his mind while the child continued going through the books. Josef pursed his lips to prevent an angry outburst. A child was stopping him from performing his most vital job function, keeping critical information from the public. To help calm himself, Josef closed his eyes and drew a deep breath. He accepted his lack of physical control in the situation, but he could still attempt reason.

"Even if you learned how to read the language," Josef said casually, betraying his emotions, "you won't get many people to believe you. We'll make sure it gets buried under a hundred similar stories and theories. And we won't let you distribute it. The public will continue believing in the world we devised for them."

"Now you are being annoying," Freddy said without turning.

Josef thought he heard irritation in the child's tone.

"Have you considered letting us help you, and you help us?"

"I did not have to wake you, Josef," the child said, his finger swiping across the screen at the same fast pace. "I do not need your help and you definitely do not need my help."

"Let me guess," Josef said. "You don't like what you *think* we're doing in the world?"

The child tapped on the final stand and opened its book. Josef's eyes opened wide. What happens after he's finished going through its pages, he wondered in a panic. Josef had only a short time left.

"Well, *Josef*, I do not like how the world *is*," Freddy said. "Has lying so much to the public blinded you to the lie you tell yourselves? All your actions are not to build a better society, to help humanity. You are afraid of losing your stuff."

"Someone has to control society, Freddy," Josef said as though he had no other choice. "If we lose that control, someone else will take it, and I'm sure you can understand that usually causes a very dangerous situation for everyone."

"Fear cannot build a better society," Freddy snapped with his sweet child voice. "Corrupting the youth cannot build a better society. You profit through deceit. You decimate public funds. You write corrupt laws then profit from the millions of people in prison. You promote poison then profit from sickness. You do not just lie, you marginalize those seeking truth. I could continue, but what is the point?"

The child closed the final book and returned to the home screen showing all of the pedestals behind the glass. When he turned to Josef, his sunglasses showed Josef's reflection. The probe remained motionless.

"Yes," Josef said. "There are problems and we're dealing with them one by one. Maybe you're not aware, but we have enemies who prevent progress. You can help us."

"You do not even know your real enemies," Freddy said. "You *think* you are manipulating society, but you are also being manipulated. Your profit and success are just blinding you to it. And you think the *public* is stupid."

Josef had no immediate response. The child's confidence put doubts into his mind, uncertainty about his motivations and his life's work. While Josef desperately searched for another tactic, anxiety for the immediate future fought for his attention.

"Who are our real enemies then? Maybe you can help us."

"Maybe," Freddy said, facing the glass again.

The probe floated half a meter away from the glass that shielded the cave entrance, and then Josef heard a soft hum and felt a low vibration in his chest.

"What are you doing?"

"I'm taking one," Freddy said. "People should know their origin. No more secrets."

Josef's attention turned to a shimmer in the glass. After a few seconds, it melted, forming a hole large enough for the probe. While smoke rose from the molten edges of the opening, the probe floated into the cave, approached the stand holding the largest book, and pulled the book into it with the tendrils of light. Josef watched with a feeling of impotence as the probe turned slowly and then exited the cave.

After passing through the hole, it shot from his sight like a missile, and the collapsing air made a loud clap. Moments later, a security alarm began beeping from inside the cave. The atmospheric sensors in the cave must have interpreted the sound as something breaking, Josef thought. Security would come to investigate soon. In his peripheral vision, he saw Freddy fade and then disappear.

SEVENTY-NINE

Taylor

Although she knew they could still vaporize in the atmosphere, Taylor felt a great sense of relief. "Get in your seat, Gerald," she said, turning from the door and launching herself toward the pilot's seat.

"Okay," he said.

Before strapping herself into the seat, she opened the *Maneuver* folder and clicked on the file named *falling_emergency*. The program initiated a powerful braking procedure, pressing Sadi and Gerald hard into their seats. She imagined her spine compressing. While decelerating, the cabin began filling with air in preparation to open the airlock door to the cockpit.

"So Sadi wasn't real," Gerald said, looking at the controls in front of him. "The machine was disguised as Sadi the entire time?"

"I don't know, probably," Taylor said. "And at this point, I don't care. That was a close one."

Five minutes later, Taylor heard the machine voice speaking to them. "The cabin has reached target pressure. You can safely open the door."

Before unlocking the door, Taylor hesitated a moment but then ignored the irrational paranoia. If the machine had wanted to harm them, it could have broken the door and let their air escape into the vacuum of space.

"What just happened?" Taylor asked after opening the door.

While speaking, the machine hovered a few centimeters over the floor but did not enter the cockpit. "Your host was sending a message to the parasites who just tried to kill you. She has a plan to prevent their control over you. These creatures have much more experience than Freddy, and he was no match for them, not yet. The situation required her intervention."

"So Sadi was never here?" Gerald asked.

"No."

"She never came to my room last night?"

"No, she did not," the machine answered again. "That was only in your imagination."

Gerald slumped in his chair, disappointed. Taylor wondered what had happened, then she wondered what had not happened. Before losing control of her thoughts, she decided to change the subject.

"So their connection was Freddy's extra body?" she asked, the words feeling strange on her tongue. For some reason, the information about Freddy inhabiting multiple bodies did not surprise her, although the thought caused some anxiety. She planned to discuss the subject with Freddy later.

"Yes," the machine answered. "And through that connection, they influenced Gerald, who was allowed to unwittingly install the virus to the jet's computer."

"I don't remember doing that," Gerald said, looking at Taylor. "But there's been a lot of gaps in my memory."

"It was allowed, Gerald," the machine said. "Do not feel guilty. After the reconfiguration, you will be strong enough to resist their manipulation."

"Allowed!" Taylor said, aghast. "Why would she, it, allow such a thing?"

"They are playing a high-level game, Taylor. It was a trick disguised as a trick. All that matters is now they know who is superior."

"Wait a second," Taylor said, turning to Gerald. "Were the flying lessons your idea?"

"I thought it was your idea?"

EIGHTY

Gerald

While Taylor flew the jet back to the station, Gerald struggled to fully engage in their conversation. A daydream of living in prison competed for his attention. He was sharing a cell with another inmate on death row. Taylor ignored his lapses in coherence, acting as though their conversation was flowing smoothly. At one point, she said something about how their experience had probably traumatized him further, worsening his condition. He only remembered agreeing with her.

Enjoy the now, his cellmate said in the background. *Cause it's all downhill from here.*

Gerald listened to Taylor while also listening to his cellmate fantasize about the foods he wanted for his last meal. Thinking about food helped alleviate Gerald's imaginary experience of living on death row and the time when someone would strap him to a table.

Just before they entered the hangar and landed, Taylor said something, temporarily removing Gerald from his imaginary prison cell. As usual, the imaginary experience kept playing in the background, continually fighting for his attention.

"I don't know how I can trust my senses again," Taylor said. "Not even after the reconfiguration. The complexity of it all makes my head hurt. And I don't know if I even want to understand it. Hallucinations within illusions."

"Me too," Gerald said, glad for the brief moment of clarity. "It's all my fault. I should have kept up with the treatments. I'm sorry for almost getting us killed."

"It's not your fault, Gerald," Taylor said. "It was that fucking Doctor McGraw. It's too bad I didn't get to see Audrie knock her out. Maybe when we get back, I'll have her tell us the story again."

Gerald pretended to smile, but no matter what Taylor said, he was guilty. If he was a stronger person, they couldn't have damaged him. He decided to keep that bit of logic to himself. Taylor would only act nice and disagree with him.

Everyone claims to be innocent, his cellmate said. *At least you own up to it. You'll end this life with dignity!*

The time between entering the hangar and landing on the solid floor passed quickly. Then Gerald was descending the steps behind Taylor and into the crowd of his fellow refugees. Before they had arrived, the machines had informed everyone about what had happened on the jet. Seeing Sadi in the group felt strange, disorienting, since he remembered leaving on the jet with her.

"Are you guys okay?" someone asked and Taylor answered in the affirmative. Maybe Gerald answered too. He could not remember.

When Sadi put her arms around him, he stiffened involuntarily and could only think about the night he had spent with her, the night that never happened. Maybe Sadi knew about everything. He feared to ask what she knew and felt embarrassed and ashamed for being so weak.

"They'll miss you," his cellmate said from the bunk above him.

A moment later, the machine began speaking, focusing Gerald's attention on the physical world again.

"After what has transpired, you probably have many questions and concerns," it said while beginning to float away. "Freddy is preoccupied until tomorrow, so I will meet you in the dining hall for a discussion after dinner. Consider sending the children away, as the discussion might disturb them."

Their internal discussion began in the hangar after the machine left and after Taylor retold the story from her perspective. Gerald did not remember some of her account, probably the parts when the creature had hijacked him. That frightened him, and he wondered how much of the conversation he was missing. His memory of flying the jet was blurry.

"That's basically what the machine told us," Cesar said.

"It is difficult to understand," Dominga said, dramatically pressing her fingers against her temples. "It has given me a headache, actually! A creature from Earth was controlling Freddy's clone while simultaneously using Gerald to install a virus to the jet, and our host, whoever it is, was fooling you all and killed him. Incredible! Simply incredible!"

"We're dealing with things beyond our understanding," Taylor said, about to continue but interrupted by Susan.

"Well, now we know they can't be trusted," she said. "They've been lying to all of us from the beginning. They can make us see things that aren't there."

"Withholding information is not always motivated by malicious intent," Cesar said, briefly glancing at Susan, then shifting his focus to Sadi and Taylor. "Parents do it all the time for their children's benefit."

"Well I still trust Freddy," Sadi said. "He's the only person I would trust with the ability to control what we experience. It must be an overwhelming responsibility."

"Don't take this the wrong way, Sadi," Susan said, "but you are biased. He brought back your son. He claims to, at least."

"And," Sadi snapped, barely controlling her frustration. "I've known him the longest. He's put his life on the line for me and my family numerous times. You do not understand. And he did return my son!"

Gerald stood next to Sadi and could almost feel her emotions. They helped keep him focused on the conversation. His cellmate was still talking to him but only as a whisper he could ignore.

"We don't even know it's the same person," Susan said with irritation. "I don't understand why I keep having to say it."

"The story is consistent with what we've been told," Cesar said calmly. "And you're right, Susan. We can't be sure about anything. We understand that now more than we did before."

"We have no way of opposing that thing from Earth. Gerald and I talked to it." Taylor suddenly hugged herself as if reacting to a cold breeze. "*That thing* was controlling the jet through Gerald while simultaneously pretending to be Freddy. It didn't care about dying. And that machine, or whatever it is, *saved us*. They're fighting in some other realm and it seems we're on the right side of the fight."

"They've been through a lot this morning," Dominga said, then turned to Gerald. "You especially, Gerald. Do you need anything? I could make you a cup of tea?"

"I think I need a nap."

—※—

When Sadi knocked on his door and called to him, Gerald kept his eyes closed. Her voice was like an explosion in his dream world, leaving only her image in his mind. Then the voice of his cellmate spoke from the bunk above him.

You're lucky to have so many visitors.

"Come in, Sadi," Gerald said after rising from the bed. The door opened and Jacob stepped into the room, followed by his mother.

"Did you get a good rest?" she asked.

"I feel rested," Gerald said, rubbing his eyes.

He turned his attention to the toddler standing at her side. Jacob smiled silently at him, and Gerald attempted to remember why he had felt so afraid at his introduction. Now, he felt only curiosity and admiration. The child was beautiful, and Gerald kept catching himself staring.

"I didn't want to wake you," Sadi began, holding the door open, "but it's time for dinner and then we were going to discuss the reconfiguration with one of the machines."

They walked side by side to the dining room, Gerald mostly listening to Sadi on the way. During the conversation, he kept worrying she would ask more about the flight and how the creature had tricked them into believing she was present. She began the conversation by telling him that the girls had already gone to dinner.

"Earth seems like a lifetime ago," she continued. "It's funny how our memory works, and our sense of time."

"It is," Gerald answered, pausing a moment before continuing. "It feels like we've been here much longer than we have."

Gaps in your memory can explain that, said his cellmate. *People want to forget what they've done.*

Gerald required a moment to remember that the voice existed only in his head. But it seemed more distinct than in previous days. In his peripheral vision, he saw Jacob watching him with curiosity, analyzing his response, searching for relevance to the question and consistency with previous comments.

"It does feel longer," Sadi said and her wistful smile transformed into a frown. "I'm excited about the reconfiguration, but also a little scared. How about you?"

"The same," he said, feeling Jacob's gaze still. Then he remembered his dream in the cave at the psychiatric hospital and being encased in stone. "I don't want to think about it. Just want to get it over with."

Who are you talking to, Gerald?

—※—

A few minutes after most people had finished eating, the machine entered the dining hall. It hovered to the head of the table and waited, motionless. Sadi and Susan told the children to go play somewhere, let the adults have a boring conversation. Gerald almost expected Jacob to stay, but his sisters took him with them. Even before the machine began speaking, Gerald's heartbeat increased.

"The reconfiguration can begin tomorrow," it said. "After I explain how the procedure will work, we can determine who will go first. Feel free to ask questions."

It waited for a few seconds before continuing.

"As a simplified overview, you will inhale special organisms that will enter the blood and be carried to every cell. These organisms will reset your genetic code to the original configuration."

You don't need to know the details, Gerald's cellmate said, causing him to miss part of the machine's explanation. *Only the outcome matters.*

"After inhaling the powder," the machine continued, "you will begin breathing a specialized gas mixture to feed the organisms and direct their activities. You will be unconscious while your genetic code resets to the original configuration."

"How long will the process take?" Sadi asked.

"Approximately ten hours."

"Will it be painful?"

"It will feel like sleep and without physical pain," the machine answered, "but you may experience some strange or disturbing dreams."

"After what happened this morning," Susan asked with impatience. "Are they still offering the pardon?"

"They told each of you directly about that. They did not discuss it with us," the machine said. "After the reconfiguration, we will pursue the best options for those who want to return."

Gerald lost interest in the conversation, or at least he lost the mental strength to keep following along. He was sick of discussing things, hearing questions asked and then answered. He wanted to feel different. He wanted to participate in conversations again, have fun with people again. His cellmate was right. Gerald did not need to know the details.

"I want to go first," he said, interrupting Cesar mid-sentence. Everyone turned to look at him. "I know Sadi probably wanted to go first, but I should be the one, to make sure it works."

"Thank you, Gerald," Sadi said, placing her warm hand on his knee.

He was afraid to look at her. He wanted to prevent discovering that she did not exist.

After his outburst, Gerald did not participate in the discussion and only half-listened to the following emotional discussion between Susan and Taylor. In the end, Susan acquiesced and decided not to make decisions about returning to Earth until after witnessing the procedure's result on Gerald. After the discussion, Gerald went to bed and fell asleep quickly.

At four in the morning, he woke up unexpectedly and decided to use the bathroom. Before returning to bed, he looked at the view of Bodn in the display on his wall, appreciating the stars above the horizon. He never grew tired of seeing them shining in his dark room. After lying back in bed and closing his eyes, he listened to the soothing, familiar voice of his cellmate.

It's been a pleasure, friend, the voice said from the bunk above him. *See you on the other side.*

Less than a minute later, Gerald heard a soft knock on his door.

EIGHTY-ONE

Gerald

"Hi, Gerald," Freddy said from the hallway. "Can I come in? I'd like to begin the process now if that's okay."

For some reason, Gerald remained lying on the bed when Freddy opened the door. In the dim light of the hallway, Gerald saw only Freddy's silhouette. He walked into the room, followed by Sadi and Jacob, and then Taylor, Cesar, and Dominga. They all entered quietly and followed Freddy to the bed. One of the machines entered the room last, and the door closed behind it. Gerald felt many pairs of eyes looking at him.

"It's time for your recovery," Freddy said. "I'm sorry about what happened yesterday, and that we couldn't have helped earlier."

"I thought we were going to..." Gerald said, stopping when he met Jacob's gaze.

"I know," Freddy said. "We planned this for later in the morning, but I wanted to spare you the extra anxiety of waiting. It's early and you will sleep more naturally if we begin this now. Don't talk, just lie back and relax."

The machine hovered to the side of the bed next to the flower, then used an appendage to place a strange instrument on the table beside it.

Gerald turned his head to see a stone box with a round metallic tube on top, coiled like a snake. Small lights on the side of the box pulsated to the beat of his heart, alternating between red and blue. There were other lights and aspects of the box he noticed, but the machine interrupted his inspection.

"You won't need the flower anymore," it said.

When the machine floated behind Freddy, Gerald noticed the tray in another of its appendages. On the tray sat two glass vials with a small amount of powder inside, one white and the other black. Freddy picked up a thin metallic straw lying between the vials.

"The procedure is pretty simple, for you at least," Freddy said, holding the straw in the air above Gerald. "On the tray are two powders. You will inhale them through your nose, starting with the white powder. You'll want to lay the vial on its side so the powder can be inhaled more slowly. Do you understand?"

"Yes," Gerald answered, turning from Freddy to glance at everyone around his bed.

In any other situation, he would have felt more self-conscious. None of his friends were smiling, not even Dominga. Everyone appeared nervous and tense. Gerald could feel their combined focus on his body. Their emotions felt like a light shining down on him.

"Sit up and we'll begin," Freddy instructed. "Before taking the powder, take a few deep breaths. Then puncture the top of the container with the straw and inhale."

Gerald sat up and took the straw from Freddy's hand, then drew two deep breaths through his nose. He laid the vial horizontally on the tray and tapped it until the powder fell into a line. After another deep breath, he pushed the metallic straw into the vial through some rubbery material and began inhaling the powder. The powder stung a little as it entered his lungs, but the sensation quickly dissipated. When finished, Freddy handed him the container holding the black powder.

The black powder stung more than the first. Gerald winced and attempted to shake the feeling away. The sensation soon passed, however, and he began to feel lightheaded and dizzy. But he kept staring at the vial as if nothing else existed. He felt warm hands on his back, guiding him softly to the bed again. Then a small mask slid over his nose and mouth, followed by a sweet smell.

When Freddy began talking again, Gerald could not understand his words. He felt as if his head was sinking into the pillow and people were getting farther away. Everyone was leaning over him as his eyes closed.

—※—

Gerald dreamed about escaping from prison in a hot air balloon and forever rising into the sky, passing the clouds, and ascending until the sky turned black. After an eternity of floating in darkness, the balloon exploded and he fell back to Earth, back into the prison cell. He spent another eternity staring through the bars and listening to his cellmate sleep.

Familiar people walked past his cell and looked at him like an animal in a zoo. Several clients brought their kids and friends to look at him. His aunt brought his young cousins. His law partner brought his wife and their new baby. While gazing at him, no one smiled or spoke. They reminded Gerald of scientists recording their observations in notebooks. Fortunately, no frightening aliens visited him.

When a pair of guards appeared in front of his cell, Gerald stood and waited to be taken away. *It's that time, eh?* his cellmate asked from his bunk. As Gerald watched one of the guards open the cell door, he realized that he had never seen his cellmate's face. He had only ever heard him speaking, always out of sight. Gerald did not feel the need to see him now.

As he walked down the hallway, he noticed the other prisoners silently watching. No one heckled or said anything to him. As he passed their cells, they just stared. They looked like lizards in cages, little cold-blooded killers.

The guard took him to a small room where an inclined hospital bed sat next to a drug delivery machine with tubes extending from it. One of the room's walls was made of glass and all of his refugee friends were sitting on the other side.

They wore nice clothes as if attending a church service. The women wore simple dresses, each a different color and style, and all the men wore dark blue suits with black ties. The children sat in the front row with their mothers, all except Jacob. He was sitting in a chair in the corner of the same room as Gerald. When Gerald looked at him, the child smiled sweetly.

As the guard strapped him to the hospital bed, Gerald did not struggle. Then a nurse stepped from behind him and gently inserted a needle into his arm, which he could not feel. When finished, the guard and nurse stepped away and stood motionless at the side of the glass wall.

When the machine delivered the first liquid into his veins, Gerald clenched his teeth in pain and instinctively closed his eyes. A moment later, he felt another liquid enter him, then his heart stopped and he felt nothing. The lack of sensation was surprisingly peaceful.

With his heart finally still, Gerald opened his eyes again and stared at his friends. Not only did he feel nothing, the room had become perfectly quiet as though he had entered a static universe. The glass was now tinted, so that he barely recognized his friends on the other side. They appeared submerged in a murky liquid.

While peering through the glass, trying to recognize his friends, a sudden movement caught his attention. Jacob had stood from his seat, walked toward the bed, and quietly extended his hand toward Gerald, touching his chest. When the tiny hand made contact, his eyes burst wide open, and the lethal injection room vanished, replaced by his bedroom ceiling.

—※—

He turned his head and noticed Sadi sitting in a chair beside him, the only other person in the room. The life monitoring machine sat on his nightstand as before, the blue and red lights still pulsating with his heartbeat. The frequency was noticeably faster than before he fell unconscious. Gerald sat up and stared at Sadi, waiting for her to speak.

"Hi, Gerald," she said finally, her eyes wide with anxious anticipation. She removed the gas mask from his face and waited.

Gerald peered closely into her eyes and recognized her emotions, fear of what he might say, fear of what he might have become. He turned from her to look at the bed, then his arms. While stretching them above his head, he focused on the amazing sensation in his muscles. He took a deep breath. He exhaled. After returning his attention to her, the beautiful sight brought tears to his eyes.

"Hi, Sadi," he said, throwing the covers off him.

"Hi," she said, eyes even wider than before.

She was holding her breath.

After standing from the bed, he glanced at the machine and noticed the blue and red lights pulsating even faster. He extended his hand to Sadi, then helped her stand. The touch of her hand electrified his whole body.

"I feel great," he said. "Actually, I've never felt better."

EIGHTY-TWO

Taylor

After lunch, while waiting for Gerald to wake from his genetic re-configuration, Freddy gave everyone a tour of his private garden, a place they had not yet visited. In Taylor's opinion, the garden contained nothing mysterious or worth concealing, and though she wondered about his reason for keeping it a secret, she assumed he was just too busy. It was not worth asking for confirmation. For almost two hours, the adults talked pleasantly under the pavilion and the children played. Even Susan refrained from arguing and Taylor wondered if her amiable mood was the result of an agreement with Mark.

The pleasant garden atmosphere was probably an intentional positive influence, intended to prevent further argument and strife. There were no breaks in the conversation, only silent times where they enjoyed the view of the plants and trees, the cool breeze, and warmth from the artificial sun. Taylor especially enjoyed the chatter from the birds.

She was having an extremely relaxing afternoon and did not want to leave. All of the stress from the previous day seemed to melt away and disappear into the soil below her feet. While in the garden, even her anxiety about going through reconfiguration seemed insignificant.

After a while, the children grew bored of the garden and went to the observatory, and then some of the other adults left too. Taylor remained with Cesar, Dominga, Susan, and Mark. No one spoke about Gerald undergoing the reconfiguration process, but as the ten-hour time limit approached, Taylor felt an almost overwhelming anticipation to see him again. At one point, Sadi said she was going to check on him and asked Taylor if she wanted to join.

"You go ahead," Taylor responded.

When she saw Gerald walking down the trail, holding Sadi's hand and Jacob walking beside him, she waved and forced herself to smile. As they walked toward the pavilion, Taylor experienced a strange anxiety. She did not know what to say to Gerald, so she planned to let someone else speak first.

She also had several disturbing concerns she knew were irrational. What if Gerald no longer considered her as a friend? What if the reconfiguration had failed to help him? She missed the old Gerald, the old Max, and the reconfiguration was her last remaining hope in their recovery. She hated to see how indecisive they had become, their inability to concentrate. The psychiatrists responsible for their condition had completely infuriated her. They filled her with dreams of vengeance.

When Gerald reached the shade of the pavilion, everyone at the table just stared at him. Not even Dominga said anything. Taylor spent the time attempting to decipher if Gerald looked any different, but she could not identify any dramatic change. He appeared more alive, and his skin seemed to radiate something, confidence perhaps. But when she saw Sadi's wide smile, her heart beat faster, and her next breath was deep, sending chills through her core.

"Gerald is like me now," Jacob said, looking at each of the five adults under the pavilion, then glancing up at his mother. "It worked just like Freddy said it would."

"Yes it did, Jacob," Gerald said after a glance at the child, then Sadi. When he turned his attention to the group, he focused on Taylor and smiled wide. "Don't let the boy fool you. I'm still the same Gerald you remember. Sure, I have superior genes now, but I'll try not to remind you of it."

Before she could stop herself, Taylor jumped to her feet and hugged him, tears forming in her eyes. As he returned the affection, Taylor did not expect to feel so relieved. She felt like his arms would squeeze more tears out of her, as if all the trauma since leaving Earth had gathered, and the dam finally broke. To stop the intense emotions, she needed to speak.

"It's so good to have you back, Gerald."

Gerald, Sadi, and Jacob sat with them for a while and talked. As he told about his dreams during the procedure, the experience of waking, and his improved disposition, Taylor felt more excited for the reconfiguration process. Jacob listened to the conversation for a while but then grew impatient and asked Sadi to take him on a walk in the garden.

"Yes, it is beautiful, Jacob," Sadi said after standing. "You lead the way. Excuse me, everyone."

Taylor and the rest of the group watched Sadi follow her son down one of the paths leading away from the pavilion. No one spoke until they were out of hearing range.

"So, Gerald," Dominga said. "You and Sadi seem to enjoy each other's company. Is that going to be a more permanent situation?"

"We haven't talked about the future, yet," he said while staring at Sadi in the distance. Taylor followed his gaze. Jacob was touching the trunk of a small tree while his mother inspected the branches and leaves. "I plan to discuss the subject after she goes through the procedure."

"How are male-female relationships going to work?" Susan asked in a more serious tone. "I mean, people who live forever can have an infinite number of children. After just a few hundred years, Bodn is going to be overpopulated."

Taylor felt tension begin to grow inside her chest. She hoped to think of something to divert an unpleasant confrontation. She had not thought about that issue. Gerald spoke before anyone else.

"These are just my initial thoughts, Susan, because I haven't really thought about that yet." Gerald scanned everyone in the group with narrow eyes, finally returning his attention to Susan. "The answer to your extremely valid question depends on your confidence in predicting how a couple will feel when presented with eternal youth. Would you plan to have an infinite number of children?"

Taylor and the others braced themselves for another argument. Before responding, Susan looked at Gerald with a mixture of curiosity and outrage, as if trying to interpret his tone. Although the question sounded like an insult, Gerald had a sincere look in his eyes.

"I'd prefer not to think about that," Susan said, finally and laughed. When she turned to Mark, he laughed with her.

"I don't mind thinking about it," Mark said, then Susan elbowed him in the ribs.

"Mortal creatures often feel an urgency about things," Gerald said, thinking out loud. "Women in particular feel an urgency about having children. But perhaps, when we're not subjected to a limited lifetime, we won't have children as often. This is a very good question, Susan!"

"Hmm," Susan said, nodding. "Good point."

"And we won't be stuck on Bodn forever," he said as if in sudden realization. "Bodn will be our home, but we'll be able to explore the universe, which might just be a big enough place to handle an infinite number of people if it ever came to that. But considering all of the possible things that can happen, I'm not going to predict the future too far in advance."

EIGHTY-THREE

Christine

In her spare time between helping customers, Christine prepared for her quiz the next day on the *Head Start* early education program. Although she felt prepared for the quiz, she had difficulty caring as much about college anymore. After her adventure rescuing Franklin, three weeks previous, she had less motivation than ever for school and her future as a teacher. She still loved children and fantasized about educating them, but she could not eliminate thoughts of seeing Freddy and Franklin again and joining them in whatever they were doing. She hoped for their safety, of course, and she also did not want to forfeit the opportunity for other interesting experiences.

After so long without hearing from Freddy or Franklin, Christine began to doubt their re-appearance in her life. If not for her new Lexus, the car Freddy borrowed from his friend and loaned to her, she would have abandoned hope of seeing them again. At the very least, she expected to see the owner of the vehicle.

While reading her textbook, she caught herself wondering how to become the permanent owner of the car. That seemed like a big problem though. She would eventually have to get the tags renewed. Could she find someone who could help her? Maybe forge some documents or hack into the state licensing database and insert her name as the owner? That logic always returned her thoughts to Franklin. If she saw him again, she might not care about ownership of the Lexus anymore.

Ten minutes before eight, when Christine usually closed the clothing shop, the front door opened. She did not look up from her book, but she watched the new customers in her peripheral vision, two people wearing baseball caps who walked behind a clothing rack in the middle of the store. Judging from their height and hair, they were a man and his wife or girlfriend. They were the only customers in the store.

"Excuse me, ma'am," said a tiny voice behind the counter.

Christine looked away from her book and saw the top of a child's head, covered in blond, nearly white hair. After leaning over the counter, Christine smiled at the child who was looking up at her. He had dark brown eyes set in a pale face. He seemed familiar.

"Hi, little man," she said, glancing at the couple who remained on the other side of the clothing rack. "Can I help you?"

"When do you close?" he asked. "My grandma wanted to know."

"In just a few minutes."

"Oh, okay," he said.

The child cocked his head to the side and looked at her with only one of his eyes, reminding Christine of a bird. While staring into his eye, she could not distinguish the pupil from the iris. His eye looked like a black hole surrounded by a brilliant white crystal. Christine saw her reflection on the clear surface and became temporarily paralyzed when she remembered those sightless eyes. The mirror reflection stared back at her, and she gulped.

"What's your name?" she asked finally.

"Freddy," he said, looking straight at her again, and her reflection vanished.

An intense adrenaline rush caused Christine's eyes to burst wide open. She jumped off her stool and looked to the middle of the clothing store where the last remaining customers now stood in full view, both staring at her.

"Hi, Christine," Gerda said.

"I said we'd be back," Franklin said.

"Holy shit!" Christine said while walking to the front of the store. She flipped the sign in the window, then locked the door. "That was three weeks ago. I was beginning to doubt I'd ever see you again."

"How could we forget you?" Franklin asked, chuckling as a little kid might.

Christine looked at him curiously. She had not expected to see him so happy and carefree. He seemed recovered from the effects of incarceration at a secret military base with such a bleak future before him. She shuddered at the thought, then turned to the child.

"What have you guys been doing?"

"We are gathering people who want to go with us," the child said. "Those who already escaped have friends and family members they want to bring."

"I've convinced my son and his family to go," Gerda said proudly. "We're all staying at Freddy's home."

Gerda's excited tone lacked any trace of concern. Christine thought again about the rescue operation, going with Freddy into the secret military base to get Franklin. She remembered having fun, but over the past few weeks, the danger of the situation had begun to replace some of the excitement in her memory.

"You guys don't look worried at all," she said, glancing at each of them. "What if they catch you again?"

"We are safe," Freddy said, grasping her hand and squeezing. "They will not find us."

"That's all I needed to hear," she said and squeezed his hand in return. Christine had complete faith in whatever Freddy told her. She felt a sudden burst of energy, urging her to move. "This is so exciting. I know you're not a child, Freddy, but can I hug you?"

"Anytime," he said, walking into her open arms.

"You're enjoying that," Franklin said.

"Are you jealous, Franklin?" Gerda asked with a smile.

"Still want to go with us?" Freddy asked after Christine released him.

"Oh my God, yes," Christine said, drawing a deep breath. She ignored the temptation to doubt the reality of the situation. If she was just dreaming, she hoped it would last forever. "I'll need your help to convince my sister to come too."

"I do not expect that to be a problem," Freddy said cheerfully.

EIGHTY-FOUR

Helen

Helen loved the task Max had given her, polishing the outer surface of the new spacecraft. She loved feeling the vibration of the tool in her hand, turning the rough surface smooth and shiny. It allowed them to more easily locate potential defects. She stood on the ladder, five meters above the ground but did not feel afraid. The climbing harness provided security.

Whenever she saw her clear reflection on the surface, she could move to the next part. Although the machines could do it faster, and probably better, she had begged for Max to give her some way to help. Maybe by helping them build the spacecraft, her mother would change her mind and allow Helen to travel to Earth with the rescue party, as she called them, to get the ones they left behind.

When Helen began working on the wings, she thought about their curvature and wondered about their aerodynamic properties. She knew they would use the craft to travel through the void of space to Earth and then return to Bodn, but she never thought they would need to consider aerodynamics. She carefully descended the ladder and then walked to the other side of the spacecraft where the adults were working.

"Hi, Helen," Mark said. "You're doing an excellent job up there."

"I know," she said, laughing.

"Still glad you decided to stay with us and not go on that camping trip?" Mark asked, bringing her attention back to the present.

"Oh yes. This is fun."

Helen glanced at the ceiling, grateful for its shelter from the frequent storms battering the area. Shortly after moving to Bodn with the other refugees, she'd watched machines larger than Miss Poofie build the hangar forty meters from the entrance to their cave dwellings. During their work, she had felt a strong desire to learn how to build. She'd watched in fascination as they incorporated the living trees into the frame and built an immense sliding door on the opposite side to block the wind. She especially loved watching them drill a tunnel into the mountain, creating an extra connection to their homes. Whenever Helen looked at the ceiling, ten meters above her, she imagined the cliff ascending far higher.

"A girl after my own heart," Taylor said. She stood at the top of the stairs leading inside the large spaceship. She stretched while descending the stairs, holding both hands high above her head. "Do you need a break, Helen? I'm hungry and need to stretch my legs."

"I guess so," Helen said. "But I had a question. Why does this thing have wings? You don't need wings in space and we don't need them to get there either."

"Taylor just wanted to give us more work, I think," Mark said, smiling and watching Taylor approach. "And all just so it would look more like a bird."

"I know you're just joking," Helen said with a smirk, then turned to Taylor questioningly. "Right?"

"Don't listen to him," Taylor said. "We're going to use this for more than just space travel. Flying in the atmosphere is more energy efficient by utilizing aerodynamics. We shouldn't be lazy engineers, just because we have a nearly limitless energy supply."

"I'm not lazy," Helen said, just in case Taylor was referring to her.

"You are definitely not lazy, Helen." Taylor turned to the top of the stairs and yelled. "Max. Helen's hungry, so let's have dinner."

"Good plan, Helen," Max said, his voice resonating from deep within the spacecraft. "I'll be right out."

While Max descended the stairs, Mark got the cooler with their food and drinks and then met them at the giant door on the other side of the hangar. Taylor, Helen, and Mark waited while Max stepped outside to quickly check for predators. Max had one of the stun guns they used to frighten dangerous animals away.

Helen hoped they would see one of the wolves, which claimed the area as their territory. She enjoyed seeing them and especially liked to hear the loud electric discharge of the stun gun. The disturbing noise always gave Helen a small adrenaline rush. Before her reconfiguration, the sound probably would have frightened her.

After Max claimed the area was free from danger, they followed the short trail to a little round pavilion near the top of another cliff. As the adults started a fire and spread some food on the long table, Helen walked close to the cliff edge. She loved the view of the valley from there. A large river flowed from the canyon far away to the left, and she liked to count the number of times the river split into smaller rivers and streams.

She turned to the overcast sky, her attention drawn to a patch of exceptionally dark clouds. While staring at them, she wondered if the rain would begin again. The lack of wind seemed to indicate a high probability. Helen did not mind the rain. Then they would have a cozy dinner accompanied by the crackle of the fire and the sound of raindrops splattering on the leaves and wooden roof of the pavilion.

While considering the pleasant possibility of a cozy evening, Helen noticed a dark object emerge from the clouds. As it got closer, she hoped it was Freddy coming for a visit, descending from the orbiting space station. After thirty seconds, she recognized the BMW.

"Freddy's coming," Helen said, keeping her eyes fixed on the car in the sky.

"Where?" Taylor asked after joining Helen at the cliff.

Helen pointed to the sky, then she started waving. Although they saw Freddy nearly every week, she was still excited every time she saw him. She and Taylor watched in silence for the next minute as the BMW flew directly toward them. When the vehicle arrived over their heads, it stopped and began descending slowly into an opening in the trees. Helen ran to the driver's door and peered through the window.

"Hi, Freddy," she said as the door opened. "You came just in time for dinner."

"I know," he answered with mock smugness. After shutting the door, he grabbed her by the shoulder and smiled. "I wanted to have dinner with you."

As usual, Mark acted as the cook and fried the fish over the fire then distributed the sizzling meat onto everyone's plates. Helen added her favorite fruit, then took a glass of water and sat in the chair next to Freddy. No one asked Freddy any serious questions until after they began eating.

"So what's the news?" Max asked.

"Yeah," Taylor said. "You always have news."

"I just talked to your mother," he said, looking at Helen. "They are doing fine, still camping. She wanted me to say hi."

"Hi, Mom," Helen said while biting into her favorite fruit, a drop of red juice running down her chin. She wiped the liquid away before it fell onto her shirt. "When's Cesar coming back with more fruit?"

"They will be back in a couple of days, I think," Freddy said. "Don't worry, Helen, you will not run out."

"Is everyone still doing okay back home?" Max asked in a more serious tone. "Still ready for us to come and get them?"

"They are still safe at Mr. Smith's house, just waiting for you all to stop goofing off and finish this thing." Freddy smiled mischievously but kept his gaze on the flames.

"We're almost done," Taylor said, rolling her eyes. "We'll probably begin diagnostics testing tomorrow night."

"Maybe," Mark said.

"So you're still taking us through the portal by yourself?" Max asked.

"I am ready," Freddy said, turning from the fire and looking at Max. "I have practiced the procedure many times."

Mark was watching the fire, not seeing to notice Freddy's gaze. "And you don't expect any trouble back on Earth?"

"I don't think they're happy with us," Taylor said, chuckling.

"I am getting extra help for this rescue operation," Freddy said, turning to the fire again. "And everyone is immune to their influence now, so I will not have to worry about them hijacking you."

Helen glanced at the other adults around the fire. She did not entirely understand what Freddy meant and was hoping someone would ask a follow-up question. No one did. Everyone was still smiling at Taylor's comment.

After turning back to the fire, she imagined traveling to Earth with the rescue party and finding Jen, her old nanny. She missed her immensely. Before her reconfiguration, she remembered being afraid of so many things, but now Helen looked to the future with excitement. She was confident in her ability to handle whatever happened.

"After we return with everyone," Freddy said finally, "you might not see me for a while."

"Why?" Helen asked, forgetting Jen for the moment. "Are you going away?"

"No, I will be busy. An old friend sacrificed himself so I could get your brother back. I need to find him. Audrie's coming with me. She wanted to help."

"Will I get to meet him?" Helen asked.

"Sure."

Freddy turned back to the fire and stared at the flames. For many minutes, no one said anything, the crackling of the fire the only sound, until a soft rain began falling around the pavilion. Helen enjoyed watching the raindrops hit the ground and hearing their tiny impacts. As the flames ascended straight into the air, turning into smoke, Helen watched Freddy and felt a strange impression. He was seeing more than just the fire.

End of Book 3

Visit hyrumjones.com to learn more about the continuation of the series and Hyrum's other works.

About the Author

Hyrum is the product of a large family and the Utah desert. He's an Eagle Scout, has degrees in chemistry and chemical engineering, and spent a few years as the Libertarian Chairman of his county. After he and his wife raised their family in the Pacific Northwest, they all moved to Kentucky, where they now reside. Other than the people in his life, he loves exploring the world and creating things

www.ingramcontent.com/pod-product-compliance
Lightning Source LLC
Chambersburg PA
CBHW070728120726
47910CB00001B/25